Please re[...]

MW01579533

4700 NE Leverich Place
Vancouver, WA 98663-3664

WOLF CREEK

Wolf Creek

Arline Faro

Spirit Lake Press

FIRST EDITION

To Michele, Andrius,
Alarik, Holeri and Carey;
And to Frank,
who made them all possible.

Acknowledgements

The author is grateful to Carey Moore for directing me back to Minnesota, the state of my childhood for the story; to Alarik P. Faruolo for the many productions of "Sit Pax," the play on which this novel is based; for Carey Maki for insisting I write *Wolf Creek*, for Holeri Faruolo, all-around consultant, Michele Migro, first reading, Andrius J. Faruolo, promoter-at-large, and Frank Faruolo, a dictionary wiz. The author is indebted to A. Nannette Taylor, Willy Clark, Lettie Lee and Michael Whelan for their support and belief in my ability; and to Susan Larson for researching the Minnesota statutes. Many thanks to Kurt Smith for inviting me to join the Main Street Writers: Kurt Smith, Margie Senechal, James Patton, Virgil Birdsall, Eva Mae Sparley and Geri Hoekzema, whose criticism and weekly company I cherish. My gratitude to Father Paul Luger, Rosalee and Don MaCrae, Pauline Peotter, Mary Jane and Ethan Granum, Susan Aschim, Angie Schultz and Aune Koski for their help and support. A big red rose for Jonathan Trotta and a blue ribbon for the staff of Fort Vancouver Regional Library. And above all, to my publishing editor, Gail Anderson, who helped bring the manuscript to its final course, a very special thank you for her optimistic attitude and unwavering support of my writing. Working with her has been exciting and creatively stimulating.

PROLOGUE

"DO YOU THINK HE'LL COME?" he asked.

She took her foot off the pedal of her sewing machine and looked at him, in the old wheelchair with the broken spokes and shredded rattan upholstery. His green wool robe, now bleached to a dull gray, was open in the front, exposing the hairy chest under his unbuttoned mismatched pajamas. At one side, the collar of the robe was carelessly turned in. That was Charlie Skinnar, her husband, the charismatic, dashing six-footer of long ago, whose right eye floated off to the side, had always a certain magnetism for young ladies. Signe went to him, with a mother's touch, turned out his collar and pulled the front of the robe together. "Father Myhre always comes." She yanked the two ends of the sash together and tied them, then took a comb from her pocket, and handed it to him.

Charlie combed the frazzled whisks of gray hair

on his head, and pocketed the comb. With trifocals perched over his nose, he flipped through the old photograph album that he had on his lap since breakfast.

Signe stood in front of him. "This is the third day in a row that you've been looking at that old picture book, at those old faded snapshots. Why?"

"I like what I see," Charlie replied. "Our whole family together." She looked down, almost sorry she had spoken. "Here's you and me," he added, happily, "by the milk house just finished."

Signe smiled, as she cut slices out of her homemade bread. "Putting that building up was some job."

Charlie took another long look at the snapshot. "But you're smiling." He gazed at her. "And always so beautiful."

Signe couldn't resist the temptation to take a look. She blushed, embarrassed at her vanity. "Don't say such things."

Charlie flipped over another page. "And here's a picture of some children." He studied it. "Oh, that's Hugo and Violet, but who're these little girls here?"

Holding the bread knife in her hand, Signe came back to take another look. "Why that's our Elma and Elsie!" she answered softly, pointing at the figures with her knife.

"They're little, aren't they?"

"Yes, children are little," she answered wistfully, "until they get big."

Charlie shook his head with wonder. "Elma and Elsie, our youngest. I'd kinda forgotten about them.

Why don't they come visit us?"

"They have their jobs. You just can't leave a good job and go prancing 'round the country."

Charlie was troubled. "To think that I should almost forget my own children, my living offspring!" He raised his left hand to his head to feel if he had remembered to use the comb that she had given him. Satisfied that he had, he handed it back to her. "I spend too much time thinking about the dead." He pondered a moment. "The three. All my seed."

"Yes," she said, staring at her husband with her once gray-blue eyes, which the years had turned to the gray of cold steel. She returned to her sandwich making, buttering her whole-wheat bread, cutting the headcheese, and spreading the mustard with the efficiency of a caterer.

"And here's the whole family, the day we left Minnesota. But where's Eldon?" Charlie asked. He flipped the sheet over expecting to find Eldon hiding on the next page. "Why isn't he here?"

Signe stared at the breadboard, as if counting the crumbs from the cuttings, pinched her eyelids together to stop the tears that clouded her vision as she recalled the day they left Minnesota for Oregon. Over a half century has passed since Eldon closed their gate for the last time, leaving behind their home and his dog, Buster. If she had known what was in store for them, she would never have consented to go. Signe wiped her eyes with her apron. "Eldon snapped the photo, remember?"

"I found him!" Charlie shouted, with his index finger on his son's picture. Signe scurried to his side again. "Lookit how Eldon holds his little brother. Like a proud father. I didn't know Hugo very well. There wasn't time. If he was to walk in here, I probably wouldn't recognize him. Wouldn't know what to talk to him about."

"He's dead." Signe spoke softly.

Charlie nodded, and paused. And after a deep sigh, continued, "Here's our house that Oscar Salo built. With two bedrooms. One for the youngsters and one for—" Charlie flipped the page over quickly and looked away. "Do you think we have enough money to buy it back?" he asked, his eyes, the color of dark chocolate, gleaming with hope.

"It's no longer there."

"How do you know?"

"Hilda Mattson wrote me," Signe answered. "She said that a young German couple from Fargo bought the place sometime ago. They took down the house, made firewood out of it, and put a mobile home in its place."

"Firewood! Out of my house!" Charlie's head shook. He put his hand over his mouth as if to quiet an involuntary cry, and searched for good news of some kind. He finally asked, "Am I a grandfather?"

"No," she answered almost inaudibly.

"I'd like to be a grandpa. I like children."

Signe reached for the album with its collection of faded memories and put it on top of the sewing machine. She went to the sink, wet the corner of a towel, and wiped Charlie's face carefully. "We have not been blessed with grandchildren."

Charlie, like a child, looked up at Signe, held his

hands out for her to wash, and continued his dream. "I'd read to them and tell them stories. I've even made up a few poems that I could recite. I never had a chance because there was so much work to do."

"I know. Life wasn't easy."

"I'll tell you what we'll do!" he said with renewed enthusiasm. "We'll sell this place and go back."

She looked at him with disbelief. "To Minnesota?"

"I'll go there to die," Charlie answered, as if planning a winter vacation in Maui.

Signe turned and stared at him. "To die?"

"Yes. And you don't need to send my body back here. I'll just rest with my old neighbors. In the old Wolf Creek cemetery."

Signe laughed. "Yaa, buried in the tundra." She pushed his wheelchair to the table, to the right of her — out of range of Charlie's right eye.

"Signe, I'm talking about Minnesota, not Siberia."

She tucked the white linen napkin under his chin. "I know what you're talking about. But what you're saying is out of the question, impossible, and quite foolish. I thought I could be just as silly." She sat down and began to ladle the potato soup.

"Why?"

"What you got to go back for? Everything's changed. Nobody's expecting you. And nobody's waiting for you. Why make waves on muddy waters?"

Charlie stared at his soup. He was quiet and with his lower teeth tugged at his upper lip. After a long silence, he cast his eyes down and asked, "Signe, why did you stay with me all these years?"

She gave a laugh, sat primly, straight as a cedar

post, and directed her gaze at him. "Did you think I had my eye on some other man? A lover?"

Charlie dropped his spoon. "May God strike me dead if I should ever have had such a thought. Signe, you are not that kind of a woman."

"Some other man, huh!" Signe teased, before sinking her teeth into the sandwich. "I wouldn't know if he wanted his white shirts starched or just hung up to dry. Wouldn't know whether he wanted his eggs hard- or soft-boiled." Signe stared into the distance as she chewed her food. She finished her coffee and set the cup on the saucer. "You know, Charlie, the young people these days get divorced before they've had a chance to get acquainted. It takes a long time to get to know the other one. Imagine what it would be like to face a strange old man at breakfast." Signe shook her head, and added, "With a wrinkled face like a withered cabbage."

"I have wrinkles."

"If you have lines on your face, Charlie, I have never noticed. They must've come in the night when I wasn't looking."

"You say such beautiful things, Mama." Charlie wiped away a tear with his starched white napkin. "I should want you to be with me when the end comes. I should want you to be with me in Minnesota."

Signe stiffened her spine. "One thing I'm saying right now, Charlie, you can't go back to Minnesota."

"I say I'm dying."

"Then you die here."

"Am I to be buried in foreign soil? Away from home?"

Signe cut the apple pie and dished it. She took his soup bowl and put the pie in front of him. "Oregon is America. Three of your children lie out here in the Valley of our Heavenly Shepherd. There's two plots left. One for you. One for me. All paid for."

"Even their deaths were unnatural—"

Charlie cut her short. He didn't want to hear what Signe was about to say. "I knew those empty graves should have been filled with earth." Charlie was referring to the empty graves in the east forty, graves from which a body had been removed. He had always connected the graves in Minnesota with the offspring he'd lost in Oregon. In his mind, Charlie felt that God had taken his three eldest children to fill the empty pits.

"Holes!" Signe cried, as if to convince herself that they were nothing but "Just holes. It's been over fifty years. The rains, the snows, and the fallen leaves of as many Minnesota winters have long since filled the voids."

"Just the same, I should return to Wolf Creek and shovel the dirt back into them."

"Why should you? You didn't dig them in the fIrst place."

Charlie winced. The undertones of Signe's last statement told him the make-believe was over. "Is he coming or not?"

"Who?" she asked, as she was about to hand Charlie his cup of coffee and lump of sugar.

"Who were we talking about, anyhow?" he shouted. "The priest! That's who." He whipped the cup off the saucer. It rolled on the floor and broke. And, as if suddenly energized, Charlie maneuvered his wheel-chair back and forth across the kitchen floor, sermonizing, "I like order in all things. Even in death. That's why I should speak to someone of authority."

Signe picked up the pieces of china. "You can talk with Father Myhre. He'll be here presently."

"A Cat'lic! I'm no Cat'lic. What does a priest know about us Finns?"

Signe cleared the table, poured another cup of coffee and handed it to him. "Father Myhre is Norwegian. He, too, comes from the north. He understands the workings of our souls. And, he is a man with authority. He's responsible to the Pope in Rome."

"He couldn't help Eldon," Charlie exclaimed hopelessly. "For hours they'd talk, the priest and Eldon. Eldon our first born. Dead by his own hand. Why? Why?"

"No one could help Eldon," Signe replied sadly. "He was a troubled soul. It was as if he was carrying the load of all mankind on his young shoulders."

"He had no right," Charlie shouted.

"What right?"

"To take his own life."

"He saw no other way," Signe replied softly.

"It was selfish."

"We are not to judge."

Charlie was deaf to reason. "He is gone and we are left with the burden."

Signe grew tired of his wheeling back and forth. She went to the back porch and returned with two long pieces of wood, and placed one block in front of the wheelchair and the other block in the back of it. Charlie was secured to the spot. "He asked nothing of you," she replied.

"I was his father," Charlie declared in injured tones.

"He knew that."

"He avoided me."

Signe drew back the curtain and looked out to the road, then went back to her sewing machine and picked up where she had left off. "Bah. Your imagination. Eldon was a loner. Born alone, lived alone, and died alone. He shared no thoughts and related no dreams. He became a stranger even to me, his mother."

"It was just the Finn in him."

"But when he was a child," Signe recalled with a smile, "he always laughed and sang."

"Yaa."

"He had a good voice."

Charlie sat peacefully, with his hands under his chin and smiled. "Yaa."

"Until he started drinking."

Charlie was immediately on the defensive. "It wasn't my fault. I was good to him."

Signe responded tenderly. "You were good to all our children. Always kind and understanding."

"I can say this now. Eldon was my favorite," Charlie confided, "my pet."

"They say you always lose the one you love the most."

Charlie shook his head at the enigmatic order of things, and the reasoning — if any — behind it. "But we lost three. And all so young."

"There were five children in my family, and we're all still here," Signe mused.

"Ten of us, and nine left," Charlie added. "One killed in the war. You don't count that."

"No, you don't count that." Her voice was soft. Once again she made her way to the window, drew the curtain aside and looked down the road. Father Myhre was always on time. She was worried, but said nothing. She tiptoed back to her machine and sat down to work, but Charlie wanted to talk.

"I miss Minnesota, the ice fishing in the winter and the first snowmelt in the spring."

"It was your idea to come here," Signe reminded him. "'We will go to Oregon. Oregon by the sea,' you recited day in, day out. You couldn't wait to sell everything, leave your house and home and your good position with the United States government."

Charlie embarked on a new high and waxed on like the chamber of commerce about the health benefits of having two distinct seasons—a cold winter and a hot summer. "Remember how I'd run out after a good steam bath and roll in the snow. That is what cleanses the body and tempers the soul."

"Run!" Signe stared at the man who, years ago, relegated his legs to the safety net of the wicker backed wheelchair. "Charlie, you are talking about a world that is now history and about a man who occupied that world. We live in the present and must plan for the future."

"I have no future. I have only memories." Charlie again made a mental switch to the land of his youth.

"All my relatives are there."

"If I'd known," Signe responded, as she rewound the bobbin, "that the children," referring to her two youngest girls, "would return to Minnesota as soon as they were old enough to leave, I'd never have let you sell the farm."

Charlie shook his head. "We cannot read the future."

"The hardest thing was leaving Buster behind. I can still feel my heart hurting." Signe added, and put her hand over her heart.

Charlie reddened, but tried to keep his temper. "With five kids, there was no room in the car for a mongrel dog."

"I don't know why you always called him a mongrel. Maybe because you're pure Finn." It was hard, she recalled, "Eldon loved Buster so."

Charlie angrily kicked the block of wood in front of the wheel and swung his chair around. "What was I to do? Leave one of the kids behind so that mongrel dog could sit in the back seat?"

Signe was immune to her husband's shouting. She could shut him off like the draft with a closed door. She pulled away from her sewing and rested her chin on her hands, which were clasped as if in prayer. "You know, Charlie, dogs have been known to follow their owners hundreds of miles."

Charlie laughed with satisfaction. "If he hasn't showed up yet, I don't think he will do so anymore."

"It takes time to cross the Rockies," she said.

"Woman, you just said it's been fifty years."

"Has it?" Signe asked, with a vague look. Recalling the past, the trip to Oregon in the old Model A seemed as recent as last week's drive to the county courthouse to pay the property taxes.

"Eldon's been gone forty-seven," he reminded her. "Died in 1936."

Signe nodded. "That's right. And Violet went two years later. Hugo a year after her."

"Just like that!" Charlie tried to snap his fingers as was his habit in youth, but the snap was gone. He stomped on the floor with his age stiffened right foot to the accompaniment of "Boom, boom, boom."

"All lying there side by side in the graveyard, like babies in their cradles. With their eyes closed. My babies."

Charlie looked around and sighed. "That's why I have to go back. Back with the living."

"And leave the dead behind? They cannot fend for themselves. I brought them on this earth. It is up to me to care for them while I'm alive."

Charlie shook his head. "The dead need no care. They feel no pain."

"I feel their pain."

"But why, Signe, why did it happen?"

"We are not to question His workings. Our Heavenly Father has His reasons. Maybe some day we will know. Maybe not." Signe left her sewing and took the towel off the pulla, as the Finns called the cardamom pastry, rising on the drain board. Satisfied that the loaf had risen enough, she carried the pan to the old wood burning range, opened the oven door and slipped it in. "Charlie, the hole between the firebox and the oven is as big as my fist. The flames are about to leap into the oven."

"Mother, I wouldn't worry if I were you. Your breads and cakes are as good as ever. Not even a burned crust."

"The stove must be as old as I. It was here when we bought the place. All other housewives have had electric ranges for years."

"Think what we've saved in electricity."

Signe went to the window, drew back the curtain and looked for the expected guest.

"Are you sure he'll come?" Charlie asked again.

Signe adjusted the curtain and went back to her sewing. "He'll come."

"Like the assessor and the tax collector," Charlie added, "to appraise and collect."

Signe laughed nervously as she fed the material to the foot of the machine. "You always have something funny to say, Charlie. I like that. You have the answer. No matter what. You are a fast thinker."

The pause that followed rankled Charlie. He did not like silence. Signe had taken out her remnant bag and was searching. "What are you digging for?" he asked, infuriated.

"I know it's in here because I saw it just the other day."

"What?"

"A piece of pique," she answered.

"What's that?"

"A remnant of material from Jenny Lindroos' sun back. 1954."

Charlie groaned. "Why don't you get rid of those rags?"

"My remnants? I can't. They're my files."

"What files you talking about?"

"The records of my life," Signe explained, as she tenderly lifted various scraps of material from the worn-out old pillowcase and reviewed their histories. "You know, like lawyers have files for all their cases. These are all the dresses, suits, and coats I've made. I remember each garment and for whom and for what occasion." Signe's happiness came to a halt. "Charlie, there's none for—"

"What?"

"Eldon's burial."

"Why not?"

"We ordered a suit ready-made from Chicago Mail Order. Remember?"

Charlie nodded.

"It's a pity we couldn't have open casket," she said.

"But we couldn't," he confirmed, in barely audible tones.

"No, we couldn't," she repeated. Signe then pulled out a large safety pin with three swatches of material: red, black and white. She held the swatches for Charlie to see. "These are from the Marks widow's last dresses."

Charlie blanched. His unsteady right eye began to quiver. "Put them away!" he ordered.

Signe continued her reminiscing as if she had not heard his admonition. "The dresses I never got to finish—"

Now out of control, Charlie screamed, "Woman, are you going deaf on me?"

Signe quickly stuffed the remnants into the bag and took it to the bedroom.

"What'll I tell Father Myhre?" he asked, when she returned to her chair by the sewing machine.

She looked him in the eye. "Say you're dying and want to clear the records."

"What if I don't die?"

"Oooo. You will. We all die. If not today, then tomorrow. And the records will be straight. Meanwhile, you and Father Myhre can have a good chat. An honest talk never hurt any body."

Her response did not seem to alleviate Charlie's concerns. "Signe, I never asked you this and you don't have to answer if you don't want to. Do you think there is a heaven?"

His question did not surprise Signe, even considering that her husband had once been a church member and a believer in God. After some thought, she answered, "Yes."

"What about Hell?"

"There must be."

Charlie finally came out with what was rankling him. "Do you think that idiot is still alive?"

"Who?"

"Reino."

"He was no idiot," she replied. "He was smart."

"Too smart for his own good."

Signe glanced up from her sewing. "Why do you say that?"

"Could land him in a lot of trouble." Getting no response from Signe, Charlie became impatient. "Well, is he?"

"What?"

"Dead or alive?"

Signe's main concern at this point was cutting the trim for the dress she was making. "Dead. Of course."

Charlie was happy. Only momentarily. "How do you know?"

"He should be. He's almost as old as you."

Charlie gave an irritated shriek. "I'm still here."

Signe thought for a moment. "That's right. He's alive," she added, with authority.

"How do you know?"

"Because no one has mentioned him in their letters. If he had died, someone would have written me and enclosed a notice from the Finnish American News. You know those columns in the newspaper with a black wreath—" Signe formed a circle with her arms—"on top, saying he had passed on to his eternal home, and was buried in the old Wolf Creek cemetery alongside of his beloved father and mother leaving behind eleven sisters and brothers—"

"I didn't ask for his obituary," Charlie screamed. "All I wanted to know was if he's dead. If he's alive, he should be dead. Buried in the bowels of the earth instead of our Eldon."

"Reino was always good to Eldon. Like a big brother." Signe spoke softly.

Charlie wheeled his chair around to the table. "Woman, I said that WHORE'S SON should be DEAD." He pounded on the edge of the table with his fist, with the energy of a young man. "Dead. Dea-"

Charlie's ranting was interrupted by a loud knock. Signe hurried to the door. It was Father Myhre, the young priest, now aged and fragile, who had be-friended Eldon in his time of need.

"I thought you'd died," Charlie shouted across the room.

Father Myhre ignored Charlie's remark and apologized to Signe as he handed her his hat and raincoat. "I was so absorbed in my packing that time sorta slipped by me—"

Before he could finish the sentence, Charlie asked, "Where you going, Father Myhre?"

"Florida."

"Florida!" Charlie echoed, and laughed heartily. "I thought they were all Southern Baptists in that part of the country."

"That I wouldn't know," the priest replied. "I've retired and look forward to spending the rest of my days basking in warm sunshine."

Charlie became dispirited. Even the priest had crossed him.

"Charlie, here, is thinking about dying and would like a passport to Heaven," Signe told the priest. "I said you were the person to issue him one."

Father Myhre laughed. "I don't have that much power, but I can perhaps write some clearance papers and give him a good reference."

At this point Charlie was cantankerous. He looked at the priest and asked, "Do you want to hear my story or not?"

Father Myhre stared at Charlie. He finally replied, "All right, Charlie. Tell me your story."

"In my bedroom," Charlie replied. "In private."

Signe opened the bedroom door, and Father

Myhre pushed in Charlie's wheelchair and closed the door.

Chapter I

"WAKE UP. WAKE UP!" Signe felt herself being shaken.

It took a moment for Signe to remember where she was. She bounced to a sitting position. "Was our ship hit?"

Hilda laughed. "No torpedoes. But I want you to witness an unforgettable scene. Such a beautiful sunrise! The sea gleams like a mirror. Ships racing to the harbor. People laughing. People crying. Others on their knees supplicating to God. What a picture! Come. We'll soon be landing."

Signe's heart danced with excitement. "That the sun is bright and the sea smooth is a good omen."

Their conversation was drowned by children shouting, "Let's go see the lady with the crown on her head." Another voice responded. "It's the Statue of Liberty."

Signe quickly dressed in her navy blue alpaca suit,

put up her long flaxen hair, buttoned her high shoes, and pinned on her hat. "Do I need a shawl?"

Hilda shook her head. "It's like Midsummer's Day."

Making their way up to the top deck wasn't easy. Trunks, bedding, bundles of kitchenware, and keepsakes cluttered the passageways. Eager passengers wanted to be ready at landing, first to get off the ship.

"They shouldn't get too excited," a male voice behind them commented. "We're lucky if we don't have to spend the next few days on board. Wait till they see the number of ships lined up to enter the harbor."

"What'll we do for food?" an old lady whimpered. "I've been hungry since we left Stockholm."

"You'll eat first class," replied the Swedish gentleman, who introduced himself as Sam Feldman, returning to the United States for a permanent stay. "All paid for by the steamship company."

"What happens when we reach Ellis Island?" the woman asked. "What will they do to me?"

"A simple medical examination of the head, body and eyes and a few questions. That's all. Nothing to worry about," Feldman assured her.

In the spring of 1917, seventeen-year-old Signe Maki left by boat her home in Helsinki, Finland. Five days later she arrived in Stockholm, Sweden. In her tiny purse she carried the ticket to America, which her older sister Gertrude had sent from Minneapolis, Minnesota, for the trip. At dawn the next morning Signe boarded the Swedish ocean liner *Gripsholm* for

America. The journey took nine days.

Immigrating to the United States had not been on Signe's agenda when she enrolled at a technical institute in Helsinki, the city she loved. She enrolled at the institute at fifteen and completed the course in two years, graduated with honors and was promptly employed.

In the summer of 1916, Saul Maki, a cousin of her friend Selma, came to Finland for a visit. He told Signe about the possibilities in United States available to people with skills such as hers. "America is the land of opportunity," Saul kept repeating. "Look at me, the son of an ironworker, now professor of Linguistics at Columbia University. That can only happen in America."

Signe's two sisters in the United States felt they had done the right thing by leaving Finland and encouraged her to make the move.

Crossing the Atlantic during World War I was risky. German submarines prowled the ocean. Sweden was not at war, but accidents could happen and a seagoing vessel might suffer the fate of the *Lusitania*. Still, Signe was determined to go to America.

Having lived all her life in Helsinki by the sea, Signe loved the water. Now on board an ocean liner, she spent much of the day on deck. As she watched the sun come out of a dark, heavy cloud she noticed a short, dark complexioned, buxom young girl, about her own age, looking out to the sea. She'd seen her there the day before. Perhaps an Estonian—too dark for a Swede—Signe thought as she approached and in halting Swedish greeted her fellow traveler.

The girl shook her head, indicating she didn't understand, and pointed to herself, "*Suomalainen.*"

"Finnish!" Signe gave a squeal of joy to find a fellow countrywoman on board. "Where from?"

"Evijärveltä. From your height and fair coloring I thought you were Finnish when I first saw you, but waited to approach you."

Signe introduced herself and gave a few facts about her background and work.

"My name is Hilda Halme," her new friend responded, saying her folks were country people. "I have no education except confirmation school, but I can read, write, cook and sew. That's all a farm wife is expected to know."

"What's your destination?"

"Wolf Creek, Minnesota."

"Sounds like a lonely place," Signe commented wistfully, as she envisioned a dark copse inhabited by wild animals. She could almost hear the mournful cry of the loons in the meadow.

"I'm going there to marry my childhood sweetheart, Gust Mattson. He's already bought a farm and two cows."

Signe nodded and smiled. "I expect to live in New York City the rest of my life."

The two spent the next six days together talking about their childhoods and their hopes for the future. It concerned Signe that no one was meeting Hilda at Ellis Island. How could she make it all the way to Minnesota, not understanding a word of English?

Hilda laughed at Signe's fears. "I made it this far

without a word of Swedish."

Signe admired Hilda's spunk.

As the *Gripsholm* approached New York Harbor, all eyes focused on the Statue of Liberty in the horizon on the left. Such activity on the water—sloops, tugboats, barges, freighters and ocean liners coming and going. The excitement was contagious. Fear and hope intermingled in the hearts of the newcomers. The fear of rejection clouded joy and anticipation. Some could not contain their happiness without shedding a few tears. Signe's heart hammered uncontrollably. "I think we should go down and gather our things," she said.

"Won't take me long," Hilda responded. "Mine is a small bundle."

Before leaving the ship, Signe gave Hilda a piece of paper. "Here's my name and the address of the man who is meeting me today. Please send me a note when you arrive at Wolf Creek. I want to know that you have reached your destination safely."

Hilda took the slip, put it in her traveling bag and promised to write Signe as soon as she arrived there. When the ship docked, the first- and second-class passengers disembarked. Signe and Hilda and the rest of the steerage passengers were directed to the gangplank near the stern and then across the pier. Each immigrant was given a tag to wear with his name and manifest number. Signe's tag read: Signe Maki - L 14. Thirty people, not necessarily of the same nationality, made up a manifest. Hilda's number M11 sent her off with another group. The last Signe saw of

Hilda was her hand waving as she was swept along in the crowd.

Barges hired by the steamship companies carried the steerage passengers to Ellis Island. On the island, barge attendants directed them according to their manifest numbers to the main building.

Each interpreter took his manifest group to the registry room where the immigrants sat on long benches and waited for their examination.

Immigrants needed to be healthy, able to support themselves and not become public charges. The doctors watched for signs of mental defects as well as physical symptoms such as conjunctivitis, trachoma, goiter, hernia, pregnancy, lameness and senility. Special attention was given to the heart, back, neck, face, feet and scalp. Children over two years were made to walk on their own. Any suspicious symptoms were chalk marked in code on the immigrant's coat that more examinations were indicated.

So far, Signe had easily passed all tests. One more remained—the eye examination. At the front of the line, the immigrants were greeted by two white coated doctors, flanked by nurses holding towels. On the tables behind them were basins of disinfectant solution. The passengers ahead of Signe were getting jittery about the test, a horrendous procedure which consisted of turning the eyelids inside out with a button hook to detect contagious diseases like trachoma, which could cause blindness.

On seeing the buttonhook, the woman in front of Signe fainted. The orderlies lifted the woman aside and Signe took a deep breath to steady herself for the examination. A nurse dipped the buttonhook in a basin of disinfectant, wiped it on a towel and handed it to one of the doctors who flipped Signe's lids inside out—a painful procedure, but brief. The doctor gave a pleased nod indicating she could move on.

Having passed her literacy test and with more than sufficient funds—five hundred Finn marks—Signe was ready to enter the United States.

"Is someone meeting you?" the interpreter asked.

Signe was surprised to hear the interpreter speak Finnish. She had just spoken in some strange, unfamiliar tongue to a man ahead of her. "How many languages do you know?" Signe asked.

Originally three—Finnish, Swedish and Estonian with a smattering of Russian. I grew up in Karelia," she added. "I married a man who migrated from Naples, so I had to learn Italian. My Jewish landlord is teaching me Yiddish. In my work, every foreign word helps. Did you say someone is meeting you?"

Signe nodded.

The interpreter put out her hand. "A letter perhaps?"

Signe took Saul Maki's photo and card out of her handbag and handed them to her.

"Professor?"

Signe nodded.

"Brother or cousin?"

Signe nodded again, unable to lie out loud.

"Which?"

The name Maki in Finland was almost as common as Smith in the U.S. Saul was no relation to her, but Signe having heard many conflicting stories con-

cerning rules about men picking up girls on the island, murmured, "Cousin."

The interpreter looked at Saul's photo. "I see the
resemblance," and gave it back to Signe. "You can
exchange your money at one of the wickets."

Signe thanked her and walked to the end of the
registry room to trade her marks for dollars. From
there she went to the baggage room to make arrangements to have her trunk sent to Saul's address in
New York City. She left the building and as she
hurried along the wire-fenced walk to the ferry, her
face lit up in a smile. I'm free to enter the United
States of America!

Saul met her at the ferry, which took them to the
terminal at the Battery. He looked her over and
seemed pleased with her appearance. He asked how
her crossing had been, but Saul was not a talkative
person and usually kept his conversation to a
minimum.

The view of New York City from the Battery left
Signe without words. It was a solid block of sky-
scrapers, taller than anything she could have
imagined. "That's the Singer Building," Saul informed
her, "with forty-seven stories. That other is the
Woolworth Building. Sixty stories."

Signe worried about Hilda. "She had nobody to
meet her and she doesn't know a word of English.
How will she ever manage to reach Minnesota?"

"I wouldn't worry about your friend," Saul
responded. "She either had a ticket voucher or purchased a ticket when she exchanged her money.
Immigrant aid societies have representatives who

assist travelers to the right railroad. Someone will see that she buys a box lunch large enough to feed her the length of the trip."

Signe was pleased with the room Saul had reserved for her in a residence hotel on Madison Avenue. "Here you'll be safe and in good company," he told her.

"Men and women have separate floors," the desk clerk explained. "Women occupy the lower floors. The men's rooms are on eight and nine. The solarium is on the tenth where tea is served every afternoon from five to six. I hope you will join our other guests at that time," he added with a smile as he handed her the key to room 714.

Signe smiled and said, "Tenk you," and followed Saul to the lobby. "What did the nice young man say?"

Saul translated the clerk's conversation and added, "You'll have no cooking facilities. There's a coffee shop downstairs, however, it might be a bit expensive. I will show you the closest Horn and Hardart Automat where you can have a meal for ten, fifteen cents or a feast for twenty-five."

Signe took out her coin purse and looked over the various coins. "A dollar, a fifty-cent piece, a twenty-five-cent coin—"

"We call that a quarter," Saul interjected, "a ten-cent coin is called a dime and a five-cent a nickel."

"Very easy."

"What should be uppermost in your mind is to learn the language," Saul said. "I have a second year student who is thinking of starting an English class

for immigrants. He hopes to get space at the settlement house on Third Avenue. I'll see that he reserves
a spot for you."

Signe showed Saul her little Finnish-English/
English-Finnish dictionary she'd bought in Helsinki.
"I know many words, but don't know how to say
them. They're not pronounced as written."

Saul laughed. "You discovered that early."

Signe was delighted with her new home. Room
714 had a lovely view. Looking toward the East River
in the early morning, she could see the rising sun. The
furnishings—bed, desk, dresser, two chairs and
sink—were finer than any she'd seen. The closet was
spacious. Bathrooms were down the hall.

Signe took to New York and the residents of the
hotel took to Signe. It seemed almost everyone knew
of a job for her. She was employed within a week by a
dress shop owned by Jay and Miriam Goldberg,
friends of Stephanie Levi, an artist, resident in room
713.

She visited the museums on weekends and went
to a dance at the Finnish Hall on a Hundred and
Twenty-Fifth Street a couple times a month. Signe had
a proposal of marriage from a young man who was
apprenticed to a piano tuner, but told him she wasn't
ready to settle down. Life had too much to offer and
she wanted to partake of the offers. Her most mem-
orable occasion was hearing Caruso in Mascagni's
"Lodoletta" at the Metropolitan Opera House as guest
of the Goldbergs. Mrs. Goldberg lent her a mink stole
for the occasion. The Goldbergs and Signe had dinner

at the Delmonico and went home in a taxi.

In December, Signe received a Christmas card from Hilda with a note saying she'd been married soon after arriving in Wolf Creek and expected a child in early spring. She wrote that her pregnancy had been most difficult.

Signe felt sorry for Hilda. She recalled her own feelings when Hilda first mentioned Wolf Creek. She could almost hear the lonely calls of the loons she'd envisioned then.

With the new year, Signe's life took an unexpected turn. At Christmas dinner at his club on Fifth Avenue, Saul was unusually talkative and said he considered Signe an important part of his future. "I have much to offer a woman," he said. "You are what I seek in a wife. I already noticed that when I visited Finland."

Signe blushed. Although she'd sensed that Saul thought of her as more than a casual friend, his putting his feelings into words rattled her. He was twice her age, settled and circumspect. She wasn't interested in what he might wish to share with her. She had come to America to seek a new life of her own, not to settle into someone else's.

Before Signe could put her thoughts into words, Saul told her that the English classes for immigrants would start the second Tuesday at the settlement house.

Early to arrive in the classroom, Signe sat in the front, with paper on the desk before her and pencil in hand. The room filled quickly—twenty-nine men and eight women. All eager to learn.

The teacher arrived, a young man in his early twenties, tall and slender, with dark hair, violet blue eyes and sweeping eyelashes. "I'm your instructor," he announced. "My name is Gael Hugo." He looked at Signe in front of him. She cast her eyes downwards. He took roll. When he called Signe's name and she raised her hand, he avoided her eyes. The class met twice a week. During the first three weeks, the two made no eye contact.

In the fourth week, at the end of class, as Signe was putting on her coat, her ring caught her necklace and broke the string. The faux pearls rolled over the floor. Gael got down on his knees to gather the beads and said, "Miss Maki, I would like to take you to see a moving picture. Will you go with me?"

Signe said yes without understanding where he was taking her. She'd never heard about people in pictures moving like humans in real life.

The film was "Little Princess" with Mary Pickford. Signe would never forget the event. Seeing people on the screen was like magic, but the thrill of that magic would be eclipsed by incidents to come.

Once the film began, Signe felt Gael reach for her hand. She was taken aback and almost withdrew her hand. She looked around. All eyes were following the events on the screen, but she noticed a couple with the man's arm over the girl's shoulder and decided that holding hands must be acceptable in America. Gael's hold was steadying and tender.

The best was yet to come. When Gael brought Signe home, he kissed her on the cheek when he said goodnight. The only sign of affection Signe had seen in Finland was between Russians. They seemed to hug and kiss without reservation, which met with raised eyebrows and headshakes of the Finns.

Signe could not have imagined happiness such as hers now. Language wasn't a barrier. Gael had a way of making her understand English and she recalled words in French she'd learned in school. She and Gael spent many evenings and weekends together—as many as he could spare from his studies—exploring the city. They attended a concert in Brooklyn featuring Berlioz' *Symphonie Fantastique*.

"Did you enjoy the music?" Gael asked Signe.

"Very much. It was . . . wild."

"My favorite composer," Gael told her. "People think Berlioz was mad, but he was a genius. His creative imagination was intensified by the use of opium, which was very popular among artists at the time."

Gael wanted to know about her family and said, "My mother is Irish and my father French. They live in a quaint little town in Pennsylvania called New Hope. Not too far from here."

"New Hope," Signe repeated. "Sounds like a lovely place."

"I will take you there when spring comes and the trees begin to bloom. And I'll show you where George Washington crossed the Delaware." They sat at the Automat and drank coffee while Gael gave Signe a brief resume of early American history.

By blossom time, Gael had been drafted into the army, briefly trained and sent out of the country. "I will never kill anyone," he assured Signe when he kissed her goodbye. "I'll do my duty as a medic."

No substitute could be found to replace Gael as English instructor and the evening classes at the settlement house were discontinued. Life in New York wasn't the same for Signe. The streets, the buildings in mid-Manhattan—even the air she breathed—reminded her of Gael Hugo. Without Gael, there was no life for her except his letters, which she read and reread.

In May Signe received a letter from her sister Anna saying she was getting married in Minneapolis in June and wanted Signe to be her maid of honor. The invitation was good news. Signe wanted to leave New York until Gael came back. She was due a week's vacation with pay and the Goldbergs consented to another week without pay.

On learning of this turn of events, Saul Maki shook his head and warned Signe not to get too friendly with any farm boy. "You know how it is in the spring. Birds, bees, and young people begin to look for a mate."

"Me, marry a farmer?" Signe exclaimed. "I've never even seen a cow up-close, much less milked one."

On the first of June, Signe went to Pennsylvania Station and boarded the train to Chicago. There she transferred to another to the Twin Cities. When she got to Minneapolis, a letter from Hilda was waiting for her. "You must come to see my son," Hilda wrote.

"Arthur is such a good-looking boy."

After Anna's wedding, Signe took the train to Detroit Lakes. There she was met by Hilda's husband, Gust Mattson and another young man, Charlie Skinnar, the owner of a secondhand Model T Ford.

Charlie gave Signe a whirl. Almost every night after chores, he'd show up at the Mattson home where he'd sit till eleven o'clock spouting his plans for the future while enjoying Hilda's homemade pastries and strong black coffee, his eye always on Signe.

"Charlie Skinnar will be a fine catch for some lucky girl," Gust said, looking at Signe across the supper table one evening.

"Yaa, for some backwoods farm girl," Hilda retorted, stabbing a baked potato with her fork, "but not for Signe. She deserves better."

Gust gazed at his wife with his mild blue eyes and in his soft-spoken voice asked, "What's 'better?' Charlie's got forty acres with a house, barn, livestock, and a car. What more can a girl want?"

"An educated, enlightened man," Hilda snapped.

"Hilda, I don't know what you're talking about. Charlie graduated. He talks English good. Mark my words, he'll go places and do things."

"I don't like him."

"Why not?"

"Well—" Hilda shot glances around the room. "For one thing, I don't trust him. I get this feeling here—" She patted her heart, which was protected by a well endowed bosom.

"Mama, you're always getting feelings there—"

"And am I not always right?" Hilda shot back. "Remember when Lahti's cow disappeared and everyone said she'd wandered to the Reservation and the Indians probably made Fourth of July barbecue out of her? I said Indians don't steal. The cow most likely drowned. A couple of weeks later the cow showed floating belly up in Shell Lake."

"Just because you don't like Charlie Skinnar isn't any reason why Signe can't marry him. You got me!" Gust blushed at his daring repartee. "Besides, New York City is no place for a young woman in time of war."

"What are you talking about?" Hilda retorted, her black eyes flashing like ignited coals. "There's been no shots fired in New York City."

"The Germans could come any time. Here in Wolf Creek we sit as in God's lap in peace and security."

Two months had gone by since Signe had received a letter from Gael. None since she left New York. "No letter for me?" she asked Gust when he returned from the mailbox.

"Why should he write?" Gust asked with a gleam in his eye. "He sees you 'most every night," referring to Charlie Skinnar. Seeing the sad look on Signe's face, Gust put on his cap. "Don't remember if I closed the chicken coop door. Don't want the skunks to get in," he muttered, and went out.

"Maybe the hotel isn't forwarding my mail," Signe said.

"Write them a letter," Hilda suggested. "Maybe they've misplaced your forwarding address."

"I can't write English that well. Perhaps I should ask Charlie Skinnar to do it for me."

Hilda's eyes flashed at the idea, but she caught herself. "I'll ask Ellie Lahti. She graduated last year. She will know how to write a proper letter."

Before Ellie could be reached, Signe received a note from the Goldbergs saying the weather had been hot in the city and business was slow. They were going to the Peekskills for the summer and wouldn't expect Signe back until the first of September.

In the same mail she received a note from Saul Maki. He said he missed her and wondered when she would be returning to New York. Lastly, Saul wrote, "You remember the young man who taught the immigrants' English class at the settlement house on Third Avenue. He was killed in action in France."

Signe fainted.

Wolf Creek was lovely in the spring. The wild plum and lilacs around Hilda's house perfumed Signe's room. She recalled Gael's promise to take her to New Hope when the trees were in blossom. She gathered large bouquets. Each one assured her that Gael would return, and every day she expected a letter saying the notice of Gael's death was an error. The letter never came.

Other than eager notes from Saul and correspondence from her family, Signe's only mail was a card from Miriam Goldberg saying her husband had suffered a stroke and they had to sell the store. That ended any desire Signe might have had to return to New York.

"Perhaps I should go to Minneapolis," she told Hilda and Gust at breakfast one morning. "I think I'd soon find employment." Minneapolis, as a city, held no fascination for Signe. Besides, her sister Anna had moved to Michigan and Gertrude was dictatorial and demanding.

"Minneapolis!" Gust cried out. "Come July and you'll feel like an egg in a hot frying pan. What's wrong with Wolf Creek?"

"I need to make a living."

"Have Saul ship your sewing machine here. You'll get plenty of customers in this corner of God's creation. Besides, now that Hilda is baby-way again, we sure could use help."

Signe stayed. The Mattsons had no money to pay her, for which Gust often apologized, but she had no expenses, either.

She had a good home. She was learning how to care for children, a new experience for her. Spring and summer slipped by uneventfully. At the end of September Hilda gave birth to their second son, Raymond.

Soon after, Gust had a second bit of good news to any who would listen—especially Signe. "Did you know Charlie Skinnar is taking Mr. Gilpin's place as mail carrier now that Gilpin is retiring?"

"Where'd you hear that?" Hilda, suckling Raymond by the kitchen table, demanded to know.

"At the creamery. From Charlie himself. He just invested in a brand-new Model A. He was sporting a new suit. Mighty fine looking gentleman that Charlie Skinnar. Tall, slender, and well built. With a good head of hair."

"Gust, you need glasses," Hilda lashed out.

"Hildy, I know you think I'm the best as far as men go," Gust teased, "but there's only one of me and I have no brother. Give Charlie a chance. There's talk that he'll be made Justice of the Peace one of these days."

"Time to feed the chickens," Hilda said, after glancing at the clock on the lamp stand.

Gust grabbed his blue and white striped cap off the hook on the wall behind the kitchen stove and hurried out.

Signe laughed at the husband-wife repartee she heard daily. She enjoyed living with them and taking care of Arthur and Raymond, but she had to think of her future.

What made up Signe's mind was Charlie's invitation to Signe and the Mattsons to visit him on a Sunday afternoon. When they arrived, the table was set for coffee with all the pastries and coffee breads any elder Finnish lady would serve. After lunch, Charlie showed them the extra bedroom he built for his mother. "But she died before the house was finished," he said. "She was a good mother, a fine woman."

Charlie then took them to see the outside buildings and finally to the well he'd had drilled. "The best in the county. Plenty of ice-cold water all summer long. Next on my list of projects is a new icehouse."

On the way home, Gust related how Charlie worked two summers on the county road to pay for the house he had Oscar Salo build. "Charlie said he still owes for the acreage, but the house is paid for. There aren't many young men his age who can claim that," Gust added.

"I realize there's a shortage of men, especially here," Hilda told Signe, and that professor in New York doesn't seem to excite you. If you've got your heart set on Charlie Skinnar, don't let me stop you. All I ask is that you have me as your matron of honor. It would make me very happy."

Signe and Charlie were married in July 1919, with Hilda and Gust as attendants.

Chapter II

ELDON SKINNAR WAS BORN in April, 1920. The baby's birth was long and hard. Eva Korppula, the midwife who had delivered Charlie himself was in charge. She worried for both mother and infant. Signe's water had broken the day before, and labor had begun. But now the contractions had stopped. Every time Eva tugged at the infant's head, he'd push out his shoulder. He does not want to enter the world, Eva told herself. Charlie, unlike his father who had hidden in the granary at Charlie's birth, was constantly underfoot eagerly waiting for his first-born. "Charlie," Eva finally said, "you're of no help around here. Why don't you sharpen your ax and split some wood." Charlie went out.

Once the door closed, the midwife hurried to her old leather pouch sitting on the kitchen table, took out a pair of crude metal forceps and went to work. She latched on to the infant's cranium and pulled. Signe screamed. The child appeared and let out a cry. "A boy," Eva announced. Charlie, standing outside the kitchen door, rushed to Signe's side. "Did you hear that?" he asked. "It was like the voice of an angel."

Eva righted the infant she was holding upside down, and looked in his eyes, shook her head, and with her right hand flailed the air as if smacking invisible fruit flies before her face. Eva was Lutheran, but she was Finnish, too, and forever watching for signs or omens.

"Is he not perfect?" the anxious father asked as Eva grabbed a pair of shears to snip the navel.

"He is," she replied as she tied the cord. Handing the newborn to Charlie, she muttered, "Come."

Charlie followed the midwife to the kitchen, gingerly holding his precious son, while Eva got the baby's bath ready.

A veteran caretaker, Eva seemed to know the workings of everyone's household. She went right for the dishpan hanging on a nail behind the stove, opened the lid to the hot water tank at the end of the range and dippered some water into the pan. After cooling it with some cold water from the pail on the wood box, she grabbed the bar of brown naphtha soap sitting next to it and set the bath works on the kitchen table. Eva pulled up the sleeve of her blouse and dunked her elbow in the pan. Satisfied that the temperature was right, she took the baby and washed him. After bundling him in flannel, Eva nestled the infant beside his mother, went to her bag and took out a document. "What are you going to name him?"

"Eldon, an American name," Charlie proudly announced.

"I was thinking Eldon Hugo," Signe voiced from her bed.

Charlie shook his head. "The first-born son should always be named after his father. Eldon Charles Skinnar."

"Can't spell it." Eva said, and handed the paper to Charlie.

Eva was exacting about records. While some midwives of the time were haphazard in recording births, Eva Korppula made sure that every child she delivered had a birth certificate on file.

Charlie went to the cupboard, took out the bottle of ink, the pen, sat at the kitchen table, and in big, bold letters inscribed Charles Eldon Skinnar in the space provided.

Eva put the paper in her bag along with her forceps. "Charlie, go warm up the car. It's getting late. I will not travel in the dark." With Charlie out of the way, she proceeded to take care of the mother. When everything was done, Eva took a white sheet, tore it into wide strips and wrapped them around Signe. "That oughta pull you back in shape," Eva declared, as she yanked the ends of the strips together over the new mother's loose belly and tied them together with large safety pins. "Stay as you are," she ordered. "I'll be back in the morning. Have Charlie pick me up at eight."

"But Charlie leaves for his mail route at seven thirty," Signe said.

"The mail can wait," Eva replied, as she tied a scarf over her braided head. "Take my bag," she commanded Charlie who had just come in. "I won't be delivering anymore babies," she announced, not looking at the young couple. "You'll have to find someone else. May Heaven help you."

Chapter III

LIFE HAD BEEN GOOD to Charlie Skinnar. His farm at Wolf Creek had grown and prospered. He'd cleared most of his forty acres, built a new milk house and added to his barn. This had been possible with Signe's help. She always worked at his side. The mail carrier's job brought in the extra cash they needed. Charlie now was a Justice of The Peace, secretary to the school board, and on the board of directors for the new Co-op creamery.

Next to cream, oats had been the main source of income for the Finnish farmers since they migrated to the area. Some grew a little wheat, a little barley, or clover, "but oats one could depend on," unless there was a drought, a flood, hailstorm, tornado, or a heavy rain at harvest. The trick was to get the t'rashers on time.

Earlier Signe had read in some farm magazine—maybe it was Successful Farming, she couldn't recall—about a hay that had more protein than clover and was palatable enough for humans. The plant was called alfalfa. This spring, at Signe's insistence, Charlie ordered alfalfa seed from a company in South Dakota for spring planting.

Signe's hunch paid well. The first year they harvested two cuttings. They swapped Ed Koski two stacks of the hay for two newborn Holstein heifers to build up the dairy herd. The second season was even more successful. Charlie cut the first crop for hay and left the second for seed.

Charlie was excited about their new adventure. He consulted Ed, an expert on clover seeds, who leased a section of land on the Ponsford prairie, about getting the t'rashers in a couple of weeks when the alfalfa seed should be at its prime.

T'rashers is Minnesotan for the threshing machine, a noisy contraption that separates the grain or seed from the straw. It includes the machine operator, its crew, and all the hungry countryside folks who follow the clanky vehicle down narrow roads from one farm to the next, expecting to have their bellies filled with beef stew and pumpkin pie. There was only one threshing machine in the area. It was owned by Sam Isaacson & Sons, who also were well drillers and barn builders and had the capital to invest in this humongous apparatus that served several townships.

The acceptable policy was to feed the crew a substantial diet consisting of meat, potatoes, pie, cake, puddings and fruit sauce with coffee hours in mid-morning and midafternoon.

"You have to come up with the cash upon completion of the harvest," Ed Koski warned Charlie when the two men met at the creamery. "Sam and his boys expect their money when the last straw flies into the pile. Deviation from this policy could mean the delay of next year's harvest."

Charlie nodded as he stared at the cream check on which the ink was barely dry. The low butterfat marking shown on the stub disturbed him. Perhaps he should swap his Holsteins for Jerseys. Recalling that he'd bought the last two Holstein calves that Ed had, Charlie said, "You got mostly Jerseys now. Right?"

Ed pursed his mouth and nodded. "Jerseys and Guernseys. Not as much milk, but much higher butterfat."

"There's been some talk that Land O'Lakes is going to be buying whole milk."

"Yaa. Wouldn't that be a blessing. I hear they would have a truck come by every morning. All we'd have to do is put the milk cans by the road. No need for ice in the milk houses."

"You're forgetting, Ed, we still got to keep the evening milking cold overnight,"

Ed laughed. "That's right. Seems there's a bug in every potato seedling."

"You pay them t'rashers prompt," Ed repeated when the two men parted company. "Or next year watch'em go rumbling and clanking past your place to your next-door neighbor while you stand at your driveway by the open gate chewing on a wad of Copenhagen. And they won't be back until the end of the season after the fall rains have soaked the crop and mildew has set in."

Charlie knew Sam Isaacson from previous business dealings. When Charlie's well went dry one summer, he hired Isaacson & Sons to dig a new shaft. The bill came to five dollars more than what had been estimated. Sam wouldn't wait until Saturday, when Charlie took his cream to the creamery, to get paid. Charlie had to drive to Fargo to a pawn shop to hock the gold watch his mother had given him for his eighth grade graduation to get the five dollars.

Charlie puckered his mouth, nodded his head in the tempo of Ed's elocution, and stared into the distance. "I hear what you're saying."

"How many do you expect for dinner?" Signe asked her husband when she planned the menu for the threshers.

"Anywheres from twenty-five to fifty."

"It takes that many men to operate the machine?"

Charlie laughed. "Only five or six men for that, but you wouldn't want to offend the neighbors by not offering them something to eat."

"Won't a cup of coffee and biscuit do?"

"Not after they've had a whiff of your beef stew. I'll get the meat. We've got the potatoes."

"Takes more than meat and potatoes to make stew."

When Signe ran into Hilda Mattson at the meat

counter at the Co-op, she told Hilda about the up-coming event.

"Be sure you got plenty of food," Hilda said. "One year I made ten pies and ran out before the school kids got home. It was such a disappointment to them. You know how the kiddies look forward to the t'rashers. To them it's like a second Christmas."

"Give me five more pounds of beef, please," Signe told the butcher, "and a pail of leaf lard."

Sparked by the news that the threshers were coming in three days, Charlie got up before dawn to observe the skies. It had rained early in the summer, but August had been dry to this point, allowing the seed to ripen well. The air was cool, almost breezeless. The moon setting in the west seemed to forecast a fair day, but fickle Mother Nature was not to be trusted. She could drum up a fall hailstorm that would thresh every kernel of grain off the stem, leaving only the straw to be gathered and hauled into the hay barn, or she could whip the mowed grass free of its seed. Charlie had no choice. The threshers were coming. He would cut today.

Signe spent two days making pies — pumpkin, green tomato and sour cream raisin. The weather had turned warm again, and having a big fire in the kitchen stove all day long to bake the goodies made the small three-room house unbearably hot.

She was eight months pregnant with her fourth child, nauseous every day of the term. The smell of coffee, cooking meat and vegetables made her ill. Her legs were swollen and painful, and her normally slim body now large and cumbersome.

"Hire somebody to help you," Charlie suggested.

"Who's there to hire?"

Before the crew got to the Skinnar farm, help for Signe, in a limited sort of way, arrived in the person of Reino Koski, Ed's retarded nephew. Signe was glad to see him. The children liked Reino.

"I come to help."

"Reino, you're a godsend. The children are tired, and I don't have time to take care of them. Could you rock Hugo?"

"You bet'cha. Can I sit in your rocking chair?"

"Of course."

Reino sang as he moved back and forth. The monotony of the two words, "Home, sweet home," soon sent Hugo to dreamland. Reino carefully carried him to bed, and sat down with Violet. "Do I sing pretty good?" he asked Signe after he delivered the sleeping girl to her bed.

"Very good. You have a nice voice."

"Yaa. I can carry a tune all right, but the words get lost."

Eldon was quick to jump into Reino's lap. "I want "Yankee Doodle.""

"I don't know that."

"Not even the tune?"

"Nah. I'll tell you the story of the two bears—"

"Three!" Eldon shouted.

"Two. One got lost."

"Which one?"

"Papa Bear."

Eldon became worried. "But Mama Bear is with Baby Bear?"

"Yaa."

"That's good."

Reino didn't get far with the story before Eldon fell asleep. "I make a good father, don't I?" Reino asked after he took Eldon to the bedroom and laid him beside his brother.

"You sure do."

"Even idiots can be good fathers."

"Don't call yourself an idiot," Signe said in a shocked voice.

"Why not? Most everyone else does. What do you want me to do now? I can carry water, sweep the floor, go to the mailbox, peel potatoes—" Reino rocked himself to and fro as he enumerated on his fingers the things he was capable of.

"Good. I need potatoes peeled. A sack of them."

"What you making, Signe?"

"Stew."

"Yum, yum. I bet I can eat three plates full. You know what?"

"What?"

"I'm going to have three pieces of pie, too. One of each kind."

As she browned the meat, Signe watched Reino carefully slide the knife under the peeling. The clumsy overgrown boy had nimble fingers.

"Notice," he said, holding up a peeled potato, "I don't leave any eyes."

Signe nodded. "You're doing very well,"

"And I cut the peelings very thin. My mother taught me. That was before she died."

"She taught you good."

Reino laughed. "I'll say. You know, I used to be able to do all kinds of things before the horses trampled me." He stared into the distance as he recalled that fateful day. "There wasn't any sign of rain, but all of a sudden lightning hit a tree as close to me as that wall. That's when the gelding reared up on his hind legs and the mare followed. They turned the hay mower over with me on the driver's seat. I don't know what happened then. After that I started having fits—"

Charlie rushed in. "The t'rashers are here!"

Signe and Reino hurried to the window. By now they could hear the rumbling and the clanging of the machine as it lumbered down the hill like a giant black beetle. "It sure is exciting, isn't it?" Reino declared as he settled back to work. He was on his last potato. "Do you want me to do those carrots, too? I know how."

"That would help me a lot," Signe replied as she poured Charlie a cup of coffee.

"Mind if I eat one? I sure like carrots and cabbage. Me and Mother used to grow them, but she's dead."

Signe told Reino he could eat all he wanted.

"I have to open the gate for the t'rashers," Charlie announced as he rushed out the door, leaving most of his coffee.

"Don't make me peel them!" Reino warned Signe when she opened a sack of onions. "They make me cry and a man isn't supposed to cry."

Signe laughed. "A good cry cleanses the soul, " but her words were lost on Reino.

An hour and a half later, the men came in the house in single file, led by Sam Isaacson himself. They had come for their morning coffee, but the four-quart blue enamel pot was not enough. Signe had to make another potful.

Charlie had made a birch table that would accommodate five on each side, with one at each end, and wooden benches to match. "We'll initiate it at harvest," he said to Signe, "and use it for our growing family later. "

The rumblings of the threshing machine stopped promptly at twelve o'clock and five minutes later the crew was seated at Signe's table, passing the stew and bread to each other. Sam wanted milk to drink, but his boys asked for strawberry Koolade. Before Signe had finished filling the glasses, the threshers were holding up their plates for refills of stew.

The pies disappeared as fast as the stew. Sam topped his pumpkin pie with whipped cream. He left the table saying it was the best meal any "t'rasher" had ever been served. Charlie quickly took Sam's place. Reino, now the dishwasher, kept his eye out for a vacancy. When Karlo, the youngest of Sam's sons, put a toothpick in his mouth, Reino took it as a sign that Karlo was full, grabbed a towel, wiped his hands and waited for his chance. It came. He moved in. "Pass me the stew, Charlie."

Signe, cutting bread at the cupboard, watched Karlo, seated on the rocking chair, take a can of Prince

Albert from his pocket to roll a cigarette. She wished she could tell him that the smell of smoke made her deathly ill now, but she couldn't. It would offend Sam, perhaps to the point that he'd pull out his rig before the threshing was completed. She put the plate of bread on the table, went outside and sat on the granary steps until Charlie came out. "What are you doing here? There are men to be fed."

Signe said nothing, but got up and went back in the house.

The table was surrounded by diners until the afternoon coffee hour. The guests were mostly neighbors "come to look the situation over," except for a small, middle-aged, shaggy haired man who came in, slipped to the table and filled his plate, without a word to anyone. Reino stared at the newcomer in overalls and worn-out tennis shoes, and whispered to Signe, "Who's he?"

"Don't you know him?"

Reino shook his head. "Not from these parts."

Signe went to the newcomer and greeted him in English.

He smiled.

Signe spoke a few words in Finnish and got the same foolish grin. She offered him some coffee and he held out his cup. Once he finished his piece of pie, the unknown guest went out the door.

"He had two plates of stew, six pieces of flatbread, pie and coffee," Reino exclaimed, "and didn't even say thank you."

Signe shrugged. There was nothing she could say.

Hilda Mattson stopped by and had a cup of coffee, said she'd just had dinner and was too full to eat. She commented that Signe should not be doing all this work considering her condition, but offered no help.

By two o'clock Signe and Reino had cleared the table and set out the coffee cups, rusks and cupcakes. By five minutes after the hour, the threshers were seated in their usual places, slurping the brew from saucers and discussing the world situation. "We're lucky to be on the farm instead of standing in a bread line in some big city," Sam Isaacson declared. "Things have never been any better here, and they can't get any worse."

"Yaa, cow manure is pretty much the same, one year to the next," his son added. Clarence resented working under his father, but didn't have the gumption to go out into the world to seek his own fortune.

Signe felt it was time to change the subject and told the men about the stranger who came and ate his fill.

Ed Koski, who had joined the threshers at the table, laughed. "Him! The rascal with the bush of gray hair? Just a hobo who shows up every fall from nowhere, follows the t'rashing machine from farm to farm, and stuffs himself for the winter."

"Is he mute?" Signe asked.

Sam Isaacson shrugged and said, "Pass me the butter."

The Skinnars cleared fifteen hundred dollars. Now everyone wanted alfalfa seed, but Charlie sold to a seed company in the Twin Cities. "Let them buy from a store. That's where I got mine," Charlie told Signe.

They paid off Adolph Jacobson, or Miser Jacobson, as he was known, the money they'd borrowed for the alfalfa seed and the loan for the mail car. That left ninety-five dollars for the new enamel-coated cooking range that Charlie ordered from Chicago through the Co-op, and fifteen dollars for an Atwater Kent radio for Signe to listen to and improve her English.

Chapter IV

IT WAS THURSDAY, the day that the Post Tribune came out.

Charlie left early. "I want to be at the post office before the cock crows so I can pick up the mail and be on my way," he told Signe. "Having to stop at almost every mailbox on my route makes the day twice as long."

Signe went back to bed after Charlie left— something she'd never done before. She didn't have the energy to stay up just yet. The cows had to be milked and the cream separated, but that would have to wait. She was glad that the children hadn't awakened.

Cooking for the threshers yesterday had made her

ill. She had been too tired to sleep last night. In the early morning the nausea had ceased and the swelling in her legs had gone down. Feeling better than she had in months, she rolled over on her side and hoped that the remaining month would be easy. She pulled the wool comforter to her chin, fell asleep and dreamt that she was having labor pains. She gave out a cry. Half asleep, she turned on her other side, but the pains persisted and she gave another cry.

Eldon came to her bedside and shook her arm. "Mother, you hollered so loud that you frightened the baby!"

Not quite awake, she asked, "Which baby?"

"Hugo!" Eldon cried out. "We got only one baby."

"Go tell him Mother's coming,"

"Well, hurry then. We don't have all day." Eldon copied his father's testy behavior and language. He stood by the bed and waited impatiently.

Signe sat up and with her right foot tried unsuccessfully to locate her old bedroom slippers on the floor, somewhere close by. She stepped down, pulled her weathered robe over her shoulders, and was about to bend down to look for the mules when a gush of water came out of her and flooded the floor. She gasped.

Eldon's rage turned into remorse and dissolved into tears. "I'm a bad boy. A real bad boy," he cried. "I hollered at Mama and made her wee-wee on the floor. God will punish me."

Hugo, led by Violet, had come to their mother's bedside. The sight of Eldon weeping made them both cry. Signe bent down to comfort her children. A stabbing pain in the pit of her stomach, followed by the downward movement of the placenta anchored her to the spot. "Eldon, get me some dish towels," she cried. "In the top drawer of the cupboard. Hurry!"

Eldon rushed to the kitchen. "I can't reach!"

"Stand on a chair."

Signe could hear the scraping of the bench legs on the floor as Eldon dragged it across the kitchen. He returned with a couple of bleached flour sacks.

"More. I need all of them. Violet will help you."

"Me, too!" Hugo called out.

Violet and Eldon piled the towels on the bed. Hugo, whose towel had unfolded, got tangled in it, fell on the floor and screamed.

His sister separated the boy from the flour sack, went into their room, returned with a wad of recycled Juicy Fruit and gave it to him. All was quiet.

The birth had begun without the usual series of contractions. Signe didn't have time to explain the happenings to her children. She had to act quickly to keep up with the spontaneous delivery. The children watched.

Eldon was apprehensive. "Mama, are your insides coming out?"

"No, Eldon. Mother's having a baby. I need my scissors. Would you get my sewing basket?"

Eldon didn't move. "What you going to do?"

"Cut the baby's navel."

"That'll make a hole in the baby's stomach."

The baby was out. Signe slapped the child and it gave a lusty cry. "See, the baby has a long cord. It needs to be cut and tied."

"Sure does." Eldon answered as he raced to the sewing machine and got the basket.

"Can you reach the rubbing alcohol bottle in the cupboard?"

"Sure. I got the bench there already."

Signe sterilized the scissors in the alcohol, cut and tied the cord and wrapped the newborn in flour sack dish towels, fresh from laundering, sterile from boiling. Signe, like all farm wives, boiled the whites in the summer and froze them on the line in the winter to bleach the cottons.

The children had watched the birth process with amazement. Eldon broke the silence. "Is the baby a boy or a girl?"

"A girl, a beautiful girl." Signe kissed the infant on the cheek and let the children each kiss her.

After careful scrutiny of his new sister, Eldon said, "She looks like me, doesn't she?"

Signe nodded.

"Me, too," Hugo chimed in .

"Like you and Violet, too," Signe assured the little ones.

"We already have two boys. Now we have two girls. And a mother and a father," Eldon explained to his siblings. "You can't have two mothers and two fathers."

Violet and Hugo shook their heads in unison with Eldon. "Since your father is gone," Signe told Eldon, "you'll have take his place and care for your sister and brother and make them something to eat."

"I'm hungry," Violet announced.

"Me, too." Hugo seconded.

"Come to the table," Eldon ordered.

"Next time your father goes to the store," Signe told her children, "he'll bring you a big bag of cookies for being good."

Elated by his new position in the family, Eldon cut the bread as best he could, and chopped hunks of butter and rubbed it on the bread with his delicate little fingers. The diners were happy.

"I like your butter bread," Violet told Eldon.

Hugo swallowed and called out, "More."

Signe placed her new daughter on the bed beside her to nurse. "Eldon, after Hugo and Violet have finished their bread, you can help them climb up on my bed."

"Can I come, too? I'm the father."

"Of course."

Signed was about to doze off when she heard a strange swabbing sound by her bed. She turned around to look.

Eldon was wiping the floor. The long handle of the mop hit him on the head, but he was persistent. When the job was done to his satisfaction, he gave a sigh of relief.

"Thank you, Eldon. You're a good worker," Signe told her son.

"I don't want to grow up lazy. Papa hates lazy people."

When Signe woke up, Reino was standing by her bed, grinning. "How long did I sleep?" she asked.

"A minute," Eldon replied, "just a minute."

"Signe, I'm sorry I'm late," Reino apologized. "I told myself I'd better hurry, but sometimes I'm so slow."

"Why are you here?"

"To help you when the baby came."

"How did you know — ?"

Reino chuckled. "I just knew. What you want me to do?"

"The children haven't had their breakfast. Could you build a fire?"

"You bet'cha. I'm about the best fire maker in the county. Come, Eldon, let's go chop kindling." Reino looked at Violet and Hugo. "Eldon, I think you'd better stay here and take care of everybody."

The fire was crackling, and the water in the tea kettle boiling. "Signe, I'm making you tea," Reino announced. "A lady in your condition shouldn't have coffee. Besides, it excites the little one." He served tea and rusks. "Now you kids, what do you want — eggs or oatmeal. I know how to boil eggs and oatmeal."

Before Sign could tell Reino that they had no eggs, the children had voted on eggs.

"I'm making porridge," Reino announced, "It's better for you."

Reino dished the oatmeal and poured some skim milk into each bowl, leaving the sugar available for self-service. He sat at the head of the table with Hugo on his lap. "Now, don't you pee on my pants," he cautioned the child. "This is my only pair of overalls and washday isn't until Monday." He proceeded to feed the boy and himself, one spoonful into his own mouth, and the next into Hugo's.

After breakfast Eldon asked, "Reino, have we been good kids?"

"You bet'cha."

"You going to tell us about the two bears?"

"Three bears."

"Yesterday you said it's two bears."

"Today it's three bears," Reino replied in a voice that ended the debate. "First, you and Violet get your clothes on and bring Hugo's stuff to me so I can dress him."

The changes were made quickly, and Reino at the head of the table, held Hugo on his knee and began the story.

"Once upon a time there lived three bears—"

"What's a bear?" Violet asked.

"Don't interrupt," Eldon told her.

"It's an animal that looks like a big dog, and eats people," Reino replied.

The answer satisfied Violet.

"The three bears' names were Papa Bear, Mama Bear and Baby Bear. 'Hurry up and eat your porridge so we can go to church,' Mama Bear said. She had put raisins in the oatmeal because it was Sunday. They put on their Sunday clothes and set out, carefully walking on the cow path so they wouldn't get lost in the forest. They had not gone far when Papa Bear said, 'I don't want to go to church.'

'Where do you want to go?' Mama Bear asked.

'I want to go to Little Red Riding Hood's house. It's our turn to visit her.'

Mother Bear said, 'Okay.'

They had not gone far when Papa Bear said, 'I smell huckleberries. I think I'll go pick some.'

'Go right ahead,' Mother Bear said, 'I don't want to stain my hands with berries or tear my silk dress in the brambles. We'll go visiting.'

Little Red Riding Hood was mighty glad to see the two bears. 'Where's Papa Bear?' she asked.

'Who knows!' Mama Bear answered.

They had a wonderful time. Little Red Riding Hood served them cookies, honey and brambleberry tea and said, 'Come back soon.'

Mama Bear said, 'It's your turn to come and see us next.'

Papa Bear was never seen again. That's why there are only two bears.

"Do you know what that means? " Reino asked. Eldon shook his head and two younger ones copied him. "It means never go on a wild-goose chase."

"Yoo-hoo!" Hilda Mattson called in as she opened the kitchen door.

"Shhhh. Signe's sleeping," Reino whispered.

"Did the baby come?"

Reino smiled and nodded.

"Boy or girl?"

"Girl, I think."

"Is it all right?"

"Looked all right to me," Reino replied.

"Can I go see Signe?"

"You bet'cha."

Hilda went into Signe's bedroom.

"Why do you always say, 'You bet'cha?'" Eldon asked Reino.

"So people will think I'm English."

"What's English?"

"It's what the King and Queen speak. Like when the Queen wants to fry potatoes for supper, she says, 'King, get me some kindling so I can make a fire.' He says, 'You bet'cha.'"

After thinking it over, Eldon asked, "It isn't swearing, is it?"

"What a dumb question! " Reino retorted. "Would a King swear?"

Eldon shrugged. "I don't know. Maybe, if the Queen made him real mad."

"She came early — an eight month baby, isn't she?" Hilda exclaimed as she stepped into Signe's bedroom. "I knew by the way you were working yesterday that no good would come of it." Breathless from hurrying, Hilda was perspiring. She took off her coat, loosened her patent leather belt and kicked off her oxfords before dropping herself into the rocking chair by Signe's bed. "They say it's much better to have a seven month baby than an eight month baby. Their chances to make it are better." Getting no response from Signe, Hilda asked, "Is she perfect?"

"Perfect as an angel," Signe replied, happily, "my second daughter."

"And that should be enough," Hilda announced in a voice that would have rattled the dead. She went to Signe's bed, picked up the infant and began to unravel the flour sacks around it. "I don't believe in kids by the dozens. After Raymond was born, I told Gust, 'This is it. Two's enough. If you want more, go knock at some other door.' I see you did a pretty good job of the navel." After a thorough inspection of the baby, Hilda asked, "Don't you have any clothes for this little one?"

"In the box by the dresser," Signe replied. "I couldn't get to it."

Hilda was as excited as a little girl rummaging through doll clothes. "I'm glad you've got some pink. I've seen plenty of blue in my day. I'd hate to put it on a girl." She diapered and dressed the infant, kissed her on the cheek and handed her to Signe. "If you'll get up, I'll make your bed. Got any clean sheets?"

Signe had expected to sleep, but now she had orders. She got up and sat on the chair that Hilda had just vacated. "Bottom drawer of the dresser."

"You'd think that having a husband with a government job, you could afford real bed linens," Hilda grumbled as she deftly spread open the bleach-ed flour sack sheets and made Signe's bed.

Signe was tired of making excuses for Charlie's growing miserliness and didn't comment. Instead she thanked Hilda for helping.

"Don't say another word, Signe. I can never repay you for your help when I was expecting Raymond." She rolled the used bedding into a ball and tossed it in the corner. "Guess I'll go home now. You don't need me since Reino's here to keep an eye on the children."

Signe was hesitant about her real concern, but it had to be said. "The cows haven't been milked yet."

Hilda lifted her nose. "I don't do barn work. I've

learned that the more the farm wife does, the more she's expected to do. I told Gust, 'Don't ever expect to see me pushing the wheelbarrow with a load of manure.' I'll speak to Reino and tell him what needs to be done. I'll be back tomorrow."

Reino was on his hands and knees romping on the kitchen floor, giving the kids horseback rides. "Only two at a time," he hollered. "What do you think I am, a mule?"

"Get off the floor and listen to me," Hilda ordered.

Reino stood up, dropping the two little ones on the floor, and looked at Hilda. Violet and Hugo knocked heads and began to scream.

"Look what you've done now," Hilda chastised Reino. "I want you to behave like a grown man, which is what you are, and get a pail and a couple of cream cans and milk the cows. You know how to milk, don't you? I should hope so. After you're done, separate the milk, take the cream to the icehouse, and feed the skimmed milk to the calves, pigs, whatever. Eldon knows what's to be done. If not, you can ask Signe."

Reino, red-faced, getting angrier by the second during Hilda's long list of commands, blew his cheeks into a balloon before answering.

"I know what needs doing, but I'm not getting under any cow. I won't be kicked in the head again."

Hilda took a deep breath, exhaled and decided it was no use.

She got her coat and tied a scarf around her coal black, stiffly bunned hair and went out the door.

Reino went into the bedroom. "Signe, you want I make you some more tea?"

"Thank you, but all I want is some rest. Would you take care of the children?"

"You bet'cha." Reino paused to formulate his question and thought it would be better to present some pertinent facts first. "You know, Signe, my mother always wanted a girl, but she never had one." He shifted his feet and gazed at the floor. "Nobody named for her. Her name was Elma." Reino scratched his eyebrow. "Could we call your baby Elma? Sounds so pretty."

Signe smiled. All through his laborious reasoning she had known what Reino was driving at. "I think it is a beautiful name. We'll call her Elma after your mother."

Reino's happiness was beyond bounds. He went into the kitchen and grabbed his cap and returned saying, "I'm going right home and tell her."

"Your mother died many years ago, remember?"

Reino took off his cap and gently brushed the top of his head with the tips of his fingers. "Yaa. Guess I got too excited. She died long ago. Should I go to the graveyard and tell her?"

"What about the children? Would you leave them alone?"

"Oh, I forgot. I'll stay until Charlie gets home, and tonight I'll tell God and he'll pass the word along to Mother."

When Charlie drove into the yard late in the afternoon, Reino rushed for his cap, opened the door, and greeted Charlie with, "The cows have to be milked, the milk has to be separated and the cream be put in the icehouse. And don't expect Signe to do it. We just had a baby girl. I named her Elma."

Chapter V

CHARLIE ADORED HIS NEW DAUGHTER, and had no trouble with the name Elma, "but her first name will be Miriam, the name of my mother, " he said. "Miriam is a Biblical name. We must baptize her as soon as possible, hopefully next Sunday. I will talk to the pastor." But Reino had named her Elma, and Elma she remained.

Signe was weak from giving birth to a premature baby and had lost much blood during the night. She was surprised but pleased that Charlie got up at four the next morning to do the milking and feed the animals. He had absented himself from dairy chores since he became mailman. "I don't want people to get the idea that farming takes priority over my government job," he told people.

Signe got out of bed to make Charlie's favorite breakfast, an omelet with home smoked bacon and baking powder biscuits. She had barely gotten the buns in the oven when Charlie, sweaty and disheveled, his right eye quavering in its socket, came thundering in. "That's the last you'll see of that cow!" he yelled as he threw his bloody, sweaty leather gloves into the wood box by the kitchen stove. "She's done for. Pitchfork through her belly."

Signe felt as if she had lost all control of her body. She couldn't think. Her knees were dissolving. She clung to the doorjamb for support. "You didn't! Not with a pitchfork!"

"Not once, but five times."

"Is. . . is she alive?"

Charlie gave a raucous laugh as he took off his denim jacket and hung it on a nail behind the kitchen stove. "Alive but no longer kicking. I told the bitch, 'Kick Charlie Skinnar once, and that's your last kick.'"

"Quiet! Don't wake the children. It wasn't Queen, was it?"

Charlie wouldn't be hushed. He raved like a lunatic. "She was Queen, but no more. Now she's shit." He took his gloves out of the wood box, lifted the round lid on top of the kitchen range and threw them into the fire. "Soon she'll be worm food in the manure pile."

Signe stood frozen to the spot. What was happening? She couldn't understand Charlie's uncontrollable anger, and least of all, his actions. "She was Eldon's cow. Our best milker. She must have had a sore nipple—"

Charlie interrupted her. "I don't care if she had a sore—"

Her eyes flared with anger as she confronted him. "Charlie! Not another word. You have crossed the line. Not even a beast of prey would do what you have just done. Where's your religion? Have you forgotten that God created all living creatures, not only Charlie Skinnar. We are how we behave, not what we say we are. What happened to the Charlie Skinnar I married—the thoughtful, helpful man? You'd better have a long talk with the Pastor."

Signe could feel the blood trickling out of her, life fluid that as a nursing mother she couldn't afford to lose. She went to the bedroom and changed, grabbed her barn coat and scarf from the hook behind the stove, and pulled on her old galoshes. "I'm going to finish the milking while you're here with the baby. Your food is in the warmer on top of the stove. The biscuits are in the oven and should be ready by the time you're shaved." She tied the scarf over her head and went out into the deep, dark night.

The lantern was hanging from the spike on the tamarack post in the center of the barn. The cows were agitated, but quiet. Not one of them was chewing on her cud, or eating hay. Signe couldn't bear to go look at Queen, whose stanchion was the last in the row, but took her pail and placed the stool under Molly and began to milk. Assured by Signe's presence, the cows, one by one, began to munch on the alfalfa. Repeated low moans from Queen broke the silence.

Signe had feared the sight of the mangled animal.

It was beyond her imagination. She gasped, but couldn't cry. Nausea once again overcame her. Queen's hide was horribly torn. Her ruptured intestines oozed blood, water and offal. Signe wished for a gun to put an end to the cow's suffering, but there was none to be had. If the animal were slaughtered soon, some of the meat could be salvaged. Signe would can the best parts and grind the rest into hamburger. There was no way she could lessen Queen's pain.

The milk had to be taken to the house to be separated. Signe got Eldon's red wagon from the sand pile, emptied it, hoisted the five gallon cans on the cart and pulled it to the house.

The fumes from Charlie's burning gloves intensified her nausea.

Charlie was leaving as she reached the kitchen door. He said nothing to her, but got in his mail car and drove off. The scent of his after-shave lingered in the kitchen.

The children had been awakened by Charlie's stormy entrance. They stood barefooted in their underwear behind the chintz curtains that substituted for their bedroom door, and listened to the contention in the kitchen. Eldon would take an occasional peek to view the situation.

Hearing their father drive out, they marched into the kitchen and one by one went up and hugged Signe who was sitting by the table, weeping.

Somewhat cheered by the endearments of her offspring, Signe got up and buttered the remaining biscuits and gave them to the children. She poured herself a cup of coffee and sat down to consider her options. If she could get in touch with Ed Koski, he would probably come to butcher the mangled cow. But she had no phone. She couldn't walk to any of the neighbors with four little children, two of whom had to be carried. All she could hope for was a visit from Reino. He'd be glad to do a favor.

Signe watered the cows and let them out into the alfalfa field as she had been doing since the crop was harvested, then separated the milk and washed the separator parts. Luckily the baby had slept through the morning.

"She's a good little girl, isn't she?" Eldon said, gazing at his new sister.

"All my children are good."

"I'm the goodest," Violet spoke up. "I even put on my own shoes."

"Me, too." Hugo added.

"Yaa, but you have to learn your right foot from your left foot," Eldon told his brother. "This shoe matches this foot and that shoe matches that foot."

"You bet'cha."

After bathing, nursing and rocking Elma to sleep, Signe cleaned the house and washed the dishes, keeping an eye for Reino. But he didn't show up. Charlie dropped the mail in his own box at noon, but didn't stop at the house. The dying cow refused to leave her thoughts, but there was nothing Signe could do about Queen, so she began to work on Miss Keksi's suit. The teacher wanted "something new and warm" to wear at the conference in Moorhead in November, and Signe had found green wool tweed at Blandings in Detroit Lakes that was "just Miss Keksi's color." She had copied the design of a ladies' suit in the Sears & Roebuck catalog, made a pattern, and was ready to cut it when Hilda walked in, carrying an old shopping bag.

"You look surprised," Hilda said, "I told you I'd come today."

"What do you have in your bag," Hugo asked Hilda before Signe could answer her, "your rubbers?"

Hilda took off her coat and headscarf and sticking her hand in the bag pulled out a delicious apple for each child and a bottle for Signe. "This is for you."

Eldon and Violet thanked Hilda, but Hugo took a look into the empty shopping bag and asked, "What about Papa?"

"He can get his own or wait for Santa Claus."

Intrigued by the bottle labeled Elixir Compound 500, Signe hadn't heard the repartee between Hilda and Hugo. "What's this?" she asked.

"Medicine for whatever ails you. "

"Where did you get it?" Signe asked

"From Aram. He gave me three bottles one year for us letting him sleep in our hayloft. You can have that one."

"Aram? Who's he?"

"The dark-skinned peddler who used to come each spring with his horse and buggy. You bought the Finnish alphabet book for Arthur from him when Arthur was a baby. Remember?"

Signe laughed. "Oh, yes, the Bible salesman."

"It was Bibles that year. Horse collars, umbrellas and jackknives the next. I haven't seen him for a couple of years. I wonder what happened to him."

Signe, reading the small print on the label 'For all female complaints,' said, "Probably took a dose of this!"

Hilda didn't get the quip. "Keep reading."

Signe continued. "For labor contractions, parturition, miscarriage, hemorrhaging, queasiness, flatulence, melancholia—" Most words Signe couldn't read or pronounce, hardly any of them could she understand. The list went on: insomnia, fatigue, muscle spasms, constipation, sleeplessness, hallucinations, depression, nightmares, incontinence—" She shook her head at the marvel of the miracle medicine.

"I take it for everything from headaches to swollen ankles. I even gave some to Gust when he was having trouble with—" Hilda left the sentence up in the air.

"With what?" Signe asked.

"Never mind. I have to go home now. It's time for Gust to begin the chores." Hilda put on her coat, tied the scarf over her head and left.

Signe went to the cupboard, took a tablespoon from the drawer, filled it with Elixir Compound 500 and swallowed it.

After eating their apples, the children amused themselves by inventing games. Eldon was paternal toward and protective of his siblings, would regularly check on Elma to be sure she was breathing. He had a fear that she might quit breathing and die. After a couple of hours had passed, he insisted his mother, too, take a good look at the baby although Signe was going in and out of the room continually to get her sewing supplies.

It was four o'clock when Charlie came home. He was in good spirits. Said he'd spoken to Pastor Kivi and arranged Elma's baptism for Sunday.

"But that's only two days away," Signe exclaimed.

"The sooner the better."

"I wanted to make her a christening gown."

"What's wrong with the one you made for Violet?"

"Each girl deserves her own."

"This is a Christian ritual, not a fashion show."

"Who did you have in mind for godparents?" Signe asked, as she put her sewing away. "I was thinking of Reino. He was here at Elma's birth when I so desperately needed help, and it would make him very happy."

"An idiot?" Charlie thundered, his face turning crimson.

"God doesn't categorize."

"Godparents should be important people."

"All people are important," Signe snapped. "If you won't agree on Reino, how about Hilda and Gust Mattson?"

"Hilda will be suitable; after all, she is your best friend. But Gust—" Charlie shook his head with disapproval. "I say Ed Koski. He's Reino's uncle. That should satisfy you. I'll stop by Ed's place and the parsonage tomorrow."

Signe left Charlie with the children and went to do the evening chores. She wondered how she could manage when the days got cold and the cattle had to be fed in the barn three times a day. It was clear to her now that Charlie was not a farmer.

Chapter VI

THE NEXT MORNING when Signe went to the barn, the battered cow was still alive, a pitiful sight such as she could never even dream. The cow's moans now were weak and sparse.

Signe had a hard time believing that it was the same Charlie who had met her at the train station with his Model T that now had so cruelly destroyed an innocent animal. She wept as she milked the others.

Signe was washing her hands when Eldon ran in the house. "Papa just went by in the mail car!"

"Did you talk to him?"

"Nah, he just put our mail in the box, and when I ran down the hill to see him, he waved goodbye and went. I brought you the catalog. That's all there was."

A sickening wave went through Signe's body. Charlie stopped to drop off a Montgomery Ward catalog, but didn't bother to come inside to see how his family was doing. It couldn't be that he resented the new arrival. He loved his children. Maybe it was the crises that she'd heard men go through at a certain age. Perhaps he couldn't face her because of what he'd done to Eldon's cow. "You know your father takes his lunch bucket with him."

"Yaa, but I thought he'd stop to look at Elma and then I could give him part of my Baby Ruth bar that I've been saving."

Reino opened the door. "I came early, but I waited till I saw Charlie go round the corner before I came in."

"Why?" she asked. "You're welcome anytime."

"He doesn't like me, I don't think." Reino shifted from one foot to the other, and grinned nervously. "I come to see Elma."

Signe took him to her bedroom where the baby was asleep.

Reino looked at the child and began to giggle with happiness. "Elma's the prettiest baby ever born."

Eldon, who with Violet and Hugo had followed Reino, said, "Mother told me I was a pretty baby, too."

"Me, too," Violet declared.

Pointing at his nose, Hugo added, 'Too."

"You were all beautiful and still are," Signe assured her children. She then asked Reino to go to his uncle Ed's place and ask him to come over with a gun.

"What for?" Reino asked.

"To shoot my cow," Eldon replied. "Papa got angry and tried to kill Queen with the pitchfork but she wouldn't die. She's full of holes and her stomach is leaking. Have to shoot her dead."

Signe looked at her son, a child so innocent, having witnessed a terrible crime. How much of Charlie's and her conversation had he understood and when had he made his trip to the barn, she didn't ask, thinking it was better to drop the matter as soon as possible.

Reino had listened to Eldon's story with a set jaw and squinting eyes. "I go now," he said.

Ed Koski came with his rifle within the hour.

"Can we salvage any part of her?" Signe asked, as Ed stared at the half dead cow. "We could use the meat."

Ed shook his head. 'Too late. The meat's begun to spoil. Why didn't you call me right away?"

"We have no phone," she replied and left it at that.

"I'll have to get my horses to pull her out of the barn," Ed said, as he closed the barn door. "Be back soon."

Signe returned to the house, glad that Ed had asked no questions and made no comments. She knew that by midnight the story of the brutally battered cow would be aired on the party line, and common knowledge by sunup.

Ed hauled the carcass to the back of the barnyard, dug a holed and buried it.

"I don't have the money to give you today," Signe told him when the job was done, "but after I finish the teacher's suit, I'll pay you."

Ed nodded, took the reins in his hands and followed his horses home.

When Charlie returned from his mail route, Violet and Hugo climbed into his lap to be hugged and cuddled. "Where's Eldon?" he asked.

"In the toilet," Violet answered.

"Hiding," Hugo added.

"Give your father a chance to drink his coffee," Signe told the children. "He forgot his Thermos and hasn't had any all day."

"I don't know what's come over Ed Koski," Charlie commented after his first saucerful. "Yesterday morning when I dropped by his place to ask him to be godfather, he was very cordial. This afternoon at the creamery he ignored me."

Signe turned her head and looked away.

Later that night Signe was awakened by fretful sobbing in the children's room. She jumped out of bed and rushed to see. It was Eldon. "I'm crying for Queen. She's killed, shot and buried. I'll never see her again. Why did Papa do that?"

She had no answers. Signe took the child in her arms, rocked and sang to him. An occasional tear of her's joined his on the boy's soft pink cheek.

Chapter VII

ELMA'S BAPTISM HAD BEEN MOVED back twice—first when the church furnace had to be replaced, and again when Pastor Kivi went to Michigan.

It rankled Charlie that the Pastor would just tell the congregation that he'd be gone for a whole month and not offer a more explicit explanation other than he would be attending the ministerial conference in Ishpeming for three days. "Isn't it unusual?" Charlie asked the members of the Men's Choir. "What's he got in mind for the rest of the time?"

His question was answered with shrugs and mumbles.

Charlie brought the matter up to the church council at a meeting a week later. "We need to know what's going on so we can decide if we should get a replacement for Pastor Kivi during his absence. I hear

Pastor Lindquist in Sebeka is retired and would be available."

"Four Sundays isn't that long," Pete Huttu, the choir director, responded.

"Five," Charlie corrected. "He'll be gone five Sundays and I have a daughter to be baptized."

"You could take her to the church on Norse Hill. I understand you were a member there once," Pete added.

Charlie nodded. That's where he really belonged, he had often told himself, the Old Apostolic Lutheran Church, the church of his father, where Charlie himself had been baptized. The Finns called it "*Laestadiuksen Kirkko*," the church of Lars Levi Laestadius, minister of the state church of Sweden, started by the Finnish immigrants in the Calumet, Michigan area.

It was a conservative church where men were men, women knew their place, and displayed no yearnings for doing outrageous things such as bobbing their locks or driving an automobile. They wore their hair in simple buns in the back of their heads, covered their bodies with long-sleeved dresses that kissed the tops of their oxfords. No fancy frocks, jewelry or outside ornaments except for a gold wedding band after the ultimate ceremony.

The followers of Laestadius, like all Lutherans believe that faith, not good deeds, paves the road to salvation. The church stresses confession of sins, absolution, and regeneration. Confessions can be heard by fellow Christians, but major transgressions require public confession before the congregation for absolutions.

Charlie had been promised the position of cantor, a station of prestige, at Old Apostolic, but his father had died before Charlie's voice was mature enough. After his father's death, his mother had announced, "Enough is enough," left the church and moved her family over to the Wolf Creek Lutheran Church, where Signe and Charlie were married.

After they were married, Charlie mentioned that he would like to go back to the church of his childhood, the Old Apostolic Church on Norse Hill, but all he'd gotten from his new bride was a blank stare. It made Charlie realize that Signe was so much like his mother that he thought it best not to bring up the subject again.

What grated Charlie was the fact that Kivi didn't stick to his job, ministry. He was a do-it-all. Not only did he serve as pastor, but quite often cantor as well. Pete Huttu was the choir director, but Kivi chose the music and frequently changed his mind with only a moment's notice to Pete. As the normal Sunday service was concluding, the Pastor would hurry to the front door, admire the ladies as they departed and tickle the babies' chins, paying little heed to the men who drove their wives to church and later filled the collection plates. Somehow Kivi failed to notice that it's a man's world after all.

At Charlie's insistence, Ed Koski called a meeting to discuss Kivi's absence.

"Should we try to find a substitute for the next five Sundays?" he asked.

"It's a little late now," Wayne Siren replied. "There's also the question of money. Where do we get the extra cash?"

"Take it out of Pastor Kivi's salary," Charlie volunteered.

Ed Koski shook his head. "Can't do that. He has a contract saying exactly how much his yearly salary will be, which I think is very little for a man with his education."

"We're not paying for education," Charlie snapped. "We're paying for a service."

John Granlund, who'd been sitting in the corner, enjoying his pipe, spoke up. "Personally, I would leave well enough alone. Pastor Kivi will be back before we know it. Meanwhile we have five Sundays to go fishing. I hear it's been a great season up north for walleyes. My cousin Willy drove to Ely last weekend and came back with two gunny sacks full."

Charlie looked at Ed. "What about my daughter's baptism?"

"Is she ill?"

"No, she's not ill. Elma is a very healthy little girl."

"So what's your hurry?"

"It's the principle of the thing," Charlie retorted as he put on his Mackinaw. "I must go now. Have to be up at five."

With Charlie out of the way, Ed Koski looked at his fellow church officers and pondered a question heavy on his mind. "Boys—" The aging youth of the Finnish male population liked to be called boys. It was like a shot of testosterone to their pork greased, butterfat clogged veins. "Boys, there's a bottle of sacramental wine in the crate in the supply room.

Been there for sometime. It should be used up or thrown out."

"I'm glad you brought it up," Pete Hutto said. "The room is small enough as is but the extra crate takes up space we so badly need."

"We had to keep the box. You can't have a bottle of wine in open view," Ed explained. "People get ideas."

Pete rubbed his hands together. "That's what I was trying to say."

"Should we get rid of the wine?" Ed asked for assurance.

John Granlund blew a long trail of smoke into the air. "Get rid of it. You can order some more."

"We have a full case, right next to the empty one," Ed said. "I'll open the orphan bottle. If it's bad, better to throw it out than have someone poisoned at sacrament."

Luckily, the wine had not turned, but since it was opened, it had to be used or thrown out. Finns, by nature, are a frugal people, and the members of the council in their conscience felt that throwing out good sacramental wine was wasteful if not sacrilegious. They would share it.

The men passed the bottle in an atmosphere of camaraderie as they discussed the proposed new Highway 34 that would cross the county from Park Rapids to Detroit Lakes.

"I saw the surveyors by Charlie Skinnar's place the other day," Ed said. "Guess they mean business."

Granlund cleaned out his pipe, put the ashes in the cuff of his overalls, and refilled it with fresh tobacco. Then scratched a kitchen match on the seat of his pants and lit his pipe. "We'll sooner see a highway linking Heaven to Hell than the proposed road. They've been talking about Highway 34 since Coolidge was president."

"What's the latest on the electrification?" Ed Koski asked.

Granlund took a puff. "What electrification?"

Pete passed the bottle to Ed. "I heard they were planning to run lines from Park Rapids as far as Wolf Creek by the end of the year. Some rural areas in the southern part of the state have had electricity for a coupla years now."

Ed, who had the largest dairy farm in the township, took a swig. "Electricity will be a godsend. We won't have to pull and squeeze any longer. We'll have machines to do the work. That's something to look forward to." He put the bottle to his lips again. It was empty. "Should we check the full case?"

Pete took out his gold pocket watch and glanced at it. "Might as well. We've got the time."

The delay of the christening had given Signe a chance to make a lovely baptismal gown for Elma, a new plaid cotton dress for Violet, and pants for the boys from dark wool remnants that she'd saved. She had no time to think about herself. But since she wouldn't be taking off her coat in church, people wouldn't notice that she was wearing the same navy rayon dress she had worn for the past three years, summer and winter. It was loose and comfortable.

On Wednesday before the baptism, Charlie hired

his replacement to take the mail route in order to go to Fargo on business. He returned with a new suit.

"If I had known that you were going shopping for clothes," Signe told Charlie, "I'd have had you get shoes for the boys. Eldon's left oxford has a hole in the sole, and Hugo's shoes are worn out and have no laces."

"I'll see what I can do," Charlie replied. He shined Hugo's high tops and shortened a pair of laces from his own discards. Then found a piece of cowhide and cut out inner soles for Eldon's.

Hugo promptly took off his bedroom slippers. "Thank God for shoes," he said and went to Violet for help.

Charlie was a proud man. He envisioned the males of the congregation coming up to congratulate him after the service. He had to look good. The new suit would show him off. People would talk how well Charlie Skinnar must be doing to afford such an outfit.

The Wolf Creek Lutheran Church was a plain building with plastered walls, birch floors and pews, and a simple cross in front. There were no stained glass windows or other decoration to detract the faithful. Pastor Kivi followed the liturgical format of Lutheran worship precisely. He was given to lengthy sermons and many hymns, and, naturally, gave preference to those written by Martin Luther.

The church was full as Charlie had expected. His heart was pounding in anticipation of what was to come. He had presumed that the Men's Choir would sing this Sunday, and secretly hoped that Kivi would call on him to sing a solo, but such was not the case. When Hulda Laine pumped the organ and the strains of "A Mighty Fortress Is Our God" hit the plaster, it was Pastor Kivi's tenor that drowned the individual voices of the congregation.

> A mighty fortress is our God,
> A bulwark never failing:
> Our helper, He, amid the flood
> Of mortal ills prevailing.
> For still an ancient foe
> Does seek to work us woe;
> His craft and power are great,
> And armed with cruel hate,
> On earth is not his equal...

Pastor Kivi then gave the public announcements. "Karl Lindgren, who in my absence had an emergency appendix operation at the Park Rapids Hospital, is now able to have visitors. Since Karl can't speak English, time lies heavy on his hands. His wife said Karl would like some Finnish books to read. He will return them once he gets home. He's particularly interested in the *Kalevala*. Anyone going in that direction should visit Karl. He's in room #210.

"It has been brought to my attention that the church is almost out of firewood. We will take bids; however, if you have it in your heart to donate a cord or two, it would be most gratefully received. The church is low on funds, and our building will need painting next summer. I will ask for volunteers later. Meanwhile, see Ed Koski about the wood.

"I would also like to announce to the young people that confirmation school will begin next Saturday. The hours are from eight to one o'clock. Since it will be a long session, I would suggest that you bring a sandwich or two. One of the mothers will come and make the coffee."

When the Pastor called for silent prayer, Reino, sitting stiffly in his new Montgomery Ward suit next to Eldon, gave a loud sigh.

Eldon, in a loud, clear voice, said, "Reino, if you're tired, just close your eyes and go to sleep. This is going to take a long, long time."

Pastor Kivi looked over his congregation . "Let us prepare for worship with prayer:

We are your people O God
Redeemed by your Son Jesus Christ:
We come to the gift of your grace
Help us examine ourselves and acknowledge
Our condition with repentant heart."
The people responded.
"Forgive us, Lord;
For all that separates us from you,
For all that separates us from one another,
For all that violates your creation . . . "

Hugo got off the bench and began to jump up and down. Violet whispered in her mother's ear, and Signe, who was nursing Elma, reached over and poked Charlie indicating that Hugo had to go. Charlie reluctantly got out of his seat, put on Hugo's coat and hat, took his hand and led him to the cloakroom where his own overcoat was hanging. A couple of farm wives gave Charlie a smile of sympathy as he hurried out the door. It made him feel better. The climate outside was windy and blustery with intermittent hail, and the outhouse was out yonder by the cemetery. Charlie was not used to taking children on these little trips. Signe usually took care of all such incidentals.

Returning to the building, Charlie heard his favorite hymn being sung. "Blessed Is He." How he would have loved to sing that solo. He opened the door as quietly as possible and carried Hugo in. There, in front of the church stood a stranger—a tall, skinny young man with a high tenor voice—warbling the last measures of the hymn. The congregation sat entranced.

Lowering Hugo to his feet, Charlie led the boy back to his seat, and sat down. Charlie's humiliation was beyond words. Kivi had hired a young whippersnapper from out of the area to sing at Elma's baptism, knowing that Charlie would've made a large donation to the church had he been given the honor to solo. He tried to get Signe's attention, but she was listening to Kivi's sermon on family values and the role of the church in family life.

Charlie was deaf to the rest of the service until Signe poked when the organist started the baptismal hymn. Signe with Elma in her arms, with Charlie, and the two sponsors, Ed Koski and Hilda Mattson, gathered at the front.

Reino, refreshed from his nap, shook with excitement as the pastor addressed the baptismal group and the congregation. "In the Holy Baptism our gracious heavenly Father liberates us from sin and death by joining us to the death and resurrection of our Lord Jesus Christ. We are born children of a fallen humanity; in the waters of Baptism we are—"

Eldon looked at Reino. "I told you it would take a long, long time." He slouched down to take a nap.

"Elma Miriam, I baptize you in the name of the Father—"

Eldon opened his eyes as the minister dribbled water on Elma's head, and continued, "and of the Son, and of the Holy Spirit. Amen," sprinkling her head after each phrase.

"He poured water on her head three times!" Eldon told Reino. "I'm afraid Elma's going to have a bad head cold."

Reino was deaf to Eldon's concerns. The pastor had made a mistake. He'd named the baby Elma Miriam not Miriam Elma. Reino was too happy to hear anything else.

Chapter VIII

TWICE DURING THE NIGHT, Charlie swore so loud in
his sleep that he made the baby cry. "Wake up and
turn over, Charlie," Signe ordered. "You've frightened the baby and will wake up the other children."

Charlie was cantankerous when he woke up. He
had slept poorly. Things had not worked out the way
he had expected at Elma's baptism. The proud father
that he was, Charlie felt he had been snubbed by the
men after the service yesterday. They behaved as if
Elma were of virgin birth. Instead of putting out a
hand and congratulating him, they hurried to their
cars to wait for their wives and kids—all except Ed
Koski, Elma's godfather, who made a point of
complimenting Signe on her beautiful, well behaved
children, with no mention of the father.

Although he wouldn't acknowledge even to himself, Charlie knew that the cold treatment he'd received from the farmers was because of the cow episode. Farmers were an odd lot in that respect. They had their own codes of behavior.

As he funneled warm water from the tank in the kitchen stove into the washbasin for his morning shave, Charlie told Signe he didn't think Eldon should be spending so much time with Reino.

"Why?" she asked.

"I don't like him or his influence on the children, especially the boys. I wish he'd stay away." Charlie lathered his face, guided by the dim mirror that hung over the wood box, made a couple of swipes down his cheek with the straightedge and asked, "Why does Reino come here anyhow?"

"He doesn't have friends his own age. His childhood companions are married with families. He likes to visit us and play with the children. Why shouldn't Eldon have him for a friend?"

"Reino's not a kid. He's as old as I and a half-wit to boot."

"Better a half-wit than a jackass."

Charlie whirled around as if hit by an arrow in the rear and faced Signe. His face was crimson, his unsettled right eye uneasily quavered in its socket. "Signe, I don't like your choice of words."

"And I don't like what you're saying. You realize the neighbors are too far away for the children to visit. Reino tells them stories and makes up games for them to play. He helps me by rocking Elma when I'm sewing. Besides, nobody else has time for Reino. Where's your Christian spirit?"

Charlie finished his dressing and ate his breakfast in silence. He grabbed his lunch pail and went out the door.

As she prepared to nurse Elma, Signe heard sobbing in the children's room. She hurried there with the baby in her arms.

Eldon was lying face down on his bed, crying, "I'm a bad boy."

"What makes you think that, Eldon? You're a very good little boy." Signe laid the baby on the bed. Then turned her son over, sat him up and wiped his tears with the corner of the baby's blanket. "You help me. You take care of Violet and Hugo, and you watch Elma. You're the best son a mother ever had."

"I hollered at you and made you wet the floor and made Elma be born early. Now Papa is angry. He hates Reino. . . and he's my only friend. I wish I die."

"I wish I die, too," Violet cried.

Hugo, about to join in the death wish, spotted Reino standing by the doorway, and shouted, "You bet'cha!"

With Reino's help, Signe was ahead of her daily schedule. She would feed the children their lunch and make a big sandwich with a bowl of yogurt for Reino and he might decide to stay for the rest of the day. She'd get several hours of sewing in.

The children were playing school with Reino as the teacher when Hugo announced, "I hear a car," and rushed to open the door. "It's Papa! He's come home for lunch. "

Reino was gone.

Violet and Hugo rushed to greet their father. Eldon stayed behind.

"What's wrong with you, Eldon—the cat got your tongue?" Charlie asked but didn't wait for an answer. "See what Papa's got for you," he said, as he handed a stick of red licorice to Violet. "You have mother cut it in three, so you all can have a piece."

Signe looked up from her bread slicing and thought, Charlie spent a penny on three children.

"Papa, did you come home to eat with us?" Hugo asked. "Mama's making the sandwiches—"

"No, Son, I have my lunch in the mail car."

"But it won't take time at all. Look, she's already cutting the bread pieces."

Charlie shook his head and turned to Signe. "I just happened to stop at the General Store and got wind of the news that the Men's Choir from our church has been invited to give a series of concerts in the churches in the Twin Cities area. Nobody's contacted me as yet, but Pete Hutto will probably bring it up at tonight's meeting."

"Who told you about it?"

"Wayne Siren. 'This is the time to do it,' I told him, 'before the spring planting is upon us.' For me it works real well. Mr. Gilpin likes to go fishing in the summertime and doesn't much care to substitute for me then. I told Wayne, 'Sure I'll go. I'll take my vacation early. I haven't been any place for many years.'"

"Did you talk to Mr. Gilpin?" Tom Gilpin was the old Irishman whom Charlie had replaced as mailman.

"Not yet."

"Since you have a brand new car," Signe said, "I thought we might drive to visit my sister in Ironwood this summer during your vacation. I haven't seen Anna for five years."

"In the mail car?"

"Yes. Isn't that what you're planning to use to go to Minneapolis?"

"But this is for the church, not personal use. Besides, Miriam is too young to be taken on a trip, especially in the summer when it's hot and muggy. Michigan is a two, three day drive from here."

"I know how far it is," Signe retorted. "We went there in the old pickup when you first got it. Eldon was only a couple months old, but we had a good time. Remember?"

"This is not the time to be thinking of good times. We have four youngsters to feed and clothe. When they're grown and married, you and I can drive a-round the country whenever and wherever the notion takes us."

Signe dropped the subject. With Charlie gone, she could catch up on her sewing. She had a ladies coat to make besides a number of dresses. Dr. Hicks had ordered a wool tweed coat for his wife, as payment for his services, and said that if the garment met his wife's expectations, he'd have Signe tailor a topcoat for himself.

Early Monday morning, Charlie put on his new overcoat that he'd bought in Fargo for the trip. "There'll be four of us in my car. Who the other three choir members will be, I don't know. We'll decide at the church." He took the four bags of sandwiches that he had Signe make—two sandwiches for each man. "They'll all have their own Thermoses with coffee," he said. "We plan to be gone ten days, but if we have additional bookings, we'll stay for the full two weeks. Who knows what this might lead to! Maybe a tour of Finland."

Signe listened to Charlie's spiel. Then gave a disinterested nod.

Eldon was delighted to have Mr. Gilpin back on the job. Mr. Gilpin was his friend.

Early in life, Tom Gilpin, living next to a Finnish community, had realized that if he was going to deal with them, he'd have to learn their ways and their lingo. That he had. He spoke Finnish quite fluently and accepted their abrupt mannerisms as part of their heritage. His patrons liked and trusted Mr. Gilpin, the mailman.

"How old are you now?" Gilpin asked Eldon on his first day's run when the boy met him at the mailbox.

"Five. And then I'll be six."

"How would you like to have a dog?"

"What kind of a dog?"

"A gray, longhaired mongrel."

"What's his name?"

"Buster. But you could change that to whatever you like."

"I like Buster."

The mailman smiled. "I named him that."

"Does he bark?"

"Yes, when strangers come around or he hears a noise."

"Good. Does he bite?"

"No. He doesn't bite, fight, or mess in the house."

"How many dollars do you want for him?" Eldon asked.

"He's a gift."

"What's a gift?"

"A present."

Eldon was overjoyed. "Buster is a present for me? Where you got him, in the trunk?"

"No. At home. You ask your mother if she will let you have him. If she says yes, you tell me tomorrow and I'll deliver the pooch next evening."

Tomorrow was too far in the future for Eldon. "You wait here," he told the mail carrier. "I'll go ask Mother and if she says yes, you can bring Buster tonight."

Eldon ran down the hill to the mailbox. "I can have Buster! You bring him over as soon as you get home. Mother's going to make a cake so we can have some coffee. Be sure to bring your mother."

Mr. Gilpin covered the grin on his face with his palm. He knew Eldon meant wife, not mother, but didn't know the word. "I'll see if she can come. Thanks for the invite."

The arrival of Buster to the Skinnar household was like Christmas and Fourth of July combined, a truly joyous occasion. Eldon wanted the dog to shake hands. Violet wanted him to lie down, but Hugo, the quickest, jumped on Buster's back to take a ride.

Eldon had made sure that Reino was there when his gift arrived. "You're going to scare the daylights out of Elma if you act so wild," Reino, rocking the baby, warned.

"Buster's real good with children," Gilpin told Signe as he cut into the piece of gingerbread with his fork. "My son has five. But Chuck felt he couldn't take the dog with him when he moved his family to Minneapolis for his new job. 'An apartment in a big city is no place for a farm dog,' he said, so he left Buster with me and the missis."

"I'll never leave Buster," Eldon vowed.

Chapter IX

SINCE BIRTHINGS HAD BEEN almost an annual event in the Skinnar family, and the household chores and sewing took most of her day, Signe was only able to give a small portion of her time and attention to Eldon, but the love his parents showed him made him feel like a star in the heavens.

At the age of two, Eldon could count to ten in Finnish. By his third birthday, he had memorized the alphabet. What he felt lacking was a sit-down-at-a-desk formal education, but now that he had Buster almost anything was possible. The gray, shaggy haired canine was his companion, guide, and guard.

At eleven o'clock one morning, when his mother went to feed the chickens, Eldon changed into his best pants and shirt and with Buster set off to get educated.

"*Mina olen tullut oppimaan*," Eldon announced as he opened the school door. I've come to learn.

His reception was mixed. Some kids giggled nervously. Others sat straight faced in awe. Eldon had broken the primary rule; he had talked Finnish in school. This infraction was punishable by "after school", which meant staying after classes were dismissed at 4:10, until the teacher had corrected all the papers, swept the floor, washed the blackboards, and written the various assignments for all grades, one through eight on a fresh slate, and carried in the next day's supply of firewood.

Who should break the rule next? It was evident that someone had to. Miss Keksi, the teacher, took it upon herself to instruct in Finnish the new student as to school rules and deportment.

Eldon nodded. He understood. No Finn spoken in school.

Despite the fact that he was given no text to read, and no problems to solve, the young scholar felt the experience rewarding and elucidating. Frank Linden, a big eighth-grader, rode Eldon piggyback around the schoolyard. Jenny Siren pushed him on the merry-go-round until he was dizzy; and Mary Linden shared her fried egg sandwich with him.

When Signe got back to the house, she found Elma fussing in her cradle with four-year-old Violet trying to appease her, and Hugo standing on a chair by the window looking out. "Come down from that chair before you fall," she said, and took Elma in her arms.

Hugo obeyed. "Eldon go," he announced.

"Go?" Signe asked. "Go where?"

"Out."

"When?" she asked, immediately realizing how foolish the question was. The children had no conception of time.

"Today."

Signe panicked. How could anyone have enticed Eldon to leave, and how had that person been able to contact her son — unless that person was Reino. But Reino would not leave the three younger children in jeopardy — unless he'd gone off the "deep end." And where was Buster? Eldon and the dog were inseparable. Buster had probably gone for the ride.

"What was Eldon wearing when he left," Signe asked.

"His new black pants that you made for him, and his new blue shirt," Violet replied.

"He wash his face and comb his hair," Hugo added.

Signe's thoughts ran in circles. Her mouth was dry. She could hardly talk. "Did he say anything before he left?"

"Sure did," Hugo volunteered. "He say, 'Be good kids and don't fight and don't touch the matchbox.'"

"Is that all?"

"He told me," Violet added, "take care of Elma until Mother comes back from the chicken coop."

"Did you see anybody else or did you hear a car?"

Hugo shook his head. "Nobody. No car."

"Did you see which way Eldon went when he got on the road?"

"Out the door. I'm hungry. I want two eggs, two

breads an' cuppa cocoa." Hugo thought for a while. "An two pork sops and six peas."

Signe stood motionless in the middle of the kitchen holding Elma, now secure and asleep in her mother's arms. "I'll cook as soon as I figure what I can do."

"Don't worry, Mama. Eldon knows the road. You jus' make my breakfess."

Signe had many questions, but her children could only answer the most simple ones. But who could? "Did Eldon put on his hat and coat?"

"Sure did, an' he comb his hair like this." Hugo pulled his hair back with the palms of his hands.

Signe had no phone. It was a mile and a half to the nearest neighbor. How could she possibly take two little children and an infant to go look for her son? But if that was what she had to do, that's what she would do."

She gave Violet and Hugo a slice of buttered bread and put on their coats and hats, and was bundling the baby when Reino walked in.

"Where you going?" he asked.

"Eldon's disappeared."

"Not like a ghost," Hugo explained to Reino. "Eldon go out the door."

Signe broke into tears. "I'm afraid someone lured him—"

Reino interrupted her. "Who'd be crazy enough to drive here on that muddy road to snatch a poor farm kid? There's no percentage in that. Eldon probably went to school."

Hugo piped up, "Yaa, Eldon wash his face and

comb his hair like this."

"School?" Signe exclaimed.

"He's been talking about it for a long time, but said he couldn't go alone. Now he has Buster. I'll go find them."

When Reino opened the door of the school porch, he almost stumbled on Buster stretched out on the floor, sleeping on Eldon's coat. Eldon was inside, seated by Jenny Siren, coloring a picture of a horse. He motioned to Reino to come to him, and whispered in his ear, "*Älä puhu Suomea elikkä joutut olemaan jälkeen koulun.*" Don't talk Finn or you'll have to stay after school.

Eldon refused to leave before dismissal time, but when he got home he felt it was a day well spent. Never had he been the object of so much attention. His mother cried with joy just to see him. Violet wanted to know if he had learned to read. Hugo asked him if he'd seen any of the three bears on the way to school. Reino bragged about Eldon's fine singing voice.

Tired from the long day, Eldon took off his coat and sat on the bench beside Reino and asked his mother, "When I go to school, can I bring a fried egg sandwich in a lard pail, like the other kids?"

Signe nodded wistfully.

Chapter X

IN OCTOBER, 1925, the ground around Wolf Creek, Minn., was mostly bare, but cold rains and freezes at night had stunted the new growth of alfalfa in the field, and Signe had to feed the cows dry hay twice daily, which doubled her workload. It could snow any day now, and the cattle would have to be fed three times and watered twice.

Her nausea had returned. "Mama, I heard you vollop three times this morning," Eldon told Signe, as she sat by the kitchen table, trying to down a glass of buttermilk. "Did you eat rotten meat?" Since he learned to talk, Eldon had pronounced vomit as vollop.

Signe smiled and ran her fingers lovingly through his blond curls. "No, Eldon, I haven't eaten much of anything."

She was saved an explanation to Eldon by Hugo's

"Me, too!" wanting attention. Signe patted the feathery wisps on Hugo's head, and hugged Violet. "I have to check the baby before I go back to the barn." She hurried to the bedroom, followed by her brood.

"Her name is Elma," Eldon reminded his mother. "And you don't have to worry about Elma. I'll be here."

That evening Charlie was drinking coffee with Hugo seated on his lap, when Signe told him she suspected she was pregnant.

"Again!" he gasped. His unstable right eye quavered and he dropped the cup on the saucer from a height that made the cup rattle and spill its contents on the green and blue plaid oilcloth.

With dishcloth in hand, Signe rushed to the table to see if any of it had gotten on the child and to wipe up the coffee.

Charlie, a true Christian, promptly recovered. "It's God's will. 'Be fruitful and multiply,' He said, 'and replenish the earth, and subdue it: and have dominion over the fish of the sea, and over every living thing that moveth upon the earth.'" Charlie clasped his hands, shifted his eyes up toward the heavens that overspread the tarpaper roof of his house and addressed his Maker, "Thank Thee, Lord, for thy bountiful blessings. I love the fruit of my seed, my children. Amen."

Little Hugo, trying to clasp his hands as he'd seen his father do, kept repeating, "Amen . . . Amen. . . Amen. . ." as he adjusted his tiny fingers into their proper slots.

"What's multa pie?" Eldon asked his mother.

"Multiply," she corrected. "Something added many times."

"How many?"

"Hard to tell."

Pushing the wheelbarrow full of manure from the barn to the pile several yards away, day after day hurt Signe's back, and kept her away from the house and children too long. When Reino came to visit, Signe was shoveling manure. She asked him if she could hire him to do it once a day.

"I don't want to be kicked on the head by a cow." Reino took off his blue and white stripe cap, and felt his scalp. "I was clobbered on the head once and that's enough. Haven't been the same since."

"You can clean the barn when I let the cows out for watering."

"Why doesn't Charlie do it?"

"He has his mail route."

"He's lazy, that's why. Why doesn't he leave the farm if he doesn't want to deal with the shit?"

"I'll pay you—"

Reino turned his head sideways and looked at Signe from the corner of his eyes. "Real money?"

"A dollar a week."

"That much?"

Signe nodded. "That's what I get for making two dresses—two cotton dresses."

"I'd have to put it in the bank, and get a bank book."

"Or you could spend it."

"Nah, I'm not a big spender," he said, shaking his head to emphasize the point.

"You'll take the job?"

"If you promise Charlie won't hit me with a pitchfork."

"Charlie won't touch you."

Reino looked her in the eye and said, 'Signe, you're baby-way, aren't you?"

She nodded and blushed.

"My uncle Ed said Charlie used to be a real hard worker when he was a kid. Guess the government jobs have gone to his head. Reino put on his cap. "I have to run over to Uncle Ed's and tell him about my job."

"Don't you want to see Elma?"

He took one step toward the house, but changed his mind. "I have to tell Ed. He said, 'Reino, you must tell me anything that's important,' and getting a job is real important." He took off, running clumsily like a bear on two feet. Then turned around, waved back to Signe, and continued on to the main road.

With five dollars in his savings account at the First National Bank in Frazee, Reino had fresh concerns. "I didn't ever think I'd die a millionaire, but that's the way it looks now," he told Eldon as he pitched the manure soaked straw into the wheelbarrow.

"What's a millionaire?" Eldon asked.

"It's a man who has so much money he doesn't know what to do with it."

"You can put it in a wheelbarrow and dump it in the lake."

Reino shook his head as he stared at his young buddy. "Oh, you kids, you don't know the meaning of life."

Eldon wouldn't be dismissed so easily. He simply changed the subject. "You like cows now, don't you?"

"Yaa, they're kinda nice. When you get to know them. But I wouldn't want to milk one." Reino took off his cap, massaged his head and bent down. "Feel this bump. It's a horse kick."

Eldon ran his hand over Reino's scalp and exclaimed, "That's your head."

Reino slapped his cap back on and muttered, "Go inside, Eldon. You're keeping me from my work."

Charlie was pleased with Signe's choice of a hired hand. Reino did his job well, avoiding Charlie as much as he could. He removed himself from the place before Charlie got home in the afternoon, and on Sundays Reino came while the family was at church.

After the death of Eldon's cow, Queen, Charlie had never entered the barn, or tossed a forkful of hay to the cattle. Everything related to the dairy was left to Signe, and it was more than she could handle in her condition. "Would you help me feed the cattle their hay?" she asked Reino.

"With a pitchfork?'

Signe nodded.

"They can't kick my head when I'm standing, can they?"

"No, but cows like you. Haven't you noticed?"

Flattered that he was liked by the dairy herd made Reino giggle and shake. "Yaa. I like them, too. I put my hand on their backs and rub them like Eldon showed me how, and they want to lick my hand."

"I'll pay you fifty cents more each week for two feedings a day, morning and noon."

Reino figured on his fingers. "Three dresses' worth altogether. Cotton dresses."

Signe nodded.

After a noon feeding, two days later, Reino, out of breath, ran to the house calling for Signe. "Beauty is trying to calve, but I think she's got troubles."

Signe hurriedly changed into her barn outfit. "Eldon, Mother has to go to the barn."

"You need help?"

"Yes, take care of your brother and sisters."

"I'll tell them the story about the two bears," Eldon announced as he went to his bedroom to get stools for Violet and Hugo to sit on.

It was Beauty's second calf, a breech birth. For two hours Signe and Reino worked trying to pull the calf out of its mother without any luck. At first Reino balked at helping—said he didn't want to get his hands all gooey—but he felt sorry for Signe. "A lady in your condition shouldn't be doing man's work," he said.

"Maybe you could get your uncle Ed to help us," Signe suggested.

Reino shook his head. "Not today. He went to Fargo and won't be back until who knows when."

Signe suddenly had no more strength to continue. Her body became limp from exhaustion. Her legs buckled and she collapsed beside the cow that was trying to give birth.

Reino picked her up in his arms. "Don't you worry, Signe, I won't drop you. I never drop anything. I'm going to get you help." He carried her to the house and set her on the bed beside Elma.

The children were frightened.

Eldon tiptoed into the room, afraid to look. "Is she dead?" At the word "dead," the two younger ones who had followed him, started to cry.

"No, Mother's not dead," Signe answered. "I just need rest."

Hearing the good news, Eldon gave his brother a push up to the mattress and the children joined Elma and their mother on the bed.

"Now don't you kids suffocate Elma," Reino cautioned. "I'm going to get help."

"Signe, you could hemorrhage to death," Hilda Mattson shouted as she hung a clothesline above the kitchen stove. "Those cows aren't worth it. What's to become of your children if something happened to you? Charlie would go chasing after some mindless young skirt and your little ones would be left to shift for themselves or be sent to an orphanage. And where does Charlie's money go, anyhow? I've often said to my husband, 'Gust, what do you think Charlie Skinnar does with all his money that Signe has to kill herself running the farm?'"

"Charlie is very thrifty."

"A skinflint! That's what he is."

The children were in their room listening. Eldon, behind the curtains that substituted for a door, kept an eye on Hilda through the slight opening in the middle.

"Furthermore," Hilda continued when she returned to Signe's room, "you have four beautiful youngsters now. You don't need any more. I, as you know, had the two, but after Raymond I told Gust, 'Keep your peeper hidden if you don't want it snapped off.'"

Eldon, behind the curtain, placed his little hands in front of his blue corduroy pants and listened for more.

"There's a doctor in Park Rapids who specializes in women's problems, such as yours now. He's very reasonable, they say. Only two dollars in the early stages. You'd have to stay in bed for a couple of weeks, but that's where you are now. Gust could take us to town. We'd tell him we're going shopping for shoes—"

Hilda's monologue was interrupted by Charlie's entrance into the bedroom. "Why, hello, Mrs. Mattson. Reino tells me that you've been having trouble—"

"Not me," Hilda flared back, "You," and pointed at Signe. "Your wife is in bed ready to miscarry and one of your cows is about to die in the process of calving. I suggest you get out of that monkey suit and get to the barn. Where's Reino? Get him to take care of the kids. I'm going home. I have bread dough rising." She put on her hat, coat, and arctics, and was in the process of pulling on her mittens as she went out the door.

"I have to stay with you kids while your father goes to get somebody to help him with the cow," Reino complained as he seated himself at the table. "I sure hope your father drives me home. I don't like walking in the pitch-dark."

"You can stay overnight," Eldon volunteered. "You can sleep with me and I will make you some cold cocoa before we go to bed. I will put vanilla in it. Wouldn't you like that?"

Reino smiled. "Guess I would. Now sit down and listen. I have a new story."

"What's the name of it?"

"Don't interrupt," Reino ordered. "It's impolite. I was coming to it. The name of the story is ITSY, BITSY AND MORE. ITSY, BITSY and MORE were three horsemen —"

"What's horsemen?" Eldon asked.

"It's men that ride on top of a horse."

"Don't they have wagons or buggies?"

"Horsemen don't ride wagons or buggies. Wagons and buggies are for ladies and old men."

"I would want to go in a buggy. I'd hold the reins in this hand and the whip in this," Eldon said, demonstrating as he spoke.

"For the last time, do you want to hear the story or not?"

"Not," Hugo shouted. "not, not, not."

"Hugo is just a little kid," Eldon explained. "He doesn't know what he's saying. We want to hear the story."

Reino was eager to continue and appreciated the vote of confidence.

"These horsemen were different from other horsemen. ITSY was indivisible and so was his horse."

"What does indivisible mean?" Eldon wanted to know.

"It means that you can't see him. Like the wind. You know the wind is blowing, but you can't see it."

"Like a ghost."

Reino was elated. "Now you're using your brain, Eldon. BITSY was indivisible but his horse was visible."

"Did the horse have a saddle?"

"You bet'cha. But guess what. MORE was a great big, fat man but his horse was indivisible."

"Did he break the horse's back?"

"Course not. It was strong like steel. The man was so fat that there was no belt in the world long enough. He had to tie a hanging rope around his waist to hold up his pants.

"The three horsemen would ride all around, like from here to Sebeka to Menahga and Thief River Falls, getting people excited and all they could see was BITSY'S horse and MORE.

"People would shout, 'Hey, we have a tornado coming!' but wise men knew better. 'It's the three horsemen.' Some people only saw a horse without a rider and a fat man flying in the wind, but Mr. Sandvick sensed all three.

"Mr. Sandvick was pumping water for his cattle at the barn well when he felt this great gust of wind and the cattle scattered like chased by a herd of wild dogs. He saw BITSY'S horse and he saw the fat man who looked like he was sitting on air while the horses drank from the cattle tank. Mr. Sandvick said, 'Good morning, gentlemen. Where you traveling today?'

"All three answered most politely, 'Good morning, sir. Brainerd is our destination. And then to Anoka. We wish you a very fine day.' They got on their horses and rode away."

The children, satisfied with Reino's story, sat quietly.

"Do you know what it means?" he asked.

The children shook their heads.

"It means that just because you can't see it, doesn't mean something can't be there."

Eldon thought for awhile. "Like a ghost."

Violet raised her hand as if in school and said, "Like the sun."

Reino paused and thought over her answer. "You can see the sun."

"Not the warm of the sun."

"The heat of the sun. Now can you beat that?" Reino was elated. "I've always said Violet is the smart one. Why, you're almost as smart as me. You're a genius."

Hugo, who had been unlacing his boot, closed his eyes and kicked the shoe in the air and squealed, "You bet'cha."

"I'm sorry to hear that you're not feeling well," Charlie told Signe when he finally entered their bedroom, after Hilda's chastisement.

Signe didn't answer.

"Guess I'll have to find somebody to take care of the cow," he added.

"It can't be just somebody. You'll have to go to the neighbors and call Dr. Swanson."

"His'll be a costly visit, I guarantee."

"It'll cost you more if we lose the cow and calf."

'I'll see what I can do," Charlie grumbled and left.

As soon as their father went to his pickup truck, the children rushed to Signe.

"Reino told us a story about the horsemen you can't see," Eldon said. "Have you seen them?"

Signe smiled. "Not yet."

"They should be in Anoka by now. They drive fast. Like the wind."

"Would you ask Reino to come here, Eldon?"

Eldon got down on all fours, Hugo got on his back and the two left the room.

Reino came in smiling. "Signe, you want me to rock Elma? Is that why you want to see me?"

"Not right now, Reino. But on your way home, I'd like you to go to Lahtis and ask Mrs. Lahti to send her boys to do the milking until I feel better."

Reino took off his cap and massaged the imaginary bump on his head. "Can't do that."

"I know it's out of your way—"

He interrupted her. "They have a mad dog. Can't take anymore chances with my life." Reino wanted to please Signe, but it took some heavy concentration on his part to come up with an idea. "I know what. You write a letter to my uncle Ed and tell him what he's supposed to say on the phone when he calls Mrs. Lahti and I'll take the letter to Ed. What do you think of that?"

"Sounds good." Signe called for Eldon, who was

traveling around the house on his knees with Hugo on his back, to get a pencil and tablet from the cupboard.

"You writing to the teacher to see if I can go to school?"

"Not yet, Eldon, you're only five."

"Going on six. Guess I'll have to wait until I'm an old man with a long beard."

"Get the tablet and pencil like your mother told you," Reino ordered. "I don't have all day."

Eldon returned with the goods, looked at the pencil, and asked, "Would you like me to sharpen it? I have my knife in my pocket, ready to go."

Signe shook her head, wrote the message on a piece of paper and handed it to Reino. "Be sure to thank your uncle."

Reino slipped the note in his pocket. "Now you kids be good. If you're real good, I'll buy you licorice when I get rich." He left the three dreaming of the day when Reino struck gold and would come over with sacks of mouth-watering strips of black confection.

"Eldon," Signe said, holding out the pencil and tablet, "would you put these back where they belong?"

"Don't you want to write the letter to the teacher? It will only take a few minutes."

"You're too young to go to school."

"I know. I'll put the letter in the box under my bed to keep it safe."

"So, why do you want me to write it now?"

Eldon began to cry. "You're sick and might die and I'd never get to school."

Violet and Hugo joined in the funereal chorus.

Signe held out her hand to help get them up on the bed. "Eldon, Mother doesn't have a disease. I'm sick because I'm going to have another baby."

"Holy cow!" Eldon whisked away the last tear with his sleeve. "You'd better watch out or you'll have as many babies as Porker." Porker was Gust Mattson's sow who had a litter of fifteen earlier in the year.

Signe laughed and hugged her brood.

All was quiet. The children had dozed off. Signe could hardly move on the crowded bed — much less sleep.

She heard the kitchen door open and close. She thought it must be Charlie, but Reino's figure zoomed at the poorly lighted doorway. "You back already?"

"I didn't go. It was dark outside. I don't go on the road in the dark. Somebody might run over me."

"What about the cows? Who's going to do the milking?"

Reino straightened himself. "Don't you worry about a thing, Signe. I took care of all matters. I helped Charlie get his pickup running and then told him what to do. I'm not afraid of Charlie Skinnar. He's almost a year older than I, but I'm stronger. I could push him down and sit on him for a day and there's nothing he could do about it." Reino laughed. "He even thanked me for helping him!"

"You must be hungry."

"Yaa, but that can wait. First, I have to move the kiddies into their own beds. I see you're pretty crowded over there."

"Two of the slowest milkers I ever saw," Charlie hollered from the kitchen, when he finally came in that night lugging cream cans full of milk to be separated. He was referring to the Lahti brothers who had come to do the evening milking. Charlie washed his hands, grabbed a towel and stood at the bedroom door. "They charged me fifty cents each for just one milking. You'd think the neighbors would be willing to lend a hand in time of emergency without digging into your pocket. People seem to think if you have a government job, the money just flows like gravy over mashed potatoes."

"How much was the veterinary bill?" Signe asked.

"I didn't want to bother old Doc Swanson. He's getting up in years. Besides, his services are very costly. I called Cal Peterson from Ed's place. He came over with a wire coat hanger and we had the calf out in no time. We lost the calf, but we saved the cow."

Signe couldn't bear to hear more. "Charlie, would you bring me a cup of water and the aspirin bottle from the second shelf of the cupboard?" She swallowed two tablets with the water. Then turned her face toward the wall and fell asleep to the whirling sound of the cream separator as Charlie turned the handle.

"So what did you decide about the matter I mentioned yesterday?" Hilda asked Signe when she returned the next morning.

"I will not kill."

"Up to you." Hilda was miffed. "You might

instead be the victim. You're hemorrhaging to death, have a young one at your breast and expect another in a few months. Have you given any thought to what would happen to your living children if you should die?"

"Yes, I have. I will not die. After you've hung up the laundry, I want you to go home and call Dr. Gates in Perham and ask him to come to my home as soon as he can."

"It'll cost you a pretty penny to have him drive here. Much cheaper to have Charlie run you there."

"I'm not in the running mood, Hilda. I'll pay the bill somehow, and as for your help, I'll make you that winter coat you've been talking about."

Hilda reddened. "Oh, it's not entered my mind."

"Yes, it has and that's quite natural. We all need to be paid for our services. Give the doctor explicit directions so he won't get lost."

At the mention of a new coat, Hilda moved like a sixteen-year-old. "I'll wash the sheets and pillow cases tomorrow," she called to Signe in the bedroom, as she flipped the laundry on the line that hung over the kitchen stove. "It's supposed to be warmer tomorrow and I can hang them outside."

"Mother, can Mrs. Mattson boil us some milk?" Eldon asked. "I've got the cocoa and sugar mixed in cups."

"Of course, Sonny," Hilda volunteered, as she grabbed the milk jug from the table and poured some into a pot. "No trouble at all."

"Can we put some vanilla, too?"

"What's cocoa without vanilla?' Hilda said, as she

reached into the cupboard and plunked the bottle on the table for Eldon to help himself. She put on her coat and stocking cap while she waited for the milk to heat. "I'm going to warm it just enough so you kiddies won't burn your little tongues."

Hilda poured the lukewarm milk into the three cups Eldon had prepared, and after saying goodbye to Signe, she left.

"Ick! This is terrible," Eldon exclaimed after a sip of the lukewarm liquid. Mrs. Mattson doesn't know how to make cocoa."

"Turrble! Turrble!" Hugo echoed and spat out his drink.

Eldon emptied all three cups into the pot and set it on the stove to heat. "No other lady knows how to cook good like Mother."

Hugo shook his head, and repeated, "No lady."

Reino rushed into Signe's bedroom. "Those dumbbells — referring to the Lahti boys who had been hired to do the milking — left the morning milk for me to separate. Okay, I'll separate it but I won't wash the separator parts. I'm not a dishwasher. Charlie can do something around here to earn his keep. What's more, those boys don't strip the cows good enough. First thing you know, they'll all go dry. But the worse thing that can happen has happened." He waited for Signe's reaction.

"What's that?" she asked.

"The cow died."

"Beauty? No!"

"Darn doodin' she did. What do you expect?

Those two geezers putting that old rusty coat hanger in her. Blood poisoning, that's what. Anyone with any brains knows better."

Signe couldn't cry. She had shed her tears.

Reino shook his head. "Charlie is getting so tight, he'd sell his mother for a nickel if she were alive."

"Two of our best cows dead," Signe thought a-loud. "How will we get her out of the barn?"

"Charlie! Put an old horse collar on him and say, 'Giddyup, Charlie.'" Reino giggled till he shook. "Think I'll tell my Uncle Ed that one. He'll get a kick out of it."

Dr. Gates in his new green Studebaker arrived at midafternoon. He gave Signe a complete examination. "Too many babies in too short a time," he said. "You stay in bed, day and night, until I return. That'll be two weeks from today. If your condition should get worse, have someone call me. But bed rest should do it."

"But the children need —"

The doctor interrupted Signe. "Hire someone to take care of the kiddies." He put on his coat and hat, picked up his satchel and left.

"I sold the cattle!" Charlie bellowed joyously as he set foot in the bedroom.

"You sold our cows?" Signe exclaimed in dis-belief. "All of them?"

"Every goddamn last one."

"Don't swear, Charlie!" Signe, face white with an-ger, commanded. "The children will hear you. What will we do for milk and butter? Did you think of that?"

"Buy from the neighbors. No more milking, no more separating, and no more worrying about the damn cream turning sour before getting it to the creamery. Best of all, no more cow shit."

The baby, awakened by Charlie's hollering, began to cry.

Signe sat up in bed, spine straight as a fence post. Her gray-blue eyes lashed with anger. "Charlie, you have frightened Elma. I've had enough. You're making nervous lunatics out of me and the children. I won't listen to any more of your ranting. Go warm up the sauna, heat a vasta and beat out the poisons in you. Now!"

Charlie turned on his heel and left the bedroom. In the safety of the kitchen, he took off his hat and shook his head. Then went out, and closed the door after him.

Chapter XI

SIGNE WAS IN THE HOSPITAL awaiting the birth of her fifth child.

Reino, taking care of the Skinnar children, was seated at the kitchen table with Elma on his lap, playing checkers with Eldon when Charlie returned from his mail route. Violet and Hugo were rolling marbles over the floor.

"What are you doing?" Charlie asked Reino.

"Playing checkers."

"You smart enough?"

"Sure. Aren't you?"

"Isn't checkers the same as cards —"

"Nah, cards are square and thin. Checkers are round and thick." Reino knew what Charlie meant, but he wanted to nettle Charlie.

Charlie gritted his teeth. "I know the difference."

"Then why did you ask?"

"I don't want my boy learning sinful pastimes."

"Checkers aren't sinful," Reino said as he jumped over Eldon's. "I jump you."

Elma put her tiny fingers into Reino's mouth and he responded with a "BLURRRR" and shook his head dizzily. She laughed and shook her head, trying to imitate him.

Violet got up from the floor and clutching her favorite marble, went to her father. "Papa, isn't this the most beautiful thing you ever saw?"

Charlie gave a vacant nod.

"Look, it has blue and green and a little bit of lavender." Violet closed her left eye and put the marble in front of the right one and gazed at it. "When I grow up and get rich, I'm going to have Mama make me a dress this color."

Charlie wasn't in a listening mood. "Where did you get all this junk?"

"From Pastor Kivi's son's auction. They had lots of nice things for sale. The pastor said to me, 'Reino, since you spend so much time with the Skinnar kids, why don't you buy a few playthings for them.'"

Nothing Charlie heard was what he wanted to hear. He was about to ask Reino if the pastor had really called his children "kids" when he noticed that Elma was wearing pants. "Is that my daughter?" he asked.

"That's what you told the pastor," Reino replied, and began to giggle. He laughed until his whole body shook, shaking the baby on his lap.

Charlie tried to control his anger. "She's wearing

boy's pants."

"They're not boy's pants. See," he demonstrated by putting his hand in the trousers, "no hole in the front."

"She's a girl!" Charlie started to yell, but caught himself. He didn't want a confrontation with Signe.

"I know. I change Elma's diapers."

Charlie's right eye quivered and his head shook involuntarily. "What's the use? I'll see what Mother has to say." He rushed into the bedroom but was back in the matter of seconds, his face the color of a turnip. "She's gone!"

"I jump you," Eldon squealed.

"Where is she?" Charlie thundered.

"No, you can't," Reino told Eldon. "Look, I show — "

Charlie went to the table and with one swipe of his arm scattered the pieces of the game. "Where did Signe go?"

"To Park Rapids,' Reino answered, as he tried to pacify Elma who had been frightened by Charlie's outburst.

"Why didn't you tell me?"

"You didn't ask," Reino replied as he walked the hysterical child.

"Having another baby. Don't you know?" Hugo replied as he rolled a marble across the floor.

Charlie changed his aria, and began to pick up the checkers. "I have to go see Mother," he told the children. "Reino, it'll be late by the time I return. We'll make a bed for you here in the kitchen, so don't worry about walking home in the dar — ."

The kitchen door sprang open. Hilda Mattson, breathless from her mile-and-a-half walk, stood holding the doorknob. "I'm glad you made it home in daylight, Charlie. Put on your coat. Let's go."

"Go where?"

"To the Co-op to get some groceries."

"Too late."

"They're open until five and after that Vernon will let us in if we knock on the back door."

"I have to go to the hospital. Signe is about to have the baby."

"She won't need your help," Hilda snapped, "but the kiddies need food. Up and at'em, Charlie." She followed him out.

"I'm tired of playing marbles," Violet said. "Can we play school?"

"Nah," Eldon moaned. "We don't have books or paper or pencils. How can we play school?"

"Easy," Reino said, as he fed Elma buttered flatbread dunked in coffee. "We'll do it all oro."

"What's oro?" Eldon asked.

"It's all talk. Like when the teacher gives a test and says it's an oro test, that means no paper or pencil. We'll start now. I'm the teacher. It's the first day of school. Who wants to be first?"

Eldon raised his hand.

Reino directed his eyes at him. "The boy in the blue shirt. Tell us your name, age and what you want to be when you grow up."

"My name is Charles Eldon Skinnar. I'm six years old. I want to be a professor when I grow up."

"What's a professor?" Reino asked.

'I don't know, but that's what I want to be."

"Besides, you mustn't fib in school."

"I didn't fib."

"Eldon, you said you were six years old."

"If I want to go to school, that's what I have to be."

"Say, I'm five years old, almost six. Next, the girl in the speckled dress."

Violet stood up prim and proper. "My name is Violet Katri Skinnar. I'm four years old. Will be five soon. I plan to study hard so I can be a teacher when I grow up." She curtsied and sat back on the floor.

"Good work, Violet."

"You mean I was bad?" Eldon asked.

"There's room for improvement," the teacher responded and called on "the little boy in the blue shirt."

"My name is Hugo. I'm t'ree. I'm going to be a aeroplane driver brrrrr." He grabbed ahold of an imaginary wheel and burred around the house.

"Hugo, sit down," Reino ordered.

Hugo turned off his engine and dropped himself on the floor. "You bet'cha."

Reino tapped on the table with a spoon. "Hugo, I'm tired of you always saying, 'You bet'cha.' Can't you say something else like 'yes' or 'okay?'"

"Okay."

When Hilda Mattson and Charlie came back, Reino could see that Hilda had not been easy on Charlie's pocketbook. She hauled in a box of groceries big enough to feed all the poor at the poor farm, and

Charlie was dragging in a mattress.

"Charlie, you should've left the mattress in the pickup until you had the bed frame and spring put together." Hilda looked at Reino and shook her head at Charlie's stupidity. "The mattress goes on last."

Charlie didn't answer, but his hands trembled and his eye quivered uneasily as he went out the door.

Hugo went up to Hilda who was unpacking the box of groceries. "What did you bring for supper, Mrs. Mattson?

"Pork chops."

"Can I have two? I a growing boy."

"We'll see."

"What else did you buy, Mrs. Mattson?"

"Peas."

"Can I have ten?"

"Yes, you may have ten. Now go talk to your father. He looks like he could use some company."

"Who's going to sleep on the new bed?" Hugo asked Charlie.

"Ask Hilda," his father replied. "It was her idea to buy this junk from the secondhand store."

Hugo eyed the bed frame for some moments. "Looks new to me."

He went back to Hilda. "Whose bed is that?"

"It's for you and your brother. I can't see everyone in the family cuddling up in one bed like immigrants in the bottom of a ship. I even got a crib for the new baby that's coming, but there wasn't enough room in the truck to bring it home tonight. Charlie can pick it up tomorrow."

Hugo went to his brother. "Did you know that me

and you are going to have a new bed? We can sleep together all by ourselves." He then remembered Reino who was sitting by the table holding the baby. "You can sleep with us. I will sleep at the end of the bed. Eldon can't reach to kick me. He's too short."

Reino listened without answering, trying to figure how well he'd like the arrangement. "I have to go change Elma's diapers. Seems the bigger she grows, the more she wets." He BLURRED on the baby's cheek as he took her into the bedroom.

Elma tittered with delight.

Violet, helping Hilda set the table, became concerned about Signe. "Will my mother die?"

"Don't you worry about your mother. She's in a big hospital with the best doctor and lots of nurses running around like headless chickens. The rest will do her good."

"When will the baby come?"

"When it's good and ready."

Violet went back to rolling marbles on the floor.

Hugo neared the stove as Hilda dropped the pork chops on the skillet. "Aren't you going to boil any potatoes, Mrs. Mattson? I always eat potatoes with my meat and peas. It keeps the gravy on the plate."

"Of course I'll cook potatoes. What's meat without spuds."

"Can you make gravy without bumps?"

"I try," Hilda answered wearily.

"My mother makes good gravy. I like to dip my bread in it."

"Go see how your father is doing. He might need your help."

"Okay." Hugo took hold of an imaginary wheel and drove into the children's bedroom where Charlie was trying to put the bed frame together. "BRRRRRR . . . Is Mama going to have another baby?"

Charlie nodded.

"How many more?"

Charlie looked up at his son. "As many as the good Lord wants us to have."

"That much?" Hugo wanted to have more of a conversation, but Charlie had said all he had to say. Hugo missed his mother who never ran out of answers to his questions. He went back to the cook. "Mrs. Mattson, your cooking doesn't smell like Mama's."

Hilda was ready to snap at him, but changed her mind. "I don't look like her, either. She's tall and skinny and I'm short and fat."

"I like short and fat ladies, too," Hugo said sweetly.

Hilda smiled. She took out a package of gum from her pocket and handed Hugo three sticks. "Here." She gave him a loving pat on the bottom. "Go play marbles with your sister and brother."

"Black Jack," he exclaimed with joy. "You eat Black Jack, too? Thank you, Mrs. Mattson. I'll give half of my stick to Reino. He likes Black Jack."

Signe's baby was born at two o'clock the next morning. She had long thought she'd like to name one of her daughters Elise, after an Irish girl she'd known in New York. When the doctor came to her with papers and asked, "What do you want to name the newcomer?"

Signe said, "Elise June."

"How do you spell the first name?"

"E-l-i-s-e."

When Signe got the birth certificate, it read ELSIE JUNE SKINNAR. Charlie, however, was pleased. "Elsie is a good name for a farm girl."

Chapter XII

ELDON'S FIRST DAY OF SCHOOL was a big event in the Skinnar household. The night before, Signe warmed the sauna. Charlie broke in the new birch vasta—a ritual consisting of placing the switch on the hot rocks and throwing cold water on it to soften the leaves. The vasta is used to switch one's body clean. Before the switching, soaping and washing it is necessary to perspire profusely to bring out the body's accumulated poisons.

Charlie, undressed, climbed to the top step of the stairs of the steam room, threw a coffee can full of cold water on the hot rocks and sat down to sweat.

Eldon followed.

"No, Eldon, it's too hot for you up here. You'd better stay on the first rung.

"Don't worry. I won't faint." Eldon sat by his father. "The bottom steps are for the ladies and children. They can't take the heat like we men can."

Eldon had marked the days until his sixth birthday on the calendar with his father's flat yellow carpenter pencil, and colored the day after—which was Friday—red. Friday was the day.

"Why don't you wait until Monday?" his mother suggested.

"Can't. I will wait by the mailbox and walk with the big kids."

"What would you like for lunch?" Signe asked, as if there were much of a choice.

"Two fried egg sandwiches, a piece of jellyroll and a jar of milk. I have to eat good so I can learn."

Friday morning Eldon was outfitted with real wool pants and a white shirt. "I won't have my son going to school in overalls," Signe had told Charlie when she ordered the trousers from Chicago Mail Order. At the same time, she'd gotten her son a red and black Mackinaw. "He won't need it much now that the weather is warming up, but it'll come in handy next fall," Signe told Charlie.

Eldon went to the stove and poured himself a cup of coffee, added plenty of cream and sugar and sat at the table to wait for his breakfast. When his mother set the stack of saucer sized pancakes in front of him, Eldon saw tears in her eyes. "Why are you sad, Mother?"

"I'm not sad." Signe pulled up the bottom of her blue checkered apron and wiped away the droplets.

"I'm happy. Soon you can teach me the Constitution and I can get my citizenship papers."

Eldon swallowed a bit of pancake saturated with his mother's chokecherry jelly and took a sip of coffee. "I hope I don't forget to count right."

"Don't worry. Everyone makes mistakes."

"On the first day of school?"

"Especially on the first day."

Eldon shook his head, determined not to err.

Having finished the hotcakes, Eldon put on his jacket, picked up his tablet, pencil, lunch bucket and kissed his mother.

She hugged and hung on to him as if she'd never let go. Once released, happy that his siblings were still asleep and not fussing over him, Eldon hurried out the door. He waited until he had passed the woodpile to look back. His mother was standing at the kitchen window, waving to him with one hand and wiping her eyes with the other. He was about to turn back when Art Kivi by the gate yelled, "*Eldoni, hopusti elikkä me olemme myohasiä*," Eldon, hurry up or we'll be late!

Eldon ran down the hill, swooped under the gate, and joined Art, Karlo Koski and Senia Mattson.

"You can't bring Buster to school," Art said. "Dogs mess up the yard."

Eldon turned around. Buster was at his heels. "Go back, Buster. Mother needs you. I'll be home soon."

The dog crossed the road and sat by the mailbox.

"Now remember, you don't speak Finn in school, not even in the schoolyard," Art reminded Eldon, "because if you do, you'll have to stay after school and walk home alone."

"I know."

Before opening the school gate, Art gave Eldon final instructions in Finnish. "We leave our lunch pails in the porch. Put yours on the shelf so if any stray dogs get in, they can't reach it. In the winter when it freezes we take our lunches inside, but not now. When you open the school door, you say 'Good Morning' in a loud voice so the teacher can hear."

"What if there's nobody there?"

"Makes no difference. You don't just sneak in. Do you know what 'Good Morning' means?" Art asked.

Eldon nodded. "That's what Mr. Gilpin, the old postman, says when you meet him at the mailbox."

The group entered the porch where they deposited their lunch pails and Art opened the door to the classroom. "Good morning," they vocalized in unison.

Miss Keksi, standing at the blackboard writing the day's assignments, turned around. "Good morning, children."

Eldon followed the group to the corner where the encyclopedias were kept. "Hang your coat on a hook under the shelf," Art said. "Don't just throw it on the floor."

Eldon hadn't understood Art's instructions in English but followed the examples of the others and carefully hung up his new Mackinaw. He knew it had cost his mother many hours of tailoring. He then went to the desk he'd occupied when he visited the school and sat down.

Miss Keksi went to the long rope that hung by the

front door and pulled on it, ringing the final bell which meant that school was in session.

Eldon was cautious. He didn't want to miss anything or act stupid. His eyes followed the teacher's moves. When she went to the flag, everyone stood up, put his hand on his chest and muttered something like 'ayebledchaleenstodtaflakg . . .' Eldon listened and imitated what he thought he was hearing and wished the teacher would give him a book.

His wish was soon granted. Miss Keksi reached over to the bookcase next to her desk, took out a reader and gave it to him. It had pictures of a red mother hen and her chicks. Eldon felt his heart dancing as he gingerly flipped over the pages. He was finally going to learn to read.

"Primary reading," Eldon heard Miss Keksi announce. Eldon looked at Art, who motioned that Eldon should take his book and join Bertha and Richard who were going to the front of the room. Richard sat at one end of the long bench and Bertha at the other. Eldon sat by Bertha. The other kids giggled and Bertha's face turned red. Eldon, confused, didn't know what to do. Richard tapped on the bench at his end indicating that Eldon should sit there. Eldon moved. The teacher talked to the kids. Eldon didn't understand what she said, but she looked severe. He'd had his first lesson in school etiquette: Boys don't sit by girls.

Learning to read English was not simple. The teacher showed printed cards with words like HEN, RED, NOT, I, which Bertha promptly pronounced. She'd been in school since September and understood

English, having learned it in Hibbing where her family had previously lived. Richard, however, was struggling with the language, barely able to read his own name.

First recess was fun. The big kids took turns carrying Eldon piggyback and turning him on the merry-go-round. He had never had so many play-mates. He felt a bit hungry and thought about taking a nibble out of his jellyroll, but the fifteen minutes were over too quickly.

After recess Eldon's academic luck turned. The teacher called Primary for arithmetic. Eldon followed Bertha and Richard to the front of the room and sat next to Richard. When Miss Keksi said "count," Eldon recognized the word and shot up his hand.

She nodded and said, "Eldon."

Eldon rose to his feet and counted to ten in English as fast as his tongue would move and sat down. The teacher smiled and said something in a voice that made him feel she was pleased.

Miss Keksi looked at the clock on the wall. "Classes dismissed. Walk. Do not run."

Eldon rushed to the porch to grab his lunch. Art Kivi was waiting for him on the steps outside. When Eldon opened his pail, he discovered a surprise. His mother had put in a penny Baby Ruth—one of those miniature candy bars that sold for one cent each and made you wish for more.

Since he could remember, Eldon had dreamt of eating lunch at school, but now the fried egg sand-wiches held no appeal for him. He nibbled on the jellyroll and recalled his mother's face at the kitchen window when he left. When he thought how much she missed him, his stomach felt as if he had turned a somersault. She probably was still standing at the window crying, waiting for his return.

"Aren't you going to eat your sandwiches?" Art whispered in Finnish.

"I'm not hungry."

The fifth- and sixth-grade girls wanted to push Eldon on the merry-go-round again, but he shook his head. He didn't feel like it.

"Aren't you going to eat your sandwiches?" Art asked again, after making sure no one was listening to them talking Finnish.

Eldon shook his head. "You can have one of them if you want."

Art quickly consumed the sandwich. "What are you going to do with the other?"

"Take it home to Buster."

The bell rang. It was time to go inside. Eldon hesitated as he viewed the half open gate. If he ran all the way, he could be home in twenty minutes. Seeing him again would make his mother wipe her tears and smile with happiness.

"Come," Art snapped. "What are you loitering for? Didn't you hear the bell—almost on top of your head?"

Eldon closed his lunch pail, put it on the shelf in the porch, and went to his seat. The recurring scene of his weeping mother at the kitchen window now became a recollection he couldn't bear. He laid his head on the desk and began to cry.

"What's the matter?" the teacher asked him.

Eldon only sobbed harder.

"Why are you crying?" Art whispered in Eldon's ear.

"*Minun hammasta pakottaa.*" I have a toothache. I have to go home and put liniment on it.

"He has a toothache," Art told the teacher.

Miss Keksi shook her head in sympathy. "Would you take him home?" she asked Art.

"Will you count me absent?" he asked.

"Of course not."

Art got up from his desk. "Come, Eldon, put on your jacket. I'm going to take you home."

Eldon expected to find his tearful mother still at the window, but she was bent over the big aluminum pan kneading bread dough. "I'm glad you're home," she said. She covered the pan and washed her hands to give him a hug. "How did you do in school?"

"I counted to ten. Didn't make any mistakes. And the teacher smiled at me."

Eldon learned fast, but he learned by rote. He had read through three pre-primers before he knew the meaning of the words. It was one afternoon when he was silently re-reading about the little red hen that he understood the story. To Eldon it was like finding a pot of gold at the end of the rainbow. He had learned to read English.

Chapter XIII

SIX YEARS HAD GONE BY since Elsie was born, and with all of the children in school, Signe had been able to increase her business. Her clients came from small towns around Wolf Creek.

Charlie was no longer interested in farming. Besides his mail route, he had civic duties and church activities that took up his time. He'd kept his team of horses, which Signe called hay burners, for turning over a small bit of ground for the garden each spring. Signe had Ed Koski harvest the hay on shares. Half for the landowner, half for the operator. "Let Papa keep the horses," Eldon had recently told his mother. "Next summer I'll be thirteen, big enough to do the haying. I'll get the Lahti boys to help me."

Signe and Eldon had replenished the dairy herd in a small way. They'd bought a cow and a heifer at an auction sale five years ago. The heifer, herself, had since had calves. They now had seven milkers. "The children need fresh milk," Signe had told Charlie when Ed Koski delivered the first cow and calf. Charlie condescended to taking the cream to the creamery once a week. It kept him in touch with the "boys." And after all, he was a stockholder.

The children were doing well in school. Eldon, who excelled in math, planned to become an engineer. Violet had her sights on becoming a schoolteacher, "just like Miss Keksi." Hugo was training to become a runner. He wanted to follow the trail of Paavo Nurmi, the great Finnish athlete. Elma and Elsie still played house.

When the children brought home their report cards, Signe studied them and Charlie graced them with his signature. It was always a serious, but happy event.

Reino arrived with the children when they came home from school, smiling as he scraped the mud off his shoes. "I got a dollar," he told Signe, who was mopping the kitchen floor, and took the silver coin out of his pocket to show her.

"Where did you get it?

"I earned it." He carefully wrapped the money in his red handkerchief and stuck it in his pants pocket.

"Good for you. How?" He was standing right where she wanted to mop. She motioned for him to move.

Reino stepped toward the bedroom. "Working for the new lady."

"What new lady?"

"The beautiful one." He looked at her and corrected himself. "The other beautiful lady."

"You know two beautiful ladies?" Signe teased.

Reino blushed and looked away. "Yaa."

Violet smiled. "Mother, he means you and Mrs. Marks," Violet poured herself a cup of coffee and disappeared into her room.

"Who's Mrs. Marks?" Signe asked, as she mopped the area under and around the table,

"The lady who bought the old Lindbom place. I have a job now. I shovel. She treats me real good, just like I was normal. I told her I have epilepsy, but I take medicine for it. She said she has arthritis and wishes she could find something to make the pain go away." Reino sat himself by the kitchen table, took off his blue and white striped denim cap and placed it on his knee, and smiled. "After Charlie sold all your cows that time, I never thought I'd get another job, but now I'm employed. I had been worried when Mother died that I'd be sent to the poor farm. But things have picked up, wouldn't you say?"

"They have, indeed. Is Mrs. Marks an elderly lady? Does she plan to live there alone?"

Reino laughed. "No, she's young like you, with two nice children."

"The children haven't mentioned anything about new students in school."

"That's because her kids came down with the measles when they moved here and have to stay home until the bumps go away. Do you want to hear how I met Mary? That's her name—Mary Marks."

Signe nodded and took her mop and pail outside.

"I was passing her place when I saw this lady trying to set her mailbox up straight. I stopped and said, 'Good morning, that's no job for a lady. If you'll get me a shovel, I'll do the job.' I dug the hole halfway to China, put the post in there and packed it with mud and stones. Once it dries, the earth around it will be rock hard and that post won't go anywhere. It'll rot right where it is — some fifty years from now. It's a good thing that the ground was no longer frozen, or I would've had a devil of a time digging."

"Would you like a cup of coffee? I made a new pot just before you got here."

Reino lowered his head, gazed at his feet and grinned with happiness. Signe had hit the spot with her offer. He'd stopped by to announce the good news, but coffee made the stop all the sweeter. He took the handkerchief out of his pocket, unraveled the bundle and gazed at the shiny silver dollar. "Sure's pretty, isn't it?"

Signe smiled and nodded as she set the cup before him.

With the coin safely back in his pocket, Reino smelled his brew before adding cream and sugar. "Aren't you having any?" He liked socializing — Signe's company especially.

She shook her head. "I've lost my taste for coffee. In fact, it makes me sick to my stomach. Have you eaten today, Reino?"

"Oh, yes, Mrs. Marks made me a mighty good sandwich with—" Reino began to enumerate on his fingers, "bread, meat, butter, mustard, lettuce, and soft black marbles, I've never had before, with stones in them. It was a big sandwich."

"Olives."

"Yes, olives. And tea. You know something, Signe? All my friends except Eldon are ladies."

Signe went to the cupboard, got a glass, and poured herself a glass of buttermilk. She sat across the table from Reino and sipped. "That makes you a ladies' man."

Reino's face got red and he began to giggle. "Charlie used to be my friend," he said after he got control of himself, "but not lately. 'Hello, Reino,' he would say, 'How's everything?' And we'd have a good talk. In school, I remember, he was the most friendly kid. Now he spits out, 'Hi, Ray' and doesn't wait for an answer. My name isn't Ray, it's Reino."

"Charlie's so busy these days—"

"Not so busy that he can't pronounce my whole name. Do you know what people are saying?"

Signe blinked.

"They're saying Charlie Skinnar isn't the man he used to be. He's changed."

"He's older."

"So he should get better."

Signe didn't pursue this line of talk. Reino was speaking the truth. Charlie was moving away, not only from his friends, but his family. He was a businessman now, a government employee. "Where did Mrs. Marks come from?"

"Some place else. I told her I know a nice lady she should visit—meaning you. I said, 'Bring the kiddies. Signe makes good gingerbread cake and puts lots of whipped cream on top.'"

The winter had been a hard one with record low temperatures and many blizzards, but it was over, and the world was awakening from its long white sleep. Last night Signe had thought she'd heard a frog, a single frog, heralding spring. Tonight it was a whole a capella chorus as she walked to the house from the barn. She stopped to listen. A note of a different instrument was coming through the woods—Jacob Niemi's accordion, and songs such as she not heard before.

She drifted back to the land of her childhood, to the city of her first love, Helsinki, where she had danced from sunset to sunrise. Now there was no more dancing. Charlie didn't believe in such capers. To him it was a sin of the highest order.

The accordion segued into a classical number. It reminded Signe of the Berlioz concert she'd attended with Gael Hugo. Gael's face, long repressed in her memory, now appeared before her eyes and she felt a pang of deep sadness. Then it came—a sudden kick below her heart. There was no mistaking the movement. She straightened with a start.

Charlie was in a tizzy when he got home from his mail route. Choir practice at the church started at seven. It was five fifteen and the sauna was not hot enough. "What's sauna without a full head of steam," he complained.

"Eldon gets out of school at 4:10, you know. He ran to build the fire as soon as he got home," Signe countered.

Charlie's mind already was on other matters. "What we need here in Wolf Creek is a club, a fraternal organization."

"What about the Order of Kalevala?

"It's for men and women."

"You could say, 'No women wanted,'" Signe quipped.

"You can't go against the bylaws. Besides, there's bound to be some poor farmer who will insist on bringing in the wife."

"I don't know what to say," Signe murmured as she dished Charlie his mashed potatoes, meat loaf, and cabbage. "Sit down and have your dinner before it gets cold."

Signe tucked her children in their beds. She was glad of this time to herself, a time to think. Nature pulls tricks out of her sleeve, Signe told herself, capers that change our lives, just as hers was now being changed. She would have to tell Charlie, but not yet. She drifted to sleep to the melodies coming through the meadow, along the creek, and dreamt that Gael Hugo had returned from France.

Chapter XIV

Signe roused the children out of their beds earlier than usual. It was Palm Sunday and their father was going to sing the solos with the Men's Choir at church.

Charlie was proud of his good ear and strong baritone voice. Using the human voice musically was to glorify God, he believed, but playing a man-made instrument other than the organ was a sin. These were tenets he had absorbed early in life, and never questioned.

It was Violet's duty to get her sisters fed and dressed on Sunday mornings. Signe had stayed up nights to sew new dresses for her pretty daughters. She'd bought ribbon for their hair. Ribbons, ornaments and short sleeved dresses on girls or women were something of which Charlie strongly disapproved, but Signe knew he would overlook them on his own daughters because he loved them and was proud of them.

In the next room Signe could hear Eldon saying he wished he were a heathen so he could sleep in Sundays, and his father reminding him, "You have to think of your soul, Eldon, your everlasting soul."

Pastor Jalmer Aho, the new minister, made a practice of welcoming his parishioners at the front door as they arrived. He praised Signe on her fine family, and patted each child on the head. They then took seats in the front row left and the children eagerly waited for Charlie's solo.

The church was packed, as it usually was on Palm Sunday, Easter and Christmas. Many of the farmers felt that hard work made up for the remaining Sundays. Pastor Aho welcomed the congregation, made his opening statements and asked for silent prayer. After the organ prelude, Aho, as usual, segued into "A Mighty Fortress Is Our God" in a strong tenor voice that fervently expressed his gratitude to the Almighty. The other male voices joined in zealously.

The pastor was defining the meaning of Palm Sunday when Reino Koski marched down the aisle in his blue and white striped overalls and matching cap, and sat beside the Skinnar children. He took off his cap, and told Violet to move to the other side so he could sit with Eldon. "I brought a dollar," he announced in a voice clearly heard by the pastor, "to put in the collection plate so I can go to Heaven when I die." Pastor Aho smiled at Reino and continued his sermon.

His words were soon lost on Signe. With clasped hands and closed eyes, she thought of the new life within her and wondered how Charlie would take the news. This was not the time to tell him. He was not in a receptive mood. As Reino had said, Charlie was somehow changed.

Little Elsie poked her mother in the ribs and whispered, "You sleeping?"

"No, Elsie, just thinking."

" 'bout God?"

"His workings."

"Oh. Then you can go back to sleep."

Reino spotted Mary Marks seated across the aisle from him. He caught her attention and waved happily to her. In a voice loud enough to reach the preacher's ear, Reino announced to Signe, "See that pretty lady across from us with the two children, that's the Marks widow. Her name is Mary. The boy's name is Robert. They call him Bob. And the little girl is—"

Reino's introduction was cut short by a jab in the neck by the strong index finger of Hulda Peterson, angry because she had missed the better part of the new minister's sermon.

Interruptions like this did not shake Pastor Aho's ardor at delivering the word to his flock. Activity among the congregation while he was sermonizing only added adrenaline to his already strong life fluid. He continued.

Signe thought about the happenings in the past few weeks, and recalled her illness back in January when she couldn't keep food down. She had blamed the red beets she canned last summer and thrown all fifty quarts in the manure pile. Good food wasted, she realized now.

The pastor asked the congregation to stand and join the men's chorus in singing, "All Hail the Power of Jesus Name!"

Signe could hear Charlie's rich baritone voice as he sang the praises of his Lord.

> All hail the pow'r of Jesus name!
> Let angels prostrate fall!
> Bring forth the royal diadem,
> And crown him Lord of all;

The pastor made a few announcements. Then called for prayer.

"When is Papa going to sing?" Elsie asked.

"Shhh! Your father's getting ready."

Pete Hutto, the choir director, signaled for Charlie to begin, but the soloist had his eye glued to the front seat, right-hand side, mesmerized by what he saw.

Pete cleared his throat to get Charlie's attention, but the baritone was deaf to grunts.

In a loud voice, the choirmaster then announced, "The Men's Choir will now sing, 'He Leadeth Me,' Charlie Skinnar singing the solo."

Charlie woke up, stood bravely, like a man facing his Maker, and in a voice that would alert the heavens, sang:

> He leadeth me! oh, blessed thought!
> Oh, words in heavenly comfort fraught!
> Whatever I do, wherever I be
> Still 'tis God's hand that leadeth me.
> The choir responded:

He leadeth me! He leadeth me!
By his own had He leadeth me!
His faithful follower I would be,
For by His hand He leadeth me.

The pastor offered another prayer. Ed Koski and Sam Peterson came around with the collection plates, Ed on the left and Sam on the right-side of the church. Signe dropped in the half-dollar she'd earned for making Emma Siren's burial dress. Eldon donated his nickel, and Reino kissed the silver dollar Mary Marks had paid him, and dropped it in Ed's basket.

Ed stood in front of Hugo waiting.

"What you got in your hand?" Reino demanded to know.

Hugo opened his fingers slightly.

"A quarter," Reino exclaimed. "Put it in the basket."

"No."

"It's for Jesus."

"Let Jesus earn his own money. I'm saving my money for college."

"Farmers don't go to college," Reino snapped.

"I'm not a farmer. I'm going to be a country gentlemen like Thomas Jefferson."

Meanwhile, Ed had passed the collection plate to the girls who struggled to untie their handkerchiefs to get their pennies. Elma had dropped in her donation, but Elsie's coins had fallen on the floor. Signe was searching. Ed got down on his knees to help.

When all matters were taken care of and the Recessional Hymn was being sung, Pastor Aho hurried to the back of the congregation to give the Benediction and to say goodbye to his flock. He praised Charlie Skinnar for the fine solo, and made no mention of Charlie's distraction.

Once outside the church, Reino followed Signe and the children to the old green Mack truck with the red door, which Charlie still used for pleasure and family errands. Regardless of the weather, the children sat in the bed of the truck. The new Model A Ford was only for mail, for government business. Charlie didn't mix family with federal, although the car was bought and paid for by Charlie's and Signe's earnings and the government had no claim on it.

When Charlie joined his family in the parking lot, his eyes searching for something or someone, Reino helpfully blurted, "If you're looking for the Marks widow, she's gone home."

Chapter XV

IT WAS TEN O'CLOCK IN THE MORNING on Good Friday and the children were home for Easter vacation. Signe had just come in from the barn and was washing her hands when there was a knock on the door. "It must be the constable," Hugo whispered to Eldon.

"Why would the constable come to our house?" Eldon asked.

Hugo shrugged. "Who else would knock?"

Signe wiped her hands, flung the towel over her shoulder and opened the door. It was Reino, Mary Marks and her two children. Reino giggled with happiness. "Signe, this is Mary Marks. Shake hands."

Signe was stunned. This lady didn't belong in her house or in Wolf Creek. She belonged in another world, a world Signe had almost forgotten. Signe gazed at Mary's face and saw the soft, unweathered skin and lustrous dark hair, and unconsciously ran her hand up her own cheek and to the tight bun at the base of her neck, then extended her hand to her guest, "How do you do," and gestured to a chair by the table.

"Come, fellows, let's go throw horsehoes and leave the ladies to themselves." Reino said, and herded the boys out.

Violet following Reino's example, invited Janie to her room. "We'll show you our dolls and we can play house."

"Violet sews pretty things for our dolls from Mama's scraps," Elma told Janie as she and Elsie followed Violet and Janie to their room. "She can already use the sewing machine and she never puts the needle through her finger."

Signe and Mary were left alone in the peace of the kitchen that smelled of cinnamon and cardamom from the Easter breads that Signe was baking. At first Signe was hesitant to say much. She was self-conscious of her broken English, as she put it; but Mary was easy to talk to, like the people in New York, and Signe soon found herself chattering as if she spoke English every day.

Looking at Mary, Signe decided they were about the same age, both with big city backgrounds. She told Mary about her early life in Helsinki and her immigration to New York. Mary said she was originally from Chicago. They talked about city life and the things they missed, their loneliness.

"I have no one to tell my dreams," Signe confided to Mary, as she took the breads out of the oven and turned them onto a board. "No one to share my tears."

"At night I lie awake recalling what life was like before my husband died and wonder if I'll ever know such happiness again." Mary went on to tell about her husband's death in an auto accident two years ago, and how she inherited the old Lindbom place through his distant cousin. "I think Wolf Creek is a good place for a single mother to raise her children."

Signe nodded as she counted the spoonfuls of coffee she was putting in the percolator on the stove. She flipped the pot lid shut, closed the can, and put it back in the lower part of the cupboard. She set the table with cups, plates, butter and jelly, and sliced the fruit loaves.

"Have some bread while it's still warm," Signe said as she filled Mary's cup with the steaming brew. "And put plenty of butter. It's fresh. I just churned it this morning."

Mary shook her head. "I gave up butter a long time ago. I don't want to put on weight."

"Goodness, your bones are barely covered." Signe covered her bread with a generous layer of butter.

The two smiled as they listened to the girls playing house and giggling in the next room. "They're having a good time, aren't they?" Mary said.

"It's good to be that age. No worries, no concerns. Being a city girl, do you mind the desolateness of Wolf Creek? Are you ever fearful at night?"

"I try to be brave, but one night, I believe it was Sunday night I had a bad dream, one that has been haunting me all week. I dreamt I was murdered."

Signe gasped. "I've had dreams and dreams, but nothing that frightful. But you needn't worry, there hasn't been a killing here since one way back in 1888, as I recall, on the Indian reservation north of here. The story goes that a lowly chief stole the horse of a higher chief and the thief chief was scalped. We never lock our doors, even at night. Very few strangers come this way except a hobo or two in the summer, but they're harmless. Would you like another cup of coffee?"

"No thank you. I limit myself to one. I've been thinking about getting a telephone," Mary added, still brooding about her nightmare.

Signe replaced Mary's cup with a clean one. "A good idea. I would like one, too, but Charlie says if God wanted us to have a telephone, he would have installed one somewhere between our necks and our noses." Signe went to the door of the children's room. "Violet, will you call the boys in for coffee."

Mary was shocked. "Coffee for children?"

"What else?"

"Milk, of course."

"We have plenty of that," Signe said, and when the boys came in she asked Eldon to get a jar of milk from the icehouse.

"Can I come, too?" Robert asked. "I've never seen an icehouse."

"Sure," Eldon replied, and led Robert down the path, "but it's nothing special, just a small building packed with huge chunks of ice. I'll show how it works." He opened the door. "In the winter Pop goes to a lake and cuts huge hunks of ice that he piles there in the back half of the shed. Then he covers the ice with sawdust so the ice won't melt when the weather turns hot. This front part of the shed is made of concrete. There's a tank filled with ice to keep the milk and cream cans cold. Look at the butter in that bowl. It's hard like ice."

Violet seated Jane at the table and sat next to her. Elma and Elsie sat on the other side of Jane. Reino sat on the other side of Violet, took off his striped denim cap and laid it on his knee as usual.

"Can I sit next to you?" Hugo asked Reino.

"Sure, but I'm not anything special."

Hugo slid up on the bench, next to Reino. "Eldon always gets to."

Reino looked at Mary. "These kids really like me."

Mary smiled. "I've noticed that."

"Reino is a good neighbor," Signe added as she filled the cups and glasses, "and a good friend."

The attention made Reino uncomfortable. He started to giggle.

Eldon entered with a half-gallon mason jar of milk which he set on the table. Robert was right behind him. "Mom, they have ice even in the summer," Robert told his mother, and sat beside Eldon at the table.

Mary smiled and nodded. "How old are your children?" she asked Signe.

"I'm seven next week," Elsie volunteered.

"I'm eight already," Elma spoke up.

Hugo took the two lumps of sugar out of his mouth and announced, "I'm nine. I'm going to be a aeroplane driver when I get big."

"I thought you wanted to be a runner," Eldon

reminded his brother. "In church on Sunday you said you were going to be a country gentleman."

"Was Thomas Jefferson just a slave driver?" Hugo retorted.

"How old are you?" Mary asked Violet.

"Eleven."

"She's the smartest one in the bunch," Hugo told Mary. She's going to be a teacher and an old maid like Miss Keksi."

"Miss Keksi is not an old maid," Violet responded in her serene way.

"So where's her husband? Besides, she's got gray hairs all over her head. I saw when she bended down to pick up her eyeglasses."

Mary covered her laugh, and looked at Eldon. "You must be about twelve."

Eldon nodded. "This month." He dunked his bread in the coffee. "Gee, it feels funny to be speaking English at home."

"Don't you usually speak it at home?" Mary asked, surprised.

Eldon shook his head. "First you have to think in Finnish, then translate it into English. Too much trouble."

"Let's go play baseball," Hugo said as he left the table.

Reino bolted. "I don't like baseball."

"Ah, come on, be a sport," Hugo urged, as he tugged Reino off the bench by the table. He got the ball and bat from the children's room and the two went out. Eldon and Robert soon followed, and the girls returned to their dolls.

"Mary, would you like to see the suit I'm making?" Signe asked.

"Oh, yes, I've never done any sewing myself."

Signe brought the almost finished garment to the kitchen and Mary was admiring it when Hugo ran in. "Papa's home!"

Signe excused herself and went into her bedroom, taking the suit with her. "Now?" she asked Hugo who had followed her. "He's never come home in the middle of the day."

"He stopped by the mailbox and put our mail in, and when he saw Robert, Papa called to him and asked, 'Is your mother here?' Bobby said 'yes' and Papa said, 'Eldon, open the gate.' Eldon opened the gate and Papa drove in — "

Hugo had not finished his story when Signe heard Charlie's booming voice greeting Mary. Signe laid the suit on the bed and hurried to the kitchen to introduce her husband. "Mary, this is my husband Charlie. He's the mailman."

"We've met," Mary replied, briskly.

Signe was puzzled. "Oh?"

"He came to my door the other day to deliver mail."

Bewildered by the situation, Signe quickly explained, "It's the law that the mailman has to deliver registered and insured mail to the patron, and not leave it in the mailbox."

"It was a Sears and Roebuck sales catalog," Mary responded.

"Welcome to our modest home, Mrs. Marks," Charlie boomed like a chairman of the board at a stockholders meeting after a year of stupendous sales.

Signe asked the inevitable question, "Would you like a cup of coffee, Charlie?"

Charlie was not hearing, but the girls had left their play and the boys, including Reino, were gathered in the kitchen and listening with both ears. Papa was expounding on his plans for the future, two new bedrooms, a living room, a dining room and an inside bath.

Eldon, with his palm pressed over his mouth, tried to figure how they could have an inside bath without running water.

"I will run a pipe from the well to the kitchen and put a pump by the kitchen sink," Charlie added, as if he'd heard Eldon's thoughts.

For his young age, Eldon was a boy with a lot of savvy. He now wondered how the water could be siphoned to the bathroom with a hand pump in the kitchen. Ice-cold water was not his choice for a morning dip. He'd rather warm the old sauna any day.

Signe stood befuddled. Why was Charlie cruising on this flight of fantasy? Was he trying to impress Mrs. Marks or were those really his plans? Maybe that was why he was hoarding every penny he could nab.

Reino, who had been listening to Charlie's prattle, was shaking his head as if to clear cobwebs from his brain.

Charlie gawked at Mary expecting her to praise his plans. She said, "Signe needs a phone. I'm calling the telephone company on Monday to have them install a telephone at my home. Shall I order one for you, too?"

"You have read my mind, Mrs. Marks. I've had it in my head for months, but you know how it is. I leave early in the morning and return after office hours—and time goes. Days turn into weeks and weeks into months." Charlie smiled and said, "Can I run you home, Mrs. Marks?"

"The Mack has a flat tire, Papa," Eldon spoke up. "It needs a new inner tube. The old one's busted to smithereens."

"Not the truck!" Charlie snapped. "I'm going by Mrs. Marks' place on my mail route. This is no weather for a lady to be in."

"Mary isn't ready to go yet," Signe countered. "We have lots of talking to do and this is the children's chance to play with each other."

Charlie acted as if Signe hadn't spoken. "Are you ready, Mrs. Marks?"

"No, I'm not."

Charlie stiffened. His right eye quivered. He turned and tramped out the door.

Chapter XVI

THE PHONE HAD BEEN ON THE WALL for two weeks. Charlie had ignored it; but to Signe, Alexander Graham Bell's invention had been a blessing, a means to communicate with her friends. She'd first called Hilda, who had promptly blasted Charlie Skinnar on the party line—not about anything in particular, but many things in general.

Signe was grateful to Mary Marks for getting the phone, and they chatted almost daily after the children left for school. She no longer was timid to speak English.

A week ago Mary had brought two dress lengths of material for Signe to design and sew. One was floral print cotton. The other was a blue rayon. They copied designs from dresses illustrated in the Sears & Roebuck summer catalog. Signe had finished the blue dress except for the hem.

It was a beautiful spring day and Signe was in the mood for company. She got on the phone and rang Mary's number. Mary was in the house and answered promptly. After discussing the weather and other small talk, she told Mrs. Marks her blue dress was ready for a fitting. "Would you care to come today? The children won't get out of school for another four hours. You'd be back in plenty of time.

"You've spoken my thoughts," Mary said. "I felt like taking a nice walk, but didn't know where to go, and I didn't want to interrupt your work. I made oatmeal cookies for the children's lunches. I'll pack a few along for our afternoon repast."

Signe had the table set and the percolator dripping when Mary arrived. "I haven't been able to stand the smell of coffee for the past three, four months," Signe said when they sat down at the table, "but now it smells like it never did before. I'll have a second cup."

Mary was pleased with Signe's creation, the sky blue rayon with slightly puffed sleeves and a flaring skirt brought out the best of Mary's slim figure. "It fits like a dream, a beautiful dream, and I feel like a princess."

"You look like one." Signe was proud of her creations, but it wasn't often that she had a client who showed off the garments as well as Mary. Standing there critiquing her own work, Signe suddenly felt as if she were supporting a bellyful of lead. "Would you mind getting up and standing on the bench, so I can pin up the hem. It's hard for me to kneel down on the floor."

Mary did as Signe requested. While pinning, Signe had to stop to adjust the bun in the back of her head. "My hair is getting too long. It's unmanageable."

"Why don't you have it cut?'

"Oh, no."

"A short bob would be most becoming on you."

"What would people think?"

Mary shrugged.

"And what would Charlie say?"

"What can he, once it's done?"

Signe thought for awhile. "Who'd do it? Barbers here work only on men."

"I will," Mary volunteered. "I cut my children's hair."

Signe thought for awhile. "Why not? I'll get my dressmaking shears."

Far from regretting her choice, Signe felt a tiny weight falling off with each clip of the scissors. When Mary was done, Signe took a tray from the cupboard to look at herself.

"What's that for?" Mary asked.

"It's my mirror." Signe smiled as she viewed her new self on stainless steel. "T'enk you, Mary."

I hear you're making a big addition to your house," Ed Koski said, as he cornered Charlie at the creamery.

Ed's seeming friendliness surprised Charlie since Ed had spoken only a limited number of words to him in the past five, six years — since Queen's unfortunate death. It was good to be acknowledged by Ed Koski.

"Yes, I've had it in mind for some time, but you know how busy I am. With a family as large as mine, three rooms is not enough."

"How much of an addition do you have in mind?"

"Two more bedrooms, a dining room, living room, porch and a full basement. A finished basement."

"That's quite an enlargement. You'll be showing up the rest of us."

Charlie thought he noted what looked like a smirk on Koski's face, but probably just a tinge of envy. Charlie's face turned crimson as he concluded that it was the Marks widow who'd told Koski of his plans — an indication that she was interested in his project. "Yes, quite an undertaking. I expect to add a bathroom, also. I have a deep well with no shortage of water even in dry years."

"I hear Land O' Lakes is finally set to buy our milk whole," Ed said, changing the subject unexpectedly.

Charlie didn't want to discuss milk, cows, or manure, but he had to respond to Ed's remark. "Finally."

"They plan to start about the first of next month."

Charlie excused himself and hurried to his mail car. It made him feel good that Ed Koski was on talking terms with him, but Charlie somehow felt that he'd been pumped dry.

Instead of starting the engine, he got out and crossed the road to Rontty's General Mercantile. Jacob Rontty, the proprietor, was shooting the breeze with a couple of old poor farmers — a designation given to those hard-working souls who'd given their lives to working their forty, eighty acres with nothing to show except broken bodies and wrinkled faces. Charlie took this opportunity to roam around the store. He passed the drug and makeup shelf — next to the hardware — twice, taking note of the beautifiers, enhancers, and scents. On the third round he stopped, looked and opened containers and smelled them. A cobalt blue vial labeled "Evening in Paris" caught his eye. Dazzling. Just what he was looking for. Charlie unscrewed it, sniffed it, and found the contents quite exciting. She was sure to like it. He put the top back on and returned the bottle to the shelf, then picked up a fresh one. When the two old farmers left, Charlie took his selection to the counter.

"Signe's birthday, right?" Rontty volunteered as he slipped the bottle in a brown sack.

Charlie nodded, but fumed inside. The storekeeper had stuck his nose into Charlie's business and ruined his day.

"Will there be anything else?"

Charlie shook his head.

"How about some candy for the kiddies?"

"I don't have time." Charlie pulled out his gold pocket watch and looked. "I'm late."

"Won't take any time at all. I've got some orange slices all bagged and ready to go." Rontty went to the glass case and returned with a sack.

"How much?"

"The total is — "

"No, I mean for the candy."

"Fifteen cents for the candy," Rontty replied.

"Too much. I can get a box of Farina for that."

"Yaa, but Farina won't make the kiddies smile."

Rontty smiled wryly. "If spending a dime and a nickel on your children is going to break you, I have suckers two for a penny —"

"I'll take the sack." Charlie threw a five dollar bill on the counter, pocketed the change Rontty gave him and left. He reached his car and was opening the door when the storekeeper, standing on the stoop in front of the building, yelled out to him, "Tell Signe I expect her to smell real pretty at church on Sunday."

The children were delighted with Signe's haircut. They wanted to know who the barber was. After she got over her initial surprise, Violet said, "Mama, you look like a schoolgirl. Can I look like you?"

"We will see," Signe answered as she went out the door to feed the cows.

Hugo was apprehensive. "I hope Papa doesn't get angry at Mama and hit her."

"Don't worry," Eldon said. "He wouldn't dare."

"Come and play, Elsie," Elma called from their room. "We'll cut our dolls' hair so they'll look like Mama."

Signe's and the children's concerns had been for nothing. When Charlie got home, his mind was on making money, and he made no mention of Signe's haircut. He sat by the table, added cream to the coffee Signe had poured him, and with his teeth cracked a lump of sugar into two. "I'm going into trapping," he announced.

"You mean catch little skunks and things?" Hugo asked.

"Not little skunks. Big skunks."

"Big skunks are the parents. The baby skunks will be orphans and die."

"Don't worry, Son. Life goes on."

"Now?" Signe asked. "You can't trap when the weather gets hot."

Charlie poured coffee in the saucer and slurped it through the sugar. "No. In late August when the weather cools."

Signe dismissed trapping as the latest in Charlie's moneymaking schemes, and said, "Mary Marks told me she wants to live like we farmers, grow and harvest our own food. I think we should help Mary plant her potatoes."

"Her little patch isn't worth harnessing the horses," he replied.

"She'll need a space plowed for her garden, too."

Charlie didn't respond. Instead, he bellowed, "Elma, where are you?" Elma and Elsie appeared from their room. "Do you and Elsie want to do some singing while Mama and Violet make supper?" After his Palm Sunday solo, Charlie had taken to teaching the little girls hymns in the evening before dinner.

"Sure, Papa." Elma went into her room, and returned with a hymn book. She and Elsie climbed on their father's lap.

"Now, what do you want to sing?" he asked.

"God Is Love, His Mercy Brightens," Elsie answered and began to sing.

> God is love; His mercy brightens
> All the path in which we rove;
> Bliss he wakes and woe he lightens:
> God is wisdom, God is love...

Chapter XVII

FOR THE PAST FEW DAYS Signe had not sensed life inside her. The nausea was gone, and her midsection felt hard, foreign. Now she was glad she had not told Charlie that she was expecting again. After Charlie left in the morning, she asked Eldon and Hugo to do the farm chores, while Violet made the lunches. "I don't feel well," she told the children and went back to bed.

The youngsters took their orders and went about their tasks quietly and cheerfully. They realized their mother never backed off doing work. Elma helped Elsie dress for school. From her bed, Signe could hear their conversation. Elma explained that their mother was sick and they should be good and do their share of the work. "Will she die?" Elsie asked.

"No, she'll be better in a few days."

"How long is that?"

"Two or three days. Depends on the weather," Elma replied.

Once they had their coats on, the children came to Signe's bedroom and kissed her before leaving. Eldon was the last to go.

At midmorning Signe awakened with severe cramps in her stomach. They were worse than any she had ever suffered. She'd given birth to five babies, and not uttered a sound, but now her screams were loud and long. As she lay there, she recalled as a young girl in Helsinki overhearing old ladies talk about their birthing experiences, one of them saying, "There's nothing so difficult as trying to give birth to a stillborn."

Suddenly it was over, whatever the cause of her pain. She wiped the tears and sweat off her face with the corner of a sheet.

"Are you all right, Mother?" a child's voice asked.

Signe raised her head from the pillow. Eldon was standing at the doorway. "What are you doing here?" she asked. "Didn't you go to school?"

"I did. I told the teacher you were sick. She said I could come home."

"I'm fine now," Signe told Eldon. "I think I'll get up and make myself some tea. A cup of hot tea and a buttered rusk."

Eldon insisted that she stay in bed. He would boil some water. But Signe got up and was about to hug her son when it happened. The placenta with its dead young fetus slid down her leg and to the floor. She gasped and looked at Eldon.

He quickly perceived what had happened. He had seen life and death in many forms. "I'll get some towels," he said.

Signe wrapped the stillborn in the bleached flour sacks, handed it to her son and wept. She wept for the child she could never kiss and wept because it would never see the light of day.

"I will put it in a wooden nail box," Eldon said, "and bury it under the plum tree that's about to bloom, and say a prayer."

She went back to bed and sobbed until she had no more tears. Exhausted, Signe was about to fall asleep when she heard singing. She wiped her eyes, went to the window and raised it high. It was Eldon, shovel in hand, standing by a freshly dug mound, singing "Rock of Ages."

From what Ed Koski said, Charlie concluded that Mary Marks was interested in his remodeling project. He felt this might be a good time to visit her. And, if the moment was right, he'd present her with the cologne. He started to sing "Red Wing." He'd heard it sung over the radio time and again. Charlie had a good ear for music, a memory for lyrics as well as his splendid vocal cords. It was a sunny spring day, warm enough to roll down the windows of his mail car to let his voice ring out.

His heart was beating wildly as he approached the old Lindbom acreage. He stopped his car behind a stand of tamaracks to calm the adrenalin-laced blood that was racing through his arteries and to prepare for his presentation. Charlie was about to run a comb through his full head of auburn hair when Sam Isaacson appeared from the opposite direction in his new bright red pickup. Charlie gave a silent curse.

"Having car troubles?" Sam asked.

"Just a little overheating," Charlie replied.

Sam parked on the opposite side of the road, hopped out of his truck and had the hood of the mail car up before Charlie had a chance to get out. Charlie now regretted saying what he had. Knowing Sam from the time he drilled the Skinnar's well, Charlie feared Sam might present him with a bill for fixing a nonexistent problem.

"Nothing wrong, far's I can see," Sam said as he lowered the hood back in its place. "Warm weather like today might make the engine heat. Maybe you were kind of heavy on the pedal."

Charlie nodded and thanked Isaacson for his troubles. When Sam was out of sight, Charlie finished his grooming and with a happy and expectant heart, proceeded to the old Lindbom place where Mary Marks now lived.

He stopped by the mailbox to view the situation. If the coast was clear, so to speak, he'd walk up and deliver her present. The children were in school, so she would be alone. Charlie reached over to the back seat to grab the bottle when Mary's front door opened and Reino Koski came out and walked toward the garden, followed by Mary.

"The mail's here," Reino called back to Mary.

"Won't you get it for me, please."

Charlie cursed to himself and stepped on the gas.

"Papa, can we sit on your lap now?" Elsie asked when Charlie took his place at the table that evening.

"After supper."

"Eldon cooked the dinner," Violet told her father as she sliced the bread. "Mama taught him how to make pot roast."

"With carrots and onions and potatoes," Elma added, as she set the table.

"And rutabagas," Elsie reminded Elma. "Papa, is it all right for boys to do ladies' work?"

Charlie thought for awhile. "Wel—"

His hesitation was interrupted by Signe who had just returned from the barn. "There's no such thing as women's work or men's work. It's all work. You do what needs to be done, and be glad you have the strength to do it."

"I guess your mother has the answer," Charlie told Elsie.

Signe helped Eldon set the roast on the table. They all sat down and Charlie said grace.

Elma and Elsie climbed on Charlie's lap and Eldon was about to go to his room to study when Charlie said, "Eldon, would you go to the mail car and get me the bag of orange slices on the back seat?"

The sun had set and it was getting dark. Eldon got on the front seat and reached over for the paper sack in the back. He was about to take the whole thing to his father, but realized it contained not only the bag of candy but a small blue bottle. He examined the container, but all he could read in the dusk was "Evening in Paris," a strange name for whatever its contents were. He'd seen cobalt blue poison bottles, but they were three-sided. Eldon was familiar with lethal substances such as cyanide, arsenic, strychnine and ones with trade names "London Purple" and "Paris Green," but "Evening in Paris" puzzled him. He looked carefully for a picture of skull and bones on the label, but it was too dark to see. He slipped the bottle back in the brown sack and placed it on the back seat where he'd found it. Eldon delivered the sweets to his father who was surrounded by the four younger children. "Eldon, have some orange slices," Charlie bellowed.

"No, Papa, I'm full. I have to study now." Eldon went to his room where he sat, holding his head in his cupped hands, and wondered what the bottle contained and why his father had bought it. He thought about his mother and what she'd gone through today. Something was not right. He was disturbed. The happy voices from the kitchen only added to his melancholy as they sang,

Jesus loves me, this I know,
For the Bible tells me so.
Little ones to him belong,
They are weak, but he is strong.

Yes, Jesus loves me! Yes, Jesus loves me . . .

Chapter XVIIII

THE NEXT MORNING, Eldon went up to his teacher and asked, "What's 'Evening in Paris?'"

Miss Keksi gave a little laugh. "I imagine it would be quite enjoyable. Better than an evening in Minneapolis."

"In a bottle?"

"Bottle? What bottle?"

"A little blue bottle," Eldon indicated its approximate size with his fingers.

"Where did you see this bottle?"

Eldon was stumped. He couldn't tell the truth and telling a lie was a sin. But he'd rather commit a sin if the bottle was something bad than squeal on his father. He could tell by the brown paper bag that it was purchased at a store. "In a store," he said.

Miss Keksi finally got it. "You mean 'Evening in Paris,' the toilet water."

Eldon made a wry face. "Toilet water?"

"Cologne. Like perfume."

"Oh, I know what perfume is," Eldon exclaimed. "It's the stuff ladies put behind their ears so they won't smell of the barn."

The teacher covered her grin and nodded.

Eldon went back to his desk, troubled. Why did his father carry "Evening In Paris" in his mail car?

Meanwhile, Charlie, passing through town on his mail route, spotted Reino in front of the creamery with his uncle, Ed Koski. Charlie quickly decided this was his chance to see the Marks widow alone. But he'd have to hurry. Reino seemed to have the ability to step from one corner of the township to another like Paul Bunyan looking for his ox. Charlie dropped only the first-class mail in their proper boxes. He had no time for the newspaper or auction notices. He'd deliver them tomorrow. He stepped on the gas as he passed his own mailbox, knowing full well that he had in his pouch a letter for Signe from her sister in Michigan, for which she was waiting. He'd give it to her tonight.

Spring was acting more like July than May. It was hot. Even with all the windows in his car open, Charlie was sweating. He decided to take off his jacket. As he was going down Cream Hill at a good speed, the right sleeve became entangled and he couldn't free his arm. Charlie lost control of the car.

When he woke up, Charlie didn't know what had happened. His nose was so swollen that his vision was impaired. He had a walloping headache. He put his hand to his forehead and felt something like a horn growing in the center. The trunk of a wild cherry tree hugged the windshield, and the windshield looked like a crystal jigsaw puzzle. Charlie was stunned, but he still had a certain presence of mind. He remembered his "Evening in Paris," and turned to look at the back seat to see if the sack containing the precious bottle was still intact. The sack had fallen down on the floorboards, but the bottle hadn't broken.

As he was appraising his fate, a brand-new green Studebaker pulled alongside. Ed Koski opened the door, stepped out and came around. "What happened here?' he hollered, announcing the mailman's mishap to the world. Charlie's gaze automatically focused on the man sitting on the passenger side of Ed's car. It was Reino, with what was clearly a smirk on his face.

"We heard that you were in an accident," Elsie said, when she and Elma met their father at the door and led him to his rocker. Just above his chair, Charlie glanced at Alexander Graham Bell's invention on the wall. The news of his accident had most likely already been broadcast via the party line. Charlie silently cursed the inventor and the installer.

"Do you want to read us a Bible story while you wait to get better?"

"Papa can't read you Bible stories," Hugo told his sister. "Can't you see his eyes are almost glued shut?" He gazed at his father with pity. "Papa, we don't have beefsteaks to put on your eyes. Do you think pork chops would help?"

Signe called the insurance agency in Park Rapids to report the accident. Charlie needed a car for his mail route. Mr. Fry, the adjuster, came the next day. He inspected the car and declared it a total loss. The news hit Charlie hard. "I still have payments to make."

Mr. Fry, a tall, portly man with a booming voice, replied, "Mr. Skinnar, you're lucky to have gotten by with a horn and a couple of shiners. In fact, you're fortunate to be alive. Have the car towed to a junkyard, and we'll make arrangements for a replacement. You're lucky to get a new model. The one you wrecked was less than a year old."

Ed Koski had the proper equipment to take the junker away. Charlie felt he'd save money by hiring him, but was disappointed. Ed charged him by the hour. "It's a long haul to Osage," Koski said, when he presented the bill.

"Koski scalped me," he told Signe after Ed left. "Where's his Christian charity?" Charlie was gnawed by the fact that he'd already lost a week's pay to Mr. Gilpin who was taking over the mail route while Charlie was without a car.

Signe shrugged and plunked a bowl of vegetable soup on the table. "Lunch is ready. Wash your hands."

Koski returned the next day, right after Eldon got

home from school. He took from his pickup a cardboard box of junk. The bottle of "Evening in Paris," which had shed its brown paper wrapper, laid on top, naked like a native maiden under the tropical sun. Ed approached Eldon who was standing by the well with two pails of water ready to take in. "These things were in your father's car. I forgot to leave them yesterday."

Eldon, who'd spotted the bottle from a distance, avoided looking at it. He took the box and thanked Ed. "I'll take them in the house." He turned to go.

"I was thinking," Koski said, stopping the boy in his tracks, "I'll be needing help with the potato planting coming up. Because of the drought last summer, I've decided to use the team and plow this year. Have to get the spuds in deep. Reino and his cousin will help, but I need a couple more hands. The seed potato has to be in the furrow when I turn the next one on top of it, so you need to be fast."

Eldon nodded. "I know."

"Do you think you could help me next Saturday?"

"Oh, sure."

"I can't pay you any money. I'm broke. But I have a Holstein heifer calf—"

Eldon couldn't wait for Koski to finish the sentence. "A calf is better than money. I'm sure Mother will let Hugo and Violet come, too."

"The calf will have to be bottled. Do you have the milk?"

"We have all the skim milk the calf can drink and I have a big pop bottle with a nipple on it to feed it with. I'll name her Princess after—" Eldon stopped.

"Be at my place at eight, and bring a big lunch."

"Thank you for bringing Pa's stuff," Eldon called as Ed got in his truck.

Eldon looked at the box at his feet and chewed on his lower lip. Then proceeded to empty the box. He took out the tire pump, hacksaw, hatchet, tire patches, pliers, wire cutters, screwdrivers, a mouse trap, screws, hooks, part of an old inner tube and other castoffs. He put the cologne bottle on the bottom, covered it with the other junk and took the box to the house. His mother was standing by the kitchen stove, stirring gravy. Eldon slid the box behind the stove. "Those are Papa's tools that were left in his car when Ed Koski hauled it to Osage."

Signe nodded and kept on stirring. After Eldon went out, she moved the pan of gravy to the side of the range, on top of the water heater, and pulled out the box. This was her chance to get some of the items she needed almost daily. She took out a pair of pliers, wire cutters, a screwdriver, a Philips screwdriver, and a couple of screws and hooks. When she reached for the box of thumbtacks, she saw the bottle. Signe got her old three-pound coffee can, her storage canister for small implements, and put her newly acquired tool collection in it. She returned the can to its rightful place in the bottom of the cupboard. Signe then retrieved the elegant blue vial from its grimy quarters and read the label, "Evening In Paris." She unscrewed the top and took a whiff. She closed her eyes and smiled. She repacked the box as Eldon had it. When Charlie came in, Signe said, "Your tools are in a box behind the stove. Ed Koski brought them by this afternoon."

"Good. I wondered what had happened to my gear, but forgot to ask him."

Some other man would've taken time to convalesce, but Charlie was up at his usual time the next morning. Since he couldn't cover his mail route without a car, he decided to plant his potatoes. "The youngsters can stay home from school so we get the job done fast."

Signe shook her head. "No. They've all had perfect attendance this year. We will not ruin their records. You go and harness the horses and hitch them to the plow. You run the plow and I plant."

"You won't be fast enough. You have to get each furrow planted by the time I'm ready to turn over the next one."

"I know how it's done," she said.

They finished the planting by midday.

"I really enjoyed that," Signe remarked, as she filled Charlie's cup with freshly perked coffee.

"You mean sticking the spuds in the ground?"

Signe nodded and gave a closed-mouth smile. "We used to do everything together."

"Yaa. Now we have the youngsters to help us." Charlie's face took on a bitter expression. He pushed his coffee cup aside and grimaced. "Why does the Marks widow consider herself above the rest of us?"

Shocked at what he had just said, she turned and faced Charlie. "Oh, I don't think she does. What gives you that feeling?"

"She's cold."

"Cold? No, not cold. Just reserved." Signe paused and came up with the answer. "She must be English."

Charlie wrinkled his brow and puckered his upper lip. "What has that to do with her and me?"

"Everything. It's the way we're brought up. We do what what we've learned. The Swedes talk. The French kiss. The Italians talk and kiss. But the English are very proper. Very reserved. They would just as soon spend their time with a cup of tea."

"You sure?"

"Heed my words. Mary Marks will come around and be as neighborly as anyone. You just act cordial and neighborly. Take your time. You can't rush friendship." Signe crossed over to the kitchen range, raised a lid and stuffed the grate with dried wood — tamarack, pine and birch — to bake the potatoes and fry the meat. She thought to herself how fortunate she was to have a home of her own, plenty of food, a husband with a good government job, and five smart, beautiful children.

'What's on your mind?" he asked. "You're smiling."

"Just counting my blessings."

Charlie put a lump of sugar into his mouth and crushed it with his molars; then reached over for his cup of coffee, now cold, and sipped in silence.

Chapter XIX

THE BRAND-NEW FORD made Charlie feel like a Rock-efeller and being back on his route was exhilarating. He'd visit Mary Marks today. He'd been planning it all week. Charlie had found some of Violet's blue crepe paper and had wrapped the cologne bottle in it, real pretty.

He had gotten up at four to heat the sauna. With a hot bath, a clean shave and the fresh hair cut that Ed Koski had given him, Charlie felt young and virile.

As he pulled up to the widow's house he rehears-ed his lines so his presentation would be perfect. He got out of the car with an auction notice and the gift, and knocked. Mary opened the door. "Here," he said. "Here's your mail."

Mary looked at the printed sheet of paper. "Is that all?"

"Why, yes."

"Thank you," she said, about to close the door.

"Wait. There is something else." He shoved the package at her.

"What is it?"

"Open and see."

Mary kept her eyes on Charlie while she removed the wrapping and read the label, "Evening in Paris." She shoved the cobalt blue bottle back at him. "I don't want it." She shut the door and turned the lock.

Charlie went back to his car, started the engine, drove out of sight and parked at the end of the property. He felt rejected and confused. The Marks widow must've misunderstood him. On the other hand, Charlie didn't understand his own actions. What got him was the waste of money, the outlay of cash for the luxury item. He took out his Thermos and poured some of Signe's strong coffee into his mug and sipped. The caffeine cleared his brain. The money was not wasted. He could return the cologne and get a refund. Jacob Rontty was a sensible sort of fellow, a good businessman. He'd find it to his advantage to do the right thing. Charlie made a sharp turn and backtracked.

"You want to return this fragrance?" Rontty asked, holding up the now shopworn bottle. "What's wrong? Didn't Signe like the smell?"

"No."

"Why not? It smells real good."

"I would like my money back," Charlie said, shifting from one foot to the other in front of the cashier's counter.

"Has the bottle been opened?"

"Of course not."

"Well, how does she know she doesn't like the smell if she didn't open it?"

"Signe doesn't like perfume."

"If Signe doesn't like perfume, why did you buy it? Or was it for another woman?"

"Listen, here, Jacob, don't insinuate!"

"I didn't. I asked. And you turned red."

"I turned red because I'm getting angry."

"Charlie, anger will get you nowhere."

"Just keep the bottle and give my money back."

"We don't give refunds, but we do make exchanges." Rontty was speaking like a representative of a corporation, whereas, he was the chief, cook and bottle washer in his establishment. "Take any item in the store of equal or lesser price. Take something in a higher price range and you pay the difference."

"Where are the men's socks?"

"No."

"What do you mean, no?"

"It has to be something for Signe. After all, it's her money."

"It's not!" Charlie hollered. He then realized he'd have to go according to Rontty. "What can I take?"

"Look around. Perhaps a broom, a mop or a dishpan."

Charlie shook his head.

Rontty turned to the shelf behind him and pulled out a sack of granulated sugar. "Take that. Makes a nice gift for a lady. A woman can always use some extra sugar."

Charlie grabbed the bag and hurried to the door.

"Come back, Skinnar. I owe you some change."

Charlie, expecting nothing less than a half-dollar, returned to the counter and waited while the store-keeper dug in his pockets.

Rontty pulled out a handful of coins and with his other hand sorted them out. "There you are."

Charlie looked down. On the counter were three old worn-out Indian head pennies. He grabbed them and cursed his way out.

The next day Charlie hurried through his mail route in order to sight Mary Marks in her garden again. She would be going into the house when her children came home from school. He was undecided as to what his course of action would be. He must not rush things. That he knew. As he approached Mary's house, Charlie ran into a bit of luck. Across the road from her mailbox, he noticed the old logging trail, where he could park, eat his lunch and enjoy watching Mary without her being aware of it. Anyone coming along would naturally assume that the post-man was so eager to get the mail delivered that he didn't bother to eat his lunch until he was almost home.

Charlie kept his vigil six days a week, and as he sat in church on Sunday he closed his eyes and fantasized about the Marks widow. The pastor had concluded his sermon and the two ushers were coming down the aisle with their collection plates, Ed

Koski at the right and Sam Isaacson on the left. Sam hesitated before nudging Charlie. A pious man should not be interrupted while in communion with his Maker, Sam felt; but when Charlie dropped a five dollar bill on the plate, Sam paused — the five spot looked foreign amongst the nickels, dimes and quarters — and held his breath. Koski, the usher on the right, turned left just in time to see Charlie drop the bill. A shadow passed down Ed Koski's face, and his glance caught Sam's eye. The message that was transferred was: Charlie is trying to bribe the Lord. The cantor led the congregation in the hymn. Charlie's voice rang loud and clear as he sang:

> My faith looks up to Thee,
> Thou Lamb of Calvary
> Savior divine
> Now hear me while I pray;
> Take all my sins away...

That night Charlie had a hard time falling asleep. The image of Mary Marks working in her garden kept appearing before his eyes.

Signe, who had awakened to his flipping and tossing, asked, "Charlie, are you not feeling good? Want some Alka-Seltzer?"

"It's not my stomach," he replied. "I have things on my mind."

"Matters on the mind will sort out themselves by morning," Signe counseled, and went back to sleep.

Once in dreamland, Charlie held the widow in his arms. He was moaning in ecstasy, such as he'd never known, when he felt Signe's index finger jab him on the sternum, as was her way of waking him up. She was standing by the bed in her long white flannel nightgown, holding a bottle and a spoon. "Here, take this," she ordered.

"What are you giving me now?" Charlie grumbled, angry that his flight to bliss had been aborted.

"Castor oil," Signe said, looking at him, sternly. "I can tell by your groaning that your bowels have become inactive."

Chapter XX

ELDON SKINNAR HAD ESCAPED Urho Lahti's badgering except for an occasional demand to give up his candy bar or piece of cake so Urho wouldn't make up some humiliating story about him. Now Urho insisted that Eldon give him the pocketknife Signe had bought from the Co-op.

Urho had been a troublemaker in school since the first grade. Going on seventeen and in the eighth grade, he was hefty like a well-fed lumberjack and "dumb as an ox," quoting his peers. At his age, he was free to quit, but Miss Keksi believed the longer Urho remained in school, the more education he'd absorb. So Urho stayed on to bully his schoolmates.

At this point, only the seventh- and eighth-graders were aware of Urho's lewd mind, but they kept quiet. Bringing such matters to the attention of adults was not only awkward and embarrassing, but could result in humiliating quizzing of the informant.

"Gimme the knife or I'll tell everyone about your father," Urho threatened Eldon at recess.

"No."

"I'll tell," Urho warned

"Tell what? There's nothing to tell."

"No?"

Eldon stood his ground. "No."

"You know — the widow..."

"Mrs. Marks?"

"He wants her."

"For what?" Eldon asked.

"You know, to — "

Eldon knew what Urho was going to say. He put his fingers in his ears and closed his eyes so he couldn't see the formation of those filthy words on Urho's lips, but in his mind the bottle of "Evening in Paris" loomed as big as a five gallon cream can. He began to cry.

The bell rang. Recess was over.

Eldon's world had cracked. He went in and laid his head on the desk and shaded his face with his arms.

"What's the matter?" Miss Keksi asked.

Eldon didn't answer.

"He's got a bad headache," Urho volunteered.

Eldon was angry, angry enough to make his tears dry up like raindrops in the hot July sun. What hurt him was the possibility of truth in Urho's insinuation. The whole county must be talking. But he'd show Urho the price of gossip. Urho would learn to keep his mouth shut.

"Eldon, do you feel like coming up for reading?" Miss Keksi asked.

"Sure."

At lunch Eldon asked Urho if he wanted a piece of chocolate cake.

"You mean you're giving me some cake just like that?"

"Why not?" Eldon cut the piece in two. "I have something to tell you first."

"Really?"

"Let's go behind the woodshed."

"A secret?" Urho asked.

"Yup. You go first and I'll follow. Be sure nobody sees you."

Once behind the woodshed, Eldon told Urho, "Get down on your knees so I can whisper in your ear. Close your eyes and open your mouth. Wide."

"I don' wanna."

"You don't want to know the secret or you don't want the cake?"

"I don't want to shut my eyes."

"Then it's no secret. And no cake. But you'll be sorry."

"Supposing someone sees me," Urho said. "What then?"

"Look around. Do you see anybody?"

"Nah." Urho got down on his knees, shut his eyes and opened his mouth.

Eldon stuffed the cake in Urho's mouth, closed his fist rock solid and let loose on Urho's left eye. "That's it," and walked away.

By the end of lunch break, Urho's eyelid had pretty well sealed shut and the left side of his brow line was turning blue.

"What happened to you?" Miss Keksi asked when Urho came in.

"I fell on a rock. I mean I hit the bar on the merry-go-round."

Signe had set the table for six with coffee cups, as was her daily routine before the children came home from school. She peeked in the oven to see how the cheese was browning, then glanced at the clock on the shelf—three minutes of five. The children were late. She went to the window, drew apart the starched white curtains to look up the road.

Seeing no one, she opened the door to listen. Pleased at hearing her children's voices, she smiled and closed the door.

A yellow ribbon of sticky flypaper with a load of dead flies fell down from the thumbtack fastener in the ceiling. Signe snatched the streamer, raised the lid of the wood stove and dropped it in the fire. Then she grabbed the fly swatter and looked around for any escapees that might still be hoping to survive the winter.

"What took you so long?" Signe asked when her daughters filed in the door. "I thought the gypsies had taken all five of you."

Elsie giggled. "There are no gypsies in Minnesota."

"Nah, they've moved to North Dakota." She

nudged her sister. "Fargo, N. D. USA."

The girls tittered.

Signe smiled. She enjoyed Elma's and Elsie's childish joke.

Turning to Violet, Signe exclaimed, "So many books you brought home. Does Miss Keksi expect you to read them all?"

"No, Mother. Three are library books. We're allowed to bring only one library book home at a time, but nobody else checked out any, so the teacher let me have three books for the weekend." Violet held up the books, *Black Beauty, Uncle Tom's Cabin,* and *Lorna Doone.* She hugged the third book to her chest, "It's a romance," and blushed.

Signe was happy that Violet was a good reader and her children were doing well in school. She took the cheese out of the oven and set it on the cutting board as the girls found their places at the table.

Elma took the Black Jack out of her mouth and placed the wad on her palm. Then extended her hand toward Elsie.

Elsie opened her mouth and carefully set her gum on Elma's waiting palm. "Careful not to get them mixed up. I don't want your diseases."

"Don't worry." Elma crawled under the table to park the Black Jack. "I put yours by the leg."

Signe, coffeepot in hand, stopped pouring. "Where did you get the gum? Did you chew gum in school?"

Elma shook her head. "No, on the way home Urho Lahti gave me and Elsie and Hugo a stick of Black Jack. He offered Violet a whole package of Juicy

Fruit—he likes her—but she said, no."

"She's proud," Elsie added, "but Elma and I aren't. We'll take anything. Except Peerless and Copenhagen!" She squealed with laughter at her own joke.

"And moonshine!" Elma shouted.

The two giggled as they flavored their drink.

"Don't put so much sugar or you'll get diabetes," Elma warned her younger sister. "Ed Koski's aunt died because she ate three lumps of sugar with every cup of coffee."

The girls cut their cheese into bits and dropped them in the hot brew.

Signe set the pot on the stove and joined the girls at the table. "Where does Urho get his money?"

"His father," Elma replied. "Urho gets a penny for each cow he milks. He milks ten cows in the evening and ten cows in the morning before he comes to school. Boy, does he smell like a barn."

"He stinks," Elsie chirped.

"Urho's a good worker," Signe commented. "His parents are getting along in years. They need help. Why did he give you the gum?"

Elsie shrugged. "Guess he wanted to make friends with us after Eldon gave him the black eye. He offered Eldon a package of Sen-Sen, but he said, no."

Violet asked to be excused. She took her cup, gathered her books and disappeared into her bedroom.

"Elsie," Signe spoke sternly, "You mustn't say things that aren't true even if you wish they were."

"I don't lie. Honest. I'm almost eight years old and have never told a lie, 'cept on April Fool's Day."

"That doesn't count," Elma, coming to her sister's defense, interjected, "if you say, 'April Fool' after the person has gotten excited."

"Was it an accident?" Signe asked.

Elma shook her head. "On purpose. Urho's eye was closed and puffy. The eighth-grade boys looked and said, 'That's a real beauty.' On the way home, his face was red and blue and purple and kind of green,"

"Like a rainbow," Elsie added.

"Yaa, like a rainbow."

Signe was perplexed. "Girls, you mustn't say bad things about people. Even if you don't like them."

Elma looked at her mother. "Urho's meeeean! He told Mayme Johnson that her bloomers were falling and they weren't. She got all red in the face and started to cry."

"I like Urho," Elsie declared, "He can't help it if he's dumb."

"Don't call anyone dumb. People use what brains God has given them." Signe wiped her brow as if to clear her confusion. "Eldon's half Urho's size, how could he hit Urho in the eye?"

"Easy," Elsie replied. "Urho bent down so Eldon could reach."

"Yaa, bent down on his knees," Elma confirmed, "closed his eyes and opened his mouth."

"Where did this take place?"

"Behind the woodshed," Elsie answered meekly.

"Girls, tell me the whole story. From the beginning."

"I'll tell," Elsie squealed and held up her cup. "First, may I please have more? The hot coffee makes the cheese squeak like rubber."

"That's why we call it squeaky cheese," Elma piped.

Signe got the coffeepot. "Just a half cup." She glanced at the clock. "Almost suppertime."

"Morning recess," Elsie began, "Urho was teasing Eldon. He wanted Eldon's new knife that you bought, but Eldon said no. At lunchtime, I saw Urho go behind the woodshed. Eldon went after him. I gave the crooked finger to Elma to come and we followed them."

"To Nylund's property?"

Elma and Elsie looked at each other and nodded.

"Don't you know it's against the rules to leave the schoolyard without permission?"

The sisters looked down.

"Then why did you go?"

"Cause . . . cause—" Elsie began to cry. "We didn't want Urho to beat up on Eldon. If he did, we could run and tell the teacher."

"What did Miss Keksi say when she saw Urho's eye?"

"She asked what happened," Elsie sobbed.

"Urho said he fell on a rock and then he said he got hurt by the merry-go-round," Elma continued. "The teacher laughed."

"She did not," Elsie screeched.

"Yes, she did. I sit in the front seat and was looking to the back. After she 'samined Urho's eye, she walked back to her desk and wiped the laugh from her face with her hand."

Signe looked at the clock. "Where are the boys?

They should've changed from their school clothes."

Elsie took a homemade handkerchief from her pocket and blew her nose. "Eldon's feeding the sick pigs. Hugo went along. He's siding with Eldon."

"What do you mean — siding?"

"He's taking Eldon's side. Eldon called Elma and me names."

"Names? What kind of names?"

"Hugo said we're double-faced because we took Urho's gum and he hates Urho."

"Elsie, you said Urho gave Hugo gum, also."

"Yaa, but he spitted it out. I want you to give Eldon a whipping, Mama."

"I haven't heard Eldon's story. But I won't whip him. I don't believe in whipping."

Elma sparked up. "Papa will give Eldon a whipping!"

Elsie gave a scream. "With the pitchfork and kill him like he did Eldon's cow. Elma, I hate you. You aren't my sister anymore. I hate you, hate you, hate you!"

Signe took the hysterical child in her arms and rocked her. She wondered where Elsie had learned about the cow incident. Eldon wouldn't have told her, she was certain. "Elma, where did Elsie hear the story about Eldon's cow?"

"In school."

This was a touchy subject, but she had to learn the truth. "In the schoolyard?"

"Nah, in the big kids' class. The teacher said we should be kind to birds and animals. The boy told how Papa killed Eldon's cow with the pitchfork. Then the teacher said, "Everyone, take out your Golden Song Book. It's time for music.'"

Signe had heard enough. "Elma, go tell the boys to come in. When you come back, I want both of you to change your clothes and start on your schoolwork. She wiped Elsie's tears with her apron and kissed her.

Elma went as far as the door, but turned back. "Elsie, do you still hate me?"

Elsie smiled and shook her head.

Elma took her hand. "Come."

The girls went out, brought their brothers to the house and quietly went into their room.

Signe sat the boys at the table. "I made the cheese this afternoon."

"I'm not hungry," Eldon said.

"That means I get your share, too." Hugo grabbed two large slices and went to his room .

Signe poured the untouched coffee back in the pot and sat facing Eldon. "Did you hit Urho Lahti in the eye?"

Eldon nodded.

"Because he wanted your knife?"

Eldon shook his head.

"What then?"

"Because what he said."

"What did he say?"

"I can't tell you. It was dirty. He was saying bad things about someone."

"Who was he talking about?"

"Fath—" Eldon clamped his mouth with his hand.

"Why did you feel it was your duty to hit Urho?" Signe asked.

"Because I don't want anyone talking about my father that way. Are you going to tell him?"

Signe thought for a moment. Then shook her head. "Go change your clothes."

Chapter XXI

IT WAS SATURDAY MORNING. Charlie had gotten up before dawn to warm the sauna. Now steamed, washed and clean-shaven, he was as chipper as a bushy tailed chipmunk after mating. "Signe," he said, as he opened the kitchen door, and sat on his favorite chair by the table, expecting his coffee, "I have news I forgot to tell you last night."

Signe grabbed the pot of fresh brew from the top of the stove and hurried to fill his cup. "Good or bad?" She was referring to the news.

"I'd say in-between," Charlie answered after taking a sip from the saucer. "As I was approaching the Salo mailbox, I spotted Oscar waiting for me. He wanted to buy a hundred dollar money order. I said, 'Oscar, don't you trust me anymore? You always put the money in the mailbox and leave a note as to what

I should do with it.' He said he trusted me, but he had news he wanted to tell me before I heard it from someone else. 'I'm leaving Minnesota,' he said. Just like that—'I'm leaving Minnesota.'"

"Where is he going?" Signe asked.

"Oregon. He's moving his family to Oregon by the sea."

"Why?"

"Oscar said he was discouraged. Said he'd lost ten sheep in the blizzard last winter and this summer the rain spoiled his entire crop of alfalfa seed. He's having an auction sale, selling everything. I wished him luck."

"Aren't we going to the auction?" Signe asked as she moved the three flatirons to the hottest part of the stove.

"Of course we are." Charlie sat and watched Signe carry in the heavy homemade wooden ironing board, and a bushel basketful of rolled up starched, dampened clothes.

Seeing that he had finished his coffee, she refilled his cup. "But you wished him luck."

"Yaa. I'm going to wish him luck again after the sale."

Signe spread a child's dress on the board and picked up an iron with her right hand. She spat on the fingers of her left and lightly touched the iron to see if it was hot enough, and started to iron.

Charlie stuck a fresh cube of sugar inside his cheek. "Oscar invited me West, too."

"What did you say to that?"

"I said, 'That's thoughtful of you, Oscar, but I got

my roots here. Solid like an oak, to be moved only in a box carried by six men in black.'"

After Charlie left, Signe cleared the table and washed the dishes so she could start her baking. A knock on the door interrupted Signe's bread kneading. "Elma," she called, "come see who's at the door. I have my hands in dough."

Elma and Elsie came running, excited to see who the guest might be. "Must be someone special," Elma whispered to Elsie. "Maybe the 'ssessor." It was Mary Marks and her daughter. The sisters took hold of Janie's hand and led her to their room.

"Another batch of bread," Mary commented.

Signe gave a laugh as she patted butter on the mountain of dough in the oversized aluminum dishpan that she'd bought especially for this purpose. "It seems I end up baking twice a week."

"No wonder, with six people taking lunches daily," Mary said. "I buy my bread at the Red Owl store in Detroit Lakes, twelve cents a loaf. You can't make it for that."

"Charlie won't eat store-bought bread." After covering the pan with a towel, Signe tested the top of the water heater at the end of the stove with the palm of her hand. "Guess that's not too hot." She set the dough there to rise. She poured water into the basin on the wood box to wash her hands. "What's new?"

"I brought you something." Mary opened the brown paper sack she'd brought. "Come sit here at the table and rest yourself."

Signe wiped her hands and flung the towel over

her shoulder. "How about a cup of coffee?"

"No, thanks. I don't have time. Ed Koski's coming to plow my garden this afternoon. Your children stopped by earlier and picked up Robert. They're helping Ed." Mary unloaded her goodies.

"I brought you some Pond's Cold Cream."

Signe's eyes opened wide. She was not used to gifts, especially of this nature. She unscrewed the lid of the jar and inhaled. "Ooo, that smells good!"

"Be sure to pat some on your face before going to bed at night," Mary instructed her, "and some again when you get up. It keeps the skin soft and smooth in this Minnesota weather. And here's some Lady Esther face powder—"

"Oh, I couldn't," Signe exclaimed. "What would Charlie say?"

"It's your face. He shaves every day, doesn't he? Did he object to your haircut?"

"Never mentioned it. He acted as if he hadn't noticed."

"So what are you worried about? This vanishing cream," Mary continued, "goes on before the powder to give a nice foundation. And here's rouge to give your cheeks some bloom. I did choose the right shade, didn't I?" she asked as she dabbed on the color.

Signe didn't know what to say. This was so unexpected. She stared at the items Mary had pulled out of her bag.

"Now close your mouth. I want to see how this lipstick looks—"

"Oh, no, I couldn't—"

"Sure you can. It's Tangee. Completely natural.

Nobody will know that you're wearing it. Besides, it keeps your lips from chapping."

"You mean I should wear it every day?"

"Why not?"

Signe laughed. "The cows might leave home."

"Mrs. Skinnar, you look very pretty," Janie said when she came to the kitchen. "Did Mommy make you that way?"

Before Signe could answer, Elma and Elsie joined in admiration of their mother.

"Look what Violet made me," Janie said, laying a doll's patchwork quilt on the table in front of her mother. "Isn't it the beautifullest thing you ever saw?"

"It certainly is," Mary replied, as she examined the handwork.

"It has real wool inside," Elma pointed out. "Mrs. Mattson gave us some. Janie's doll will never be cold."

"Your sister is very talented," Mary said.

"She makes paper flowers, too. Her roses are so real looking that you wanna smell them," Elma said, and turned to Jane. "Come, I'll give you one."

Mary glanced at the clock on the wall. "Girls, you'd better hurry. We have to be back home by the time Mr. Koski comes to plow."

When Mary left, Signe carefully gathered the containers of makeup, put them back in the brown paper bag and stashed them away in the cupboard next to her three-pound coffee can of tools. Wolf Creek was not the place for a woman to flaunt her looks.

Since it was Saturday and the children were home from school, Charlie didn't expect to see Mary Marks outside, but while there's life, there's hope, as the old saying goes. Charlie parked on the old logging road, sat and waited.

Roy Niemi, who was driving home from the creamery with his father, spotted the parked mail car and asked, "Why do you suppose any man would want to eat a cold lunch from a smelly dinner pail when he could be home in minutes chomping on Signe's pulla and hot coffee?"

Jacob thought for a moment, then voiced a guess. "Perhaps he's reading the Scriptures. Charlie is a man of God, you know."

Mary Marks finally went to her garden and started to pull up last year's tomato stakes, gathering dried cornstalks and withered pumpkin vines left by a former occupant of the place.

Although there was no mail for Mary Marks, and she had no outgoing letters, Charlie drove up and stopped at her box just to be sociable and friendly.

There was something fascinating and sensuous about the widow that titillated him, and when Mary brought her sewing to Signe, he would watch them jealously. He almost hated Signe at those times. Hated her because in fitting the garments, she got so close to Mary.

As he sat parked by the widow's mailbox, watching her, he could see the outline of her slender thighs, the curve of her breasts through her sweater, and he could almost feel the silkiness of her dark hair. Charlie wanted to envelope her body, but it was out of his reach. So he called out, "Looks like an early summer, doesn't it, Mrs. Marks?"

She glanced up and nodded. Then yanked another cornstalk. Not even a smile.

Charlie felt the strong tinge of hurt. A hurt that grabbed him by his innards, nauseatingly, and paralyzed his whole body, brain and limbs. He had that sensation only once before in his life, at a church picnic. Walter Jalo was choosing players for the baseball team to play against the Pickerel Lake Apostolic Lutheran Church, when Jalo ignored Charlie, and, instead, picked Bruno Lehto, the village idiot. Charlie was twelve then, but the humiliation still gave him nightmares, and, years later, when Bruno was gored to death by a bull, Charlie felt a certain elation.

Charlie was about to ask Mary if he could plow her garden for her, but decided against it. Perhaps another day she would be more receptive.

There was nothing further he could say, but he didn't want to leave, not just yet, so he reached over to the back seat for his mail bag and pretended to be sorting the letters while he watched the widow. It then occurred to him that she might have a man friend, a lover perhaps. But the fact that he'd seen no such letters consoled him.

His reverie was cut short by a blast of a horn. Ed Koski, in his flatbed truck, was coming from the opposite direction, carrying a tractor and a plow. Ed stopped smack in front of him and opened the cab door to let out his passengers—Reino, Eldon, Violet, Hugo, and Robert Marks.

"How's it going, Charlie?" Ed yelled out. "What do you think of my crew?"

"I see you have a handful," Charlie muttered, while he silently cursed himself for not taking Signe's advice to plant the widow's potatoes.

As Charlie waited for Ed to pull up his truck, Hugo stuck his head in the left window of the mail car. "Pa, can I have Mrs. Marks' mail so I can give it to her?"

"She didn't have any today."

"So, why you parked here for?"

"I'm sorting the first-class."

"I thought you did that at the post office."

"I made a mistake."

Hugo's face lit up. "You make mistakes, too? I make mistakes all the time."

"Come, Hugo," Robert Marks called. "Mother's made hamburgers for us."

"Hamburgers, wow! I hope you get the letters all sorted, Papa," Hugo said, and made a running start for the house.

The mail had been light. Charlie finished his route early, but he avoided going home. He didn't want to confront Signe. The widow was on his mind, and to come face to face with Signe would be onerous.

Charlie drove around aimlessly for some time. As he was about to pass Ernie Yoki's place, he recalled that it was Yoki who owned the forty acres east of his own. The county road separated the two parcels of land. Charlie drove in the driveway and parked in front of the barn. Seeing the top half of the Dutch door open, he called, "Ernie, you in there?"

"Sure, 'nough," came the answer, and Ernie, hammer in hand, appeared in person.

"Taking up carpentry, I see," Charlie wisecracked.

"I'm adding more stanchions."

"What for?"

Ernie blinked in puzzlement at the stupid question. "To make room for more cows, what else?"

"Don't you have enough work to do?"

"Sure. But I could use some more money. I don't have a soft government job on the side like you do. But with Land O' Lakes hauling the milk, I figure dairy business will be tolerable." Ernie eyed Charlie curiously. "Got your potatoes in?"

Charlie nodded and paused. "I was wondering what you were planning to do with the forty across the road from mine."

"Why?"

"I might just be interested in buying it."

"A year ago I would've said, no deal. But now I'm willing to listen."

"What do you want for it?"

"What's your offer?"

"Three hundred."

"My God, what do you take me for? A darn blasted fool?"

"Name your price," Charlie said.

"Eight hundred, with terms."

"I didn't say anything about terms. I asked you what you wanted. I'll give you four."

Ernie shook his head. "No deal. Make it seven."

"Seven hundred for forty acres of brush! No

decent timber to speak of."

Ernie peered over his glasses. "Who said it was timberland?"

"I'll give you four fifty. I bet I could get that piece west of mine for a coupla hundred."

"Then why don't you? I'm not pressing you to buy."

"Four fifty, take it or leave it," Charlie said and started to walk to his car.

Ernie followed. "Make it five and I'll shake."

Charlie stopped in his tracks. "Too much. Way too much, but I don't have all day." He opened his wallet, took out a bill. "Here's a hundred. You get the papers drawn up and call me."

"You want a receipt?"

"Not necessary. You've got the hundred."

When Charlie got home, Signe was making pies. He had nothing to say to her, but he sat by the table and forced himself to ask, "What kind?"

"Rhubarb. We got a nice crop this year."

He hoped she didn't realize how ridiculous his question was since he faced the pile of rhubarb stalks she was cutting on the table.

But Signe's mind was on her work. "I wish the wild strawberries would ripen earlier. Strawberries with rhubarb makes a real tasty pie."

The door flung open and Hugo burst in. "Boy, did we have fun today."

"What did you do besides plant potatoes?" Signe asked.

"We had popcorn. Mrs. Koski made us a whole

bunch and Reino had two big bowls by himself. Mrs. Marks made us hamburgers with real ketchup and I had Dr. Pepper with mine. Papa, have you ever had Dr. Pepper?"

Charlie shook his head.

"It's real powerful. Mrs. Marks asked if I wanted root beer, but I said, 'No. It's sinful to drink beer and whiskey.' She laughed. Guess she thought it was funny." Hugo went to his father and took his hand. "I want you to come see Princess, Eldon's new calf. She's real pretty."

"Not now."

"Oh, come on. You can have a talk with Mr. Koski and Reino, too, before they go home."

"Didn't you hear me?" Charlie raised his voice. "I said, 'Not now!'"

Signe, rolling piecrusts across the table from Charlie, puckered her lips and stared at him, eyes squinted, but said nothing.

Hugo, with tears swelling in his eyes, went silently out of the house.

Signe, her whole body trembling, stood up straight, with rolling pin vertically poised, "Charlie, don't ever treat my children like that!"

Charlie quickly changed his mood and behavior. "I feel a bit high-strung. I'd like a cup of coffee."

"Help yourself."

Chapter XXII

ED KOSKI PICKED UP REINO on his way to Mrs. Mark's place. Koski was driving Mary to town to do her business and Reino was to stay with the children and pick the bugs off the potato plants. "Ed," Reino spoke out, "do you think it's possible for an idiot to learn new things?"

"I would think so," Ed replied after mulling the matter for a moment. "What makes you ask?"

"Well, since I've been working for Mrs. Marks, I've learned practically all she wants me to do for her. She never asks me, 'Can you do this?' She always says, 'Ray'—she calls me Ray as if I were English— 'will you please do this?' And I do it. I do it without thinking. Like I was smart."

Ed looked at his nephew sitting next to him in the pickup. "Why do you call yourself an idiot?"

"That's what lots of people call me."

"They're the real idiots."

Reino sighed with relief and started to giggle. "What should I do? Punch them in the nose?"

Ed shook his head. "Just ignore them."

When they arrived at the Marks' home, Reino was greeted by a crew of seven—the Skinnar children and Jane and Bob Marks. "Did you all bring pails?" he asked, in English—the Marks children were not Finnish. The answer was a loud enthusiastic yes. "Now, what we gotta do is to go row by row and pick every potato bug you see. If you leave even one little bug, it'll grow up and make a whole bunch of babies who will eat the stems off the plants and Mrs. Marks won't have any potatoes to fry. Is that clear?"

The bug pickers gave another animated yes.

Reino continued, "The reason we are picking the bugs instead of spraying them is that poison is bad for you. Listen carefully. I'm the head boss and Eldon is next to me and Robert is the low boss. We go according to age."

"How old are you?" Janie asked Reino.

Reino gave her a disapproving look. "Never, never ask a boss how old he is. If he's your boss, he's old enough to be your boss. Is that clear?"

Janie nodded.

"What are we going to do with the bugs when we get a pailful?" Elma wanted to know.

"Drown'em in kerosene," Reino replied, "like a sea burial."

Mrs. Marks came out and followed Ed to the

truck. Before climbing in, she turned to Reino. "Don't forget the potato salad. Eat it all. It won't keep. Children, be good and listen to Ray." Jane and Robert rushed to kiss her as she stepped up to the pickup.

"Are we going to eat here?" Elsie asked Elma.

"Guess so."

"Of course, we're going to eat after we do the work," Reino announced. "Workers get lunch. That's the rule."

"Ask him what we're going to have," Elsie whispered to Elma.

Reino heard the question. "Potato salad, tuna fish sandwiches and olivers," he announced.

"Olives, not olivers," Janie corrected.

"What's tuna fish?" Elma asked.

"It's like salmon, only not pink," Reino answered.

"Who caught it?"

"A fisherman sitting in a boat in the ocean," Jane replied.

"Don't forget the chocolate cake," Robert reminded Reino.

Reino wanted action and he wanted it fast. His mind was on the potato salad. "Come, kids. I give you girls each a row. Pick clean. Then us bosses will come after you to inspect. Is that clear?"

Each day brought new hope to Charlie Skinnar, the hope that he could get close to the Marks widow. This morning was no exception. He had a letter for her, postmarked Chicago, Ill. This was the third to arrive. Charlie had presumed that the first two were business letters. This one was handwritten, but the stationery was the same. From a lawyer? Relative? A lover! He examined the seal and decided that the envelope could easily be steamed open. But not yet. There were other ways of finding out.

Charlie drove slowly to the Marks' mailbox. No one was in sight. He would take the letter to Mary. Her face would reveal the nature of the sender. Charlie got out of his car as noiselessly as he could, but closing the door brought the bug pickers out like a noonday whistle. "The mail! The mail!" the Marks children sounded. "Hi, Papa!" sounded the five Skinnars.

"A letter for Mom," Janie announced and snatched the letter from Charlie's hand.

Charlie was angry, angrier than he had been in years. He felt like slapping the girl across the face, but instead he asked, "Where's your mother?"

"She's gone to town on business," Janie replied. "Ray's taking care of us. He's our boss."

"Some boss," Charlie muttered under his breath. He looked at Eldon, "What you kids doing here?"

"We're picking potato bugs," Elma volunteered.

"Don't you kids have enough work at home?" Charlie didn't wait for an answer. His mind was on the widow. "With whom did your mother go?"

"Mr. Koski."

Charlie turned on his heel, went to his car and drove on.

Back from town, Ed stopped at the Skinnars' to drop Mary off. Signe offered him coffee, but he said he didn't have the time. He wanted to look at the property across the road.

Mary looked unusually happy. As soon as Ed was out the door, she said, "Signe, I have news."

"I can see by your face that it's good news. A man in your life?"

Mary nodded.

"Someone from Chicago?" Signe knew it couldn't be a local farmer.

"The boy next door when I was growing up. He had heard that I am alone now, and found me through relatives."

"I'm happy for you. Does he plan to come see you?"

"He wants me to go to Chicago around Labor Day."

"School starts the middle of August," Signe reminded Mary.

"I know. I was going to ask you if you thought Ray could take care of the children for a week or so."

"Sure. And I'll be here to check up on things on my way home from Gertrude's. I told you my sister is planning to live permanently on the old Kivi place which she bought sometime ago. She had the rest of her furniture shipped here from Minneapolis. I go there almost daily to help her out."

Mary nodded. "How does she like Wolf Creek?"

"She complains."

Mary gave a laugh and took out the three lengths of fabric she had bought—red, white and black—to show Signe. "Next time I come we'll go over the catalogs for patterns to copy."

The two women were having coffee when Ed

returned. "What do you think Charlie would charge yearly for me to run some sheep in the forty across the road if I fenced it in and cleared some of the brush?"

"It's not for Charlie to charge," Signe said as she filled Ed's cup. "That belongs to Ernie Yoki."

Ed sat at the table. "Not anymore. Ernie said he sold it to Charlie."

Signe added more rusks to the plate on the table. "It's the first I've heard and I haven't signed any papers."

Charlie was cantankerous when he returned home, but his mood was mild compared to Signe's. He could feel the disturbed molecules of air whizzing by him when he opened the door. He sat at the table and made small talk. "Looks like an early fall. How are the tomatoes doing?"

Signe stood at the other side of the table, her eyes blazing with anger. "When did you buy the forty acres across the road?"

"A few days ago."

"Why didn't you tell me?"

"Guess it just slipped my mind."

"Where are the papers?"

"They'll be here."

"Where are you going to get the money to pay for the acreage?" she asked.

"I have money," he answered cockily.

"So when are you going to build the children's bedroom?" Signe didn't mention the other bedroom, living room, dining room, and inside running water that he'd bragged about earlier.

"They have a bedroom."

Signe raised her voice in anger as she exclaimed, "Five children in one room."

"I haven't heard them complain."

"They don't even have a table on which to do their homework."

"They can always put their tablets on their laps. And what's wrong with the kitchen table? That's what I used when I was a kid."

Signe knew she was losing the battle of words against Charlie on the subject of a new bedroom for the children. She went to the stove, took off the round lid, stoked the embers and threw in a couple chunks of wood. She gave the lid a whack with the poker to set it back in its place. She was angry, but anger would not remedy the situation she told herself. "If fenced, we could use the new forty for pasture and plant this forty in clover or alfalfa," she told Charlie. "Remember how well we used to do with alfalfa? Alex Nieminen, I heard, made over twelve hundred dollars in clover last fall."

Charlie did not like to be doubted, questioned, quizzed or compared to other males. "I've had my share of gazing into horses' asses at the plow, on the mower and the harrow. I don't want it anymore."

"I've been thinking we might hire — "

Charlie's face had turned purple. "You leave the thinking to me. I'm buying more traps with my next paycheck."

"Don't forget I'm fifty per cent of this corporation."

A shock wave passed through Charlie's body. He

looked around as if he had been hit by a thunderbolt. What was happening? His immigrant wife was talking about percentages and corporations.

A year ago, Charlie had bought a number of traps and planned to make big money selling pelts. "With all the beaver, muskrat, mink, skunk and wolves a-round here, a man could make a haul in just a few seasons," he had told Signe. When he spoke of wolves, she didn't know whether he was referring to timber wolves or common coyotes. But when he got out the Montgomery Ward catalog and showed her the picture of a lady wearing a coat with a wolf collar, priced at $19.95, Signe acknowledged that there might be water in Charlie's steam, not just hot air.

The season, however, had not been lucrative. Besides the one skunk that Charlie had mangled bad-ly while skinning, his only other catches had been a jackrabbit that had frozen stiff—Charlie had forgotten exactly where the trap was and it was a couple of days before he located it—and Leo Hendrickson's dog, Kaiser, which froze its foot and later lost it. The three-legged dog became a daily reminder to Charlie as he passed Hendrickson's place in his mail car. Now Leo, the dog's master, called Charlie a crackpot.

"If the skunk had been pure black," Charlie had explained to Signe, "it would've earned much more—maybe $1.25 or even $1.50, but the ones with the white stripe bring less." He hadn't told Signe that the buyer had said Charlie butchered the hide while skin-ning the animal. And it was only after some heavy dickering on Charlie's part that the bookkeeper at the Minnesota Hide and Pelt Company wrote Charlie a check for sixty-five cents.

That was last year, Signe told herself as she set a pot of water on the stove for the potatoes she was about to peel; maybe this year would be different.

Charlie got up, went to the cupboard, got a cup and saucer and served himself coffee. "I told the Marks kid to ask his mother if I could trap in her pasture."

"What did Mary say?"

"She gave me permission."

Charlie tucked a lump of sugar in his right cheek as he rehashed his last year's mistakes and almost cracked a molar cursing the day he sprang open the trap to let the hound go. One more night in the clear Minnesota moonlight at forty below would have ended the howling and preserved Charlie's reputation. Burying the mutt would have been out of the question, the ground being frozen solid six feet deep, but he could have thrown the mongrel's frozen carcass in a brush pile and torched it come spring. And no one would've been wiser. Truth and honesty aren't always the best course to follow, Charlie concluded, as he saucered his coffee. He got up from the table, put on his cap and denim jacket and headed for the door.

"Where you going?" Signe asked.

"To check my traps."

Chapter XXIII

SIGNE AWAKENED to the excited twittering of the swallows.

The birds were preparing for their flight south. The green edged light of dawn was beginning to filter in through the screens on the windows of her bedroom. Signe stretched her hand to touch Charlie's shoulder, but he was gone. She folded back the old wool quilt. A cold draft enveloped her as she got out of bed. She shivered. About to close the window, she inhaled the crisp autumn air. The smoke from the sauna chimney and the sweet smell of the toasted birch vastas hit her nostrils. Charlie had heated the sauna.

She decided to leave the window open. Might as well enjoy the last warm days of summer, she told herself, there can't be many left.

Signe hurried into her barn clothes, lit the fire in

the kitchen stove, put on the coffeepot and woke up the children, telling them "only two more days of school after today and then it's Saturday and you can sleep in."

She closed the screen door gently, her eyes focused on the stand of trees across the barnyard. The poplars were turning from chartreuse to yellow. The birches, oaks, and maples in various shades of crimson and scarlet were blushing from Jack Frost's nocturnal visit. The box elder stood naked like little children in a sauna bath, waiting to be washed.

Signe hurried to her flower garden. Protected from the cold by the lilacs on one side and the corn on the other, the bachelor buttons, zinnias and petunias were still bravely standing at attention. Later, she would come by and pick a bouquet for Gertrude. Signe hummed to herself as she went down the path. When she passed the sauna with its doors flung open, she realized that Charlie had already gone.

Charlie had told Signe it was "just a couple of miles" to Gertrude's house, but Roy Vester, Gertrude's bachelor neighbor, said that it was a good four miles. Signe told Mary Marks, "In June it seems like two and come January, I wager it will feel like ten."

Every Thursday Signe went to help her sister with the housework. Not that Gertrude was indisposed or indigent. She was in good health and very comfortable. But Gertrude had certain standards and she wanted those standards met. There were times when Signe had to show up every other day.

A maiden lady, ten years older and a mother

figure to Signe, Gertrude was a university graduate who had worked as a secretary and legal assistant to a solicitor in Helsinki. When he died some twenty years ago, leaving her his worldly possessions, she decided to migrate to America and begin a new life. She'd chosen Minneapolis, a cultural center with many Finnish residents for her residence. She now was a permanent resident of Wolf Creek.

Being the high-toned lady that she was, Gertrude mingled little with the local folk. She had no phone. Didn't' want to hear the local gossip; but, surprisingly enough, knew everything that went on. She was not a church person. Her sole entertainment consisted of a couple, maybe three concerts by the Minneapolis Symphony, when Roy Vester would drive her the two hundred miles to the Twin Cities to hear Beethoven. They would stay at the hotel.

Signe hoped that Gertrude would keep her all day. Gertrude paid her by the hour, and every hour helped. Violet needed new shoes for school.

When she opened the door and handed her sister the bouquet of garden flowers, Signe knew that Gertrude was on to something, something that she, Signe, didn't want to hear. And it would concern Charlie. Gertrude and Charlie had locked horns at their first meeting when he picked her up at the railway station. He had not opened doors for her, as she expected a gentleman to do and when she'd gotten her luggage in the truck, he added insult to injury by saying, "Hop in, let's go."

"Shall I begin with the kitchen?" Signe asked.

"Set yourself on a chair," Gertrude began. "What's this I hear about Charlie quitting his government job and going into trapping full-time?"

"Where did you hear that?"

"He bought out all the traps they had at the Co-op and had Emil order more from wholesale. What does he hope to catch?"

Signe was at a loss. She didn't know how to answer her sister, but she didn't need to.

Gertrude railed on. "Traps! Buying traps when his boy doesn't have shoes. When Eldon came to fertilize my strawberries, the sole of his oxford was flapping. I had to give him a pair of my old tennis shoes to wear so he wouldn't get chicken manure on his stockings. What does Charlie hope to catch?" she asked again.

"Skunks, I guess. Maybe beaver. Or mink. Musk-rat? Weasels bring a good price. Ermine coats are very popular now," Signe rattled on nervously. "Maybe even a bear."

"Bear?" Gertrude shrieked, forgetting her Finnish parlor manners. "I would gladly give ten years of my life to see Charlie wrestle a black bear." The humor of such a possibility threw Gertrude into convulsions of glee, after which she wiped her eyes with a fine linen handkerchief, lit a cigarette and inhaled. "Oh, my, this is all too good to be true. Charlie Skinnar gets better by the year."

Signe rushed for an ashtray. Her sister was the only woman she'd seen take a puff. Gertrude had told her she had learned to smoke on her trip to Paris where all educated and cosmopolitan women smok-ed. Hers was not a common American brand such as

Chesterfield or Lucky Strike, but a long, thin English brand — a blend of rare Turkish tobaccos — which she ordered from a shop in Minneapolis.

Gertrude inhaled, tapped the ashes off the cigarette into the tray, exhaled, arched her right eyebrow, and asked, "What about the new truck?"

Signe was stunned. "What new truck?"

"The new Ford pickup he ordered from the dealer in Osage." It was clear to Gertrude that Signe was unaware of these new developments in her life.

"His truck is very old," Signe replied in her husband's defense, as she worked to open a long closed window.

"Good enough for his purpose, whatever that may be."

Gertrude classified men into categories: spendthrifts, indolents, dipsomaniacs, and philanderers. It rankled her no end that she couldn't peg Charlie into all four groups, but she had never caught him nipping. As for adultery, he would if he could, she liked to say.

Signe was impatient. Time was fleeting, and Gertrude would not clock her until she had brush or broom in hand. "Shall I start with the kitchen?" she asked again.

Gertrude pointed to a chair. Like a reluctant child having to obey her mother's wishes, Signe sat down.

"What about the hogs? They should be ready for the market."

"We've had problems," Signe confessed.

"Problems. What kind of 'problems'?"

"Cholera."

"All ten sick with cholera?"

That Gertrude remembered how many pigs had been in the litter surprised Signe. "No, just five —"

"Thank God."

"The others died. Charlie —"

"I don't want to hear anymore about Charlie," Gertrude snapped.

Signe sighed with relief.

"You still taking in sewing?"

"Oh, yes. I like to sew. I earn enough for my household expenses and my children's clothes. I like to work on lovely materials, especially brides' dresses, but the weddings in Wolf Creek are simple. No long gowns, no veils and what orders I get from the nearby towns are for suits and coats."

"How much do you charge?" Gertrude didn't hesitate asking personal questions.

Signe didn't mind the interrogation — Gertrude was like a mother to her — but she resented losing precious time. She didn't let her voice betray her feelings. "Fifty cents for a cotton dress, seventy-five for rayon, dollar for a suit and dollar and a half for a woolen suit with bound button holes and a lined jacket."

Gertrude told Signe she was working for nothing.

"That's all the market will bear," Signe said. "I'm competing with four big mail order houses. A woman can order a ready-made cotton dress for $1.79 to $1.98 from a catalog, but I do all right. I copy their styles. When a customer comes in, I hand her the latest catalog and tell her to look at the pictures and choose her pattern. Mary Marks says she's never seen one I couldn't duplicate." Signe looked at Gertrude and asked, "Have you met the Marks widow?"

Gertrude gave a noncommittal nod.

"I'm making three dresses for her, a red, a white and a black one. She's planning to go to Chicago on a holiday."

Gertrude got up from her chair. "You can start with the kitchen. The windows all need washing, inside and out."

Signe was home by the time Charlie got back from his mail route. He took off his jacket and hung it behind the stove. "Did you go to Gertie's today?"

"I did, but she didn't need me for long." After pouring his coffee, Signe sat down at her Singer and started a seam on a white dress.

"Stingy old girl, your sister."

"Her place is clean. Gertrude has no husband, no children. Who's to bring in dirt?"

"What news did the female herald have about Charlie Skinnar?"

"She mentioned the traps."

"So I'm adding some here and there. You knew that. I'm even putting a few in the widow's woods."

"You're not leaving your government post?"

"And lose my government pension! Woman, are you crazy?"

"What about the new truck?"

Charlie was stunned. He became angry. Marv Stubblefield had broken his word to keep quiet about the deal. Nobody crosses Charlie Skinnar, he said to himself. Stubblefield Brothers now had lost Charlie

Skinnar's patronage. Tomorrow he'd go to Marv and
cancel the order for the new Ford, and come spring,
he would requisition a Chevy, next year's model,
from the dealer in Frazee. "What new truck?" he
asked Signe. "Have you seen me driving one? You
can't believe everything your sister tells you."

Signe had finished sewing the side seams of the
dress and held it up to view. "I wonder why Mary
Marks chose three plain colors this time. No florals or
prints."

Charlie stared at the garment. "White! Why
white? She's no virgin."

"What are you talking about? A woman with two
children? And it makes no never mind. The sheiks of
Arabia wear white—" At loss as to words, she used
her hands to outline a robe. "And who knows?"
Again she gestured with her hands bringing them
together and opening her palms as if to say, and who
knows what they do.

"Sheiks are men."

"So what?" Signe shot back impudently, and went
on to her favorite subject. "That royal blue dress I
made for her in the spring, didn't she look pretty in it?
It brought out the color of her eyes and the soft lines
of her neck."

Charlie's eyes were fixed at the garment in a
mesmerized stare. "That soft goods will show her
breasts."

Signe pulled a length of thread from the bobbin,
bit it off with her teeth, pulled it through the eye of
the needle and knotted the end. "Of course. What do
you want do you want her to do? Cut'em off?" She

laughed. This was one of the times when Signe felt Charlie was receptive to a little banter, which she enjoyed. They seldom had a chance to talk, and she sensed that he liked discussing the widow.

"It's sinful for a woman to flaunt her intimate parts."

"Phooey. She's young. Her husband's dead and won't come back. Mary needs to get out and live. Find someone and go dancing. Oh, how I loved to dance. When I was whirling around the dance floor, I felt like a bird floating on air."

Charlie pushed the empty cup and saucer away from him.

"Useless bouncing. Besides, it's against the scriptures."

Signe stood up and clasped the dress with both hands and held it close. "I think when your mother looked into your cradle, she said to herself, 'I have given birth to an old man.' Charlie, you have never let yourself experience the joy of life. Each morning brings to you another day of toil. I remember those dances at the Finnish Hall on a Hundred and Twenty Fifth Street—in New York City, you know—"

"I know," Charlie grumbled, cutting short her thoughts. "I've heard the story before."

"There was this Polish boy—"

Charlie interrupted her again. "What was the Polish boy doing at the Finn Hall?"

Signe gave Charlie a puzzled look and answered, "Dancing." She slipped back into recollection. "The accordion began to play "The Blue Danube" and he came to me—" Signe made an elaborate bow with flourishes—"and asked me to dance. I didn't know how to waltz. I could do the polka, mazurka, schottische, and the haampo, but had never waltzed. I shook my head. He looked so sad. I said to myself, 'What the Dickens." He took me—" Signe held the white dress in front of her, "and we waltzed." She sang as she whirled around the room. Out of breath, she stopped. "Hooh, I'm not used to dancing anymore."

"Finish that dress before you wear it out," Charlie growled.

Still glowing from the memory of a sweet moment in her youth, Signe took her seat by the sewing machine, with the dress on her lap. "I've been thinking, it'll soon be time to pick the potatoes."

"Yes," Charlie agreed. "The nights are getting cold."

"We ought to give Mary Marks a hand. Since the seed potatoes were plowed in, the crop has to be plowed up. The spuds are too deep to dig up by hand. You could turn over the soil and the children and I would pick. We'd be finished in an hour or two."

Charlie glowered. "The widow doesn't need our help. Let her call Ed Koski. He has the equipment and the crew."

"Crew—you mean the children." Signe laughed. "They had a feast they'll never forget after the potato planting last spring, dishes they'd never tasted."

"Better get those dresses made. The widow's coming for a fitting on Thursday, isn't she?"

"Yes, after I return from Gertrude's. I should be back early."

Charlie was contentious and irritable. "I don't think you should encourage Eldon to spend so much time there," he said, as he got up to refill his coffee cup.

Signe was puzzled. "Eldon hasn't seen my sister for weeks. Every time he goes to Gertrude's house, she finds some odd chore for him. Last time she had him clean out the old chicken coop. What for? She hasn't any chickens and doesn't have plans for getting any."

"I wasn't talking about Gertrude," Charlie said in demeaning tones. "I meant the widow."

"Mary Marks? Why?"

"Eldon might get ideas."

"They were picking bugs off potato plants," Signe countered. "What ideas can you get from picking bugs?"

"The widow is—" Charlie hesitated. "seductive."

"What does that mean?"

"She causes desire in men."

"Men!" Signe laughed. "Eldon is twelve years old. A baby. He and Violet sometimes play checkers with Mary's children. Eldon doesn't have much time for play, you know."

"The less time for play, the less time to transgress the law of God."

The door flung open. The children were home from school. The girls, led by Violet, walked in without a word and went straight to their room. Eldon arrived, lunch pail in hand, carrying Hugo on his back. He let down his brother and put his lunch pail on the wood box. Charlie gazed at his son, not at all like himself at that age. Eldon's like his mother, Charlie would say, but Signe was tough and resilient. There was something ephemeral about Eldon that disturbed Charlie at times, something unearthly about his older son, which he could not put into words. He had never forgotten the look on the midwife's face when Eldon opened his eyes for the first time.

"What do you want me to do?" Eldon asked his mother. "It's too early to start the chores."

"Go to your room and study," Charlie said. "You can always read more."

Signe flipped over the skirt she was hemming. "I think you should go out and play with your brother. Hugo doesn't know he has a big brother. He sees little of you."

Eldon was happy to be let loose. "Come, Hugo," he called and ran out, only to return promptly to get the ball and bat.

"Eldon," Charlie spoke up, "I had a talk with your teacher the other day. She says you have a fine voice. She wants you to sing at the Christmas program."

"Okay." Eldon hesitated. He had something else on his mind. "Say, Father, can I go to the school board meeting with you this evening?"

Charlie shook his head. "They run late into the night. You need your sleep. Besides, why do you want to go, anyway?"

"So I can learn. When I grow up, I want to be on the school board like you."

"School board? That's chicken feathers. You can be the governor of Minnesota."

Signe looked up from her sewing. "Governor? I

say President."

"Mother, how do you know?"

"I've been to civics class," she answered proudly.

Eldon was dumbfounded. He had never envisioned his mother in school. "Civics class?"

"Yes, so I could get my first naturalization papers. The constitution says if you have been born in America and are at least thirty-five years old, you can become president."

With a wave of his hand, Charlie dismissed his son. "Go now, play with your brother. Remember, in America you can become anything you want if you have a good education and work hard."

Eldon was all smiles. "President! Gee whizz," he said as he went out the door.

Charlie was in no hurry to get to the board meeting. He took out the Minneapolis Tribune and sat by the table with his cup of coffee. He stared at the newsprint without reading it. Signe had placed a plate of homemade cheese, his favorite food, in front of him but Charlie's mind was not on cheese, regardless of how delectable. His coffee had gotten cold.

Yesterday a large package had arrived in the mail for Mary Marks. He'd offered to carry it to her house instead of leaving it by the mailbox. She'd refused his help. Today she had been in her garden, digging potatoes. Charlie had called out to her and tried to make conversation. She merely waved.

Even from his mail car he had been able to see the outline of her shapely legs, the fullness of her breasts under the light summer dress. The vision would not leave Charlie's mind.

Chapter XXIV

IT WAS THURSDAY, a beautiful, balmy August morning. The sun was warm, but in the shade one could
feel the nip of fall. Charlie took nature's glow as a
portent of the day, as a forecast of things to come. He
was happier than he'd been since his early youth. He
felt a jubilation, a euphoria that he would have considered sinful at one time of his life, but now he was a
changed man. He felt entitled to happiness, and love.
Even love illicit in intent.

Thursday was his favorite day. The week was half
over, and the mail was usually light. The Finnish
American News came on Mondays, Wednesdays and
Fridays. And Signe went to her sister's on Thursdays,
so he was free to come and go.

Yesterday after work, Charlie had gone to the

barber, and this morning he'd heated the sauna so he could bathe before his mail run. He'd gotten up at four to heat the rocks that would make the steam — after which he'd used one of his new birch switches to beat and cleanse his body. He was clean.

The image of the young widow digging in her garden had not left Charlie's mind. He dreamt it at night and visualized it during his waking hours. His face was flushed by the anticipation of what was to come. He felt young and virile.

Signe had gone to Gertrude's place as soon as the children left for school. And the widow was expecting to come for a fitting. Two facts which perfected his plan for the day.

Charlie was running early according to his planned schedule and had only a half dozen stops to make before he was through with his mail route; but in order to give himself more time, and decrease the chances of any foul-ups, he decided he could drop off the post at those boxes tomorrow. What difference could a day make to the recipients, especially since it was mostly bills and flyers advertising Co-op Specials? He began to whistle as he cut off the main road and turned onto the old logging road across from Mary Marks' house. He hadn't whistled a tune since he could remember.

He opened his lunch box, took a bite of the meat loaf sandwich Signe had made for him, and was about to open the Thermos of coffee when he thought about the time. Charlie took out the gold pocket watch his mother had given him for his eighth-grade grad-uation, and revised his schedule. He jammed the par-

tially eaten sandwich back into the bucket, drove to
the Marks widow's mailbox, and blew the horn. He
had a letter and a Sears & Roebuck fall catalog for her.
He knew she was waiting for the letter as she had
waited for the others which would never come.

Charlie decided to take the mail to her house. If
she was amicable, he might consider giving her the
letter. He stepped lively and tried to whistle, but his
mouth was dry. As he neared the end of her driveway, his heart began to pound. He was short of
breath. Charlie stopped to fill his lungs with air. His
right eye wiggled erratically, and he had double
vision. He paused before entering her porch, closed
his eyes and breathed deeply. Charlie had never been
inside Mary's house. He could only imagine its
interior. In fantasy, he'd often visited her bedroom.

Mary Marks appeared at the door when he
knocked, "Yes?"

A cold cloud suddenly enveloped his person.
Charlie felt cheated—cheated out of a common
courtesy of "Good Morning" or "Hello, Mr. Skinnar."
Ladies had always treated him with the greatest
respect and admiration. He felt he could have had any
woman he ever wanted, but he was an admirable
man. "I've come to get you." It was as if she didn't
understand what he was saying. "For the fitting," he
explained.

"My appointment isn't until later," she said,
businesslike, but coldly.

Charlie was afraid she would shut the door on
him. "Signe sent me."

She had her eyes on the black Ford. "In the mail

car?"

Charlie nodded. "I'm done for the day."

She didn't seem to hear. She kept staring at the auto. "I'll walk," she said, and turned around to go back in the house.

He grabbed her arm.

"Let go!"

Charlie held tighter. "I can't. Signe wouldn't like me to return without you." He had to hurry. School would dismiss for lunch at twelve, and the children would be scanning any movement on the road.

"I'm not ready. I have ironing to do."

"There's always tomorrow," Charlie quipped with a smile, and let go of her wrist. "We don't want to keep Signe waiting."

"I have to change."

"Here's your catalog," he announced as she was about to close the door.

Her face fell with disappointment. "Is that all?" she asked when he handed her the bible of fall specials.

"Were you expecting something more?"

He was about to follow her into the house when she turned around and closed the door on him. Charlie stood motionless on the steps, with his eye on the mail car. He had been rebuffed again. Nobody snubs Charlie Skinnar, he told himself as he took Mary's letter, one of the many that arrived, postmarked "Chicago, Ill.," out of his pocket, opened and read it. Then with a laugh, tore it up, and put the pieces back in his pocket.

She came out, wearing a skirt with a sweater the

color of a sun ripened apricot. He opened the door and she slipped into the car—her soft, warm body pressed against the door away from him. So close and yet so far.

Charlie started the engine and put his foot on the gas. He didn't want to move. He wanted to stay there forever. With his hand on her thigh, if he could. She smelled like wild plum blossoms in the spring. He wanted to let loose her luxurious dark tresses and drown his face in them, but he had to move on.

He checked his watch again. It was five till twelve. His timing was perfect. Except for the mail for the schoolteacher, his route was completed for the day, and the widow was seated by his side. He'd speed by the schoolhouse, and none would be the wiser. But then he remembered the bundle of "Current Events" he had on the back seat. As he veered to the right to drop the papers in the oversized box by the gate, he spotted Reino Koski standing by the door, posed like a doorman at the Waldorf-Astoria, with Buster, Eldon's mixed breed dog, seated by his leg.

Reino gave no sign of recognition, but Charlie could feel Reino's eyes following him as he stepped on the gas. Charlie looked straight ahead, as if he had seen nothing on the sidelines. Buster, however, recognized the mail car, and turned his head to watch. The son of a bitch, Charlie said to himself, not sure whether he meant the idiot or the mongrel dog.

Mary Marks, worried and agitated, with Charlie at her heel, pushed open the door and rushed into the Skinnar house without ceremony. "Signe, Signe!" she called breathlessly. "I'm here." Getting no response, she turned to Charlie. "Where is Signe?"

Charlie shrugged. "Maybe in the bedroom."

She searched the three small rooms of the house as if looking for a hiding child. "Signe's not here," Mary said coldly. "I arrived too early. She told me to come in the afternoon when the children got home from school. Said she'd make them little meat pies. Where is she?"

Charlie, standing by the window keeping vigil, lest his wife return early, quipped indifferently, "Probably at her sister's."

"But you said she was here. Waiting for me."

Charlie smiled defiantly. "Do you see her?"

Mary turned around, opened the door and ran, but Charlie was fast. He grabbed her by the hand and dragged her back in the house, leaving the heel of her shoe entrenched in the ground at the root of a sleeping dandelion. He dropped Mary by the stove. "Nobody pulls tricks on Charlie Skinnar," he said, as he stood towering over her sprawled on the floor.

She took off her heeless shoe as she struggled to get up. "Please let me go home," she pleaded. "My children need me."

He resumed his watch at the window, with fingers clasped under his chin, and repeated, "Today is the day of your fitting. You don't want to disappoint Signe, your friend, your only friend."

Mary tried to reason with him. "But Signe is not here." In desperation she took the dresses on their hangers off the nail. "Look," she showed him the red and black dresses, "these are merely pinned. They have not even been basted. They can't be tried on. Signe wanted to work on these today before I arrived." Charlie wasn't listening. Mary put the hangers back on the nail and rushed for the door.

He grabbed her, and pulled her to him. "I want to look at you. Close. I never had a chance to see you close." He clutched her tightly, undid the bun at her slender neck and buried his face with her silky ebony hair as it came cascading down her shoulders. "Look at me."

She jerked away from him. "I don't want to look at you."

He pulled her back, angrily. "I know. I've known that since I first laid eyes on your carnal form. Why don't you like me? Don't you think I'm manly enough?" he asked, drawing her ever closer. "Or is your lover more virile?"

Mary was startled. "What lover?"

Charlie smiled as he looked down on her, his right eye vacillating, uneasily. "The one from Chicago. The one who writes those long letters S. W. A. K. Sealed with a kiss."

"What letters?"

"The letters you've been waiting for. Twice a week, as regular as clockwork, Tuesdays and Thursdays. Passionate epistles."

Stefan didn't forget me! Mary told herself, as she stood motionless, with her eyes on the door, considering Charlie's size and strength; and speculated were he to let go, could she outrun him, going through the woods. She couldn't take the road. He'd follow her with the car.

"Twice a week he'd pour his love and lust on paper and add to my load," Charlie continued.

"You've read them!"

"I've read his. I've read yours."

Mary began to cry. "It's against the law."

"The law doesn't know," Charlie responded smugly, and kissed her on the top of the head.

"Please let me go," she cried. "Think of my children."

"Not before you've done what you came for. What I brought you for."

"What's that?" she asked in a lifeless voice.

"To try on your dresses. What else?" Charlie released his captive. He crossed over to the nail where the dresses were hanging, pulled the red one off its hanger. "Here, put this on. I want to see you in it. I've been waiting to see you in red." He was about to hand her the dress when he changed his mind, and held it up to her. "Yes, it goes . . . it goes with you. It's your color. It's exciting. Go ahead put it on. Let me look at you in it."

Mary stared at the creature before her. Charlie no longer was the well groomed, clean-shaven rake who had seized her. A thick reddish brown stubble covered his face, giving his dark chocolate brown eyes a coppery red cast. His right eye had a menacing squint. He was perspiring heavily, and his body emanated a foul odor.

She was afraid. Her legs shook. Tears clouded her vision. What could she do? She would try to appease him. "Let me try on the white frock. The side seams are sewn."

His smile was taunting. "White for you?" Charlie shook his head. "You're no virgin." His moves now were calm and deliberate. He took the white dress and gave her the red. "Go in the bedroom if you wish," he said, with a jerk of his head. "It makes no difference now. Hurry. We don't have all day."

Charlie could hardly restrain himself from rushing in after her; but not here, not yet, he told himself — Signe could return early — and went back to the window to keep watch. He positioned himself where he could see Mary Marks in the mirror of the old dresser he'd bought last week from the secondhand store.

Mary carefully laid the red dress on Signe's bed and looked around for an avenue of escape. The bedroom had no outside door. There must be a way, she told herself. She slipped to the side window and attempted to open it, but it was painted shut. She tried the first of the two back windows. It wouldn't move. The second one opened, but it was backed by a screen. Mary looked around for something to cut the screen — Signe's dressmaking shears on the dresser! She carefully cut the top and one side and was about to make the final slash at the bottom when her hand went numb and the shears fell on the floor. Charlie, breathing hard, with his body pressed against hers, had hold of her wrist and was squeezing it. "Let go!" she screamed, her mouth so dry she could hardly form the words.

He lightened his hold. "I didn't send you in here to destroy the furnishings." He dropped her arm and threw the red dress at her. "Put this on as I instructed." He closed the window and hurried to the one in the kitchen.

Mary took another look at the inviting gap in the window screen and considered her options. "I won't wait all day," Charlie shouted, as he moved toward the kitchen door to block her escape, "or do you want me to come there to get you?" Mary struggled into the pinned-together dress.

She walked gingerly to the kitchen, removing the extraneous pins from the garment. Charlie crossed his arms over his chest and gazed at her, smiling, his wayward eye capering excitedly. "I've dreamt about this moment," he said as he grabbed her in his arms, "since first I laid eyes on you. Kiss me." He pressed his foul-smelling mouth against hers. She clamped her teeth and squeezed her lips tight.

A pin on the neckline of the dress pierced her, and she let a scream that would've awakened a hibernating bear. "The pins are sticking me!" she yelled.

Charlie loosened his hold — "Here, let me help you" — and pulled out a pin. In the same action, he fondled her breast. She reached up and struck him on the face with her fist. The two pins she held in her fingers pierced his cheek, and blood oozed out. Charlie became angry. They struggled. Mary, fighting a man twice her size, decided to use the only weapon available, the pins. She whacked his cheeks, neck, and Adam's apple with her pin enforced fist. Charlie covered his bleeding face, stood and stared at her. Then smiled, a victor's smirk. "I know what'll fix you!" He grabbed Mary's arm, twisted it, and pulled her into the bedroom to retrieve her skirt and sweater.

About to stumble over Mary's shoes in the kitchen, he picked them up and dragged Mary out of the house.

Reino heard the teacher jingle the noon bell. The door from the schoolroom to the porch opened and the commotion started full speed. Forty-three kindergarten through eight, rushed to grab their lunch containers — lard pails, molasses pails, imitation grape jelly pails and a real honest-to-goodness "boughten" lunch bucket or two. Next, the porch door hit the side of the building with the force of a minor quake, energy supplied by a couple of upper grade bruisers. It was fresh air and freedom from books for thirty minutes.

Reino expected Eldon to be coming out last, with the girls and small kids. But Eldon had slipped out unnoticed by his pal. He was already across the road, headed for the woods before Reino spotted him. Reino was about to yell, "Wait for me," when he remembered that nobody should know about Eldon's leaving the school grounds at lunch. He ran to catch up with his friend.

With only the noonday sun peeking between the branches of the trees, Mary Marks' cowless pasture was as peaceful and serene as the Elysian fields. The oak, maple, birch and box elder all glowed in its own shade of gold or vermillion. Eldon ran in and out between the trees, playing joyfully, waiting for Reino to catch him. He kicked a piece of metal, one of Charlie's traps, and stopped to look down. Reino caught up and hit him with a loud slap. They laughed.

Eldon turned around and faced his friend. "Can I

tell you something, Reino?"

"Shoot."

"When you're playing tag, you aren't supposed to hit the other person so hard. Just a tap on the shoulder. Like now, you whacked me so my heart fell into my stomach."

"Eldon, that's not your heart. That's your lung."

"The heart is on the left side," Eldon explained, pointing to his own small chest. "The lung is on the right."

"Okay. Okay. But I caught you."

"Only because I had to stop. To check the trap." Eldon bent down and picked up the closed trap. "Look! The trap's shut and no skunk."

Reino shook his head. "Your father sure doesn't know how to set traps."

Eldon quickly came to his father's defense. "But he knows how to do everything else."

"You sure like your old man, don't you?"

"Yaa. He's real smart, you know. He can read anything. Even law. He's a judge, you know."

"Just a Justice of the Peace."

Eldon gazed wide-eyed at his friend. "Well, Justice of the Peace is law," and took out his penknife to whittle a branch on which to attach the trap. "I wish I had an ax. Papa always has an ax with him."

"I know."

"If there's a storm and a tree falls on the road, he has to chop it up. The mail has to get through."

"But you can't bring an ax to school." Reino thought about the matter for a moment and added, "Unless you have to split wood or make kindling for the teacher."

Eldon's mind was still on his father. "Besides, Papa is the tallest man around here."

"No, he isn't."

Eldon got up, with his hands on his hips, stood before his friend, "What do you mean 'he isn't?'"

"Because he isn't the tallest. There are many as tall as he." Reino stood up straight and grinned. "Look at me."

Eldon stared at Reino in amazement. He had never noticed how large a man his friend was. Eldon crouched down on the ground and continued his task, and in a small voice said, "But none taller," and began to reset the trap. "Did you bring the bait?"

"Sure did," Reino answered happily. He dug into the pocket of his striped overalls, pulled out a piece of decomposed pork liver and handed it to Eldon.

"Pee-uuu. It stinks." Eldon was almost sorry he'd been so eager.

Reino smiled. "That's how skunks like it."

Eldon adjusted the bait in the trap, and glanced at Reino who was poking holes in the soft earth with his index finger. "Did you like your father?"

"He's dead . . . He wasn't very tall . . . He just came to here," Reino pointed to his own armpit, "to my mother. My mother was tall." His eyes lit with love and pride at the recollection. "She was as tall as your father."

"Really?"

"And pretty."

Eldon sat next to his friend, on a pile of leaves. "How pretty?"

"As pretty as Signe and Mrs. Marks."

"Really?" Eldon asked, with wonder. "But she's dead."

"Yaa, she's dead." Reino dropped down on the leaves and stared at the sun. "Been dead for a long time."

"Since you were a little boy?"

"Forever."

Reino's mind was on the past, but Eldon's was on the future. "You know what?"

"No, what?"

"I'm going to take care of my father and my mother when they get old."

"That's nice."

"My father will be old soon."

"Nah. He isn't much older than I."

"That's old. He has some gray hairs already." Eldon looked at Reino for grizzled strands, but Reino's head was covered by his grimy blue and white striped denim cap. "Maybe you could move to our house," Eldon mused, "because you will be old, too."

"That would be nice." Reino ambled up. "We'd better get going or you'll be late for school and the teacher will ask where you've been."

Eldon liked the tranquility of the woods. He would often wander off by himself, just to be alone. "Don't worry. I can run fast."

"Did you eat your lunch?"

"Nah, it's just a fried egg—" Eldon stopped and listened. "Hey, did you hear that?"

"No, what?"

"A scream. Like a lady's scream."

"I don't hear anything. Maybe you heard a bird."

Eldon covered his mouth and listened. "There. Did you hear that?"

Reino shook his head. "What direction did it come from?"

"Over there. Shhh."

"Where?" Reino whispered.

"North. Toward Mrs. Marks' house."

As they got closer to her house, the cries became clear. Then muffled. Reino began to tremble. "We shouldn't be here." He grabbed Eldon by the shirt. "Let's make a run for it."

"We can't. What if Mattson's bull got through the fence? What if the bull got into Mrs. Marks' garden?" Eldon looked around, trying to figure what might have happened and decide his course of action. "We can't just run and not do anything."

Reino was shaking. "I want to go home."

"Are you going to have fits? If you're going to have fits, I'm going to leave you."

"Please don't leave me!"

"Then follow me. We'll make a dash for Mrs. Marks' house." Eldon started running, hopping over gopher mounds, and dodging brambles and branches.

Reino at his heels, tugged at Eldon's shirt. "What if it's the bull? What can we do?"

"Climb a tree."

Reino drew back. "I can't climb a tree. I never could climb a tree. I'll be gored to death."

"Would you let Mrs. Marks die because you're afraid of an old bull?"

"Do you think it was her screaming?" Reino asked

as he resumed his running.

Eldon didn't take time to answer. He continued racing between trees and over boulders until his right foot hit a rock and he flew into the air and on his belly. He groaned. Bubbles of tears filled his eyes. The pain was worse than any he had ever had. He felt only death could give him relief.

Reino hurried to him. "What happened?"

Eldon sat up and took off his ragged tennis shoe. "I hit that rock over there. I think I broke my big toe." He removed his sock. Blood was oozing from underneath the nail. "It hurts like heck."

Reino put his hand over Eldon's foot. "Try wiggling the toe."

Eldon managed to curl the toe a bit downward. "Auoooo."

"Not broken!" Reino announced. "Wouldn't move if it were broken."

Eldon got up and stood on his foot and the top half of the nail popped off. He stared at the half naked toe with surprise and relief.

"That's good," Reino commented as he watched Eldon's reaction. "Relieves the pressure. Doesn't it?"

"Guess so."

"Put on your sock and shoe and get on my back. We have to hurry."

"Nah, I'm too heavy."

"No heavier than a spring rabbit." Reino bent down and Eldon got on. It was not an easy ride. Reino was clumsy as a bear on two feet and his gait was uneven; but they moved forward at a steady pace until Reino's foot hit a gopher mound and he fell on his face, throwing Eldon headlong in the thicket.

"Look. My best overalls are ruined," Reino griped.

"Hey, you could've killed me," Eldon retorted, as he pulled himself into a sitting position and wiped the dirt and twigs off his face. "Could have broken my neck."

Reino stared at Eldon and grumbled, "What about me? You think my neck's made of iron?" They had reached a thicket of willow. Reino looked around. "How far are we from Mrs. Marks' house?"

"Not far." Eldon stood up to survey the area. "Hey, look."

Reino lumbered to his feet. "Why, that's the mail car!"

"What's it doing in Mrs. Marks' woods? Can you see him?"

"Maybe he's setting traps. Let's move closer and get a good look."

"I don't want to get too close." Eldon threw himself on the ground through the bushes. "Oh! Oh!"

"What's the matter?"

"Oh, my God! I never saw anything bad like this."

"Can you see his face?"

Eldon shook his head.

Reino got on his haunches to look. "I can't make out his face, but it's Charlie. This is terrible. Terrible. He's ruining her red dress. Her brand new dress." Reino scrambled up. "I'm going to get him."

Eldon grabbed him by the ankles and hung on.

"Let me go. I'm going to kill 'im."

"He'll kill you first. He's got the ax."

Reino looked down his wet pants and began to

blubber uncontrollably.

"Shhh! Reino, don't cry. He'll hear us."

"I'm going to get Ed and tell him to bring his Winchester."

"You can't. He'll hear you. He's got ears like a deer and he can run just as fast. He'll get you and me, both." Eldon gasped at what he was witnessing. Then with one hand over his mouth, he pressed it with the other to keep from crying out.

Crouching beside the boy, Reino gently placed his hands over Eldon's eyes. Finally, a "plop", followed shortly by a dull thud. Eldon's vomit showered Reino's overalls.

Reino watched Charlie jump into his car and flee, leaving Mary Marks' remains in the deserted pasture. Reino's face was gray and his body shook violently. "First he did that to her, then hit her on the head with the shovel and then he chopped off her head, her beautiful head." He wiped the vomit off his pants with freshly fallen leaves and pulled Eldon to his feet, "Come."

Mary's head was only an ax-cut distance from her body. Her face was badly scratched and her hair was clotted with blood. The right side of her head showed the brunt of a heavy blow. The eye was closed, but the left one was open. Reino gently pulled the lid down. "May you rest in peace."

Her arms were scraped, and her stockings torn. A shoe covered one foot and a heelless shoe lay a yard away. "He took her ring!" Reino shrieked as he picked up her lifeless hand and the ring finger, broken at the joint, fell limply in the other direction. "Charlie

Skinnar will pay for this."

"Will he go to prison?" Eldon asked. "To Still-water?"

"You kill somebody, you pay for it. That's the law." Reino discreetly tucked the bloodied panties under the dead woman's skirt.

"Maybe he didn't mean to kill her," Eldon said hopefully.

"Maybe he did and maybe he didn't. We saw him do it."

"Are you going to tell the constable?"

"We have to act fast," Reino responded. "Charlie will be back." Reino kneeled down by Mary's severed head, took his red handkerchief, spat on it and wiped the blood off Mary's face. "Charlie chopped off your head, your beautiful head, and ruined your new red dress," he sobbed, "but Charlie will pay."

Elsie had followed Eldon into the school porch at noon. Instead of picking up his lunch bucket, he went straight out the door and through the school gate into the woods. She motioned to Elma, who was not far behind, and whispered, "Eldon's gone into the forest, and there goes Reino after him."

"I bet they're going to check Papa's traps," Elma answered.

"Shall we tell Violet?"

"No, he'll come back before the bell rings."

After lunch, when the teacher went to pull the rope, Elma panicked and rushed to tell Violet where Eldon had gone. "He still isn't back and the teacher will wonder what happened to him."

"Don't say anything," Violet instructed her sisters.

"What if the teacher asks us?" Elsie said.

"You don't know."

Elma was shocked. "You want us to lie?"

"Or Eldon will get into trouble."

Miss Keksi closed the door to the porch, glanced around to see if everyone who'd been in school in the forenoon was present. She promptly noticed Eldon missing and asked Hugo, "Where's Eldon?"

"I don't know."

Violet raised her hand. "Miss Keksi, Eldon's outside. He's not feeling well."

Elma and Elsie buried their faces in a book, hoping they would not be called on to testify.

"I'm sorry to hear that. Wouldn't he rather come inside?"

"No, Miss Keksi, he wants to be in the fresh air."

"Where in fresh air?" Benny Lahti asked. "I didn't see him nowheres all noon hour."

Violet blushed and said, "The boy's room," meaning the two-holed privy at the bottom of the hill.

"I just went to toilet and there was nobody there," Art Kivi informed the teacher.

Miss Keksi, eager to go on to other subjects, said, "Eldon will come in when he's ready. Time for fourth grade spelling."

All three of Eldon's sisters kept their eyes on the clock on the wall. It was one thirty but no sign of Eldon. Two o'clock, still no Eldon. At five minutes of three, the door opened and Eldon walked in and went to his seat. He laid his head on the desk and wept. The stench of the stale vomit on his clothes proved that

Violet had been telling the truth. Eldon was sick.

"Would you like someone to take you home," the teacher asked.

Eldon shook his head.

Chapter XXV

IT WAS WAY AFTER two in the afternoon when Signe finally left her sister's house. She had planned to leave promptly at one, but after cleaning the kitchen, doing the weekly wash and hanging it on the line, Gertrude handed her two hangers with dresses and said, "I need them altered since I'm getting so skinny. Take them with you." Before any alterations could be made, the dresses had to be fitted, and that took time. Once out the door, Signe walked as fast as her legs would move.

Now, on the long nail next to Signe's sewing machine were four garments on hangers: a white dress, a black dress, and two print dresses. Gertrude liked prints. "Flowers on the cloth," she said, made her feel young. In a hurry to make up for lost time, Signe didn't notice the red dress missing.

Mrs. Marks was coming for a fitting when her children got out of school. Signe had promised to make the kiddies little meat pies—a total of seven pies, including those for her own children. Knowing how much time it takes to make the crust, chop the meat, onions and potatoes, Signe set to work at once.

She was cutting the lard into the flour when Reino walked in, his clothing disheveled and dusty. He had lost his striped denim cap, and his hair was heavy with perspiration. Pine needles and pieces of twigs clung to his old blue chambray shirt. Shaking and trembling, with one shoe partially on and the other in his hand, he hobbled to the closest chair, stared into space, and said, "May God have mercy," in English.

Signe grabbed a towel hanging by the stove to wipe her hands and rushed to him. "My Lord, what happened?" His exclamation in English, since they normally spoke Finnish, stunned her. She brushed the hair from his eyes with her hand. "Your face is the color of skimmed milk. Did you see a ghost?"

Reino didn't answer. He stared vacantly into the distance.

"I know!" Signe speculated, nervously, "You were in Mrs. Marks' pasture, weren't you? Resetting Charlie's traps. How many times have I told you that you'll be killed by Joel Mattson's Jersey bull if you keep going there? A barbed wire fence means nothing to an animal like that. You can talk to a Holstein bull, but reasoning with a Jersey bull is like looking into the eye of a tornado and expecting it to calm down." Signe was breathless from talking. She paused and looked at Reino. "You weren't hurt, were you?"

"N-no." He began to cry. His body shook painfully.

"Take that shoe off," she ordered, "and step outside. I have to sweep you off."

Reino removed the shoe, leaving his big toe exposed naked to the world, and got up from the chair. His nose was dripping. He reached to his back pocket for his handkerchief; then remembered he'd discarded it after wiping the dead woman's face. He gave his nose a long swipe with the sleeve of his denim jacket and went outside.

Signe grabbed the broom standing by the kitchen stove and started to sweep. "Turn around so I can get the other side of you. Lying on the ground! Lucky thing the weather's still warm, or you could have caught pneumonia. Come in, sit by the table and put your shoes on. I'll fix you a cup of coffee."

Reino followed Signe back into the house, took his place at the table and started to put on his stockings.

Signe watched him as he tried to cover the big toe with the torn sock. "Wait one minute," she said. "I'll get you some clean stockings." She went to her bedroom, returned with a pair and handed them to him.

"These Charlie's?"

"Of course. Who else in this house would wear men's socks?"

"I don't want them." He shoved the hose back at her and slipped the shoes on his bare feet and the old socks in his pocket.

Signe had set the table and was slicing the bread when she paused and asked, "Where's Eldon?"

"School."

Her chest heaved with relief. "For a moment I thought he might have been with you in the pasture. You could have been killed, the two of you."

At that Reino began to cry. He laid his head on the table and sobbed.

Signe went to him and messaged his spine like a loving mother. "Now, now, Reino, there's nothing so bad that a good cup of coffee and a sandwich won't fix, but first we have to clean you up a little." She went to the washbasin, poured a dipperful of water into the basin, soaked the end of a towel and wiped his face with it. He held out his hands, palms up. She gave them a light going-over. "Now, eat," she said. "Eat plenty. A big man like you needs lots of nourishment. Did your doctor ever tell you that?"

Reino laid two large slices of bread on the blue plaid tablecloth instead of using the plate Signe had provided, and looked around.

"What are you looking for?"

"You forgot the butter. I always put butter on my bread. I don't eat bread without butter."

Signe got the plate butter dish from the cupboard and gave it to him. "Would you like mustard?"

"No, I don't like mustard. I don't like the color." Reino layered his sandwich with butter, cheese, thuringer and sliced dill pickle. He was about to add hunks of salted herring, but after deciding it would make the sandwich too bulky, he stuffed the fish in his pocket.

"Mrs. Marks is coming for a fitting this afternoon after the youngsters get out of school," Signe said, as she started to roll out the pie crust. "I'm making three new dresses for her."

At the mention of Mary Marks, Reino froze, dropped his sandwich on the plate and began to mumble "May God have mercy" as if hypnotized.

She looked at him and tried to decide what had caused Reino's unusual behavior. "You don't need to tell me; but you were out there in the woods and the convulsions came, didn't they? You could've died. If you had a fit, that means you forgot to take your medicine. I know it's hard to remember to do so, especially when you live alone and there's no one to remind you."

Signe wasn't one to leave a stone unturned if she was able to move it. "I tell you what, Reino. When you take off your shoes at night, stick the medicine bottle in your shoe like this." She took off her run-down oxford, grabbed the saltshaker from the table, and put it in the shoe. "So when you wake up in the morning, you'll remember to take your medicine. That way you won't forget and you won't have convulsions." She looked at him to see if he understood, but he seemed to be in another galaxy.

"Will you remember?"

"Y-yes," Reino whimpered as he got off his chair.

"You're just tired," Signe said, and patted him on the back. "You've had a hard day. Go home and take a nap. You'll feel like a new person."

Reino gave his nose a quick brush with his sleeve and went to the door. About to turn the knob he remembered something. He walked to the table, took the salted herring out of his pocket and put it back on the plate.

"Aren't you hungry?" Signe asked.

He shook his head and left.

Three thirty, she told herself after glancing at the clock on the lamp stand. I have to hurry. She stoked the fire and added more wood in the stove. She chopped the onions and was slicing the potatoes when it occurred to her that she was preparing pies for Janie and Robert, but had mentioned nothing to Mary about her dinner. Signe had gotten some nice pork chops from the Co-op for the three adults. How stupid of me, she told herself, as she went to the phone and cranked. No answer. Mary must be in the garden, she concluded.

After putting the pies in the oven, Signe checked the time again. Three minutes of four, she said to herself. The children get out of school at four ten. Mary should be in by now. She cranked Mary's ring. No answer. Signe then called the operator. "Central? I was trying to get Mary Marks. Is it two longs and a short or two shorts and a long? Hmmm. That's what I dialed. T'enks." She tried again. There was no answer. Signe hung up and stood by the telephone with the palms of her hands together and her fingertips rubbing her chin, puzzled.

The phone rang. Signe was startled. The caller was Hilda Mattson. "You scared the daylights out of me," Signe said when she answered. "I thought the phone had come to life. I just tried to reach Mary Marks, but she didn't answer. Then my phone rang. What's new with you, Hilda?"

"New?" Hilda laughed. "Nothing's new with me. Nothing new in Wolf Creek, as far back as I can remember. I take that back. Nothing new since Charlie Skinnar married Signe Maki. Now that made news." Hilda laughed again. It seemed to do her heart good to remember Charlie in a gnarled way. "I just rang to see if Eldon could help my boys pick potatoes on Saturday."

"Sure, what time?"

"Eight o'clock. I'll have Gust pick him up."

As Signe was about to end the conversation, her eyes hit the dress rack. She gave a gasp.

Hilda heard. "Signe, you okay?"

"I'm all right, Hilda, but I just noticed something. Her red dress is gone! Mary Marks' red dress is gone. It's not hanging with her black dress and white dress."

Chapter XXVI

SIGNE STARED AT THE GARMENTS hanging behind the ironing board in the kitchen next to her sewing machine. The red dress was not there. Could she by mistake have hung it in her own bedroom, next to her own clothes? She hurried to look. What she saw was a slashed window screen and her best shears on the floor. A thief!

She was about to go to the phone to ring Hilda Mattson, but thought the better of it. The party line would soon buzz with the news of a thief going around. Signe went back to the window. It was locked. If the thief went out by the window, how could he lock it? she asked herself. Signe searched for further evidence of crime, but nothing seemed missing except Mary Marks' red dress. It must have been Mary. She decided to finish the dress herself. But why didn't she call or leave a note? And why did she cut the screen?

The phone rang. It was Hilda. "Did Charlie say anything about the widow?"

"Charlie's not home yet. Why do you ask?"

"I just thought he might have seen her."

"As I told you earlier," Signe responded, "she's coming to my place with her children when school lets out. They should be here any minute."

"But she wasn't at home when her children stopped by to pick her up; so they went back to school and the teacher took them home with her. Signe, where do you think Mary went?"

"My mind is blank."

"How's Eldon feeling?"

"He always feels good. He's a healthy boy. Why do you ask?"

"He was sick in school and cried all afternoon—"

"The children are here now. I have to hang up," Signe said, cutting Hilda off. She was relieved to have an excuse to terminate the conversation. There were too many unanswered questions. She hurried to her bedroom and pulled down the shades so the children wouldn't see the torn screen.

"Where's Eldon?" Signe asked Violet when the children walked in.

"He went to pump water for the cows," Violet replied, and followed her sisters into their room.

"In his school clothes?"

"Yaa. He's a real farmer," Hugo volunteered as he set Eldon's lunch pail on the wood box. "He worries about the animals."

"How was school today?" Signe asked, hoping to

get some unsolicited information.

"I did well on my spelling test except I spelled huckleberry with an 'o'."

"English is a difficult language to learn," Signe said. "Nothing is written the way it sounds. You have to memorize every word."

After changing clothes, Violet started to set the table for dinner. She was quiet, but that was not unusual. "Anything new in school?" her mother asked. Violet shook her head.

"Let's have some music," Hugo, a western music buff, said as he turned on the radio. "I like to hear the cowboys sing."

"WDAY," the announcer trumpeted, "Yankton, South Dakota. We will now have a report—"

"Nuts," Hugo murmured and clicked it off.

Signe was uneasy. "I wonder what's keeping your father."

"The traps," Hugo replied. "He spends most of his day going from one set of traps to another. I don't think he knows what he's doing."

"Don't say that."

"It's the truth. Guess I'd better go and haul in the wood." He put on his coat and left.

The party line had been ringing constantly since late afternoon, but the calls were for other people. Signe didn't listen in.

Charlie came in, his face scratched up and swollen. He dropped his lunch bucket on the wood box and plunked himself in the rocking chair. "I'm beat."

Signe hurried to examine his face. She took off his hat. "What happened—another car accident?"

"A raccoon."

"Raccoon? How could it reach your face?"

"It was caught in my trap. I slipped and fell. And it got even with me."

"It'll bring you a pretty penny."

"He got away."

"Oh." Signe went to the stove, got a dipperful of hot water from the tank, poured it over the end of a towel and wiped Charlie's face. Then she got a bottle of rubbing alcohol and swabbed him down from forehead to shirtline.

Charlie hollered like a bull being castrated.

"Stop that," Signe ordered.

"It hurts."

"Would hurt worse if blood poisoning set in. Who knows what bacilli that raccoon had on its claws. Did it bite you?"

"Tried to."

Signe put the bottle and towel away. "You know how I feel about your trapping. I can't say anything more."

Violet had in no way acknowledged her father's presence. After setting the table and cutting the bread, she quietly took her coat and head scarf from the nail behind the stove, grabbed two milking pails and went out the door.

Charlie had been watching his daughter. "She's a quiet one," he remarked.

"Always was," Signe agreed. "When Violet speaks, she has something to say."

"Takes after her mother."

Signe didn't hear the compliment. Her mind was

on the perplexing events of the day. She didn't want to bring up the torn window screen yet, but had to know why Mary Marks didn't keep her fitting appointment. "Did you happen to see Mrs. Marks when you delivered the mail?"

"N-o," Charlie stammered, "I had this letter for her. I knew she had been waiting for it. I left the mail car, went to her door and knocked. No answer."

"So what did you do with the letter?"

"I wrote, 'Moved. Return to sender' and will take it back to the post office in the morning."

"Moved! How do you know she's moved?"

"That's the first thing that came to my mind."

"Her children are still here." Signe waited for Charlie's answer. Since none came, she asked, "You didn't, by any chance, see Mrs. Marks on the road walking this way?"

Charlie bristled. "I said, I hadn't seen her."

"Don't holler. I don't want the girls to hear."

The phone rang, three shorts, a long and a short. "That's for us," Signe said, as she hurried to answer.

"Let it ring," Charlie shouted.

"Shhh. I can't. If I don't answer, whoever is on the line will think something's wrong. Everybody knows we're home this time of day." She picked up the receiver.

The caller was Hilda Mattson. "Is Charlie home yet?"

"Yes."

"What did he say about the Marks widow?"

"He hadn't seen her."

"Something's crazy," Hilda said, and added, "I'll

call you in the morning."

"Who was that?" Charlie grumbled.

"Hilda."

"What did the snoop want to know?"

"She just asked if you'd seen Mary Marks."

Charlie was testy. He got up, took off his jacket and threw his cap toward the wood box. It landed on the floor. "What do people think? That I'm some kind of soothsayer?"

Signe tried to appease him. "You are a public servant and you see 'most everything that happens on your mail route. It's only natural for people to look up to you for answers."

Placated by Signe's flattering appraisal of his station in life, Charlie sat at the table and waited for coffee.

Signe reheated the meat pies she'd made and served them for dinner.

Eldon washed after chores and quietly went to his room without eating. Said he wasn't hungry.

"Girls," Charlie asked Elma and Elsie after he'd finished his dessert of bread pudding topped with wild plum sauce, "would you like to sing a few hymns with Papa?"

After Charlie had gone to bed, Signe saw Violet taking Eldon's supper to him.

Chapter XXVII

ELDON TRIED TO CONCENTRATE on his arithmetic, but his stomach growled so loudly that Amy Niemi giggled and covered her head with a book. He glanced at the clock on the wall. Two minutes until twelve. He was hungry but the thought of food repulsed him. He'd barely had anything but coffee since the murder. Eldon had given Hugo the potpie that Violet brought him last night.

George Koski stood facing the teacher in front of the room reading aloud *The Legend of Sleepy Hollow.*

"Put some feeling into your words," Miss Keksi instructed.

"I don't got none," George replied.

"You 'don't have any,'" she corrected.

George looked up and smiled at his mentor. "You noticed it, too?"

The commotion of closing books and clearing throats indicated to Miss Keksi that noon had arrived. She looked up at the clock and announced "dismissed" to the eighth-grade reading class, which signaled freedom for the whole school. George threw the book on his desk on his way out to the woodshed for a sandwich and a smoke.

Still seated at his desk, Eldon caught his brother's eye and nudged his head toward the porch, but Hugo was too busy explaining an arithmetic problem to Mayme Linden to notice. Eldon got up, followed the girls out the door and picked up his and Hugo's lunch buckets from the shelf in the porch. He sat on the steps and waited. With no sign of Hugo, Eldon finally opened his pail and looked at the sandwiches his mother had so carefully prepared, wrapped in wax paper. He opened the first one, roast pork with butter and mustard. Roast pork, which used to be his favorite, now left him cold. The imitation grape jelly sandwich underneath looked more appetizing. He was about to bite into it when a loud whistle from behind the gate caught his attention. It was Reino Koski.

Eldon glanced around to see if anyone had gotten sight of his visitor. The older boys were in the woodshed and the rest of the kids were scattered around the schoolyard. No one else had noticed Reino. Eldon put his sandwich back in the lunch box and went to the gate. "You shouldn't be here."

"I know."

"You can only come to visit when we have classes. This is not the right time."

"But I had to see you."

"What do you want?" Eldon asked.

"I have to speak to you about what happened yesterday."

"Not here."

"I know. " Reino looked around. "Meet me behind the woodshed on the other side of the fence. On Nylund's property."

"I'm not supposed to leave the schoolyard."

"It's important."

"Hurry, go!"

Reino plodded around the fence to Nylund's pasture. Eldon ran past the woodshed, careful not to disturb the smokers inside, and jumped over the fence to join him. "Are you going to tell on him?" he asked Reino.

"Killing is a sin."

"I know, but are you going to tell on him?"

"Murder is against the law."

"If you tell on him, he'll have to go to prison. For life!"

"It says in the Bible, 'Thou shalt not kill.'"

Eldon nodded. "What about my mother?"

"She didn't do wrong."

"I know. But how will she get along?"

"She'll get along just fine." Reino gave a brief promising smile. "I'll help her. I'm strong."

"But I'll be an orphan. Think of that."

"No, just the son of a convict."

"I would never see him."

"You could visit him. Stillwater isn't that far away. No farther than Minneapolis."

"Think of Elma and Elsie. They'd be so sad."

Reino stared at Eldon. "What about the Marks kids? Don't you think they're sad? Now they don't have a father or a mother."

Eldon listened and nodded sadly. Then an idea came to him. "Maybe nobody will ask you! They don't know that we were there."

"Wouldn't it be right to volunteer?"

"Then I should volunteer, too. But I couldn't tell on my own father."

Reino scraped the leaves underfoot with the toe of his shoe as he pondered the question. "You have to be a good citizen."

"My mother would know the right thing to do."

"But you can't ask her!"

Eldon shook his head. "She must never know. I have to go eat now. Mother will feel bad if I bring both of my sandwiches back home tonight."

Reino turned to leave. "We'll see what happens. Maybe there won't be an inquest."

"Really!"

The morning had been a trying one for Signe. Charlie had left before dawn. "Why are you leaving so early?" she asked him. He'd grumbled about having to spend so much time sorting the mail at the post office before starting on his route. The kids had been out of sorts and dawdling in getting ready for school. Violet, usually optimistic, looked like the caretaker for the world. Eldon hadn't spoken to anyone. He'd just gone to the barn, acting as if he had cut his connections with everyone except the cows. Now Signe was home alone, seated at her sewing machine, uneasily trying to sort out in her mind recent happenings. She laid down Gertrude's dress that she was altering, and went outside to the back of her bedroom. The screen she'd thought ripped was whole. For a few seconds Signe questioned her own sanity, but decided to examine the other windows. She walked around to the children's room. The screen was missing. Someone had removed it to replace the shredded one in her room.

Signe decided to make herself a bowl of dumpling soup. That is what her mother used to make for her when Signe was distressed. "Hot milk warms and soothes the troubled soul," she would say.

As she adjusted the curtain on the kitchen window, Signe saw Charlie in the mail car pass by. She looked at the clock. Lunch hour at school was about to end, and the children would be in the classroom. All was clear for what she had made up her mind to do. She was going to look for her friend, Mary Marks. Mary, a city girl, always locked her house, but Signe was determined to climb through a window to break in, if necessary. If she didn't find Mary, she'd go to the school to have a talk with the teacher about finding a temporary home for the Marks children. Miss Keksi, renting a single room with kitchen privileges didn't have the facilities to take care of two school age youngsters.

Signe put on her best oxfords and a heavy sweater and headed down the road. It was a pleasant autumn day. The air was still nippy from last night's frost, but would warm up by midafternoon. She noticed some cattails in the ditch by the road and reminded herself to pick some on the way home.

She knocked on Mary's door. There was no answer. Signe turned the knob and to her great surprise, the door opened. She paused. Mary is either in the house or left in a hurry, Signe told herself. She walked in. Her question was answered. By the kitchen table stood the ironing board with Janie's partially ironed school dress and a flatiron standing on its end. A wicker basket filled with starched, dampened linens sat on the floor close by. Signe touched the iron. It was stone cold. If she was gone, Mary had left unexpectedly.

Signe called Mary's name, and searched the small house for any possible clues as to where she might be. In the bedroom was a small dresser. She opened the top drawer. Mary's handbag was there, evidently as she had placed it. Signe took the purse into the kitchen, sat by the table and examined its contents. If I should disappear, she told herself, Mary would do the same for me. Signe found two letters—one from a Sophie Marks in Duluth and the other from a Stefan Harris, postmarked Chicago, Ill. She read both. Sophie evidently was the sister of Mary's late husband and Stefan, the man Mary was expecting to visit in September. Stefan's letter was postmarked in June and Signe couldn't find any later communications. She copied both addresses, slipped them in the pocket of her sweater and returned the purse to the dresser drawer.

Since there was nothing more she could examine in the house, Signe checked the barn, granary and the outhouse for clues, constantly calling Mary's name.

Since Mary had no cattle, Signe didn't feel the need to explore the pasture.

She had passed Mary's mailbox and was on her way to the school when she remembered the old well and decided to turn back. The pump was sitting on top of the heavy planks as it had been for years. Nothing had been disturbed.

The children were just going out for afternoon recess when Signe arrived. They greeted her excitedly. Miss Keksi was glad to see her. "I had planned to come visit you this evening," she said. "I didn't feel I should speak over the party line."

"I understand," Signe replied.

"The Marks children were fairly happy and content at my place last night," Miss Keksi continued. "Janie thinks their mother will return in a day or two, but Robert, being older, is becoming apprehensive. Since the children have no relatives in the area, I don't know whom to call. At the Moorhead Normal School, we were taught to get the names of relatives of the children to contact in case of emergency. I did exactly that when I taught in town, but here I felt no necessity for it since everyone knows each other and many are related."

"For my own satisfaction," Signe told the teacher, "I went to Mrs. Marks' house on my way here. I went through her pocketbook and found the name Sophie Marks—evidently an aunt of the children. I copied her address. I hope it will help you."

Miss Keksi thanked Signe. "It takes a great weight off my mind."

Signe then brought up Eldon's reported illness in school the day before.

"Just an upset stomach," the teacher assured her. "Nothing to be concerned about."

"But Eldon never gets sick."

"Probably a touch of stomach flu," Miss Keksi said. "Jennie Kangas was ill the day before. Eldon's growing fast. His resistance is low. Today he seems to be his old self. Almost."

Signe wasn't satisfied with the teacher's explanation. "I thought it might have been the egg sandwich I put in his lunch—"

Miss Keksi interrupted her, "Believe me, you have nothing to worry about," and got up to ring the bell. "I hope you'll stay the rest of the afternoon. The children like to have visitors. They do their best then."

The clanging bell brought the students in. Hugo, Elma and Elsie were delighted that their mother had stayed to hear them sing. Violet showed her the maps she was coloring. Eldon seemed unusually somber. Signe was proud of her smart, studious children and now felt guilty that she couldn't keep her mind on what they were doing. Mary's face kept reappearing before her eyes.

"Did you see Mrs. Marks?" Signe asked Charlie that evening when the children went outside to look at the live rabbit Buster had brought home.

"No, I haven't seen Mrs. Marks. Was I supposed to?"

"You know I was expecting her for a fitting yesterday afternoon."

"I didn't know—if I knew, I forgot. She didn't show up?"

"Did you see her on the road?"

"No, I didn't see her on the road."

"Did you deliver her mail?"

"Of course I delivered her mail, but all she got was a catalog."

Signe bristled. "Yesterday?"

"Yes, yesterday!" Charlie hollered. "That's the day we're talking about, isn't it?"

"Last night you told me she got a letter in yesterday's mail and you were returning it to the sender."

"So I returned it to the post office. What was I supposed to do—carry it in my pocket until she got back from wherever she's gone?"

"You didn't see her around the house?"

"I didn't look around the house. Why should I?"

"Mary Marks is missing."

"Probably ran away with some lover," Charlie said, laughing.

"She wouldn't leave her children."

Charlie shrugged. "Give me a cup of coffee. Haven't had any all day. And you'd better make my sandwiches tonight. I have to leave early in the morning. Days are getting short."

"Is anyone looking for her?" Signe asked as she set the coffee cup before him. "She might be ill."

"She has a telephone. She could call for help. You haven't gotten a ring, have you?"

"I mean she might have started for help and fallen by the wayside. Something should be done." Signe did not want to divulge the fact that she had searched

Mary's house and outbuildings. It wouldn't set well with the menfolk.

Charlie shrugged again. "If she doesn't show up in the next few days, I'll organize a search party. Now, get my supper ready. I have a church meeting tonight." He drank his coffee. Then got up from the table, poured hot water into the washbasin and started to shave.

The party line had been busy last evening and all day today, but no one had called Signe since Hilda rang her last night.

Signe told herself maybe she was giving undue significance to Mary Marks' disappearance, but her trip to Mary's house had reinforced her concerns. Signe realized that she had been acquainted with her neighbor for only a few months and really didn't know Mary; but Signe took pride in the fact that her first impression was always right. And her perception of Mary was that she was a loving, caring mother, an honest and forthright person, not given to impetuous decisions or actions. Something must have forced Mary to go away and she'd either come back or have someone come for her children. There, also, was the matter of the missing red dress—who could have come into Signe's house and taken it? Why only the red dress and not the black and white? Maybe Mary feared someone and was in hiding. Signe had not forgotten when Mary told her she had dreamt she was murdered. That was Signe's first thought when Mary failed to come for her fitting yesterday. God forbid! Signe said to herself.

Sunday morning when Signe called Eldon to breakfast, he refused food, adding that he was too sick to go to church.

"What's wrong with the kid?" Charlie barked, with his mouth full of pancake and strawberry jam.

"I don't know, Mr. Billy Goat," Signe snapped back.

Charlie shook his head as if shaking beetles out of his ears. "What did you call me?"

"I called you 'Billy Goat.' I can think of lot more descriptive names if you ever again call any one of my children 'kid.' Signe was short-tempered with Charlie. She felt he'd turned into a laggard, and she hated idlers. She and her children worked hard, but could see no improvement in their lifestyle. The additions to the house that Charlie had crowed about had turned into fluffy clouds that were no longer on the horizon.

After milking, Violet came in and said, "Mother, I don't feel well. I can't go to church."

Charlie opened his mouth to speak, but gave the matter some thought and closed it.

"Don't you want any pancakes?" Signe asked Violet. "I have a stack all made."

"I'll rest for awhile. Maybe I'll feel like eating later."

Hugo came in with an armload of wood, and piled it neatly in the wood box. "I think I'd better stay home and be the doctor."

Charlie cleared his throat to express an opinion, but changed his mind.

Hugo, sensing the climate not favorable to sudden

changes in ritual said, "Guess I'll go to church." He went to his room to change clothes.

The church service was long as usual, but seemed longer to the congregation. Pastor Aho had a bad cold. He coughed, sneezed, and sputtered, but continued the sermon. Signe heard only snatches of it. Her mind was on Mary Marks and the two Marks children.

Since the Men's Choir didn't sing, Charlie sat with his family. When the collection plate came around, it wasn't Ed Koski's hand holding it, but Jacob Rontty's. It seemed to Charlie that Rontty, the fat grocer, spent an overly long time by his side, sneering. Even after Charlie dropped the five-dollar bill on the plate, Rontty retained a knowing smile. Charlie wanted to put his fist into the shopkeeper's eye.

Signe wondered why the pastor hadn't mentioned anything about Mary Marks. Maybe it was because she wasn't an affiliate of the church and had attended only once, but still she was a member of the community.

After the service, people hurried to their cars and left. Signe saw Annie Virta standing by the door, waiting for her husband to come around. Signe approached Annie, and was about to bring up Mary Marks' disappearance when Annie said, "Winter must be on its way. This morning I saw a flock of geese flying south."

On the way back from church, coming up from the gate, Elma pointed to the doghouse covered with crepe paper roses in various shades, "Look! Must be Buster's birthday."

"Don't they have anything better to do than decorate a mongrel's house?" Charlie grunted, referring to Eldon and Violet. "They complained of being too sick to go hear God's word."

"It looks real pretty," Elsie exclaimed.

Elma nodded. "Yaa, like the top of a grave."

Chapter XXVIII

NOW THAT THE CREAMERY was defunct, Rontty's General Mercantile had become the farmers' gathering place. On good days, Jacob was even known to bring the coffeepot from his kitchen in the back of the store to make the meeting more jovial.

"How come you were passing the collection plate at church yesterday?" Olli Homola asked Rontty. "Is Ed Koski under the weather or something?"

"No, he went to Duluth with the schoolteacher to take the Marks widow's children to their relations."

"What makes them think that the widow won't show up in a day or two?" Otto Virta asked. "What if she comes back and finds her kiddies taken to the other side of the state?"

"That would make another trip to Duluth for Ed Koski, that's all," Rontty replied. "But as it stands, we don't know where the widow is and there was nobody to take care of the children. The teacher couldn't do it. Signe Skinnar would have been the ideal person, but she doesn't have the facilities. From what I hear, her five youngsters share a single room."

"Now, what do you suppose happened to the widow?" Wayne Siren asked. "She's been gone since Thursday, I hear."

John Granlund, sitting on the unopened barrel of salted herring, blew a whiff of smoke into the the air from his pipe and said, "That is the most puzzling thing that ever happened in these parts. Do you think someone did her in?"

Pete Hutto popped a jellybean in his mouth. "What for? She wasn't rich. Or was she?"

"If there's a killer around, who is he?" Olli asked.

Granlund stared at Olli. "What do you mean, 'killer'? No body's been found."

"If she was done in, then it was some half-wit—" Olli stopped and the men looked at each other. "You don't think it was—"

Siren chewed on his upper lip, thoughtfully. "You mean Ed Koski's nephew?"

"No, Reino wouldn't attack a fly," Rontty said. "He's not all there, but he's harmless."

"Supposing he made some advances, and the widow repulsed him. That could throw him over the deep end," Olli added.

Hutto pursed his mouth, thought and nodded. "He's strong as an ox."

"You bet he is," Olli concurred, as he opened a can of Copenhagen and put a pinch of snuff under his lower lip, "I recall when we were clearing the south side of the schoolyard, we had dug out a box elder stump that must've weighted close to three hundred pounds and were wondering what to do with it when Reino grabs it and hoists it over to Nylund's side as if it were a gigantic snowball. But that was before his accident."

"He surely had the opportunity," Hutto added. "He was at the widow's 'most every day, I hear. He was supposedly hired by the widow to tend the garden and do outside chores."

Rontty shook his head. "It wasn't Reino. He thought the world of Mary Marks and her kids. Ed Koski would bring them here to the store and Reino, just paid by Mrs. Marks, would spend his earnings buying cookies and licorice sticks for her kids."

"He could afford it," Pete Hutto, the choir director exclaimed. "Wish I was living off the county."

Granlund got off the salted herring barrel to get the blood back to circulating in his posterior. "Of course, anything is possible."

"Has anyone questioned Reino?" Hutto asked.

Granlund knocked the ashes out of his pipe into the brass spittoon in front of the counter. "That is up to the constable. According to Gust Mattson, Hilda has had several conversations with Signe and Signe is real concerned. Said the widow was to come for a dress fitting and never showed up. It was a weekday so the kids were in school. Anything could have happened."

"My wife said she heard over the party line something about a red dress missing from Signe's house,"

Siren added.

"Signe should ask Charlie," Rontty quipped as he slipped to the candy counter, got himself a package of Wrigley's Spearmint gum and put a stick in his mouth.

"Why?" Granlund asked. "He doesn't wear dresses."

Rontty rolled his eyes. "No, but maybe he knows someone who does!"

Otto Virta shook his head. "Charlie is a God fearing man. He thinks the world of Signe. He'd never as much as glance at another woman. Says he sings hymns with his girls evenings after supper."

"Could've been a hobo," Siren suggested. "They come here riding on boxcars from cities as far as Chicago and hit the farmhouses for food."

Pete Hutto perked up. "Yaa! Like the one who follows the t'rashers."

Rontty threw the gum wrapper in the spittoon. "You mean Gabby?"

"How'd you know his name?"

"I asked him," Rontty replied cockily.

"He could speak? I thought he was deaf and dumb!"

"Dumb?" Rontty smirked. "Maybe he thought the same of you."

The men guffawed.

John Granlund relit his freshly-packed pipe and shook his head. "Couldn't have been him. He got run over by a train trying to catch a freight somewhere between Detroit Lakes and Moorhead last fall."

Pete Hutto shook his head. "That's one thing I'd

never try. That is, hopping the freight."

"I should hope not," Homola cracked. "You run about as fast as buttermilk left in a can outside in—" he stopped and stared at Charlie Skinnar who had just walked in—"January."

Charlie gave a nod to the men and went direct to Rontty who was standing behind the counter, "A pack of Luckies."

Rontty was taken aback. "I didn't know you smoked."

"I don't," Charlie replied and laid his fifteen cents on the counter. "These are for a friend in Osage."

Homola gave a belly laugh. "You mean to say they don't sell cigarettes in Osage anymore?" Catching Charlie's disgusted glance, Olli added, "Caught any Airedales lately?" He was referring to the dog that froze its leg in one of Charlie's traps.

Charlie left without responding.

Rontty, still intrigued by the returned bottle of "Evening in Paris" cologne, looked at Granlund. "What about Charlie?"

"What about him?"

"You said anything is possible."

Granlund nodded.

"I think he was stuck on the widow."

"I wouldn't put it past him. Look how he snagged Signe and the way he's treated her. I've never seen such a change in a man. He isn't the person I grew up and went to school with."

Hutto flipped another jellybean in his mouth. "How do you mean?"

Granlund held his pipe in front of him as if he

were reading it. "Charlie was kind, helpful, and generous—"

Olli Homola interrupted John. "Maybe so, but he's always had a mean streak to him. He's always wanted control. He always wanted "to get even," meaning if he didn't get his way, he'd get revenge. It's amazing that Signe has lasted this long. He might be a Christian, but he's mean, spiteful and stingy as hell. His kids go around in old tennis shoes. Signe has to sew day and night to keep the family going. What's he doing with his money?" Olli shook his head. "We can't have people disappearing without a trace. Somebody better call the constable."

"I already did," Rontty spoke out. "I called Friday morning, but Winslow's gone to his mother's funeral in Grand Forks. S'posed to be back sometime today."

Signe heard a car pull into the yard. She looked at the clock and said to herself, Charlie's late again.

There was a knock on the door. It was Constable Winslow. Signe invited him in. He took a chair, laid his hat on the table and made small talk. She knew that the useless chatter would lead to serious business. She was most curious as to why he had come to her house, but waited for him to open up and come to the point. "What do you know about Mary Marks?" he finally asked.

"What do you want to know?"

"For instance, how long have you known her?"

"Well," Signe answered, "five or six months—" She paused to think. "I can tell you exactly. Since the day before Easter when Reino Koski brought Mary and her two youngsters to visit me." The constable expected more information, she realized, but she was not going to blabber about nothing or give him any more facts than necessary. Men in the legal professsion, she knew, could take plain facts and twist them into horrendous tales. "A nice lady," she added, "a good neighbor."

"Is she a friend of yours?" he asked, now making notations in his little black book.

"She was a good friend," Signe replied.

"Did she have any enemies?" Winslow asked.

Signe paused. The policeman just made a slip of the tongue or a grammatical error. "You mean," she corrected him, "'Does she have any enemies?'"

The constable nodded.

"What enemies?" Signe exclaimed in an offended tone of voice. "She's a widow. Her husband, I understand, died a couple of years before she moved here. I'm making three dresses for her. One dress—the red one—disappeared." Signe walked to the hangers on the nail and fingered each remaining dress. "Right off this rack."

"When?"

Signe looked at the constable and shook her head. "Mr. Winslow, if I knew when it was taken, I'd know who took it and why."

"Is there anything else you can say about the widow?" he asked, eager to add a few more notations in his little black book.

"Oh, yes."

Winslow perked up. "What's that?"

"She's very beautiful."

Winslow was let down. "That is of no conse-
quence."

"To me it is. My dresses look like a million dollars
on her. But why are you asking all these questions? Is
she in trouble?"

"Just routine business, Mrs. Skinnar. Nothing for
you to worry about." The constable paused to get the
right wording for his next question. "Tell me about
your husband."

Signe was proud of her husband's accomplishments, and didn't like the constable's probing. "He's a
mailman. Everyone knows that. Been a postman since
he was twenty-one years old. Works for the federal
government. He's also Justice of the Peace. On the
school board. On church committees. And a farmer on
the side."

"Is your husband friendly with the widow?"

"Oh, yes. We're friendly with all our neighbors.
When you are in public service, like my husband, you
have to be friendly whether you like it or not. Why
are you asking about Charlie? Is he in trouble?"

Signe's directness rattled the constable. "No-no-
no-no. Just routine questions."

"Like the census?"

"Yeah. Something like it."

Signe sighed with relief. "If you have more questions, Charlie should be home anytime soon. He can
answer all of them. Please make yourself comfortable.
I'll make a pot of coffee."

"No, thanks. I have to run along. Thank you for
your help." Winslow grabbed his hat and went on his
way.

The children had come home from school and changed their clothes, but Charlie hadn't returned from his mail route. He'd left early again that morning—without his usual coffee. When Signe mentioned this to Eldon, all he said was, "Yaa," grabbed his milking pails, and hurried to the barn with Violet. She looked at the clock. It had stopped at twelve. She'd forgotten to wind it before going to bed last night—something that had never happened before.

Signe was about to put on her barn gear when the phone rang. Three shorts, a long, and a short. That was the Skinnar ring. She stared at the telephone on the wall. Was it good news or bad? Milking time was not the hour for a neighborhood chat. The ring was repeated. The call must be urgent. Signe answered.

It was Hilda Mattson. Without a *hello* or *how are you*, she sprang the news. "They found the grave," she exploded, "in Mary Marks' backwoods."

"What?" Signe asked.

"They found the grave," Hilda repeated.

Signe could hear the clicks of the receivers being taken off the hook, as their owners tuned in for the evening news. Every phone in Wolf Creek now was open to the party line, and each had a human ear on the receiver. Signe's knees were giving way. "What grave?" she asked, as she grabbed a chair for support.

"A newly dug grave in Mrs. Marks' woods."

"Who was in it?"

"Nobody. The grave was empty."

Signe took a deep breath and exhaled with relief. She had expected the worst. "Then it wasn't a grave.

Just a hole in the woods. A bear dug a place for sleeping away the cold winter; but since it turned warm again, the bear left. They do that, you know," she added, trying to make light of a situation that looked most serious.

"It was freshly dug," Hilda countered, "with a shovel."

Grasping for a logical answer, Signe conceded, "Then it was people. Maybe digging for oil. They say there's oil—"

"Charlie said it was a grave, but the body was taken away."

"If Charlie said it was a grave," Signe answered quietly, "then it is a grave. Where did he say the body is?"

"He's looking for it."

Signe's mind was on Mary Marks. "Maybe she left with a sweetheart," she said wishfully, as she stared at the empty hanger on the dress hook.

"The widow had a sweetheart?" Hilda exclaimed, with new interest.

"I don't know if she had a sweetheart," Signe quickly responded. "I just hope she has. The red dress is gone. It was not ready to be worn. Maybe she couldn't wait. Maybe she'll be back in the red dress. Let's hope so."

It was dark when Charlie got home. Must be close to nine, Signe told herself. She waited to see what kind of mood Charlie was in before asking him for the time so she could set the clock. She poured his coffee and placed it on the table in front of him. "You had another long day."

He took a lump of sugar and put it in his cheek and slowly sipped his coffee from the saucer. "The mail was light, thank God. I spent most of the afternoon transferring traps from one corner of the woods to another. Some job. But it should pay in the long run."

Signe kept quiet about Hilda's call. She waited to hear Charlie's story but she had to tell him about the constable's visit. "The constable was here this afternoon."

"What was on Winslow's mind?" Charlie asked, with a note of derision.

"He asked about Mary Marks, if we were friends and if you were friends with her—" Signe stopped. The look on Charlie's face turned frightening. With his right eye quivering out of control and the coppery stubble covering his face, he looked like a primate from an ancient past. A corroded, sickening odor exuded from him.

Charlie laughed. "If the good constable comes back, tell him I found the grave."

He had just confirmed what she didn't want to hear. Signe began to rattle senselessly. "I have always said you should be constable. You have a good head on you. You can figure things out—"

"But there was no body."

She gave a hysterical laugh as she set a bowl of beef stew in front of him. "See, there is no body. No dead body," Signe said, and got herself a cup of coffee to relieve the nervous tension. "Hooh! That was hot. I scorched my throat clear down to my chest."

"Boiling coffee, what do you expect?" Charlie grunted as he pushed the food away from him without touching it, and got up from the table.

She ignored his remark. "What are you going to do now?"

"Warm the sauna. Tomorrow's another big day. Have to find the grave. The one with the body in it."

"Do you think she's dead?" Signe asked without mentioning Mary Marks' name.

Charlie put his hand in his pants' pocket and pulled out a bloodstained piece of red cloth. "Here's proof."

Signe gagged.

Chapter XXIX

ED KOSKI, JOHN GRANLUND, Wayne Siren, and Pete Hutto arrived at the church for the monthly meeting. "Where's Charlie Skinnar?" John asked, as he stepped in the vestibule.

Pete Hutto laughed. "Probably looking for empty graves."

"It's no laughing matter when someone just disappears," Ed told Pete, "especially a widow lady with two small children. It was no joy ride taking the Marks children to their aunt's in Duluth. The youngsters didn't shed a tear, but their sorrow was so deep that it penetrated right through my skin. It was like driving a hearse. Miss Keksi said the trip was sadder than any funeral she ever attended. At the final service the minister usually assures the grieving family members that the departed one has gone to better quarters, but we couldn't say whether Mary Marks was dead or alive."

"What about your nephew, Ed?" Hutto asked.

"Reino? What about him?"

"Has anyone questioned him?"

Ed turned red in the face. "Questioned him about what?"

"About the missing widow."

"Are you insinuating that Reino is responsible in some way?"

Pete shifted his gaze from man to man. "Doesn't hurt to ask. He might know something we don't."

"I don't get you," Ed snapped.

"I hear he was sweet on the widow."

Ed shot an angry look at the choirmaster. "You're inferring that Reino had something to do with Mrs. Marks' disappearance."

"You know darn well that your nephew's not counting on all ten fingers."

Ed rushed at Pete, but John quickly stepped in. "Hutto, if we weren't in church," Ed said in a calm voice, "I'd beat the shit out of you."

John spoke up. "Before we go into business matters, I'd like to make a suggestion. Why don't we all meet tomorrow morning, go over to the Marks' place and look at the grave that Charlie Skinnar claims to have found. Won't take more than an hour or two to walk over the whole property."

"Count me out," Pete said. "I have to go to Sebeka early in the day."

"And I have plans to go to Fargo," Wayne Siren added.

John shook his head. "I didn't necessarily mean in the morning—"

"Let's make it nine in the morning at the Marks' mailbox," Ed said to John. "You and I can take a walk through."

"From what I heard, the widow was on her way to Charlie's place when she disappeared, but never got there. Did anyone see her on the road?" Wayne Siren asked.

"Nobody saw her, as far as I know. I'm sure if anyone had, they'd come forward with the information. I've searched both sides of the road a dozen times." Ed shook his head. "I even rummaged through the school woodshed. According to Signe Skinnar, the widow wasn't expected until after school let out for the day. She was to come with her kiddies, but something unexpected took her away from her ironing before she finished, and she left without locking her door."

"Hell, we never lock the door," Pete remarked. "We don't even know where the key is. If they want to get in your house, they'll find a way."

"Who you talking about?" Ed asked Pete.

"Anybody."

"Come fellas," John said, and slapped his hands together. "Let's get our business done."

The following morning Ed and John met at Mary Marks' mailbox as planned. They walked through the house but found no clues except the ones Signe had sighted—the basket of dampened clothes and the ironing board standing upright with the flatiron standing on its end. "There's been no struggle of any kind here as far as I can see," Ed said. "Let's check the other buildings and the well."

John ran his hand over the cold kitchen stove. "The widow sure kept everything nice and clean. She could've given my wife some direction in house-keeping."

Ed, walking in front of John as they went out the kitchen door, stopped and turned around. "You talk as if the widow was dead."

"What else can one think?"

Finding no clues in the vicinity of the house, Ed looked at John and shook his head. "What do you say we go into the pasture?"

"You read my thoughts. We have to take a look at the 'grave' Charlie found."

They pushed open the old gate. John pointed to the ground. "Look. Fresh tire tracks."

"Could be Charlie's. Reino said Charlie had gotten permission from Mrs. Marks to trap on her property."

"Why would he drive his car here?"

"To bring it off the road," Ed replied. "You know he treats that Ford better than he treats Signe."

"But he could have left it by the house. This is no place to drive a car, especially a new one. Look how rough the ground is."

Ed laughed. "Don't quiz me about Charlie Skinnar's reasoning. He's getting nuttier by the day."

They had a hard time finding the grave Charlie had supposedly discovered. The hole was next to an old brush pile that had not been burned. John dug into the earth with the toe of his shoe. "Ed, what do you think?"

"Charlie's right. Something human or animal has been buried in that pit for a short time, and recently, too."

"What do you see that I don't?" John asked.

"Nothing. Just an eerie feeling—as if I were walking in the hollow of death." Ed turned and walked a few paces. "Hey, come around this way. Look at the ground here. The grass has been trampled on and the fallen leaves are matted. Looks as if a herd of buffalo had a conclave here." He covered his nose. "It smells."

"Whew! Had we approached this area from the opposite direction, we'd have caught the stench earlier." John picked up a piece of an old board and dug around. "I think that's blood encrusted on the fallen leaves. A living being was slaughtered here."

"Animal or human?"

"Who can tell?" John replied. "It could be a poacher. Having shot a deer off-season he buried the head and entrails in that pit over there."

"True. But why dig it up later?"

John pursed his lips and shook his head.

"I think we'd better get the constable to come take a look." Ed took out his pocket watch and glanced at it. "Time for coffee. Since the Skinnar place is on our way home, what do you say we stop and visit Signe. She serves a great cup of coffee."

John laughed. "It's not the coffee you're thinking of. It's the spread she puts on the table with it."

"Are you boys on some sort of official visit?"

Signe asked when they walked in.

"No," Ed replied. "Just stopped to say hello to Charlie since it's almost dinnertime."

"Oh, Charlie doesn't come home at noon," Signe explained. "He takes his lunch. Have you any news about Mrs. Marks?" she asked as she sat down with the coffee grinder on her lap to pulverize fresh beans for a new pot.

"We just came from what Charlie thinks is a grave in the widow's woods," Ed said, "and noticed a worn-out spot on the ground close by which looks most suspicious."

Signe stopped her grinding and stared Ed in the eye. "What do you think?"

"We have to agree with Charlie. There is a hole there with all the markings of a grave," Ed said. Then added, "The world is getting crazier by the day."

"You mean the people," John corrected. "The world is pretty much the same it's always been, but its inhabitants are turning loony."

After having served them a healthy spread, Signe watched Ed and John drive off. Charlie had passed his home on his route and the children would be in school for several more hours. The coast was clear, so to speak. She put on her coat and started for Mary Marks' place.

Signe followed the tire tracks from the old gate to the woods as it wound around the trees, and wondered why Charlie had driven his new car there when it would've been easier to walk. She assumed the tracks were from the time he discovered the empty grave.

She readily found what the men thought was an empty burial pit. As she viewed the opening in the earth she saw what to her looked like a straight pin glimmering in the sun. She eased her way down, looked at it, and attached the pin to her coat. Signe now wondered what other evidence the clay and rocks would reveal. She tried to dig with her hands, but the earth was unforgiving. She climbed out and went back to the farm. In the barn she found the spade that Reino used.

After about an hour and a half, Signe had shoveled most of the loose dirt out of the pit, and her labor bore fruit. She found a lady's heeless pump, and knew it belonged to Mary Marks. No one else around Wolf Creek wore shoes like that. Shoe and straight pin proved to Signe that dead or alive, Mary Marks had been here. Without bothering to refill the hole, she wrapped the pump in her coat and left.

Hilda Mattson entered without a sound, walked to Charlie's chair by the kitchen table, sat down and asked, "Where's Charlie now?"

Her question irritated Signe. Too many unexplainable things were happening. She didn't like the position such questions placed her. "On his mail route," she replied.

"What time do you expect him home?"

"I don't know. I never know. Depends how the roads are."

"Nothing wrong with the roads now," Hilda retorted. "Dry as last Thanksgiving's wishbone."

"What I meant," Signe tried to explain, "was that

some days the mail is heavier than others, especially on the days when the paper comes and there are magazines. Why do you ask?"

"We—ll," Hilda hesitated. "I heard that the Marks widow had been seen riding with Charlie."

Signe, standing by the table, grabbed the edge of it for support. "In the mail car?"

Hilda nodded.

"Where did you hear that?"

"On the party line."

"Who said?"

"I don't know." Hilda bit off pieces of nail on her index finger and spat them out. "I just overheard the conversation. Didn't recognize the voices."

"When was this?"

"The day the widow disappeared."

"What else did you hear?" Signe asked, not really wanting to know any of it.

"They said Charlie Skinnar had brought the Marks widow home in his mail car."

The shredded window screen and her sewing shears on the floor flashed back in Signe's memory. The table no longer was enough support for her. She let herself down on a chair by the table opposite Hilda. "Here?"

Hilda nodded.

"There must be some mistake. Charlie never lets anyone ride in the mail car, not even Eldon. I went to my sister's in the morning that day, but stayed only a short time. I waited for Mary to come with the children, but she never came."

The door opened. Charlie walked in and threw his

mailbag under the table. Signe was shocked. He had always treated the sack as if it were a personal treasure. The glazed look in his eyes sent a chill through Signe's body. It was a Charlie she had not seen before. "Hello, Mrs. Mattson," he said in a voice unusually high for him. "What's new?"

Before Hilda could speak, Signe said, "I went to the grave today."

Charlie turned white. "And what did you find?" he asked, voice loaded with sarcasm.

"No body."

"I found another grave today," he said, addressing Hilda.

"Another grave?" she asked.

Charlie nodded. "It was empty."

"Where?" Signe asked in a voice barely audible.

"Across the road." Charlie turned to Hilda. "On my east forty, that I just bought."

Chapter XXX

SAM ISAACSON HAD CALLED a stockholders' meeting to discuss the sale of the now defunct creamery to be held at the site at seven o'clock that evening. "It's chilly as hell here," John Granlund complained.

"I've always heard that hell was hot," Pete Hutto piped.

Nobody cared to comment.

"You could've had us at your place," John continued. "You have that mansion with a sitting room, dining room—"

"What housewife would want a bunch of farmers with manure on their boots to come into her parlor?" Pete asked before John had finished his sentence.

Sam took out his gold pocket watch. "It's five past nine."

He looked around. "We're all here except Charlie

Skinnar. He's usually on time."

"He's probably finding new graves or reburying old bodies," Pete joked.

His remark was largely ignored.

"Yaa, what do you all think about this missing widow?" Sam asked. He felt somewhat detached to the happenings in Wolf Creek since he lived in the next township. "Did she leave of her own accord or was she murdered?"

"I think she's dead," Ed Koski said. "Who did it, how and why, I cannot understand."

"What makes you think she was killed?"

"Number one, she left unexpectedly. Number two, she left her children behind which Mrs. Marks would never have chosen to do. Number three, Charlie found a piece of her dress stained with blood by the first grave."

"What do you mean by the first grave?" Elmer Lindgren asked. "How many 'graves' are there and are they really graves?"

Pete Hutto's eyes lit. "Charlie brags he found two. And one he claims was in his forty."

John Granlund spoke up. "Ed and I inspected both holes and came to the conclusion that a body had for a time occupied each of the pits. Whether it was human or animal, we couldn't tell."

Elmer Lindgren shook his head. "Now who'd want to keep burying and digging up a body? There's a nut loose around here."

"That's sure," Ed agreed. "But which of us is it?"

Pete brought up Charlie's name again.

John shook the ashes out of his pipe into the

spittoon on the floor in front of him, refilled it from the can of Prince Albert, scratched the kitchen match on the sole of his shoe and lit his pipe. "It can't be Charlie Skinnar. He's a good Christian, a real model for all of us. He does have a temper, but he's a loving father, a good citizen, and he's devoted all his free time to searching for the missing widow. That's more than any of us has done. We have to give credit where credit is due."

Pete Hutto had listened to Granlund's laudatory speech with a noticeable smirk on his face. "John, we've gone through this before, and I recall you saying anything is possible, and I think it's not only possible, but also quite probable."

Sam Isaacson watched as Ed Koski got up from his chair and threw a couple of sticks of wood into the small potbelly stove. Then cleared his throat. "Charlie will be here, but we might as well start the meeting. As you all are aware, we have a building here that's bringing us no income — just rotting away. We should get rid of it."

"We could sell it," Pete volunteered.

"You want to buy?" Sam asked.

Pete looked around. "Why? It's useless. Nobody would want to rent it for business. We already have a store, a church, and a dance hall, and the building isn't suitable for living quarters."

Sam smiled. "Pete, you said it all. I'll give each of you twenty-five cents on the dollar that you put down in stock."

There were groans and murmurs.

Charlie Skinnar walked in just then and was greeted warmly by the men.

"You're late, Charlie," Pete hollered. "You must've been looking for still another grave."

Charlie liked being the center of attention. He smiled. "You're right, Pete. And I found it."

"Let's finish what we started," Sam told the men. He looked at Charlie and said, "I'm offering to buy this building at twenty-five cents on the dollar of your investment. How do you feel about it?"

Charlie multiplied out loud. "Two hundred fifty dollars. I say let's find a real buyer. With cash."

Sam smiled, the same smile he used when he sent Charlie to the pawnshop in Fargo for a paltry debt. "I'm as real as you'll find. Who else will take a chance on this shack?"

"What do you plan to do with the building?" Charlie asked.

"I'll think of something."

Ed asked Sam when they could expect their checks.

"By the end of the week," he replied.

Charlie shook his head. "I'll go along, but Signe won't like it."

"When did you ever consult Signe on anything?" Sam retorted.

"Twenty-five dollars!" Pete moaned. "Ten years ago, I thought the stock would make me rich."

"Rich or poor," Ed mused, "I'm glad not to be turning the separator handle anymore."

It was agreed that as soon as the stockholders received their checks, the deed to the creamery property would be turned over to Sam Isaacson. The men then shifted their attention to Charlie Skinnar.

The limelight was on Charlie. His face became flushed and his right eye danced merrily as he related how he discovered the first grave in the Marks widow's unused pasture, the second one on his own property, "the East Forty" as he called it. and yet a third one further in from the road.

"What do you think of all this?" Sam asked Charlie.

"I wouldn't hazard a guess, except someone's having fun keeping Wolf Creek jumpy as to what's going on."

Chapter XXXI

SIGNE LIKED SATURDAYS because the children were home. Not that she minded being alone with her thoughts and memories, but her children added dimension to her dreams. For a while she had two close lady friends, Mary Marks and Hilda Mattson, but now Mary was gone and the subjects Signe could discuss with Hilda were limited. Hilda was restricted by her lack of education and experience, but she was always helpful. Mary Marks was a "woman of the world," Signe would say, intelligent, observant, and imaginative. She was broadminded and receptive to the new and the unfamiliar, contrary to the local housewives.

Elsie and Elma came in from the granary where they had been playing and found Signe standing at the open doorway looking up toward the mailbox.

"Mama, who you waiting for?" Elsie asked.

"I was hoping Mrs. Marks would come walking down the road and surprise me."

Elma stared at her mother. "Ma, she's dead and buried."

"Dead and buried and dug up again," Elsie reiterated.

Signe stood horrified. "You mustn't speak like that."

"That's what all the kids at school say," Elma replied.

"Yaa, they say they know who did it, but won't tell us," Elsie added.

Feeling uncertain ground under her, Signe changed the subject. "Reino hasn't visited us for a long time."

"I know," Elma said, pulling strands of hair on the sides of her head to see if they were long enough to reach her nose. "He doesn't want to come here anymore."

"I'm sure Eldon misses him."

"Nah, he sees him all the time in school."

"Does Reino come in the schoolyard?" Signe asked.

"No, he stays on the other side of the fence and Eldon stays in the schoolyard. Sometimes Eldon sits on the gate when he talks with Reino. Reino gave me a stick of gum because he says I'm like his godchild."

"Yaa, Juicy Fruit," Elsie added.

"Elsie, didn't he give you any?" Signe asked.

"I gave part to her," Elma said.

"Yes, she gave part to me," Elsie testified. "I like

Juicy Fruit better'n Spearmint, but I like Black Jack the best of all. Nestor wanted my gum. He's just a little kid. I told him he could have it the next day, but I swallowed it by accident so I couldn't keep my promise."

Signe was delighted by the guileless story she'd just heard, but she felt a lesson in deportment was never redundant. "Don't you know you're not supposed to chew gum in school?"

"Yes, Ma. We waited until we were out the gate," Elsie replied.

"Why doesn't Reino come visit us anymore?" Signe asked.

Elsie looked at Elma to answer. "Because," Elma said, "he hates Papa. He called Pa 'goddemsonoma-bitch.' Ma, can we go to your remnant bag and get some pieces to make doll dresses? Violet said she would sew us some if you aren't using the sewing machine."

"Yes, you can get some scraps and Violet can have the sewing machine. I'm baking today. But you know it isn't nice to swear —"

"We know," Elma cut in. "But I wasn't 't swearing. I just told what Reino said. You mustn't be mad at him. He's very nervous these days."

The girls were quick in their choice of cloth. Elsie wanted the blue pieces left over from Mary Marks' dress, and Elma the red. "What's this?" Elma asked, holding up a red swatch. It was the piece that Charlie had supposedly found in the first "grave." Forgetting her daughters' liking for cloth, Signe had hidden it in her remnant bag where no one would see it. "It's dirty." Elma exclaimed, and threw the scrap of fabric on the floor.

Signe picked up the bloodstained segment and put it in her apron pocket. The tiny piece of Mary's red dress was something she wanted to keep.

Eldon and Hugo came running in. "Mama, can we move upstairs?" Eldon asked.

"What upstairs? You mean the attic?"

The boys nodded.

"Why it's not high enough for a rooster to get on its toes to crow!"

"In the center it's high enough for me to stand straight," Eldon said, "until I grow a couple more inches."

Charlie had talked about raising the roof and building a second story to the house, but he no longer mentioned it. "How are you going to get up there?"

Eldon's eyes lit up. "Ladder."

Signe nodded happily. She was relieved to see Eldon almost like his old self. She'd been worried about his sullen demeanor the past few days.

"And, we're going to teach Buster to come up with us," Hugo supplemented.

"A dog can't climb a ladder!"

"We'll put him in a bushel basket," Eldon said, "and train him a little at a time. First day we'll lift him two feet, next day three feet, and so on until we we get him in through the window. Every day we give him a lump of sugar after his lesson. That'll make him happy."

Signe laughed. "The poor dog will die of sugar diabetes before he ever sees the top floor, but sure you can have the attic. You don't plan to sleep there, do you?"

"Of course," Hugo shouted with glee. "Eldon gets the big room and I get the small one. That way the girls can have the bedroom to themselves."

"What rooms?" Signe asked. "It's just one loft."

"Not anymore," Hugo informed her. "We made it into two."

"Where did you get the boards?"

"No boards. We used chicken wire." Hugo giggled. "Eldon said what's good enough for chickens is good enough for us. We papered the chicken wire wall with gunnysacks and left a secret hole in the middle for us to send secret messages to each other."

"Eldon and me are inventors."

"Could you sew some flour sacks together to stuff with straw to make mattresses?" Eldon asked his mother.

"If you can't have beds, at least you should have real mattresses. I'll talk to father. But will you be warm enough?"

"Mama, it's roasting in there," Eldon said. "The heat from the kitchen stove goes straight up through the ceiling. Heat rises and cold goes down. I learned that in science."

Charlie returned early from his route. "I'm going on vacation next week," he announced as he threw his mailbag under the kitchen table and sat down to wait for his coffee.

"In August?" Signe asked. "You aren't due one until next June."

"I made a deal with Mr. Gilpin. He'll do the route now and I pay him next summer when I get my check. Come June, he'll have money without having to work for it."

Shocked at the turn of events, Signe asked, "Where are you going?"

"No place. I'm staying home to work. I'm going to clear my new forty."

Signe noticed that he had been calling the acreage across the road his new forty all along. She didn't mind that now, but wished he'd make full use of the cleared land they already had. "What are you going to plant there?"

"Sheep." Charlie laughed. "Did you hear that? You asked what I was going to plant and I said 'sheep.'"

She didn't think it was funny. "You aren't planning to buy them this fall, with winter coming soon?"

"Why not? Winter always follows fall."

"Charlie Skinnar, are you out of your head? You have no place to keep them! Sheep need a barn or a shed to come in from the cold like any other warm-blooded animal. You remember what happened to Roy Gustafson a few years back. Lost all seventy-five head in the blizzard. Frozen stiff standing up on their feet. It put Roy out of the wool business for good." Signe shook her head at Charlie's foolishness. She poured his coffee and returned to her bread making.

Hugo rushed in with a bushel basket. "Mama can we have this to teach Buster?"

Signe gave a nod of her head.

Hugo turned to Charlie. "Papa, did Mama tell you

that me and Eldon are moving out?"

"Where you going?"

"Upstairs."

"To the attic?"

Hugo nodded.

"Really? How are you going to get up there?" Charlie asked.

"Up the ladder. Through the window. Eldon gets the big room and I get the small. Buster can choose who he wants to sleep with. Right now we're training Buster for the trip."

Charlie made a wry face. "You don't want a smelly mongrel up there."

"We already told Buster. We can't disappoint him." Hugo went out with his basket.

Signe was glad that Charlie had no objections to the boys' plan. "If Eldon and Hugo want to sleep in the attic, I think we should allow it. It'll be fun for them and will give the girls room and privacy. I was hoping we could get a couple of mattresses from the secondhand store."

Charlie looked at his pocket watch. "I could go now. Moe stays open until eight." Charlie put on his hat and went out.

There was a shuffling at the door. Eldon rushed to open it. Charlie was lugging in a mattress. "This double mattress is for you, boys, and the single one is for me."

Hearing the evident turn of events, Eldon's face fell and Hugo ran out without a word. Their father again had taken control of their plans.

Charlie stood in the middle of the floor and ordered Eldon, "Get the ladder so I can go up and open the hatch."

Eldon objected. "Pa, we were going to use the outside window for going in and out. That way we don't need to bring the big ladder in the house."

"It'll just be for a short while, son. I'll build a nice staircase when I remodel the upstairs. Now get the ladder." It was Charlie's habit to call Eldon "son" when he knew he was stepping out of bounds.

Eldon reluctantly followed orders. When he returned, Charlie set up the ladder and opened the hatch above. "It's going to be hell to get this damn thing up there," Charlie said.

Eldon glanced at his mother, who had just come in from the barn.

"Charlie, there's no need to swear," Signe snapped. "You should've gotten two single mattresses."

"Two growing boys need a double mattress."

"Who's the single one for?" she asked.

"Me."

"You?"

"Yaa." Charlie punched and bent the secondhand mattress to get it up through the opening in the ceiling. "I'll take the big room and the boys get the small one."

Signe listened to Charlie talking about the attic as if the "rooms" were fancy bedchambers instead of spaces partitioned by chicken wire. "You're moving into the loft?"

"I don't know why I shouldn't," Charlie replied. "We boys will leave you girls more room. Elma and

Elsie will have their bedroom and you can share yours with Violet." Charlie then addressed his older son. "But Eldon, you might as well forget about hauling Buster up. I won't sleep with a mongrel dog."

Signe poured herself a cup of coffee, sat at the table and stared at the mattress rising with hurt and anger. Charlie was wrecking plans and dreams. When she was a little girl, Signe had a romantic vision of marrying a man with whom she could share thoughts and talk over matters. At night, he'd put his arm under her head, next to the pillow, and they'd speak in whispers so as not to wake the children; and when the youngsters were gone, their conversations would be about the new families and the grandchildren. But that was not the way life had turned out. Charlie had long ago lost interest in her world, and now he'd crushed the fragile dreams of their two sons.

She looked at Charlie. He was still trying to figure how to get the double mattress through the hole in the ceiling. The boys had left the scene. Signe got up from the table without finishing her coffee and threw the cup into the empty aluminum dishpan, shattering it.

Charlie, stunned at her action, let go of the mattress and it plopped full spread on the floor.

Signe went into her bedroom.

"It won't work," Hugo told his father after Charlie got both mattresses up into the loft. Unlike Eldon, who was careful not to offend Charlie, Hugo felt free to speak whatever came to his mind.

"What won't work?" Charlie asked.

"Leaving the ladder where it is."

"Why not? It's stable."

"There's not enough room in the kitchen. The ladder's too close to the stove. Mama can't cook. Why can't we leave it outside, in front of the window?"

"Because I will be sleeping in that room," Charlie answered, "and you boys will be climbing in and out at night to go to the outhouse. It'll disturb my sleep."

"Don't worry, Pop. We won't wake you."

"What do you plan to do?" Charlie snickered. "Aim out the window?"

"We'll just take an old molasses pail up with us at night."

"That was a good pork roast," Charlie commented after dinner. "Time for a few hymns. How about it, girls?"

"No, Papa, I have to memorize 'Hiawatha,'" Elma replied.

"'Hiawatha' at your age? I was in the sixth grade before I read it."

"Things have changed, Papa. We're more advanced," Elma said as she led her sister to their room.

"Advanced," Charlie repeated. "Did you hear that?" he asked Signe who was clearing the table.

"Elma is a very bright girl. She'll go to college and get a good position."

"I want three sandwiches for my lunch tomorrow," Charlie said. "That roast with mustard would be nice."

"Sandwiches? I thought you were going to work across the road. You can come home to eat."

"I can't take the time. I want that forty cleared

before cold weather sets in. I still have to build a barn for the sheep."

"Where are you going to buy the sheep?" Signe asked disinterestedly.

"At some auction sale, probably in Fargo."

Chapter XXXII

IT WAS PAST NINE on Monday morning when Charlie came down from his attic hideaway, smelling like a skunk. The barn chores were done and the children had left for school. Signe had cleaned the kitchen and was setting up her sewing—a late hour for him to be getting up, Signe told herself.

"Aren't you going to ask me how I slept?" Charlie grumbled.

"I trust you slept well," she replied, knowing well that he had not slept much. She'd heard him cursing outside her window in the wee hours of the night. "The boys said they slept clear through till morning. They wanted to know if they could stay in the attic permanently."

"They can have that inferno. The first three hours it was hot as hell—"

"It was bound to be," Signe interjected. "I was baking until eleven last night, and as Hugo said, heat goes up and cold goes down."

Charlie wasn't listening. He had suffered and he wanted Signe to know about it. "Just as I was about to fall asleep, I felt the need to go to the outhouse. The kids had forgotten to put kerosene in the lantern. It smoked like hell and finally went out— just as I was about to go down the ladder.

"As I passed Buster's food dish I saw what I thought was a stray cat, eating the mongrel's food, I got sprayed by a goddamned striped skunk. Thank God there was warm water left in the tub in the bathhouse so I could wash. Where is that mongrel anyway? I haven't seen him for days. Maybe someone put a bullet through his head! I hope so—"

"I packed you three sandwiches, a jar of milk, Thermos of coffee and a piece of sour cream raisin pie," she said, interrupting his senseless ranting.

"I haven't had any of that pie, " he exclaimed as if he had been deprived of his due. "When did you make it?"

"Last night after you went up to bed. I didn't put any sugar in your coffee. You might want to have some midmorning, so I put a few lumps in an envelope."

Charlie looked back as he was about to go out the door. "I'll come for my lunch after I pack the tools in the car."

"You taking the car? Just to cross the road?"

"You expect me to haul the equipment on my back like a camel?" he asked in injured tones, before he shut the door.

All he requires is his lunch and an ax, Signe told herself, but when she happened to look out the window, she saw him packing an ax, a saw. a pitchfork and a pickax. What does he need a pickax for, she wondered. He isn't leveling ground, just clearing brush. Besides, Charlie was exposing his new car and its tires to unnecessary risks. Signe shook her head disapprovingly. But why should she worry? she asked herself. Every other year he got a new model and meanwhile, if the tires wore out, he'd buy new ones. In a rare moment of self-concern, Signe looked at herself. her hands dry and calloused from hard work, dress thin from numerous washings, and old oxfords with run over heels, why should she worry about a car? If her feet failed, Firestone would not come to her rescue, and if she petered out, Charlie would soon find a young replacement.

Signe went out and got Buster's food bowl, which had been cleaned out by the night visitor, and washed it. She scraped the remains of Charlie's oatmeal into it and topped the cereal with the cream left in the pitcher on the table. She set the bowl and two pieces of buttered flatbread on the kitchen steps. As soon as Charlie was gone, she'd call the dog to eat. Buster refused to come near the house when Charlie was there.

Charlie came in, took his lunch pail and drove across the road. Signe went to the door and called for Buster. He was gone. Left without his breakfast. Signe called again. Then she whistled, but the dog was nowhere to be seen.

Signe put on her coat and one of Violet's berets and headed for Mary Marks' house. She had to find out what happened to her friend. Charlie would be cutting brush in the east forty all day, unaware of her absence from home, giving her a rare opportunity to search. Signe had not told anyone about the heeless shoe she'd found in the empty grave. It was a closely guarded secret in her bag of remnants. She would bring it out at the right time.

Luckily no one else chanced to travel the county road that morning, therefore, she didn't have to reveal her destination to anyone. Mr. Gilpin, Charlie's replacement for the week, would pass by a couple hours later than Charlie usually did on the mail route. Now that he was retired, Gilpin could stop and visit with old friends standing by their mailboxes.

Signe's second search of the house revealed nothing new. The granary offered no clues, other than the seed potatoes having been recklessly scattered on the floor. Mischievous kids, Signe told herself. She inspected the area around the well, but the half-century old boards showed no signs of being trifled with. The log icehouse next to the granary seemed desolately clean and empty.

If Mary was killed here, Signe told herself, the barn would have the answer. She climbed the rugged parallel rungs of birch boughs that Gus Lindbom had nailed to the barn wall for a ladder to get up to the hayloft some sixty years ago. She found a rusty manure fork with a broken prong to sift the broken bales of moldy hay that were scattered about. The loft yielded nothing but a few toys the Marks children had left behind.

Downstairs Signe searched the feed barrels and each cow stall, then pushed open both top and bottom sections of the back door leading to the manure pile. The previous farmer had moved away several years ago and Mary Marks had no cattle, so nothing new would have been added to the mound recently. It looked like wild animals had been scratching at the earthen heap. She looked for a shovel. Finding none, she went back to the hayloft and got the old manure fork.

She plunged the fork into the decayed animal dung and kept digging until she'd dug about three feet down. There she came upon a bundle of tightly bound clothing, soiled with what looked like dried blood and mildew. The stench was unbearable. Signe quickly covered her find, hid the fork behind a feed barrel in the barn and hurried home.

"Where have you been?" Charlie asked, pushing away the remains of his lunch that he'd laid on the table in front of him.

She was startled to find him at home, but she would not show her surprise. She went to the stove, stirred the dying embers and added a few pieces of kindling. "To look for Mary Marks," she replied calmly.

"And what did you find?"

"My search isn't over."

"Looking for bodies is a man's job," Charlie lashed at her.

"It turns into woman's work when men get nowhere."

Charlie put on his cap and went out the door. When Signe heard his car go up the road, she went to her bedroom and got a pencil and tablet and sat down at the kitchen table to write the constable a letter. Calling on the party line was out of question. Signe's English was far from perfect. Spelling in English follows no logic, the schoolteacher had told her when she was studying for her citizenship papers. "You have to memorize each word," Miss Keksi had said. How could one memorize if one had never seen a word or name written? Signe did her best.

> Dear Sir: I think I have found something about
> Mary Marks. Come see me quick. Yours truely,
> Signe Skinnar

She put the note and an envelope in her pocket-book and went to the mailbox to wait for Mr. Gilpin. If Charlie should return from the east forty and see her standing by the road, she would tell him she was waiting to buy stamps to mail a letter to her sister in Michigan.

Mr. Gilpin was obliging when Signe asked him to write the constable's name and address on the envelope. "You know where Mr. Winslow lives?" she asked him hopefully.

The mailman smiled. "I'll see that he gets your letter." He asked no questions except "Where's Buster? He usually greets me when I arrive at your box. I trust he hasn't forgotten his old master."

Signe thanked the mailman profusely and bought

five two-cent stamps. He took one to put on the letter she was sending Winslow.

Three days had passed and Signe had received no word from the constable. The letter would take a day to reach him, but two other days had gone by. She couldn't understand the delay.

Friday afternoon Ed Koski and Sam Isaacson came over. "We've come to see what you know about the murder," Sam announced.

Signe's heart missed a beat. How did they know that she had discovered something and contacted Winslow? Mr. Gilpin knew not what she said in the letter he addressed. Furthermore, the old mail carrier was as tight-lipped as a mummy. Winslow's wife must've opened the letter and spread the news, Signe decided. "Where's the constable?"

"He had to go to the Twin Cities," Ed replied.

"What did you find out or what have you to show?" Sam asked.

Charlie walked in. "I was cutting brush across the road when I saw you boys drive in my yard. What's new?"

Ed glanced at Signe.

"Signe wrote the constable that she knows something about the Marks widow's murder," Sam answered.

Charlie gave Signe a cold look. "Oh?"

Signe decided to stand her ground. "On Monday I found a bundle of rags in the old manure pile behind the Marks' barn."

Charlie gave a deprecating laugh. "That's the first

I've heard of that story. The husband is always the last to know."

Ed's face turned white with anger. "Charlie, we didn't ask you. Signe, what kind of rags were they?"

"I didn't open the bundle, but I saw what looked like a man's undershirt. Cotton. Like what Charlie wears."

"What she means is that it was a brand that the Co-op sells," Sam explained. "Right, Signe?"

"Yaa."

"What did you do with the bundle?" Ed asked her.

"I didn't touch it. It smelled real bad. I covered the whole thing with earth as fast as I could pile it on. I wanted the constable to look at it."

Charlie put on his cap. "Well, let's go. boys."

"Come, Signe," Ed said. "We'll all ride in my car."

Signe led the men through the barn to the yard. Her heart sank when she glanced at the manure pile. It was evident that someone had worked the heap over since her visit, but she got the old fork from behind the grain barrel and handed it to Ed.

The men took turns in sifting the composted animal refuse, but found nothing except a part of a bleached cow skeleton.

Charlie turned to Sam and Ed. "If Signe really saw what she thinks she saw, her broadcasting the find alerted the killer to remove the bloody clothes."

Ed quickly turned to Charlie. "Who says they were bloody?"

Charlie stammered. "She did."

"She only said the rags smelled real bad."

"Well, doesn't that mean they were bloody?"

"Could have been rancid sweat or urine," Ed snapped. "Come, I'll take you home. I have things to do."

After dropping Signe and Charlie at their place, Ed and Sam decided to ask John Granlund to join them in a search on Charlie's east forty. He had now reported two empty graves on his property besides the one in the Marks' pasture. "I didn't like the way he talked to Signe today," Ed said.

"If you were the killer and your wife led a search for evidence, how would you act?"

Ed blinked in surprise. "You think Charlie—"

"Who doesn't?"

"What proof have you?" Ed asked.

"None. I have it from good sources that he was crazy about the widow, and he'd heard that she was going to see her boyfriend in Chicago around Labor Day. Signe was making new dresses for her, I heard. The widow probably repelled Charlie's advances and he finished her off so no one else could have her either."

Ed's thoughts went back to Charlie's accident and the bottle of "Evening in Paris" that was stashed with Charlie's tools in the cardboard box in the back of his car. "I'd hate to think that of a devout Christian, a good church member, but you just might have something there."

Sam was silent for a while. "Charlie goes back on his mail route next week?"

"That's what Gilpin told me."

"What do you say I stop by John Granlund's place tonight and ask him to join us—say next Monday—and we make a thorough search of the 'graves' that Charlie has found, and the surrounding area?"

"Okay by me," Ed replied, as he stopped the car at Sam's mailbox.

Sam got out of the car and slammed the car door shut. "Let's bring our lunches so we can spend the day if we need to. There's something very peculiar about the widow's disappearance. Should we give the constable a call and ask him to join us?"

"By all means," Ed replied. "But I just thought of something. We can't search Charlie's property without his permission."

"Right you are. So what do we do?"

"I'll ask Signe. She wants the case solved more than anyone," Ed said as he turned the ignition key and put his foot on the accelerator.

"And I'll talk to Granlund and give Winslow a ring," Sam called to him as he opened his mailbox.

Chapter XXXIII

MONDAY MORNING Ed Koski, Sam Isaacson, and John Granlund were joined by Constable Winslow and a host of other locals, all bent on finding the body. Whose body, it wasn't clear, but with three vacated graves and the Marks widow missing, there was bound to be a body somewhere. The meeting place was across the road from the Skinnar house. Charlie, as yet, had not gotten wind of the exploration of his property. Ed had received Signe's permission by phone.

The men came prepared with shovels, picks, axes, pitchforks, and even a scythe. Pete Hutto held in hand his newly acquired Metallascope. "What in the hell you going to do with that?" Sam asked him. "We're not prospecting for metals or minerals."

"Many of the best things are arrived at by

accident," Pete mused. "There might be copper, silver, or even gold in this area. One never knows."

"This is iron ore country," Ed told Pete.

"So Charlie's forty would turn out to be another Hibbing. I'm not the selfish type. I'd split with him."

Ed was peering into a recently dug hole. "This must be one of the 'graves' Charlie thought he found."

"Why that's not big enough to bury a newborn calf in," John exclaimed.

Sam surveyed the pit. "That's nothing. Just a hole in the ground."

"Who dug it?" Pete asked, hopefully setting his instrument at the edge of the cavity.

"The hollow we found on the Marks' property at least looked like a grave," Sam continued. "Charlie Skinnar is having some fun at our expense. He probably threw the body down his barn well."

"Charlie killed the widow?" Pete yelped. "He'll land up in Stillwater."

Ed, ever cautious, hurried to correct any false impression Pete may have gotten. "Sam is just joking, Pete. You know how reckless Sam can get with his buffoonery. We don't know who killed Mrs. Marks. We don't even know that she's dead. She might have gone to see a friend—"

Pete interrupted. "Yaa, I heard she had a boyfriend—hey, listen to the ticking," he squealed. "I found it."

"Found what?" John asked.

"Iron ore."

Ed looked down and, in his persevering manner,

said, "Pete, will you get that thing off my boot."

"Now, where's the third grave supposed to be?" John asked Ed.

"I have no idea. Let's see what we can find."

At that point, the constable left the group and went his own separate way.

Ed looked around to view the area, and said, "Men, let's do a spread-out parallel search. John, you take the area to the left of me. Pete and I will take the middle, and Sam, you and your boys cover the right as far as the south fence line."

The morning's search uncovered nothing. Promptly at twelve, the men stopped at a grassy knoll and sat down for lunch.

After his last sandwich, John Granlund lit his pipe and said, "We're wasting our time. I think we should go back to the Marks' place. What we found here is nothing but a rabbit hole. The one in the widow's pasture looked more like a grave. Furthermore, why should anyone want to transport a dead body a couple of miles in this heat just to rebury it?"

Pete Hutto blew the dust off his metal detector. "That's what I asked my wife this morning."

"What was her answer?"

"'To give you stupid men something to get excited about,' she said."

"Tekla is smarter than you think," John joshed, and got up to resume the reconnaissance.

Not content to stay with the group, Pete dashed about a few hundred feet ahead of the others aiming his instrument toward the ground. Suddenly he gave a hoot.

Ed shook his head thinking it was another false alert, but hastened to the spot at which Pete pointed. "Now this is real," he said, and blew his whistle. The two other groups came running. "Pete found another grave."

The cavity had been filled with earth, but after removing the top third of the loose soil the men found a woman's stocking. "He was in a hurry," Ed said. "He missed the sock."

Pete stared at Ed. "Who we talking about?"

"A crazy man. Does anyone here have an idea whose stocking this might be?" Their noncommittal silence told Ed that each man had an answer he didn't wish to air.

"Give it to the constable," John said. "It's valuable evidence."

By nightfall, the search group had covered the forty acres up to Lindgren's fence line. They were joined by Winslow. Ed handed the constable the stocking and explained what they had found and asked, "What more can we do? It looks like the killer has moved into another area taking all evidence with him."

The constable patted his ear as if shaking marbles out of the ear canal. "What are we looking for? We don't know. Finding a worn ladies' stocking doesn't necessarily mean there's a dead lady around. We might as well give up. I'm dead tired and about to go deaf listening to that yapping mongrel."

"Where?" Ed asked. "We haven 't seen any dogs

around here."

"By the old brush pile, near the burned shed."

Ed knew the spot. It was on the south side of Charlie's forty, the area that Sam and his crew had covered. Ed quickly led the men to the scene. "Why that's Buster, Eldon Skinnar's dog." He petted the dog and asked, "What you doing here, Buster?"

The animal would not be heartened. It kept up a mournful whine.

Ed said, "Let's see what's under the brush."

"That's ten-year-old stuff. Can't you see?" One of the men in Sam 's group moaned. "I'm not wasting my time carting that away." But the others followed Ed, and branch by branch the space was cleared showing newly disturbed earth underneath.

Charlie Skinnar arrived, dressed for the occasion, spade in hand. "You boys find something?"

At Charlie's entrance, Buster silenced and, with his tail between his hind legs, slinked out of sight.

With his eye on the fleeing dog, Ed replied, "We'll see," and stepped down on his shovel.

Charlie was right there giving a helping hand, and the others joined in the dig.

Two and a half feet down, they came upon a naked, badly decomposed headless woman's body. The men were not prepared for what they had come for. The scene defied description. All was quiet until Pete Hutto, the church choir director, lost his lunch on the Metallascope.

Charlie rested on his shovel and shook his head. "The work of a mad man. We'll have to have an inquest."

Winslow shook his head as he stared at the body before him. "I'll give the coroner a call."

Ed Koski looked at Charlie. "May God have mercy."

Chapter XXXIV

TUESDAY WHEN CHARLIE ARRIVED home from his mail route, Signe told him to call the coroner at once.

"What for?"

"Mr. Simpson wants you to conduct the inquest."

The mental picture of himself presiding at the hearing gave Charlie reason to straighten up to his full height. His right eye danced excitedly. "Why me?"

"Mr. Simpson is very sick. He's leaving for the Mayo Clinic in the morning. The doctors around here don't know what's wrong with him."

"But why me?" Charlie repeated, milking whatever laudatory utterances he could out of Signe.

"You're a Justice of the Peace and you know what should be done. Who else is capable of such legal work?"

Charlie smiled. "I guess you're right. You almost always are," he added and went to the phone. He took the receiver off the hook and rang the operator. "Central, would you get me the coroner?"

After receiving full instructions from Mr. Simpson as to procedure, Charlie gave a call to Mr. Gilpin, the ex-postman and asked him to take the mail route on Thursday and Friday.

The next morning he dispatched a warrant to Constable Winslow to "summon six good and lawful men of Becker County to appear before me at Kaisala's Funeral home in New York Mills at 10:00 a.m. Thursday, August 25th, to inquire upon view of the headless body of a woman there lying dead, how and by what means she came to her death. Hereof fail not." He signed the document, Charlie Skinnar, Deputy Coroner.

Charlie added a postscript: Since Ed Koski, Sam Isaacson, and John Granlund were with us when we discovered the body, they would be three good men to summon to Kaisala's Funeral Home for the inquest. Charlie didn't include Pete Hutto.

Seated on the school steps with his brother, Eldon carefully repacked the partially eaten jelly sandwich and closed his lunch bucket. "Don't you want it?" Hugo asked.

Eldon shook his head.

"Can I have it?"

"Yaa, and the bologna sandwich, too, if you want it." Eldon handed the pail to his brother. "Put it on the shelf in the porch when you're done."

"Gee, whiz. Thank you."

Eldon looked to see if anyone was looking in his direction. Everyone seemed occupied. He went down the steps and ran south of the building, then hopped over the fence to Nylund's side.

Reino was standing under the big elm, fidgetting. "I thought you'd never come."

"I had to eat my sandwich."

"What kind?"

"Imitation grape jelly."

"I like grape jelly. I never get grape jelly," Reino grumbled.

"Come over. I'll make you a plateful of jelly sandwiches. Mother's been saying, 'Why doesn't Reino visit us anymore?'"

"Tell her I can't stand Charlie. I'd kill him."

"You wouldn't!"

"Nah. It would be wrong."

"I wish you'd come and see us. Elma and Elsie think you're mad at them."

"When they get bigger, they can come visit me at my place."

"That's too long to wait."

"Thursday's the inquest."

"How'd you find out?"

"Uncle Ed heard over the party line. He'll have to go to the funeral parlor to look at the body."

"But he already saw it."

"Not officially." Reino took off his dingy striped denim cap and milked the straight strands of hair dangling over his forehead as he reviewed the circumstances. "Charlie might be sentenced on Thursday, and I could come on Thursday night—before dark. What does Charlie say?"

"Papa says the killer will be caught and sent to Stillwater." Eldon paused. "What do you think?"

"Sure thing. They're saying, 'Charlie Skinnar did it. Charlie Skinnar killed the Marks Widow.'" Reino lowered his voice. "They're searching for the head."

Eldon looked around to see if anyone was around. "Yaa, I know. But they'll never find it. No one else knows except Violet, and she will never tell. She had to know because we needed to have her make the roses."

"Yaa, the head had to have a Christian burial. You sang so beautiful."

Eldon smiled at the compliment. "Papa hates Buster now more than ever. Sometimes I'm afraid he'll kill my dog."

"Nah. He's too smart."

"Buster?"

"Nah, Charlie. If he killed the dog, people would say 'Charlie Skinnar killed his boy's dog because the dog found the body.'"

"Are you going to tell them what we saw?"

"Nobody's going to ask me. They all think I'm goofy."

"Mother doesn't. She says you're as smart as anybody and much kinder."

Reino smiled. "Really?"

"I don't lie. You know that. If she asked you, would you tell her?"

Reino stared at this young friend. "Why would she? Nobody knows what we saw."

"Just supposing you were asked, would you tell?"

"No, it would hurt Elma and she is the only one I have in this world." Reino began to cry.

"Don't cry. You have me and Violet and Hugo and Elsie. You even have my mother."

Reino smiled and gave his nose a swish with his sleeve. "We'll go to our graves with our secret."

"I'd feel better if I could tell someone," Eldon said wistfully. "It's a secret I don't want to keep."

"But we can't tell."

"No, we can't."

Chapter XXXV

AT 3:00 P.M. FRIDAY, the day after the inquest at the funeral home, a hearing was held at the Wolf Creek Finnish hall, a small structure designed for dances and socials, with a kitchen and a stage in the back and a coat closet by the front entrance. A large picture of President Franklin Delano Roosevelt and the American flag with forty-eight stars graced the room.

Charlie Skinnar, acting as Deputy Coroner, presided. Miss Forsland, the clerk, sat to his right. Constable Winslow, Dr. Cone, Signe Skinnar and Hilda Mattson were seated in the front chairs as were the witnesses. Newspapers around the state had been covering the story of the empty graves, and finally the discovery of a woman's headless body. The morbidly curious from as far as Fargo had come to get the details first hand, and they packed the hall.

The county attorney had examined and approved the witnesses; Charlie now was ready to administer the oath to the jury. He looked at the six men dressed in their black Sunday suits: Ed Koski, Sam Isaacson, John Granlund, Wayne Siren, Jacob Rontty and Peter Hutto. The constable had done well to include the men he had suggested, but Charlie had reservations about Rontty and Hutto.

This was Charlie's day of glory. All eyes were on him. He tapped the table with the gavel and in firm tones announced, "We are gathered here today to inquire and hear all evidence concerning the death of a female person whose headless body was found on the Fourteenth of August. Said person was located in a shallow grave on the property of Charlie Skinnar.

"The jury, upon inspection of the dead body, and after hearing the testimony and making the needful inquiries, shall draw up and deliver to the coroner the inquisition, under their hands, in which they shall find and certify when, how, and by what means the deceased person came to her death, and her name, if it is known, together with all the material circumstances attending her death; and, if it appears that the death was caused by criminal violence, the jurors shall further state who were guilty, either as principals or accessories, if known, or were in any manner the cause of her death.

"Will the witnesses, please, now stand and raise your right hand."

The six men did as instructed.

"You do solemnly swear that the evidence you shall give to this inquest concerning the death of the person you viewed at Kaisala's Funeral Home yesterday shall be the whole truth and nothing but the truth; so help you God."

"I do," the men voiced in unison and sat down.

Charlie then cautioned them not to indict anyone through envy, hatred, malice or political consideration, nor leave any person unindicted through fear, favor, affection, reward or the hope thereof of political consideration. "Any questions?" he asked.

Hilda Mattson raised her hand.

"Yes, Mrs. Mattson?"

"What are you doing here? You're not the coroner."

"Good question, Hilda. Minnesota statute number one—" Charlie's explanation was cut short by Hilda clearing her throat. "Mr. Simpson is unable to serve because of illness. I'm taking his place."

There were nods and murmurs of assent, and Hilda applauded. "Good for you, Charlie," she exclaimed. "You got that down to plain terms, simple English that we can all understand. That highfalutin legal lingo doesn't cut the mustard with us farm—"

Charlie interrupted Hilda, politely. "Can we proceed with the business at hand, Mrs. Mattson?"

"Oh, certainly."

Charlie cleared his throat. "The investigation is starting now. I hope we can keep the questions and answers to the subject at hand. We have a big job to do, and we'll need everyone's cooperation. Is that clear?"

Everyone except Hilda, nodded. She had another question.

Charlie massaged his upper lip with his forefinger. "Yes?"

"How did you know where to find the body?"

"First things first, Mrs. Mattson." Charlie switched his gaze from Hilda to Winslow. "Constable, why don't you tell us in your own words—"

Winslow stood up, adjusted his glasses and cleared his throat. "Well, when I heard that the widow was missing and was told that she had been seen riding in your mail car—"

Charlie listened, feigning keen interest in the lawman's bit of information. "Who told you that? On second thought, I think Mrs. Skinnar should be the one to start the ball rolling." He turned to his wife. "Signe, tell us what happened on that Thursday. Start from the beginning."

Signe was flustered. "What a terrible day!" She twisted her white handkerchief into knots as she related the facts as she recalled them, adding, "Then I called Mrs. Mattson, and asked, 'Have you seen Mary Marks today—'"

With her forefinger in the air, Hilda interrupted Signe to ask Charlie, "May I make a correction?" Getting Charlie's nod, she continued. 'Signe, you did not call me. I called you. Remember?"

Signe nodded. "I was going to call, but you called me."

"What then?" Charlie asked.

"I had this funny feeling here." Signe clutched at her chest. "Like an arrow through my heart."

"Forget the pain, Signe. Just tell the story, step by step."

"I called Hilda the next day—" Signe paused and looked at her friend. "What's wrong, Hilda?"

"You did not call me. I came to your house."

Signe perked up. "Right. You then told me that Mary Marks had been seen riding in the mail car."

"Where did you get the idea that the Marks widow had been riding in the mail car?" Charlie asked Hilda.

"They say she was riding in the mail car," Hilda answered boldly, "and she was wearing a bright red dress."

"Who said that?"

"I dunno. Somebody on the party line."

"Do you always believe what you hear on the party line?" Charlie asked.

"Not always," Hilda stated, defiantly.

Charlie stared at Hilda and then asked, "Have you ever seen anyone riding in my mail car?"

"I wasn't watching," Hilda retorted. She turned her head and viewed her audience with a self-satisfied look.

Charlie faced his audience and asked, "Has anyone here ever seen me driving around with another person in the mail car? With Signe? With the kids?"

The jury and witnesses avoided Charlie's scrutiny.

"Even on Sunday mornings when I take my family to church," he continued, "I use my Chevy pickup and Signe and I sit in the front, with the kids in the back of the truck. The Ford Sedan I save for the mail." Charlie then directed his gaze at the constable.

"What happened the next day, Constable?"

Winslow smoothed his wispy tresses and blinked.

"You said to me, 'I've found what looks like an open grave. I suspect foul play.'"

"Before that, Constable."

Winslow shrugged and stared blankly at Charlie.

"The schoolteacher called you," Charlie reminded the constable, "and asked what she should do with the Marks children."

"Right," Winslow exclaimed excitedly. "And I told her, 'You keep them. I don't have a wife.'"

Without the formality of a raised hand, Hilda now addressed the Deputy Coroner with the question that was on most minds, "Charlie, what were you doing in Mrs. Marks' woods?"

"Trapping."

"This time of the year?" Hilda shrieked.

"Why not?"

"The fur's no good. It's too hot. The animals rot in the traps. Even after you skin them, you have a hard time keeping them from spoiling."

"Mrs. Mattson, I can set your mind completely at ease."

"How?"

"What month is this, Hilda?"

"August," she replied, "and next month is September. So what?"

"Have you looked at your cat lately?"

"I don't have a cat."

"Have you read the *Farmer's Almanac*?"

"I have better things to read."

"It would do well for everyone to read the almanac," Charlie said. "The forecast is for the coldest winter—"

"Hooh," Hilda sputtered. "I should find out that I will freeze to death next winter!"

Charlie was pleased with himself, the center of attention, eloquent and impressive, with a confined audience. "The weasels are already turning white," he continued. "The pelts on the muskrats are thicker than I've ever seen them since I started trapping at the age of seven. Even the cows have fur like beavers. To make a long story short, Mrs. Mattson, every morning on my way to the post office to pick up the mail, I set the traps. On my way home, after the mail route, I check them. Does that answer your question?"

"Why was the body moved so much?" Hilda asked. "Three graves!"

"Four," Charlie corrected. "That is a question I cannot answer."

Hilda shook her head. "Charlie, how come you found all the graves?"

The constable spoke up. "Only three. The dog discovered the one with the body in it."

"Dog?" Hilda said.

"Yeah. He was yapping his head off by the brush pile. First I thought it was a coyote. Then I looked more closely and saw this gray mongrel — "

Signe gasped. "Buster!"

Charlie grabbed the gavel and struck the table briskly. "Order! We must have order."

The constable continued his story as if there had been no interruption. "The search party started early in the morning when Charlie was on his mail route. While the men did a parallel search, I went nosying by myself. First thing I hear is this dog howling his head off by the brush pile. As I said, I thought it was a wild coyote, and felt like putting it out of its misery with the maple stump that lay close by. But when it began wagging its tail, I had a second thought. I had the boys move the piled brush, and there she lay under about a foot of dirt. Looked like she'd just been buried there — without the head."

The room was quiet.

Signe, whose face had turned the color of a gravenstein apple in early June, began nervously waving her hand in the air.

"What is it now, Signe?" Charlie asked.

"May I, please, be excused?"

"Why?"

"I don't feel well. I have a headache."

"Take a coupla aspirin." Charlie then turned to the court reporter and instructed her to get a glass of water for Mrs. Skinnar.

Signe dug in her purse for aspirin, forced it down with water, and sat like a caged animal.

"What's become of the head?" Hilda demanded to know.

Charlie smiled patronizingly at his adversary. "That's what we're trying to learn. That's what we're here for."

Hilda's black eyes flashed as she shot glances around the room for support, which didn't appear to be forthcoming. "I thought we were here to decide who killed Mary Marks."

"We do not know that Mrs. Marks is dead," Charlie countered.

Hilda shook her head, mumbled to herself, and

finally spat it all out. "I say when you have a lady who just had a red dress made and she disappears from the face of the earth and we find a dead lady wearing the exact same dress, I think we can safely say that the two ladies are one and the same."

Charlie smiled. "Mrs. Mattson, the body we found had no clothes on." He looked at the jury. "Is that not correct?"

The six men nodded.

Hilda would not be discounted so easily. "I heard that when they found Mrs. Marks, she was wearing the red dress Signe had made and that the murderer had taken off her pink rayon bloomers—"

Charlie stopped Hilda. "She was stark naked and there were no clothes in sight."

"Let me finish!" Hilda shouted. "They say she was wearing the red dress, her bloomers, all bloodied, by her—"

Charlie was livid. "Hilda, you're out of order!"

Hilda turned to Signe. "You said you saw the piece that was torn from the dress that was found in one of the graves."

"Yes. The piece Charlie brought home was from the dress I made. When I saw it, I knew she was dead. I would give my right arm to have her walk in here alive."

Charlie closed his right eye and gave the lid a superficial brush with the tip of his little finger. "I'm sure we all feel the same but right now we have a job to do. I will call upon Dr. Cone, who has examined the body to give a professional opinion as to the cause of death. Dr. Cone, may we have your statement, please."

Dr. Cone, who was holding on to the sixth decade of his century and had seen the ravages of death in many forms, stood up. "When I was called," he began, "the remains had already been taken to Kaisala's Funeral Home. So far as I could determine, the person had been dead several days, and was in bad shape of decay, especially since it had been buried and moved several times. It was a female in her late thirties. She was wearing no rings. The ring finger on her left hand had been broken. The woman had no birth marks or distinguishing characteristics. She had been decapitated. Her head had been severed with what appeared to be a single blow from a very sharp instrument—"

"Like an ax, would you say?" Charlie interjected.

"Quite possibly," Cone replied.

Signe let out a cry.

Charlie looked at her but ignored the interruption. "Anything else you wish to add, Doctor?"

"Medical examination indicated that her person had been violated."

Not understanding the wordage, Signe asked, "What?"

Hilda moved over and whispered in Signe's ear.

The explanation completely undid Signe. "Oi-oi-oi," she moaned.

Charlie pounded angrily on the table with his gavel and coldly summoned, "Quiet! We must have order."

Hilda gave Charlie a daunting look and addressed the specialist in the matter. "Doctor Cone, do you think it was Mary Marks' body that was found?"

"I have no way of knowing," Cone admitted. "Since the head was missing, there was no way of identifying the body."

Hilda tightened the black patent leather belt around her ample waist, and focused her flashing black eyes on the constable, and asked, "Winslow, what happened to the head?"

The lawman shrugged his shoulders, shook his head, and opened his palms as if to show that he was hiding nothing.

"Did you look for it?" Hilda wanted to know.

"All over."

Charlie came to the aid of his scolded friend. "It just disappeared."

"Nothing just disappears," Hilda countered. "It was either taken away or hidden."

"There are wild anima—" Charlie started to say.

But Hilda interrupted him. "BPHHHHH! There would be some trace." Again she asked Charlie, "Why was the body moved so many times?"

Charlie smiled and with childlike innocence, replied, "Don't ask me. I don't know."

Signe waved her hand like an excited schoolgirl. "I know."

Charlie acknowledged her with, "Yes, mama."

In carefully chosen English, Signe explained what she thought had taken place, the gist of which was: The murderer buried the body near the scene of the crime. Then decided to move it to another site where no one would think of looking for it. Deciding it was too close to the road, he'd moved to another hole.

Next day, still farther. Finally, he decided to cover the grave with old brush and when fall came, he would set a match to it and "Poof, the brush pile would be burned, body an' all."

The constable applauded. "The first intelligent observation of the day!"

Signe blushed and looked down.

Charlie watched and listened to his wife's theory with fascination, and asked, "Signe, what makes you think the killer intended to burn the body?"

"Easy. We burn brush piles in the spring after the earth dries, and each fall as soon as the weather cools. Every year we burn. All the farmers do it."

Hilda shook her head with frustration. "There are too many questions with no answers. I just don't like it."

"That's what we're here for," Charlie commented brightly, "to ask questions, answer questions, and try to solve this puzzle."

Hilda sparked up again. "I say we dig up the body and take another look."

Charlie bristled. "What good would that do?"

"There is an answer," Hilda declared. "We just haven't searched carefully enough."

Charlie sighed, wiped his eyes with his large white handkerchief, and addressed Cone again. "Doctor, can we have your expert opinion once more?"

"Truly, exhuming the body would serve no purpose," the doctor replied. "The burial was only yesterday. As I indicated earlier, the body already was in a badly decomposed condition when it was discovered."

The doctor's testimony satisfied Charlie. "Any more questions?" he asked as he noticed Rontty standing for attention. "Yes, Jacob?"

"There's been talk about Mrs. Marks' lover. Who was he?"

Charlie grabbed at the edge of the bench. His right eye became agitated. "How should I know?"

"You're the mailman. The mailman sees what others don't. Like did she get little packages with perfume, chocolates or letters—"

"I do not snoop!" Charlie replied, angrily, cutting off Rontty. I don't taste, smell or read what I put into the post boxes on my route. Any other questions?"

Pete Hutto jumped to his feet as Rontty sat down. "I have a few. You recently purchased the forty acres east of your—"

Charlie cut off Pete. "That is my business, and has nothing to do with the case before us."

"The body was dragged from the Marks' place to yours?"

"So it appears," Charlie replied.

"Was the hole found on the Marks' place a grave or was it just a hole?"

"It was a grave," Signed blurted out. "Mary Marks had been buried there, I know." She stopped short. It occurred to Signe that she had not told anyone about the straight pin and the heeless shoe she'd uncovered at the site. Was she guilty of withholding evidence? She couldn't think.

"Signe, answer Mr. Hutto," Charlie commanded.

"Because it looked like a grave," she replied.

Ed Koski came to Signe's rescue. "I agree with

Mrs. Skinnar. It was not just a hole. Some form of life had been buried there for a time. A short distance from the grave we found an area which we concluded was the spot where slaughter had taken place. The grass had been trampled to nothing. Fallen leaves were coated with dried blood. The smell was sickening."

Charlie, satisfied that the inquest was over, focused his attention on the six jurors, and as he announced, "We shall await the verdict of the jury," Reino Koski entered.

Reino looked around the room from underneath his eyebrows, but made no eye contact with anyone. He plunked himself next to Hilda, and when the attention was on Reino, Eldon slipped in the door unnoticed, into the coatroom.

"Reino, what are you doing here?" Charlie asked.

Reino smirked. "Why?"

"This is a legal hearing."

"I know."

"You weren't invited."

"I know," Reino replied, daringly.

"I'll get rid of him," the constable cracked as he scurried around the chairs to Reino, and grabbed him by the arm.

Hilda slapped Winslow on the wrist. "He has as much right as anyone. This is a public hearing."

"I got as much right as anyone," Reino repeated, challengingly. Then stared at his toes and grinned.

"Let him be," Charlie told the constable, and shifted his gaze to the newcomer. "Reino, if you want to stay, you have to take an oath."

"I know."

"What for?" Hilda shouted. "He's not under suspicion."

"Stand up and raise your right hand," Charlie instructed.

Reino stood like a West Pointer, waiting for orders. "Push the hair off your forehead, so I can see your face." Reino flipped over the glossy brown strands with his right hand and raised it again and took the oath. Charlie said, "You may be seated."

Reino sat, looked around the room, and grinned.

"Why aren't you wearing a suit?" Charlie asked.

"I don't have a suit."

"Don't you have anything else?" Charlie asked, as he stared at the red shirt.

Reino grabbed the front of his scarlet flannel and shook it. "What's wrong with this? It's new."

"That your hunting shirt?"

"I don't hunt. I don't kill." Reino smiled, gratified, shook the front of his shirt some more, and asked his adversary, "You don't like it, do you?"

"It's hideous."

"It's the color, isn't it? The red color. Why don't you like the red color?"

"It is evil."

"Why is it evil?" Reino asked.

"It is the color of tarts and harlots!"

"Don't say that, Charlie," Signe protested. "It is a beautiful color. Mary Marks wore red and she was a very nice lady."

Charlie was at breaking point. "Signe, you keep

out of this," he snapped.

Reino felt exultant. He was getting to Charlie. "Signe," he said, "ask Charlie what happened to the last red dress you made."

A dead silence fell over the gathering.

"Enough of this wrangling," Hilda finally cried out. "Let's get on with the inquest. We don't have all day."

Charlie was hyperventilating. "Reino—"

"Yes, sir!"

"Where were you when the Marks widow disappeared?"

"What day was that?"

"I ask the questions," Charlie growled. "You answer them."

Reino, gratified, grinned and said, "Go ahead, shoot."

"Where were you when the Marks widow disappeared?"

"Why?"

"Just answer the question."

"What's the question?"

Charlie was agitated. His right eye jerked uneasily. "I will put the question to you this one more time. Where were you when Mary Marks disappeared?"

Reino became serious. "Here and there."

"What's here and there?"

"Around."

Charlie was shaking. "I'm not playing a game, Reino. One more crack out of you and I'll charge you with contempt. Do you know what that is?"

"I know."

"Once more, where were you when Mary Marks disappeared?"

Reino looked Charlie in the eye, and asked, "What do you want me to say?"

Charlie flinched. "Did you kill Mary Marks?"

Eldon rushed out of the coatroom, crying hysterically, and put his arms around Reino. "Father, don't say that! You know he didn't kill her." The confrontation now became a three-way scuffle.

"Take that back," Reino shouted to Charlie in a shaky voice. "Or I'll wring your neck," Reino added, as he went through the motions with his fists, grinding his teeth.

"Eldon, what are you doing here?" Charlie asked his son.

"I followed Reino."

"Why did you drag my son here?" Charlie hollered at Reino.

"Are you going to take it back?" Reino repeated.

"Are you threatening my life?" Charlie yelled.

"No, just your neck," Reino bellowed. "Are you going to take it back?" Getting no answer, Reino sprang and grabbed Charlie by the throat. "Are you going to take it back?"

Eldon sobbed and hugged Reino tighter. "Father, don't be bad to Reino. He's my friend."

Charlie, frightened, screamed, "Constable!"

Eldon, holding tight to Reino, whimpered, "Father, you can whip me all you want, but please don't be bad to Reino. He's a good man."

Winslow stood up and asked Charlie, "Want me

to restrain him?"

"Sit down, Winslow," Hilda ordered.

The befuddled lawman looked around and sat down.

Reino looked down at Eldon, took his hands off Charlie's neck, then patted Eldon on the shoulder and returned to his seat.

Hilda motioned to her husband who was seated in the back of the room. "Take Eldon home," she told him, "and stay with the kiddies until Signe gets there. I'll ride with Ed Koski."

Gust took Eldon by the hand and led him out. There was a moment of quiet. "Strike that last question," Charlie instructed Miss Forsland.

Reino grinned, satisfied that he had won the last round.

"Reino, are you married?" Charlie asked.

Reino looked up in surprise. "You know I'm not."

"Why not?" Charlie asked cagily.

Reino looked around the room, questioningly. "What would I do with a wife?"

"Explain yourself," Charlie ordered.

"How could I take care of her? I can hardly take care of myself."

"Why not?"

Reino was embarrassed. "You know why not."

"Just tell the court."

Reino looked down and murmured, "I have fits."

"What has his health to do with this inquest?" Hilda shouted angrily.

Charlie gave a satisfied smile. "We will see." He turned to Reino. "You have fits? Have you always suffered from these fits?"

"You know I haven't. It was only after that thunderstorm when I was mowing hay and the lightning frightened the horses and they ran over me that I began to have these spells."

Hilda blew her nose and wiped her eyes. "Everyone knows about his brain injury. Why bring it up now?"

"Just for the records," Charlie replied.

"You're trying to make me look like a freak," Reino observed, grimly. "I'm no dumbbell."

"When you have these fits," Charlie asked, "do you know what you're doing?"

"No."

"So, when you have these hallucinations, you're capable of almost anything."

"I'm not capable of anything," Reino retorted. "And I don't have hallucinations. I just lie there unconscious and have spasms."

"How often do you have these fits?"

"Oh, I don't have them anymore—unless I forget to take my medicine."

"Do you forget to take your medicine?"

Reino looked up. "Sometimes. Don't you?"

"I don't have fits and I don't take medicine," Charlie retorted angrily, looking sorry he asked.

"It's not bad after you get used to it."

Charlie took a new avenue. "Do you have a girl friend, Reino?"

Reino looked around, giggled and shook his head. "Nooo."

"What's the matter? Don't you like ladies?"

"Oh, yes. Don't you?" Everyone laughed. Reino enjoyed the response. He looked at person to person, and then at his feet, shaking with the giggles.

"Did you like Mary Marks?"

Reino no longer laughed. "Oh, yes, I loved her."

"You loved Mary Marks?" Charlie reiterated.

"Yes, I did, but she's dead."

"That has to be proved," Charlie restated. "Do you love any other ladies?"

Reino stared at Signe. "I love your wife."

"You love my wife?"

Reino nodded.

"Why do you love Signe?"

"Because she treats me good, just like any other visitor who comes to your house. She asks me if I would like a cup of coffee and pulla, but never waits for my answer. She says, 'Reino, come to the table,' and pours me coffee and cuts some pulla with cardamom. I like cardamom. It smells good. Sometimes Signe makes her coffee bread with cinnamon and raisins. I like that, too." Reino looked around in the silence that followed. Signe was dabbing her eyes with the corner of her twisted handkerchief.

"Reino, you said you have those fits because the horses ran over you," Charlie continued. "Isn't it true that you have a cousin who suffered from fits, too, and now is in the insane asylum?"

Reino, mortified, looked at his feet ashamedly. "I—I don't know."

"Stop, Charlie!" Hilda shouted. "That's hitting below the belt. You know as well as I that Reino was a blue baby, and there's not one here who doesn't have a skeleton or two in the closet. All any man has is his pride and his honor, let Ray hold on to his."

Ed Koski stood up. "Charlie, I hesitated saying anything until now since you have the floor, so to speak; but your treatment of my nephew is cruel, to say the least, especially since he is beyond a doubt, innocent of a crime such as we're investigating. As coroner, you have the right to question whomever you wish, but leave family histories out of your interrogations."

"Strike the last question from the records, Miss Forsland," Charlie instructed, and in the same breath asked Reino why he loved Mary Marks.

"She let Eldon and me pick the potato bugs off her potato plants. Then she'd give me and Eldon a candy bar. A Baby Ruth. Not a penny bar, but a real nickel bar. Big with lots of chocolate and nuts. I like Eldon," Reino went on to say. "He's just a little kid, but he's my friend. Sometimes we'd play checkers with the Marks kids, but they moved because their mother was murdered."

"Reino, we do not know that Mrs. Marks was murdered," Charlie reminded him in fatherly tones.

Reino shook his head, sadly. "A thump and a thud and she was gone. She couldn't even cry."

Charlie blanched, his right eye shuttering nervously. "What did you say?"

"I don't remember."

Charlie now was on another tangent. "Did Mary Marks have any boyfriends?" he asked Reino.

"Sure did."

"Did you know their names?"

"Yup! Reino and Eldon."

Charlie scratched his head in frustration. "I'm not talking about you, two. I mean real men."

Reino stared at Charlie. "We're real all right."

"Talk to a fool and get foolish answers," Charlie muttered under his breath. "Reino, you say the Marks widow was murdered. Were you there?"

Reino became fearful, and evaded the question. Holding his right hand straight before him he wildly flailed it in the air, pointing here and there. "There was the first grave, there was the second, there was the third and her pretty red dress was all muddied and ruined —"

Charlie watched Reino's demonstration with strange fascination. "Did you see it?" he asked.

"See what?"

"Her red dress."

"I sure did," Reino replied, looking at Signe. "It was beautiful. But she looked so sad riding in the car —"

"What car?" Charlie interrupted.

"In the car she was riding in. She didn't wave at me or say, 'Hi, Ray,' like she used to."

"When was that?"

"Before she died."

"Of course it was before she died," Charlie retorted. "When before she died?"

Reino looked blankly at Charlie. "I don't remember. Before the day was up, she was dead and six feet under."

"Have you told the truth?"

"I don't lie," Reino answered. "It is a sin."

"That about sums it up," Charlie announced. "Is there anyone present who has anything to add? Speak up now, for once this inquest is over, the jury will draw up and deliver to the coroner their findings." Charlie glanced at the blank, yet pained faces of the audience. Getting no verbal response, he instructed the jurors. "After inspection of the dead body, and hearing the testimony, you will now render your verdict and certify the same in writing signed by each of you, setting forth who the person killed is, if known, and when, where and by what means she came to her death; or if she was killed, or her death was occasioned by the act of another by criminal means, who is guilty thereof, if known."

Charlie handed the paper to the foreman of the jury, Ed Koski, who then returned it to Charlie once the members of the jury had made their notations. Charlie glanced at it, without any noticeable emotion, and gave it back to the foreman.

"The verdict is," the foreman read loud and clear, "Who the person killed, when, where, and by what means killed; if she was killed, or her death occasioned by the act of another by criminal means, and who is guilty is . . . Unknown . . . The verdict stands as read."

All was quiet except for Reino's sobbing.

That evening, after the supper dishes were cleared, Charlie sat at the kitchen table to complete the coroner's report, but couldn't concentrate. He felt isolated. He recalled the happenings of the day. After the inquest, he had expected to be congratulated on how well he'd conducted the investigation, but when he looked up from the paper that the foreman had handed him, the meeting hall was almost empty. He was dropped like a turd by a stump on a logging road, he told himself.

When he left the building, the parking lot was empty. The only living soul around was Reino, the damned idiot who earlier blubbered like a baby, was now grinning like a hyena.

"Charlie," Reino called out to him, "if you're looking for Signe, she and Hilda went home with my Uncle Ed." Then added, "In his new Pontiac," and smiled.

Reino is as cunning as a fox, Charlie told himself. He purposely hung around so he could give me a dig. Charlie felt like bashing Reino's head in. Instead, Charlie ignored Reino, hopped into the cab of his pickup, started the engine, and pushed the gas pedal down as far as it would go.

At home no welcome mat was laid out for Charlie. Signe said nothing to him. The girls ate supper in silence. Eldon and Hugo didn't come to the table. Violet sneaked food up to the attic. He was glad he didn't have to confront Eldon yet. Again he cursed Reino for bringing Eldon to the inquest. His children would have been unaware of the whole Marks incident had it not been for Reino Koski, he told himself.

Charlie, pen in hand, stared at the coroner's report before him.

County of Becker   )
State of Minnesota   )

An inquisition taken at the Wolf Creek Finnish Hall, in the County of Becker, on the 26th day of August, 1932, before Charlie Skinnar, Deputy Coroner of said County of Becker . . .

Charlie's reading was interrupted by the clanging of empty water pails. Signe, wearing her old barn coat, was headed out the door. "Where you going this time of night?"

"To the well," she snapped, as she stopped to tie an old flour sack dishtowel over her head. "Where did you think? To a dance?"

Her response stunned Charlie. She'd never been sarcastic.

"It can wait till morning," he said.

"The children need warm water to wash up before school." She went out and pulled the door after her.

Charlie returned to his document.

upon view of the body of an unknown female and testimony regarding thereof, by the oaths of the jurors whose names are hereunto subscribed—

Charlie thought of the jurors, six yokels in black serge suits, and spat out, "Idiots!" His mind then returned to Reino weeping at the closing and cursed, "*Saatanan, perkeleen.* Son of a bitch!"

Elsie tucked in bed with Elma, shook her sister and whispered, "Did you hear that? Papa sweared."

"Yaa. In English and Finnish."

"He's real mad."

"Yaa."

"Do you think he's mad at Mother?" Elsie asked.

"He wouldn't dare."

"He said, '*Saatanan, perkeleen,* son of a bitch.'"

"He must be mad at Jesus," Elma concluded.

"Quiet!" Violet from the next bed chastised, "Go to sleep, you two."

Charlie continued reading the coroner's report.

> who, being sworn to inquire on behalf of the State of Minnesota, when, how, and by what means the said unknown female person came to her death, upon their oaths do say, "Who the person killed, when, where, and by what means killed; if she was killed, or her death occasioned by the act of another by criminal means, and who is guilty is unknown.
>
> In testimony whereof, the said coroner and jurors of this inquest have hereunto set their hand the day and year aforesaid.

Charlie dated the coroner's report, signed his name with flourishes, Charlie Skinnar. Below his signature, he wrote: Deputy Coroner, and jabbed the fountain pen in the pocket of his suit. He was putting the Marks affair behind him and starting a new life, as it were.

Signe returned with the two pails of water. She set one on the wood box for drinking purposes, and poured the other into the tank in the wood stove.

"I'd like a cup of coffee," he told Signe, "and a piece of the green tomato pie if there's any left."

Signe obeyed his orders and disappeared into her bedroom.

Charlie stirred the sugar in his coffee and was about to partake of the pie when Signe returned with her pillow, robe, and slippers. "Where you going with that stuff?" he asked.

"I'm moving to the girls' bedroom."

"For good?"

Signe nodded and closed the door.

Charlie shoved the pie out of his way, blew out the lamp and sat there stunned. His new life had just ended.

Chapter XXXVI

CHARLIE ALWAYS LOOKED FORWARD to the school board meetings. The September gathering was no different. Although the call-to-order gavel wasn't scheduled until seven o'clock, the men usually made a point of coming a half hour earlier to discuss politics and other matters of importance. Several wives had come to bid for the job of washing the school floor twice a month. Mrs. Linden, who had the contract for the past two years was no longer interested in the job. She said getting on her hands and knees twice a month during the winter had given her arthritis.

"Good evening!" Charlie addressed the group gathered at the schoolhouse door waiting to be let in.

Only a few noncommittal murmurs met his friendly, cheerful greeting, except for Jacob Wirta, a newcomer and president of the board, who clearly grunted, "Evening," as he turned the latchkey.

"The nights are getting nippy," Charlie said.

"Yaa," Jacob replied, as he let the folks in. Without further comment, he went over to the furnace, opened the door and lured the flames with a couple of dried logs.

Charlie's right eye quivered as he looked for a desk to occupy for the evening. He chose a seat in the corner, behind Ida Wirta and Annie Hutto, two motherly housewives, who gave him a guarded smile. As he listened to the bidding for ten cords of firewood, Charlie felt like a spirit visiting its former haunts. Sam Isaacson bid two dollars lower than Ed Koski and got the contract for the firewood. Hilda Mattson wanted the job of scrubbing the school floor. She bid $6.50 a month, but Annie Wirta got it for $4.75.

As the evening progressed, Charlie knew he no longer belonged here, and when Jacob Wirta asked, "Any new business?" Charlie raised his hand and told the board members they'd have to find someone to replace him as treasurer, "I'm leaving for the West Coast. Going to Oregon." All was quiet. No one seemed surprised. He wanted reaction. He wanted them to know that Charlie Skinnar still existed, that he still was somebody. "I had an offer from the postal service there that I can't afford to pass."

It was seven thirty the next morning as Signe was pumping water for the heater in the kitchen range when Hilda, coatless, dressed in a flimsy cotton dress, came down the road at a fast clip, unusual for someone as heavy as she. "What's this I hear?" she called from a distance.

Signe released the pump handle. "What did you hear?"

Hilda stood by the well and panted. "You moving west."

Signe didn't want to acknowledge that she knew nothing about the move. "Where did you hear that?"

"Charlie made a loud announcement at the school board meeting last night when he resigned as treasurer. Said he'd gotten a good offer from the postal service. If you ask me, that's a lot of horse manure and I don't believe one word of it—I mean about the offer."

Hilda's black eyes locked on Signe's for denial or rebuttal, but Signe had no answers.

"Why would the government hire some country bumpkin with an eighth-grade education from Wolf Creek, Minnesota to work in Oregon," Hilda continued, "When, according to the newspapers, they have high school and college graduates waiting in unemployment lines?"

"Let's go inside, Hilda. It's getting cold. Feels like November. You have goose bumps all over your arms."

Hilda picked up the handle of one water pail. Signe carried two. "This is man's work," Hilda said. "Why can't Charlie carry in the water before he leaves for his mail route."

It was in the line of a statement, not a question. Signe didn't answer.

Hilda set her pail by the stove and sat by the table.

"Are you going with him?"

Signe felt as if she'd been hit on the head with a rock several times by the fast-moving incidents that had taken place lately. Charlie was acting on his own, making decisions without consulting her. Just recently he'd told Oscar Salo that his roots were here and he'd never leave Wolf Creek but the inquest had turned things around. "I don't know," she muttered.

"What do you mean, you don't know? Any woman in her right mind would have kissed Charlie Skinnar goodbye right after the inquest."

"I gave my word."

"What word?"

"To love, honor and obey," Signe replied, her voice inflexionless. "Until death do us part."

"Phooey! I know a divorced woman. She runs her own life and does very well. You don't have to worry about making a living. You've supported yourself and five youngsters this far. It couldn't be long before some good man would come around with a proposal."

Signe took out the coffee grinder, sat down and began to turn the handle. "I don't think I'd care to be honored with any more proposals." The inquest had changed their lives forever, she realized. Eldon and Violet felt friendless and suffered from rejection by their peers. Even the church felt foreign. It seemed people were hesitant to be friendly, to make small talk. Moving to the coast would be a new beginning. "I have to think of my children. They love Charlie. He's a good, kind, loving father."

"Mark my word, Signe, if you go with him, your

life will be nothing but headaches and heartaches. You'll regret the move every day of your natural life."

"Maybe so," Signe admitted, "but what future do my children have here in Wolf Creek? Eldon and Violet, even Hugo, talk about going to college. The high school is twenty-seven miles away. The road in the winter is blocked with snow half the time. Besides, how would we pay for their education? From what I've heard life in the West is easier than here. If we were close to a big city like Portland or Seattle, I might get a position as an alteration lady in a department store and the children could all go to college."

Signe's coffee grinding came to a halt as her mind wandered back in time to her arrival in Wolf Creek. There was Charlie Skinnar in his starched white shirt and bow tie, his stock of auburn hair being teased by the breeze, standing by his Model T at the railway station, expectant and ready to take her wherever she might have wished to go.

She recalled Eldon's difficult birth and the midwife's strange behavior after looking at him, the births of all the children and Charlie's love for each of them.

It was true as Reino had said, Charlie had changed, but people change at midlife, especially men. Charlie and she had built a life together—a good life as far as lives go. She had only hope.

Signe got up, pulled out the drawer of the grinder, measured eight tablespoons of coffee and dropped it in the boiling pot. "Hilda, I've made two moves in my life. I think this, the third, will be the best."

When Charlie came home that evening, he was the happiest Signe had seen him for years. He was jovial at dinner. When he finished his dessert, Charlie said he'd like to have another helping of the bread pudding with rhubarb sauce on top, but he couldn't take the time.

Elma and Elsie hurried to their room, but were called back by their father. Elsie glanced at Elma and Elma turned to Charlie, "Papa, we don't have time for hymns tonight, we have to study for our arithmetic test tomorrow."

Signe had noticed that the girls had avoided the nightly hymn singing for some time now. The change concerned Signe.

"It's not about hymns, girls, it's about our new life, the bright future that lies before us," Charlie exclaimed.

The only receptive face was that of Hugo. He was waiting to hear more, but waited in silence.

"We're selling everything and moving out West," Charlie announced with pumped up enthusiasm. Your father is getting a new position with the federal government—"

"Like vice president?" Hugo asked.

Charlie laughed. "No, son, we already have a vice president. I'm thinking more in the lines of a post-master."

Hugo murmured a disinterested "oh," took out his penknife and began to whittle on the slingshot he'd started to carve earlier in the day.

Signe looked at the sad look of indifference on the faces of her two older children and wondered if she'd be making the right decision in agreeing to go along with Charlie's plans.

Charlie looked at Elma who seemed the most receptive of the five children. "Just think, no snow in the winter. No need to wear arctics."

"How does Santa Claus travel?" Elsie piped, "In a wagon?"

Elma shook her head. "I don't think I'd care for that. I think I'll stay in Wolf Creek, Minnesota."

"Me, too," Elsie warbled.

"Eldon," Charlie said, "how do you feel about going West?"

"Who's going to take care of the cows?"

"What cows? Didn't you hear me just say that we're selling everything. We'll have an auction, sell the place and leave Wolf Creek with our pockets stuffed with money. No more pumping water or shoveling manure. What do think of that?"

Eldon didn't answer.

Charlie asked Violet, "How do you feel about leaving?"

"I don't care, as long as they have a big library in the school."

"We're going as far as the land reaches," Charlie announced, "to Oregon by the sea."

Chapter XXXVII

THE SALE WILL COMMENCE AT 11:00 O'CLOCK SHARP, the flyer read. Eldon and Violet had gotten up early to milk the cows for the last time. Their younger siblings were up just for the excitement. They had no school. Last week Signe had withdrawn the children from their classes at District 109, in anticipation of their move. Miss Keksi told Signe they would be missed and related how last year when Eldon sang "Silent Night", as the candles on the tree were being lit, many in the audience felt they could almost see Baby Jesus in the cradle before them. "Eldon should have voice lessons," she told Signe. "He has a truly magnificent voice."

"What are you doing here?" Violet asked Eldon

when she entered the barn after the chores were done.

"Just saying goodbye," he replied. As a final gesture of love, he ran his hand over the back of each cow and calf in the barn. "I wish I had a camera," he said, "I'd take a picture of every one of 'em."

Both Eldon and Violet glanced at the empty stanchion, Queen's stall, the cow that Eldon raised from a calf and Charlie destroyed with a pitchfork. "Here's your quarter," Violet said, after a long silence recalling the horrible incident.

"What for?" Eldon asked, as he gazed at the silver coin, now in his palm.

"The concession people are putting up their stand. Mother gave us each a quarter to buy something. Pop is five cents, hot dogs are ten, and bologna sandwiches with a pickle are fifteen."

"I don't want anything," Eldon said, flatly.

"Put it in your pocket," Violet commanded.

"You know what!" Elma said as she and Elsie sneaked in through the back door of barn. "Miser Jacobson came early and is snooping everyplace. He even climbed up the stepladder and went into the attic."

"Yaa, can you beat that? An old man creeping up a ladder to snoop in the attic. Wish we had bats!" Elsie added and giggled.

"That would fix him!" Elma covered her giggle.

"This is an auction sale," Eldon explained. "Anyone can go any place and inspect whatever he is interested in buying."

"I know someplace he can't look," Elsie whispered. "Mama's tool cabinet. Mama hid the lipstick and powder that Mary Marks gave with her pliers and screwdrivers under the cupboard and locked it."

"She put her remnant bag in there, too," Elma added, then turned to her brother and asked, "Do you want to go live by the ocean?"

Eldon shrugged. "I don't care."

"I do. If they make me go, I'll come back when I get big."

"Would you leave Mother?"

"She could come back here with me and Elsie."

"What I hate," Eldon said, "is leaving Reino and Buster. Papa said I had to leave Buster and Reino has no friends but me."

"Now they'll have each other," Elsie chimed cheerfully.

Eldon bit his lip to keep from crying. "I didn't even have a chance to say goodbye to Reino. Papa said Reino couldn't come to the auction sale."

"Why don't you go to his house?" Elma suggested. "You can run fast. Papa would never know. You could go now. Papa's in the house talking to the auctioneer."

"Papa would find out and he'd kill me."

"You can write to Reino," Violet told Eldon. "He can read."

Eldon blew out a long sigh, then asked Elsie, "Where's your pop?"

"We bought one to share," Elma answered as she handed the bottle to Elsie. "She wanted orange and I wanted grape, so we got strawberry." Elma, ten months older than Elsie, was the leader of the inseparable duo, who looked alike, dressed alike and acted together. They were of one mind.

The quarter was burning Eldon's pocket. He would have enjoyed a hot dog and a Dr. Pepper, but the two bits was all he had in the world and he'd have to save it for some dire purpose.

As he was trying to decide whether to satisfy his taste buds and throw himself into destitution, he spotted the new mailman's car coming down the hill. Eldon looked around to see if his father was in sight; then dashed down the path to the mailbox, stuck his hand in through the mail car's open window, and in a breathless whisper said, "Twenty-five penny post-cards, please," as he handed the quarter to Mr. Schneck.

"So you found yourself a sweetheart," the mail carrier announced in loud clear tones, as he counted the right number of cards.

Eldon was embarrassed and angered. His father would never have made a ridiculous remark to a postal customer like the one the new postman had just made. Eldon looked to see who might have heard the false herald, but nobody had. He thanked Schneck and was about to run off when he realized that he didn't know Reino's box number. He didn't want further intrusion into his life, so he said, "Do you, by any chance, have a list of your postal patrons with their box numbers?"

"Here you be, Sonny," the intrusive civil servant responded, as he handed Eldon the piece of paper. "So you're going to play the field?"

Eldon had no idea what Schneck was talking about and answered "Yaa." He thanked the mailman, then turned around and stuffed the postal cards inside his shirt and ran up the path.

Charlie was disillusioned and uneasy. The auction sale had been poorly attended by the locals. John Granlund and Pete Hutto didn't show up. Ed Koski was there, but didn't even bid on an eightpenny nail. Neither did he say goodbye to Charlie although he spent some time talking to Signe. Charlie didn't see Jacob Rontty, but learned later that he'd come, brought Signe a blue rayon scarf and the children a large bag of candy—orange slices—and shaken Eldon's hand as if the boy were an adult. The wives usually accompanied their husbands on these social occasions, but only a few came. Hilda Mattson was there but completely ignored Charlie. Kaarlo Niemi had come up to Charlie and asked what he was going to do with his place.

"I have a buyer from Fargo who wants the original forty, plus the forty I recently bought. Made me an offer I can hardly refuse."

There had been no offer and Charlie knew the east forty was nothing but rock and scrub; and with the three open graves, nobody would buy it. I can let it go for taxes, he consoled himself—meaning, he wouldn't pay the property taxes and the county would take possession.

The Skinnar children had a lesson in economics at the supper table that night when their parents discussed the financial returns of the auction. Since many of the local farmers were in debt to Miser Jacobson, the local loan shark, they had been afraid to outbid him on the farm machinery and it had all gone to the miser for fifty dollars. Charlie had owed the Miser fifteen hundred, plus interest on money he'd borrowed to purchase the machinery. Now Jacobson had his money, plus interest and the machinery for a measly outlay of fifty dollars.

"Children," Charlie said, with his mouth full of mashed potatoes and meat loaf, "don't be surprised if we decide to live in town, or a city as big as Portland. The West offers many opportunities, from what I hear. I might even end up being postmaster," he added, to show his children that he had a handle on life even on the other side of the Rockies.

"That means that we could play hopscotch on the sidewalk in front of our house?" Elsie asked.

Charlie nodded.

Signe looked at her younger son's plate and said, "Hugo, eat your cabbage. It has vitamins."

Chapter XXXVIII

IT WAS MONDAY MORNING, the tenth of October, 1932. Signe and Charlie had gotten up at four to make the final preparations for the trip. "I'm allowing ten days for us to hit the Pacific Ocean," Charlie kept repeating, as if there were a deadline he had to meet, and an appointment he had to keep.

"What's the ocean like?" asked Elma, who, followed by Elsie, had just come into the kitchen in their long flannel nightgowns and were making their way to the breakfast table.

"A big lake," Charlie replied.

"Like Moose Lake?" Elsie asked.

"Yaa, only bigger."

Elma looked up from from her bread buttering. "I don't want to drown."

"Me, too," echoed Elsie, with her mouthful of

bread. She swallowed and added, "I don't want to be buried alive."

Charlie stared at his two youngest—Elma just turned eight and Elsie ten months younger—so different from the three older children, and thought if he didn't know better, he would say they were not his. "What are you talking about?"

Elma dunked the buttered flatbread in her coffee. "Fanny Linden."

Elsie shook her head slowly. "Yaa, she went swimming in Pickerel Lake and drownded."

"And was buried alive!" Elma added.

Violet, who had been ironing on the board by Signe's sewing machine, explained. "Fanny Linden drowned, but instead of reviving her, they called the undertaker."

Signe, by the stove, stirring oatmeal explained, "People make mistakes."

At those words Charlie felt as if the blood and all life supporting fluids in his body had been drained, and only the carcass was left. He set his coffee cup on the table, went out the door and ran to the outhouse where no one would disturb him. He wanted to cry, but had no tears. He couldn't pray. He was no longer privileged to communicate with God. "People make mistakes," Signe had told the girls. Was she really speaking to him? How much did she know? What did she suspect? His desiring Mary Marks was an unforgivable sin and taking her by force was a mistake. Mary Marks' face would forever remain in his eyes and the nightmare following her death would haunt him the rest of his days. His mistake had deprived his family of a home, a livelihood and good reputation. Now they were faced with the uncertainty of a strange new world. He had nothing to offer them but words — empty words.

Hugo came running into the house "Mama, the Mattsons are here. They've come to say goodbye."

Signe's heart lightened. No one else had come to wish them well in their new venture except Ed Koski and Jacob Rontty who had done so at the auction sale. "I'm so happy to see you," she told Hilda, and would've given a hug if she'd thought it proper. "I thought I wouldn't see you again."

Hilda wiped her eyes with the back of the hand, sputtered something unintelligible between sobs and gave Signe an unexpected squeeze. Signe waited for her friend to say something, but Hilda shook her head, pulled out a handkerchief and gave a big blow.

Gust, as usual, just gazed at the scene without comment.

"We'll be leaving as soon as we get the car packed," Signe told Hilda. "With seven people in the Ford, we can't take much except our clothing. Whatever is left is yours. There are potatoes, rutabagas, cabbages, red beets and carrots in the cellar. You'd better have your boys come and get them. The steps are too steep for you. Take the quilts, blankets, sheets and whatever is left after we leave. What you don't want, give to Reino."

"I haven't blubbered like this since my mother in Finland died," Hilda sobbed.

Signe gave a quick swipe of her apron to her eyes

and laughed. "I'm not dying, that's for sure. At least not yet. I'll write you as soon as we get settled, and I expect you to keep me posted."

The children followed Signe as she saw Hilda and Gust to their car, and raced Hugo back to the house after Eldon closed the gate. Signe pulled a hankie out of her pocket, waved it at the parting guests, wiped away the tears and hurried back to the house. Her right foot hit a hard object and she stumbled. She looked down, and partially covered by earth, she saw what she recognized as a cuban heel from Mary Marks' shoe. Signe's legs gave way and she went down. Stunned, she looked around to see if anyone was looking; then shoved the heel into her apron pocket. She was puzzled at first. Then a gust of recollections rushed through her brain—the broken window screen which was replaced as if by magic, her dressmaking shears on the floor, Mary Marks' missing red dress, the straight pin and the lady's stocking in the first grave, and the bundle of soiled men's clothing in the manure pile. So Mary Marks did come for her final fitting, Signe told herself, but I wasn't here to receive her.

"What you sitting here for?" Charlie, returning from the outhouse, snorted. "We have to get going. Days are getting real short." He took her hand to help her up. She yanked her hand free. "What did they want?" Charlie asked, referring to the Mattsons.

"Just came to say goodbye," Signe responded almost inaudibly. Life was sucked out of her. She felt drawn, tired and utterly alone.

"There's one jar left," Eldon told his mother when

he returned from the milk house with a quart of home canned pork for the sandwiches for the trip. "Can I have it?"

"What for?" she asked.

"For Buster. It won't keep, you know. When the freeze comes, the jar will crack. And there's no room for it in the car, Father said." Signe nodded and took the jar from Eldon, opened and smelled it. Then handed it to Violet to spoon out as she sliced the bread.

Eldon got the remaining jar from the milk house and opened it. "I'm going away and never coming back," he told Buster as he scooped the meat into an old washbasin, which sat by the doghouse. "You have to guard your house forever and ever, until you die." The dog gazed at his master as if trying to understand the meaning of the words.

Last year, at the school exchange of Christmas gifts, Hugo had received a deck of cards from Frank Riso. When Charlie caught Hugo playing solitaire in the hayloft, he confiscated the cards saying they were instruments of Satan. To cheer him up, Eldon gave his brother a pocketknife to make slingshots. Hugo had made a dozen slingshots out of forked branches of wood and old inner tubes. He hid them in an apple box in the hayloft for the three sons he was going to have when he grew up and got married. Hugo put in his pocket one slingshot and six small rocks from the road by the mailbox.

Violet had no great regrets on leaving Minnesota. Life in Wolf Creek had not offered much and she expected no more from life on the West Coast. She only hoped for a large library from where she could get all the books she wanted to read.

The four younger children were already in the car when their father called them to come and pose for a snapshot. "I got you a present," he told Eldon who had lingered behind. Charlie handed his elder son a new Kodak box camera. "Now take our picture."

Eldon took two and handed the camera back to his father, saying, "I have to close the gate after you drive out." He wanted to take a snapshot of Buster, but knew it would rile Charlie.

By the mailbox, he watched his father coast down the incline from the house to the gravel road. When he hopped on the gate to take his last swing, Eldon looked toward the doghouse and saw Buster gazing at him. Eldon lost his breakfast.

As the car turned right, from the corner of her eye, Signe saw her son vomiting. "Look, children," she said, pointing ahead, "the geese are flying south. They'd better hurry. They're late this year."

"Eldon voluped all over the gate!" Elsie announced.

"In order to avoid any blizzards that might come up this time of the year, we're taking the southern route," Charlie explained, reassuring himself. "That'll add three days to our trip, but, hopefully, we won't be hitting snow." Nobody commented. It was if they all were in different worlds with different problems, seeking their own solutions.

When they passed Reino's house, he was standing by the mailbox, looking sorrowful, wanting to bid them goodbye. Charlie drove on as if Reino were only a fence post, stuck in the ground, waiting for the elements to make him part of the earth.

Elsie poked Elma meaningfully. Eldon looked straight ahead, as if wearing blinders. Hugo, who was sitting in the front seat between his parents, felt that something was wrong and fastened his gaze to the gear shift of the Model A. Only Signe dared wave goodbye to the pathetic weeping figure of a man.

Chapter XXXIX

THEY HAD NOT CROSSED THE BORDER into Iowa the first day as Charlie had planned, but it was getting dark, so they decided they should call it a day and stopped at the small town of Windom, Minnesota. "Are we going to stay in a hotel or sleep in the car?" Elma asked.

"I'd rather sleep on the side of the road on the grass and look at the stars," Elsie said. "I never got to sleep outside."

"What do you think your father is, asking if we're going to sleep in the car?" Charlie exclaimed. "We hardly fit just sitting up. We're going to find some night cabins with bathrooms so we can all take a bath before we go to bed."

They finally found some shacks on the other side of town. The only vacant one had two bedrooms and a kitchen. The outhouse was in the back.

When Eldon heard his father snoring, he took out the stack of penny postcards and continued his writing to Reino.

Since Schnek, the new mailman was such a snoop, Eldon decided he wouldn't sign his full name, just E.

◄ • ►

1st day. Sauk Center, Minn. CARD #1

Dear Ray,

Just stopping here. Father went to buy Copenhagen so I'm writing you. (He has started to chew snuff.) Linden's hill was muddy from the rain last night & we got stuck & had to get out and push. Mother's new suede shoes got ruined. I'm learning to read the map real good. I know exactly where we are when Father asks. I see Father coming, so I'll say goodbye for now. More later.

Your best friend, E.

◄ • ►

1st day Windom, Minn. CARD #2

Dear Ray,

We are staying at the Hawaiian Paradise, but the letters have fallen off so the sign looks like W I N E PARADISE. Somebody has added an E to the first word. It has electricity. You pull the string & the light comes on. You pull again & it goes off. Like majic. The place was just painted & stinks like turpentine & Violet got sick. Will write soon.

Your pal, E.

◄ • ►

Iowa, USA

Dear Ray,
         The seenery is beautiful & weather's warm.
We saw some really nice farms and big red barns. Have
you been to see Buster? Did you bring him food? He
needs water, too. I forgot my pocket knife at home. If you
find it, you can keep it. But be careful. It is sharp. I
counted 24 Burma Shave signs & 17 Dr. Pepper signs.
Father drives like wild. Hugo got car sick. Mother told
him to slow down.

         Yours tly. E.

◄ ∙ ►

State of Nebraska

Dear Ray,
    Today we stopped in front of a school. When Mother
went in the store to get lunch stuff, we got to play with
the kids. The teacher was nice and intradoosed us. Violet
and I talked to a 6th grade girl. Her name was Florens.
Have you ever heard that name? It's a nice name. Don't
you think? She was tall with yellow hair and blue eyes.
Real pretty.

         E.

◄ ∙ ►

Dear Ray,
    We are in Rock Springs, Wyoming. I took a lot of
pictures of big rocks & things & will send you some
when I get money. I like this state best of all. It's really
pretty. We saw antelopes run. They look like big deer.

Mother bought a watermelon. It was huge. We had 2 flat tires today & the engin got hot & we had to get water from a creek.

E.

◄ • ►

Dear Ray,
Today was not a good day. Hugo shot at a telephone pole with a slingshot & the stone hit a church window & broke it. Father said it is a bad omen (sign). Then when we were going up a big hill the engin got hot & the radiator blew up. Father went to town in a cattle truck. We are sitting by the road & eating the rest of the watermelon.

Your f, E.

◄ • ►

Dear Ray,
We are in Coeur d'Alene, Idaho now. The car needs a new engin or something, so we will stay here until it gets fixed. This town is really beautiful & I like it. There are mountains everywhere. We went to Pennys & got us some new school clothes. Mother got Violet a dark green winter coat. She looks beautiful in it. Do you know what? I don't remember Minnesota at all.

Regards.
E.

◄ • ►

Dear Ray,

I'm sorry I haven't been able to write you every day, because Father is real nervuss, & puts the light out when he goes to bed right after supper. The little kids fight. He gave Elma a whipping. She cried & said she would leave & go back to Minn. when she gets 18. I wish life was peaceful. The seenery becomes beautifuller every day. Can't wait to see the ocean.

Yours tly.
E.

◄ • ►

Newburg, Ore. (H. Hoover's home)

Dear Reino,

We came through Portland late today. It's a huge city, with street cars, trucks & cars & many rivers. You can see Mt. Hood. It's big & covered with snow. We got to Portland when everyone was going home from work. It started to rain. I never saw so many umbrellas. Papa did not like it. Leaving for Taft early in the morning. Can't wait to see the ocean & the whales.

E.

◄ • ►

Dear Ray,

Here we are! You never saw so much water in your life! The waves are much higher than in Bass Lake, 16-17 feet tall & the water is real salty. You can't drink it. Lots of huge white birds called sea gulls. There are all kinds of pretty stones on the sand. They are called aguts. I don't think this is what Father expected. The people are nice, but they keep to themselves. Maybe we should have stayed in Wyoming.

Your friend,
E.

Chapter XL

LIVING ON THE COAST, Charlie Skinnar felt as if he were on foreign soil, but he couldn't go back.

"Tomorrow we'll visit Oscar Salo. You remember, he extended me an invitation to follow him here. He will help us get located. Then I'll apply for a position with the postal service," Charlie announced in tones loud enough for his whole family to take notice.

"How are you going to find him?" Signe asked.

"General Delivery."

Signe turned to Eldon, took a dollar bill from her apron pocket, and handed it to him. "Go to the store, and get a loaf of bread, a sack of salt, a quart of milk and some hamburger with the rest."

"I'll go with you," Charlie told his son. "Have to get acquainted with your neighbors when you move to a new area."

Charlie was quick to let people know that he was a former postal employee seeking work.

"You looking for a job with the post office?" the owner of the grocery store asked Charlie, after sacking the items Eldon had requested. "We don't need nobody. Wilma Kulla has been the postmistress long as I c'n remember."

"I mean a mail carrier," Charlie explained.

"Don't need none. We have post office boxes. Pick up and carry home your own mail."

Charlie then asked about Oscar Salo.

The grocer shook his head. "You might look around D Lake. Lots of Finns there."

"My friend said, 'Taft, Oregon, by the sea,'" Charlie reiterated.

"Go ask the postmistress," the grocer suggested. "She's a walking encyclopedia."

"Sure I remember Salo," Wilma Kulla replied. "He and his family headed north up the coast for Willapa or Grays Harbor. Think he was going to try to get in on the cranberry harvest, with his crew of youngsters. But it's been several weeks." Then she asked, "You got a trade?"

"Trade?"

"Yes, like carpenter, plumber, or butcher?"

Charlie winced.

"You got family?"

"Wife and five kids," Charlie muttered. He cringed as he felt Kulla size him up.

"You're a strong, healthy looking man . Ever done any logging?"

"Logging?"

"Tree cutting."

"Only firewood," Charlie replied in a low voice.

"Well, there's not that much logging going on, anyhow. Most of the mills are closed."

The communion Charlie had expected to have with the sea did not materialize. He hated the ocean. It was threatening, overpowering and noisy. Their temporary home was an old two bedroom cabin with a kitchenette — small, damp and smelly — with strange bugs which, he later learned were fleas. There was no running water. They had to resort to sponge baths. How he yearned for a good sauna bath. With all the Finns supposedly living in the area, Charlie had yet to meet one. He couldn't sleep. The roar of the Pacific gave him insomnia; and when he finally knocked off, the broken coils of the springs reached through the mattress to jab him.

He had to make a move of some kind. He couldn't go back. He had quit his job and lost his old age pension. His farm was sold — at least on paper. He had a wife and five kids who expected him to perform miracles — that is, bring home a paycheck. He was a nobody without a future. About to turn to supplication, he recalled he no longer was in God's grace.

Charlie got up and went to the girls' bedroom. He pulled the string that lit the forty watt bulb overhead, and said, "Signe."

She slept on as if nothing had passed through his lips. He gazed at her, an angel in a white flannel nightgown. She could sleep — anywhere — she was at peace with the world and in God's grace.

He shook her. She turned her face toward him. "What do you want?"

"Tomorrow we head up north to Washington state," he said, almost apologetically.

"Did you have to put on the light to tell me that?"

"I thought you should know as soon as possible," he stammered.

"It would have waited till morning. You woke up the children," she added almost accusingly, then sat up to give a yank to the string overhead, and all was dark. Charlie went in the other room and dropped himself on the bed. A fractured spring greeted his buttocks.

"You planning to go up the coast on 101?" the man at the pump asked as he stuck the nozzle of the hose into Charlie's gas tank.

"Yaa," Charlie replied, with his index finger tracing the highway on the map in hand, "to Astoria and up to Aberdeen."

"All things considered, you'd be better-off to go through Portland and Vancouver and then take the cut-off through Oakville to Grays Harbor. That'll be three fifty."

Charlie carefully counted three ones, a quarter and five nickels. Except for the three fifties in his shoe, only a few tens, five's and singles from the auction receipts graced his deflated wallet.

Charlie retraced his route from Taft on 99W toward Portland through the cloudbursts in the coastal range, a different man from his earlier voyage a few days ago. He'd been slapped on the face by the cold hand of reality.

"Are we on the other side of the mountains?" Elma asked, as the sun broke through the clouds.

"We sure are," Eldon replied, with his eye on the map. We're now entering the town of Alder Mill, population 1,493. Holy Moses," he exclaimed. "Look at the big smokestack. How come I didn't see it before?"

"That's a paper mill," Charlie explained.

"And look at the rainbow," Elsie cried out. "Isn't it the prettiest one you ever saw?"

"It's a double rainbow," Elma corrected, pointing ahead.

"See, it's two. One above the other."

Signe looked up and smiled. "It's a good sign."

They were passing a new brick school at the edge of town when Signe said, "Stop."

Charlie veered to the right, stepped on the brake, and parked on the side of the road. "What did you say 'stop' for?"

"Look," Signe exclaimed, and pointed to the left.

- FOR RENT -
HOUSE WITH ACREAGE

Charlie looked but saw nothing of interest.

"See the sign on the fence post," she added. "The place looks like home."

"Home is where I make it, and tomorrow, early, we get back on the highway," Charlie lashed out.

"I'm tired of chasing wild ducks, and the children need to get back to their books," Signe retorted, daringly.

Charlie talked as if his mind and heart were set on going north, and it nettled him that Signe was trying to make the decisions, but he was tired of driving with no logical destination in mind, searching for a golden nugget. "No acreage, cows or chickens—or pigs," he grumbled, emphasizing the word *pigs*.

"But, we do need a roof over our heads, and I'm done with the ocean. Won't cost to take a look."

When Charlie drove into the yard, Signe stepped out of the car, alone, knocked and went in. This rankled Charlie even more. Soon she appeared at the door, coaxing the rest of the family in with her index finger.

"I'm Nelda Givens," the octogenarian volunteered, as she extended her hand to Charlie. She explained that her husband of sixty years had recently died, and she was moving to Amity to live with her daughter. "As soon as the right buyer comes along, I'll sell, but this is a bad time of the year, especially since it has been so rainy."

Instead of last year's soggy, decaying wheat stubble, what Signe saw was a field of fragrant green clover, waving in the wind, with a perennial double rainbow over it. "How many acres?"

"Thirty," Nelda replied. "Real good soil. Do you like to garden?"

Not to exasperate Charlie, Signe merely nodded, as she followed Nelda to the south window.

Nelda pointed. "I have my garden over there. Very few weeds."

"How much?" Signe asked.

"Twenty-five for the house, and another twenty-five for the acreage if you want it."

"We'll take house and acreage."

Charlie cleared his throat, and spoke up. "Just for a month. I'm expecting a position, up north, with the postal service."

Eldon and Violet glanced at each other, then looked away. Nelda, who'd seen many Charlies in her day, smiled understandingly, and said, "At least the house will be warm for a month and the place won't mildew." She looked at the children, who one-by-one, had followed their parents to the house. "And the youngsters will have a roof over their heads."

"What about the furniture?" Signe asked.

Nelda shook her head. "Except for the kitchen stove, the furniture is very old. I doubt that a second-hand store would give much for it."

Signe had eyed the stove since she came in, and she'd never had an upholstered sofa with a matching chair, nor a dining table with eight chairs. "How much?"

Nelda thought for awhile. "I could let you have it for fifty dollars, all but the rocking chair. My late husband made it for me as a wedding present."

Signe was overwhelmed. "Even the icebox?"

"Refrigerator," Nelda corrected. "It's electric."

Signe looked at Charlie, and said, "Give Mrs. Givens the hundred dollars."

Charlie, red-faced, pulled off his shoe and took

out two of the last three fifty dollar bills and handed them to his new landlady. "May I have a receipt, please."

Charlie left for Grays Harbor early in the morning. Signe and Eldon went to school and registered the children. A water pipe at the school had broken in the night, so there were no classes.

Signe liked the feeling of a metropolis. It was exciting and invigorating. She had missed Helsinki all these years. Since Portland was only a thirty minute bus ride away, Signe asked Eldon if he would like to take a trip to the big city.

They window-shopped for an hour, Signe admiring the dresses on the sculptured models, Eldon visualizing the bacon, lettuce, and tomato sandwich at Woolworth's his mother had promised him. When they came to Lipman Wolfe, a multistoried department store with beautifully dressed mannequins, Eldon spotted a placard at the window. "Look, Mother!" he called to Signe. "Look at the sign."

WANTED
ALTERATIONS LADY
FULL-TIME
INQUIRE AT OFFICE

Chapter XLI

WHEN CHARLIE RETURNED HOME after four days up north, Signe ran to the car to report all the good news: the children were now back in school—a beautiful new brick building, with inside lavatories with hot and cold water, a lunchroom, a room for every grade, and a teacher for every room; and she had gotten a job in a fine department store in Portland.

The second part of her announcement did not set well with Charlie. He had been unsuccessful looking for work in Washington and had found no trace of his friend Oscar Salo. The wood industry was shut down, mills were closed, and family men were forced to do a day's work wherever they could find it. "The wife belongs at home," Charlie said, and added that he didn't feel well.

"What about the paper mill here?" Signe asked.

"Have you thought about putting in your application for the extra board? When someone gets sick or wants a day off, you'd be called, and you could get your foot in the door, so to speak."

Charlie shook his head. "I want to be available for a job with the postal service when the call comes."

Signe went to work at her job the following Monday. Charlie stayed home to wait for the telephone installer. The children liked school. Even Violet seemed happier. Eldon continued his one-sided correspondence with Reino.

◄ • ►

Dear Reino,

We are living in Alder Mill, Ore. I like it and wish you were here. Mother got a job doing alterations in a big store in Ptld. Dad is still looking for a postal service job. I'm taking shop in school. Violet is learning dressmaking & Hugo is learning to swim. Have you been to see Buster? Is he still guarding the doghouse? Bring him a bone if you can get one.

Best regards, your fr.E.

◄ • ►

Dear Reino,

Things are going good. Mother likes her job and the people like her. She even wears the lipstick and powder to work that Mary Marks gave her. Guess what! I bought two jersey calves at the fair. We have a barn and plenty of pasture. Hugo's getting good at swimming. He runs, too. I play baseball. I like basketball, but am not not tall enough.

Best wishes, yr. fr. E.

◄ • ►

Dear Reino,
I really like school! There's a girl in my class who's really smart and cute. Her name is Crystal Grondahl. We study together in the library and will do a science project together. Dad's working part-time at the paper mill. He gave up on the gov't. Mother bought me a cow and calf for my 15th birthday. Got new buyers for our Minnesota farm. Mother wants to buy this place.

Yr.Fr.E.

◄ • ►

Dear Ray,
Remember my friend Crystal? She moved to Idaho. She wants to go to college when she graduates. I miss her bad. I have a new friend, Eric Kelly. His Mom is Norse and his dad is Irish. They make home brew. That's beer. Have you ever tasted beer? It takes bad, but makes you happy. I have 6 head of cattle. Pop's working graveyard shift. Violet gets all A's. I used to.

Yr. Pal, CES

◄ • ►

Dear Reino,
I wish I could hear from you. I don't even know if you're alive. But you can't write me. Pop would find out and kill me. This is a lonely world if you're alone.

Is Buster still alive? I wish I could see you, but you can't come here and I can never return there, so I guess we'll never see each other again. Thanks for getting me from school when I was 5.

E.

Dear Reino,

I have something bad to tell you. I've been drinking a lot lately. Once we all got drunk & slept. I dreamed about what we saw in the pasture. I heard the screams. I have the blues. Can't study. My grades are going down. Eric & I visit his uncle, Father Myhre, a Cath. minister. My last card. Bye. Take care of yourself and remember your best friend,

C. E. S.

Chapter XLII

ELDON CLUTCHED HIS LEATHER POUCH in his right hand as he walked up the five steps to the door. It was a beautiful evening, the moon almost as brilliant as in Minnesota. He transferred the bag to his left hand to knock on the door with his right. What if the priest asked what he was carrying? He couldn't lie. Eldon was about to stuff the sack in his pocket, but decided it would be too dangerous. He'd hold on to it casually.

Eldon knocked.

Father Myhre answered the door. "Hello, Eldon. Nice to see you again. Have a chair, son."

"Thank you, Father. I don't have time."

Father Myhre seemed to be in no rush. "How have you been?" he asked, although he had seen Eldon only a couple days ago.

"All right. I guess." Eldon shifted from one foot to the other, holding to his pouch so tight that his fingers were getting prickly.

"You aren't sick," Father Myhre asked, "are you?"

"Oh, no. I'm not sick. I don't get sick much. I'm quite healthy."

"You must be in a hurry to get your chores done before dark," Father Myhre probed.

"My chores are done," Eldon replied, with a note of pride and relief. "The cows are fed, watered, and milked. And the barn doors are—closed." Eldon paused. He felt like the twelve-year-old who had left Minnesota four years ago. It all came back to him now.

"So, why not sit a spell?" Father Myhre asked, with a twinkle in his eye, as he pushed a chair in Eldon's direction. "It takes no longer to sit than to stand, and you'll be doing your feet a favor."

Eldon gave a nervous giggle and sat himself gingerly on the edge of the leather covered armchair and cautiously transferred the pouch to his other hand.

"I understand you have quite a herd to take care of."

"I don't mind. I like animals, especially cows. They're peaceful and nice to be with. And they take my mind away from things."

"What—things?"

"Things that happened in the past," Eldon replied, with difficulty, and turned away. "But you don't want to hear about them."

Father Myhre sat on the armchair across from

Eldon, took out his calabash pipe, filled it with his favorite blend of Turkish tobacco, lit it and leisurely puffed away, tantalizing Eldon's nostrils with its aroma. "Do your parents know you're seeing me?" he finally asked.

Eldon faced the priest. "Of course. I don't keep things from my folks. Why do you ask?"

"We're of different faiths."

"That doesn't make any difference," Eldon promptly responded. "Same God, same Bible—and Martin Luther was a Catholic once. That's what my mother says."

"Your mother is a wise woman."

" I know." Eldon said proudly.

Father Myhre puffed on his pipe and kept the conversation on a low key. "How's school?"

"All right. I guess. But—"

"But what?"

"It's not like it used to be."

"In what way?"

"I used to really like school," Eldon replied.

"You don't anymore?"

"It's not the same."

"Our interests change as we grow older. It's only natural."

"Oh, my interests are still the same," Eldon blurted out. "I haven't changed. It's only that—well, I can't think. I can't put my mind on my studies."

Father Myhre admired Eldon's directness and veracity. The boy's reasoning was logical and mature beyond his years. "You mean you can't concentrate."

Eldon nodded.

The priest then asked, "How old are you?"

"Sixteen."

"The teens are not the easiest years of one's life," Father Myhre commented. "I wouldn't live those turbulent times for anything in the world." He paused and took a puff. "Eldon, how long have you lived in Oregon?"

"Since I was twelve. Nearly four years."

"Do you like it here?"

Eldon shrugged.

"It's hard leaving one's old home and friends," the Father said.

"I had one friend."

"He was a good friend?"

Eldon looked down and nodded.

"If a person has one good friend, that is all he needs in a lifetime," Father Myhre reflected "and it's about all any of us can ask for."

"I know."

"Perhaps you can go visit your friend one of these days."

"I can never go back," Eldon stated flatly. His grip on the neck of the brown leather sack had turned his knuckles white. He switched it to the other hand as inconspicuously as he could.

"I see." The priest paused and thought for a moment. "Maybe your friend could come and visit you."

Eldon shook his head. "He's epileptic. Besides, he has no money," he replied, impatiently, and after glancing at the clock on the priest's desk, got up to leave.

Father Myhre motioned for him to be reseated.

Eldon obeyed reluctantly.

"You have a new friend," the Father reminded him.

"Yaa, Eric."

"How did you meet my nephew?"

"Bird watching."

"Bird watching?" the priest repeated with surprise.

Eldon suddenly perked up. "Birds that sing," he said enthusiastically. "Birds with beautiful voices. Did you know that birds' voices are purest at daybreak?" And added, "I used to sing."

"I didn't know that. What kind of songs do you sing?"

"I don't. I was going to be the cantor in our church, but I can't sing anymore."

"Why not? Did your voice change?"

"No," Eldon replied. "Our Heavenly Father stopped my singing."

"How?"

"He took my voice away." Eldon looked the priest in the eye. "He did something to my throat."

"Have you seen a doctor?"

Eldon laughed. "There's nothing a doctor can do when God punishes you."

Father Myhre laid his pipe on the desk, rolled his chair toward Eldon, placed his hand on the boy's knee, and said, "God doesn't punish children. What did you think you did to deserve such severe punishment?"

"I didn't do anything. That's the reason. You

know, Father, there are sins of commission and acts of omission."

The priest nodded. "Where did this take place?"

"Minnesota."

"How old were you?"

"Twelve."

Father Myhre shook his head. "Just a child."

"A child can scream."

"A child can be too frightened to scream. We all have fears."

Eldon would not be consoled. "I should've yelled and screamed and it would never have happened. He would've run and left her. But I was a coward. I was afraid of a whipping. I pressed my mouth closed with my fists so no sound could come out."

"Did you ever tell anyone about this?"

"There was no one to tell . . . Father, did you ever see anyone die?"

The priest nodded.

"It's terrible, isn't it?"

"Sometimes. But there are circumstances when death is peaceful and even desired."

"But did you ever see a murder?" Eldon asked.

Father Myhre jerked back. "You saw a murder?"

Eldon nodded and began to whimper. "A woman. A most beautiful lady. She was my friend. But before he killed her, he did bad things to her. Real, real bad things."

The priest took out his white handkerchief and handed it to Eldon. "You witnessed all of it?"

"From the beginning to the end. I can never forget it. I dream about it at night. I see it before my eyes when I'm trying to study. I hear the thump, then the heavy thud . . . then the silence. The silence is worse then the thump and thud. He stuffed her mouth with a handkerchief so she couldn't even scream!"

"You heard a 'thump' and a 'thud?'"

"The thump was the sound of the board hitting her head and the thud was the sound of the ax as it hit the hard ground after it cut her head from her body. But the searchers never found the head," Eldon exclaimed.

"Reino—that was my friend's name—and I found an old wooden nail box. We covered the inside with pink crepe paper roses that my sister Violet made and laid the head gently on them. Then we nailed on the lid and buried the box under Buster's doghouse." Seeing Father Myhre's horrified expression, Eldon explained, "Father, we couldn't let him have her head. We gave it a Christian burial. Reino said prayers and I sang "Ave Maria." That's the last time I sang. I can still hear Buster crying."

"Who's Buster?" the priest asked.

"My dog. He'd sit on the grave and weep."

"Was the killer ever brought to trial?"

"There was an inquest," Eldon replied, and told the priest what had transpired at the trial, and said, "Reino came to tell the jurors what he'd seen, but he got scared of my fa—of the man. Real scared. The jury couldn't prove who the dead woman was or how she had died. The whispers and the gossip never stopped. The kids at school stopped playing with us. They'd just stare at me and my brother and sisters. That murder was the worst thing that had ever happened in

Wolf Creek."

Father Myhre knocked the ashes out of his pipe into an ashtray. "Was the killer a violent person?"

"Oh, no! He was a good, kind man." Eldon was getting more agitated. He kept shifting his leather pouch from one hand to the other and studied the room as if he'd never seen it before.

He stood up. "I have to go now."

The priest followed him to the door. "Eldon, why don't you get up a little early tomorrow and have breakfast with me before you go to school."

"That would be nice." Eldon folded the handkerchief, laid it on a chair and went out. The priest stood staring at the door when it opened again.

Eldon returned, took Father Myhre's hand and shook it.

"Thank you for listening to me. Goodbye, Father." He turned on his heel and was gone.

Father Myhre was puzzled. He grabbed his coat to follow Eldon, but the shot rang as he opened the door and Eldon's headless body fell to the ground. The priest crossed himself.

Chapter LXIII

"BE CAREFUL DRIVING," Signe told Charlie as he was going out the door with his lunch pail to work the 11:30 p.m. to 8:00 a.m. shift at the paper mill. "The fog is thick enough to cut with a knife."

"If it isn't the damn rain," he grumbled, "in this Godforsaken country, it's the fog."

"It's better than six feet of snow and forty below," Signe countered as she closed the door after him.

It was Friday night, three weeks since Eldon's funeral.

Violet had not been able to attend. She fainted when the constable knocked on the door and told Signe about Eldon's death. Violet had been under the doctor's care for a week.

Signe's employer offered Signe two weeks off, but she had returned to work after ten days. "It's better to be working than at home crying," she said.

At the sound of Charlie's car leaving the yard, the children, one by one, came to the kitchen. It was getting close to eleven o'clock, but it was Friday, no school tomorrow and no barn chores to do. Charlie had sold Eldon's herd the day after he died.

Violet was the first to come down. "I wrote Reino a letter," she said, as she set her stationery box on the kitchen table, "to tell him about Eldon."

"I'm glad you did," Signe said. "I haven't had time. Did you tell Reino how Eldon died?" Signe had not been able to tell Hilda Mattson in her letters, but had enclosed a newspaper clipping which said Eldon had died of a self-inflicted gunshot wound.

"I had to tell him the truth. Do you want to hear what I wrote?"

Signe nodded.

Violet took the letter from the table, stood up straight and read as if in front of her class. "Dear Reino, I'm writing to let you know the sad news. You won't be getting any more postcards from Eldon. He died the first of this month. He took his own life. Eldon was visiting his friend, a priest (a Catholic pastor) that evening. He said good night, walked out the door and shot himself in the mouth. Eldon was very sad, you know. Now he won't suffer anymore, but my life will never be the same. I miss him more than I can say. The casket couldn't be opened so we never saw him dead. I think Hugo and the girls expect him back, but I know different. Father doesn't sing hymns any more. We don't even go to church. Take care of yourself, Your friend, Violet Skinnar"

Elma, who had followed her sister to the kitchen, said, "That's an awful sad letter."

"How can I write a happy letter? I have to tell Reino what happened."

Sitting at the kitchen table, Elma put her palms together, with the index fingers over her mouth and rubbed her lips and chin up and down thinking of what she would say. "I'll tell him all the good news. Can I use your fountain pen, Violet?"

"You press too hard. Can't you use a pencil?"

Signe went to the kitchen cabinet, took out her pen and handed it to Elma. "Here, you can use this."

Hugo, who had been at loose ends since his brother's death, spent his free time playing with his yo-yo. "This is called a slippery stick," he told Elsie, showing a fancy move as they entered the kitchen. "And this one is the sliding camel. I made them up myself."

"They both look the same to me," Elsie said, in a disinterested voice.

"There's a slight difference," Hugo said, as he demonstrated the two yo-yo moves again. "It requires quick action of the eye for the looker. That's the trick. Watch carefully."

Elsie had shifted her attention to Elma seated at table with pen in hand. "What you writing?"

"A letter to Reino, a happy letter. It's almost finished. Does anyone want to hear it?"

Elsie shrugged. Hugo threw out another sliding camel.

Violet was busy sealing her letter.

Signe said, "We all do."

Elma read her letter proudly. "Dear Reino, I'm sorry I haven't written sooner, but you know how time flies. Much has happened since we moved from Minn. The saddest thing is that Eldon died. But don't cry. Eldon was a good person. He resides in heaven permanently. Mother alters at a big department store. (She fixes people's clothes so they fit.) Father is working at the paper mill temporarily until he's called for a government position. Violet is fifteen now, a sophomore in H.S. Gets all A's. She plans to be a teacher. Hugo is fourteen, tall and skinny. Looks like Mother. Hugo is a swimmer and a runner. Elsie is ten and I'm almost eleven. If we get good report cards, Aunt Gertrude will send us money to go back to Minn. when we graduate from H. S. See you then! Thank you for my name. Love, Elma"

"Can you put a P. S. on your letter?" Hugo asked Elma.

"Why?"

"I'd like you to write something to Reino for me."

"What do you want me to say?"

"Tell him to go to our hayloft and look behind the crow's nest and see if there's a box of slingshots."

"Reino doesn't want slingshots. What would he do with them?"

"They're not for Reino," Hugo explained. "They're for my boys."

"Boys! What boys? You're not even married."

"I'll be married and I'll have children. I made those slingshots especially for my boys."

"Talk like that and you'll land in the nut house," Elma grumbled as she folded the letter and licked the flap on the envelope.

Signe turned to her daughter, "Elma, we all have our dreams. Some dreams come true. Others don't."

After Eldon's death, Signe's sister Gertrude had wired Signe twenty-five dollars for flowers or whatever was needed.

Then came Gertrude's telephone call urging Signe to return to Minnesota, "back to civilization."

"Now that you have your place again," Gertrude said, "you can start over." The last buyer of the Skinnar farm—the forty acres with buildings—had not been able to make the payments and Charlie had to foreclose. Nobody was willing to buy the east forty where the graves had been found. "You're paying a hundred dollars a year taxes on the home forty and seventy on the other. That's a lot of money," Gertrude told Signe.

"My job is important to me," Signe said. "I like my work and the people in the store like me. I earn my own money. Soon I'll have enough savings to get the house remodeled and send Violet to college when the time comes."

"Have it your way, Signe," Gertrude grumbled, "but I'm telling you, living with Charlie out there in the wild will bring you nothing but heartache and sorrow," and hung up the phone.

Hilda Mattson wrote Signe that hearing about Eldon's death had driven Reino "over the edge." He'd been found wandering around the countryside looking for Charlie Skinnar saying, "Charlie killed Eldon and I'm going to finish Charlie." Reino had been taken to the county home.

"You might as well let the east forty go for taxes," Hilda added. "No one will buy it in our lifetime."

Two years had gone by since Eldon's passing. His name was seldom spoken out loud. The memory of his early death was too painful, but ever present. Hugo unconsciously tried to fill the void. He wore Eldon's boots. He even had his mother lengthen his brother's pants to wear to school. Violet no longer needed to make crepe paper flowers as she did in Minnesota. The Oregon weather afforded flowers every season. She and her mother grew a variety of annuals and perennials. Once a week they'd take a bouquet to Eldon's grave.

Signe was teaching Violet to drive. Signe herself had never steered an automobile or shifted gears, but she'd watched Charlie.

It was Friday afternoon. Charlie was sleeping, as he did during the day since he worked nights. "Let's get in the car and take Eldon some flowers," Signe said to Violet. They didn't use the word *grave*. "I'll get the keys from your father's pocket and you drive."

They'd been gone barely a half-hour when Violet became ill. They promptly returned home, awakened Charlie and took her to a doctor. A fortnight later, Signe sat with paper and pen at her kitchen table.

Dear Hilda,

Again I greet you with sad news. Our beloved daughter Violet was taken from us two weeks ago

Saturday. She wasn't feeling well on Friday, but the doctor sent her home saying it wasn't anything serious. Saturday morning she had to be taken to the University Hospital in Portland. She died before midnight of spinal meningitis. It is very contagious so her casket had to be sealed. We never saw Violet after the nurse took her to her room. My heart is heavy with grief. We miss her so much. I'm enclosing the newspaper clipping.

My best to you, dear friend.

Lovingly,
Signe

Although Hugo could not fill the void that Eldon's death three years ago had left in their lives, the family doted on him. He was a dreamer and a doer. He saw no obstacles and feared no failure. At the mill, Charlie lost no opportunity to praise his athletic son. "Hugo Skinnar is going to beat Paavo Nurmi's running record by a long shot," he'd tell his coworkers.

It was Friday afternoon. Charlie had just finished a lunch of warmed-over meat loaf, mashed potatoes, gravy and green beans and was thinking about going to bed when there was a knock on the door. He hoped it was a friend, not a traveling salesman. He could really enjoy company. Charlie felt it was unnatural for man to sleep during daylight hours, but that's what modern civilization required him to do.

The unexpected guest was Oscar Salo, the man who'd instigated Charlie's move to the west. "I had some business to do in Portland, so I thought I'd swing by and see how you folks are doing."

Charlie was genuinely glad to see the man who'd built his house in Wolf Creek and been his friend since. "What happened to you, Oscar?" Charlie shouted happily, and waved his arm toward a kitchen chair. "I looked for you in six counties and found no trace of your meandering."

Oscar laughed. "It's a long story. Reads like *Gulliver's Travels*. We hit Oregon in the middle of hard times. No work anyplace. So the wife and I and the kiddies hit the berry farms and fruit orchards and picked. Picked till our hands were raw. I even thought of mining. Went to Kellogg, Idaho. Nothing doing. Came back to Aberdeen, Washington, and with the dimes and dollars I'd managed to save, bought ten lots on the South side, built me a three bedroom house—high off the ground. But barely high enough. One winter the water came almost clear to the front door. It's low land and they have a problem with the dikes.

"Then glory be, Franklin D. came up with his Works Progress Administration to help the near starving and since they needed carpenters and me with five youngsters and unemployed, I got on right off. Been working on my property on the side. Plan to put up nine more houses as soon as the time is ripe. How's it been with you? Ed Koski wrote that you'd lost your job with the postal department."

Charlie bristled, almost dropped the coffee cups he was setting on the table. "I didn't lose my job. I quit! Don't want to have a damned thing to do with the government if I can help it. I have a good job now working for the paper mill. Paycheck every week— regular as the clock. I prefer the graveyard shift. Gives me time to work around the place here."

Having cut the coffee bread, Charlie motioned his guest to the table. Oscar promptly helped himself to a piece of the bread. Charlie pushed the butter dish toward him. Oscar shook his head as he bit into the delicacy. "None for me, thank you. This melts in one's mouth like angel cake. How is Signe?" Oscar asked, with a gleam in his eye. "Now there's a real woman! If I hadn't gone to the Iron Range to work the winter of 1918-1919, you wouldn't have had a Chinaman's chance with Signe Maki. I hear she got a good position with a big department store in Portland."

Charlie nodded. It rankled him to have Oscar talk about Signe. It hurt him that Oscar made no mention of the children he'd lost. Oscar had known both Eldon and Violet since they were born.

After small talk about the depression, Franklin Delano Roosevelt, his accomplishments, and Herbert Hoover and his failures, Oscar brought up the house in Wolf Creek that he'd built for Charlie. "I hear you had to foreclose on the last buyer."

Charlie nodded.

"Too bad you can't go back."

Oscar's last statement hit Charlie with the force of an army tank. He saw red. He felt blood rushing to his head. He was angry—angry enough to beat the shit out of Oscar. He, Charlie, was a free man, free to go anywhere he wanted. But he couldn't strike the un-invited guest. Charlie pulled out his gold pocket watch and glanced at it, then looked at the clock on the wall. "Five past three."

Oscar put the last morsel of pulla in his mouth, swallowed it down with the remains of his coffee. "I have to be going." He got up and put on his cap. "I have business to do in Portland and the stores close promptly at five. Give Signe my best regards."

Charlie remained seated. He let his guest find his own way out and when the door closed behind Oscar Salo, Charlie kicked the leg of the table and grumbled, "The son of a bitch!" Then got up and washed the cups, leaving no evidence of the visitor for Signe to see.

It was the summer of '39. Hugo was sixteen, almost seventeen. Charlie had always hoped his son would continue his running instead of swimming. "The Finns are runners," he told Hugo. "We don't take to water," and repeated the statistics Hugo had heard before, "Paavo Nurmi ran the mile in four minutes back in 1923, and won six gold medals, four in the 1924 Paris Olympics. Imagine that."

Hugo nodded. "But I'm a better swimmer than runner. I have to do what I can do the best."

"Okay, son, if you win all the local meets and get to compete at the big one in Seattle, I'll take my vacation and bring the whole family to watch you. I'll rent rooms in the best hotel."

Hugo won and Signe bought new dresses for the girls and a new suit for Charlie. Hugo left by bus on Tuesday. The four followed by car two days later.

Just before the competition was to begin, Charlie

was notified that Hugo had taken sick and been rushed to the hospital.

He died the following day. Charlie's legs buckled when he heard the news.

My dear friend Hilda,
        Death has become a regular visitor to our home. Barely a year after Violet, our remaining son, Hugo was taken. You know, Hugo always wanted to become good enough to swim in the Olympics. He was in Seattle swimming when he got sick with encephalitis and passed on. They think he got the germ from the water in Lake Washington. Charlie collapsed at the news and has not been able to take to his feet since. He lost his job at the paper mill. Death is hard, but harder still when you cannot kiss the face of your beloved child before he is put in the cold ground.

Your grieving friend,
Signe

◄ • ►

Dear Hilda,
I want to thank you for your many letters. You have no idea what they mean to me. I read them over and over. Some of them I read to Charlie. He's been confined to the wheelchair since Hugo died. The Drs. at the University Hospital cannot find any reason for his inability to walk. If we lived in Minn., we could take him to the Mayo Clinic. I also want to thank you for the chokecherry jelly. I'm saving the last jar for our French toast on Christmas morning. It is delicious and makes me lonesome for Minn. You shouldn't have done it. Postage

is so costly these days.

I apologize for not writing more often but when I get home at night I rush to cook supper. Then there's the canning and the pickling. I've canned 135 qts. of tomatoes this far & made 40 qts. of pickles. Dill & sweet. Violet isn't here to help and the younger girls are not domestic. Meier & Frank, a big dept. store in Portland had a sale on yard goods. I bought a beautiful pink print to make you a dress for next summer, also nightgown material. I will sew these up when the rainy season starts and send them with Elma and Elsie when they go to Minn. next spring. My sister Gertrude has promised them bus tickets for their high school graduation.

I hope this finds you in good health. I count my blessings every day that I'm well and able to work. I enjoy the friendship of the employees at the store. My customers are always pleasant and seem to like my alterations. I even get tailoring from scratch to do at home. That makes it all worthwhile.

In haste,
Your friend, Signe

◄ ▪ ►

Dear Hilda,

Thank you for your long letter. I'm glad your husband is feeling better. There's nothing new here. Charlie is much the same. Would you believe that Elma is graduating from the University of Minnesota already. She is graduating summa cum laude, which means with highest honors, she says. Elsie quit after two years to work in a lawyer's office. I

would like to go to the graduation, but I can't leave
Charlie. He is completely dependent on me. He can
get along when I'm at work, but he needs me the
rest of the time.

You will not believe this, but I bought a new car,
a Studebaker. I taught myself to drive in Charlie's
old Ford. Now I'm good enough to drive in Portland. Charlie does not believe in ladies driving, but
we have to do what we need to do.

My best regards to you and your husband,
Your friend, Signe

EPILOGUE

SIGNE LOOKED IN THE OVEN to see how the pulla was doing.

Besides raisins, she added candied cherries and orange peel to the pastry, as she had done for Eldon's funeral. Father Myhre liked it. Said it brought fond memories of his early childhood in Norway.

The bread had risen nicely, the crust was browning evenly and would be done, she estimated, just about the time Charlie's session with the priest was over.

Signe closed the oven door and went back to her sewing machine in front of the kitchen window and hand stitched the hem of a skirt. What could Charlie tell Father Myhre? She hoped the priest would help bring peace to Charlie, and prayed that God would listen. Signe was thankful that her work required concentration, glad her eyes were still good and her hands steady. Otherwise, she felt, there were times she might have lost her sanity.

The telephone rang. Signe smiled. Some lady wanting a new dress or suit, she told herself as she hastened to answer.

"Hello!"

"This is a person-to-person call for Signe Skinnar," the operator said.

"Not another death in the family!"

"This is a person-to-person call for Signe Skinnar," the operator repeated. "Are you Signe Skinnar?"

"That's me. But, please, no bad news."

"Good morning, Signe," the feminine voice at the other end addressed her in Finnish.

"Hilda Mattson!" Signe cried. "Let me get a chair before I faint on my feet." She grabbed one nearby. "Your voice to me is kin to that of an angel. As sweet and melodious as it was sixty years ago."

"Come now, Signe, don't flatter me too much or I'll soon believe you."

"Why did you call person-to-person? It's so costly."

"I had no wish to talk to Charlie."

"Charlie doesn't answer the phone anymore. No one calls him. He sits in his wicker chair and broods about the past."

"He's got plenty to mull over," Hilda retorted. "Is he within earshot?"

"No, he's in his bedroom with the priest."

"Admitting his sins? So he's turned Cat'lic!" Hilda chortled. "Good thinking, Charlie. Confession is good for the soul. A bit late, but Charlie's can use all the purging he can get."

"Charlie says he no longer believes in God."

"Then why waste the priest's time?"

"Father Myhre was Eldon's friend. Charlie feels the end is near and he wanted to talk with someone with authority, as he put it. I called the priest."

"I won't say anymore. The fate of Charlie's soul is not in my hands. You sound like your old self, Signe. How are you?"

"I eat good, sleep well and have plenty of work to keep me busy. And you?"

"Hold on to your chair, Signe. I have news."

"You're getting married again! It's about time. Who's the man so fortunate?"

Hilda laughed. "Not yet. I'm a woman of considerable wealth."

"They found iron ore on your place! Don't tell me it's oil."

"Neither. You know for years they've been talking about building a ski lodge on Large Mountain. They couldn't get access to the area from the north because of the Indian reservation. Our acreage lies to the southwest. We've had many offers through the years, but this time the bid was sizable. I thought why not? My husband's dead and the boys are gone. I sold the farm. The whole quarter section."

"Where will you go?" Signe asked.

"I'm coming to visit you. I know you'll never come back to Wolf Creek."

"This is too good to be true." Signe took a handkerchief from her pocket to wipe her tears. "I had no hopes of ever seeing you again."

"After the sales transaction was completed at the bank last Tuesday," Hilda continued, "I went to the courthouse to see Elma. I told her what I was planning and asked her to come with me. 'It's high time you visited your mother,' I said. But she's running for county treasurer and can't take time off now."

"Elma the county treasurer!"

"Might as well. She's run the office for years. Elma told me that Elsie is returning to the University to finish her degree and then go to law school."

"My daughters! These days girls can map their destinations and pilot their own planes. That's how a woman's life should be."

"Who knows what you and I could have done," Hilda flared, "if we hadn't thought of husbands as all important. I have more to tell you —"

"All good news?" Signe interjected.

"I have a feeling I'll not return to Minnesota after I've seen Oregon."

"Hilda, to live in Oregon, you must like water. It rains and it rains."

"But you don't need to shovel it. I'm tired of shoveling. As I started to say, I went to the cemetery to clean the plots where Gust lies. As I entered the gate, I noticed a new black Chrysler with an Illinois license nearby. I was on my knees, yanking the quack grass out of the ground when this lovely lady approached me and asked if I knew the location of Mary Marks' grave. I was about to say 'The murdered widow's' but she interrupted me by introducing herself as Jane Marks."

"Little Janey Marks," Signe squeaked, and a fresh stream of tears poured down her face. "Every day I wonder whatever became of those two dear children."

"I thanked God that I had not spilled the beans when she said that she'd been told her mother had suddenly taken ill with pneumonia and been rushed to the hospital where she died. Jane only recently found out that her mother was buried in the Wolf Creek Cemetery. I found an unmarked plot—one of many—which I can only guess was Mary's and would've helped her weed it but after all these years, weeds and vines had taken over. A job for a strong man with pick and shovel. I directed her to the care-taker at the church."

"This is a day I had never expected to see." Signe's voice caught in her throat. Eager to hear more, she sucked in her breath and continued, "Tell me about Janey. What is she like?"

"A blond copy of her mother. Tall. Soft-spoken. She's a lawyer."

"What about Robert, her brother?"

"A lawyer, too. They have their own firm in Chicago. Jane wanted to see you."

"She remembered me!"

"She asked where the nice lady lived who made them the delicious meat pies. She'd tried to find your house. 'Gone,' I said. 'Signe Skinnar left here over a half century ago, right after the auction.' I almost said, 'Right after the murder,' but caught myself.

"Jane drove me home so I could give her your address and telephone number. She said she'd look you up if she ever got out West."

Signe's mind whirled in anticipation of the coming guest. She'd have to have the house painted inside and out. "Hilda, this call is costing you a lot of money, I don't want to keep you on the phone any longer, but how is Ed Koski doing? I sent him a get-well card right after you wrote me about his heart attack."

"We buried him last Saturday. Reino was one of the pallbearers. Poor Reino, he's never gotten over Mary Marks' death.

"At the inquest, you'll remember, he rambled about seeing Mary riding in the mail car wearing the red dress. Now he says he witnessed the murder! Said he and Eldon were—" Hilda stopped short.

"Were what?" Signe asked.

"Were . . . were good friends."

"He was a friend to all our children and like a second father to Eldon."

"I'm going to Fargo Monday to get my plane ticket," Hilda said. "I'll call you Tuesday."

Signe thanked Hilda for the call and hung up. She returned to her sewing and humming an old tune, she revelled in the new information she'd just received.

Charlie whisked back the scraggly gray hairs clouding his vision and rolled his old rattan wheelchair closer to the priest seated on the rocking chair, pipe in hand. "Father, I feel death hovering nearby." Lowering his voice, he said, "I need to make confession—"

Father Myhre looked at Charlie as if studying a map. Then took a puff. "I cannot hear your confession."

"Because I'm not Cat'lic?"

The priest nodded.

"Then who can help me? I have no pastor. I have no church."

"That can be changed—"

Charlie shook his head. "Too late."

"God is eternal. It's never too late."

Charlie stared vacantly into space and stroked his hair. "Will you hear my story?"

Father Myhre nodded. "But I cannot grant you absolution."

"Guess I have to take what I can get." Charlie looked around. "What I'm about to tell you happened long ago. In my mind, I sometimes feel it is only a nightmare that has imbedded itself in my brain—" Charlie stopped and closed his eyes.

"I was a mail carrier at the time, young and virile. I attended church regularly and taught my children Christian values. It was not until this young widow moved into the area that I began to waver." Charlie got lost in thought.

"This widow became friends with Signe, and her children became friends with Signe, and her children became pals with my children—she had two, a boy and a girl. Come spring, the widow decided to have a garden. Every day she was out there in her tiny patch, weeding and hoeing. I felt she was there to taunt me. To provoke me. I was intoxicated by her presence. I was tortured between right and wrong, between sin and righteousness. Then it came—the letter! An epistle of love and desire. I was about to put it in her mailbox when I decided otherwise. I tore it open, like this" — Charlie went through the motions of angrily tearing open the envelope — "and read it. She had a lover! She waits by the mailbox. I drive by. This goes on for some time, but there is no letter, for they're in my pocket. Then one day I decide to make delivery to her house."

Charlie looked around and in a gargling voice continued. "Father, that is when God turned his back on me, and the devil took over. I told the widow that Signe was waiting for her to come for a fitting and I took her. I didn't mean to hurt her. I just wanted her for myself for a little while before she left forever. For another man.

"I'm not a vicious person. I'm a kind man, a loving husband and father. It was an act of passion. The devil performed his evil deeds through me. I didn't mean for her to die."

Charlie gazed at the priest, and continued. "God turned his back on me and death took over. Like a hawk, picking baby robins, it raided my little ones out of the nest. First it was Eldon, then Violet and finally Hugo. God, why didn't the jury do its duty and convict me? I was ready to go to prison. I would have been quite happy in Stillwater. I could have worked and paid my debt to society, and now I might be a free man. Reino, that idiot, saw me driving with the widow in my mail car. At the inquest, I taunted him, I ridiculed him, and I provoked him in an attempt to make him say those four words . . . "

"What four words?"

"CHARLIE YOU ARE GUILTY."

"Why didn't you confess it yourself?"

Charlie's eyes popped wide. "How could I? A married man with five children! He was friends with the widow. I thought he would want to come forward."

"Charlie, the widow had a name, did she not?"

"Of course."

"What was it?"

"Marks," Charlie replied.

"Her Christian name?"

"Mary."

"Named after the mother of our Savior, Jesus Christ."

Charlie seemed at a loss for something to say.

"And the children's names?"

"Jane and Robert."

"What happened to them?"

Charlie shrugged.

"Did you ever think about them?" Getting no response from Charlie, the priest lost patience. "I didn't come to give you comfort. I came because of Signe. Have you ever thought of Signe, about how she might have felt?"

"I've always been true to her."

"True!" Father Myhre shouted. "You rape a woman and you say you've been true to your wife?"

"In my heart I mean."

Father Myhre slipped his pipe in his pocket and got up from his chair. "I cannot help you."

Charlie gave a wail and began to weep. His body shook as he spoke. "You ask me if I ever thought about the two young ones I orphaned. Every waking hour of every single day." He looked at the priest and asked, "But was the body that of the widow? Did she really die?"

"Why do you ask?"

"If it was, what happened to her head?" At night I dream of her. She's complete. What we found under the brush pile was a headless corpse."

"She died," Father Myhre replied. "Eldon believed she received a Christian burial. Her head was placed in a coffin of pine and lined with pink crepe paper roses. Eldon sang 'Ave Maria,' and his friend Reino prayed for her soul."

Charlie gasped. "Eldon knew!"

The priest gave a slow nod.

Charlie let out another wail. "Eldon! What did I do to you! I killed Eldon. I killed my son and God punished me." When Charlie got ahold of himself, he asked, "Where was the head buried?"

"Under the doghouse," Father Myhre replied as he walked to and opened the door to the kitchen.

Sobbing and shaking, Charlie followed him in his wheelchair. "I am sorry. Truly sorry. Thank you, Father, for listening. You have taken the burden off my soul. I can now face whatever lies before me."

Hearing those words, Signe, seated at the sewing machine, took Mary Marks' shoe and its missing heel out of her remnant bag and hurried over to the stove. She lifted a lid, dropped the complete shoe in the flames and took the cardamom bread out of the oven.

Father Myhre came into the kitchen, went over to Signe, sniffed the bread and smiled. Then proceeded to the table and sat on a stool.

Charlie hoisted his enfeebled body out of the wheelchair on to the straight back chair he had deserted when Hugo died and sat across the table from the priest.

"You look wonderfully happy, Signe," Father Myhre remarked as Signe approached the table with her coffeepot.

"I am, Father, happier than I have been in years." She turned her eyes to Charlie. "I just received good news over the telephone. My longtime friend Hilda from Minnesota is coming here."

"Everything's going to be all right, Mother," Charlie said with a gentle smile that Signe had long since forgotten, "I have confessed my sins and am ready to face the Lord. Tomorrow we'll make a trip to Portland and buy you an electric range."

As Signe finished pouring Father Myhre's coffee, the priest stood up, looked her in the face, placed his left hand on her shoulder and murmured, "*SIT PAX.*"

"What did you say, Father?" Charlie asked.

"Now . . . LET THERE BE PEACE."

Charlie closed his eyes and clasped his hands in prayer.

Father Myhre intoned, "Amen."